The Long Chance

Peter B. Kyne

1st WORLD
LIBRARY
Literary Society

The Long Chance

Peter B. Kyne

© 1st World Library – Literary Society, 2004
PO Box 2211
Fairfield, IA 52556
www.1stworldlibrary.org
First Edition

LCCN: 2004091266

Softcover ISBN: 1-59540-684-0
eBook ISBN: 1-59540-784-7

Purchase *"The Long Chance"*
as a traditional bound book at:
www.1stWorldLibrary.org/purchase.asp?ISBN=1-59540-684-0

1st World Library Literary Society is a nonprofit
organization dedicated to promoting literacy by:

- Creating a free internet library accessible from any
computer worldwide.
- Hosting writing competitions and offering book
publishing scholarships.

Readers interested in supporting literacy
through sponsorship, donations or
membership please contact:
literacy@1stworldlibrary.org
Check us out at: www.1stworldlibrary.org

The Long Chance
contributed by the Mahaney Family
in support of
1st World Library Literary Society

The Long Chance
contributed by the Mahaney Family
in support of
1st World Library Literary Society

CHAPTER I

It was sunrise on the Colorado desert.

As the advance guard of dawn emerged from behind the serrated peaks to the east and paused on their snow-encrusted summits before charging down the slopes into the open desert to rout the lingering shadows of the night, a coyote came out of his den in the tumbled *malpais* at the foot of the range, pointed his nose skyward and voiced his matutinal salute to the Hosts of Light.

Presently, far in the distant waste, seven dark objects detached themselves from the shadows and crawled toward the mountains. Like motes swimming in a beam of light, they came out of the Land of Nowhere, in the dim shimmering vistas over west, where the gray line of grease-wood met the blue of the horizon. Slowly they assumed definite shape; and the coyote ceased his orisons to speculate upon the ultimate possibility of breakfast and this motley trio of "desert rats" with their burro train, who dared invade his desolate waterless kingdom.

For, with the exception of the four burros, the three men who followed in their wake did, indeed, offer the rare spectacle of variety in this land of superlative monotony. One of the men wore a peaked Mexican straw hat, a dirty white cotton undershirt, faded blue denim overalls and a pair of shoes much too large for him; this latter item indicating a desire to get the most for his money, after the invariable custom of a primitive people. He carried a peeled catclaw gad in his right hand, and with this gad he continually urged to a shuffling half-trot some one of the four burros. This man was a Cahuilla Indian.

His two companions were white men. The younger of the pair was a man under thirty years of age, with kind bright eyes and the drawn but ruddy face of one whose strength seems to have been acquired more from athletic sports than by hard work. He was tall, broad-shouldered, slim-waisted, big-hipped and handsome; he stepped along through the clinging sand with the lithe careless grace of a mountain lion. An old greasy wide-brimmed gray felt hat, pinched to a "Montana peak," was shoved back on his curly black head; his shirt, of light gray wool, had the sleeves rolled to the elbow, revealing powerful forearms tanned to the complexion of those of the Indian. He seemed to revel in the airy freedom of a pair of dirty old white canvas trousers, and despite the presence of a long-barreled blue gun swinging at his hip he would have impressed an observer as the embodiment of kindly good nature and careless indifference to convention, provided his own personal comfort was assured.

The other white man was plainly an alien in the desert. He was slight, blonde, pale - a city man - with hard blue eyes set so close together that one understood instantly something of the nature of the man as well as the urgent necessity for his thick-lensed, gold-rimmed spectacles. He wore a new Panama hat, corded riding breeches and leggings. He was clean-shaven and

Peter B. Kyne

sinfully neat. He wore no side-arms and appeared as much out of harmony with his surroundings as might a South American patriot at a Peace Conference.

"I say," he began presently, "how much further is it to this prospect hole of yours, if, indeed, you have a prospect as you represented to me a week ago?" His tone was fretful, peevish, complaining. One would readily have diagnosed the seat of his trouble. He had come prepared to ride - and he had been forced to walk.

The young man frowned. He seemed on the point of swearing, but appearing to think better of it, he replied banteringly, "*Por ahi. Por ahi.*"

"What in blazes does that mean?"

"Oh, I was just talking the language of the country - a language, by the way, toward which you seem most indifferently inclined. '*Por ahi*' means 'a considerable way,' 'a right smart piece, I reckon,' and conveys about the same relative amount of definite information as *manana*. Never having measured the distance to my prospect, I have tried for the past two days to give you an approximate idea. But in this country you must know that distance is a deceptive, 'find X' sort of proposition - so please refrain from asking me that same question every two miles. If the water holds out we'll get there; and when we get there we'll find more water, and then you may shave three times a day if you feel so inclined, I'm sorry you have a blister on your off heel, and I sympathize with you because of your prickly-heat. But it's all in the day's work and you'll survive. In the meantime, however, I suggest that you compose your restless New England soul in patience, old man, and enjoy with our uncommunicative Cahuilla friend and myself the glories of a sunrise on the Colorado desert."

"Damn the sunrise," the other retorted. He would have damned his tormentor had he dared. "I do not wish to be insulted."

"Listen to that coyote," replied the careless one, ignoring his companion's rising anger. "Listen to him yip-yapping over there on the ridge. There sits a shining example of bucolic joy and indifference to local annoyances. Consider the humble coyote, Boston, and learn wisdom. Of course, a coyote doesn't know a whole lot, but he does recognize a good thing when he sees it. His appreciation of a sunrise is always exuberant. Ever since that coyote's been big enough to rustle his own jack-rabbits he's howled at a lovely full moon, and if he's ever missed his sun-up cheer it's because something he ate the night before didn't agree with him."

"Sir," snapped the irascible one, "you're a trifler. You're - you're - a - "

"Say it," soothed the student of nature.

"Oh, damn it," rasped his victim, "talk business. This is a business trip, not a rehearsal for a comic opera. Talk sense."

"Well, all right - since you insist," drawled the other, smiling brightly. "In the first place, after this morning you will permit your whiskers to grow. Out here water is too precious to waste it shaving every morning. I suggested that point last night, but you ignored my polite hint. I hate to appear boorish, but I must remind you that these jacks are mine, that the four little kegs of water that they're carrying are mine, that this *mozo* - I beg your pardon - that this Indian is mine, and lastly - forgive me if I ascend once more into the realm of romance and improbability - this country is mine, and I love it, and I won't have it profaned by any growling, dyspeptic little squirt from a land where they have pie for breakfast. I positively forbid you to touch that water without my permission. I forbid you to cuss my mozo without my permission, and I forbid you to damn this country in my hearing. Just at this particular moment, Boston, the only things which you have and which you can call your own, and do what you please with, are your soul, your prickly-heat and your blistered heel. I'm fully convinced that you're quite a little man back in Boston for the reason that you're one hell of a small man out here, even if you do wear a string of letters after your name like the tail on a comet.

"You were swelling around in San Berdoo, talking big and hollering for an investment. I showed you samples of ore from my desert prospect and you got excited. You wanted to examine my claim, you said, and if you liked it you would engage to bring it to the attention of 'your associates' and pay me my price. I offered to bring you in here as my guest, and ever since you got off the train at Salton you've snarled and snapped and beefed and imposed on my hospitality, and it's got to stop. I don't need you; I don't care for you; I think you're a renegade four-flusher, bluffing on no pair, and if I had known what a nasty little old woman you are I'd never have opened negotiations with you. Now, you chirk up, Boston, and smile and try to be a good sport, or I'll work you over and make a man out of you. Savvy?"

Thoroughly squelched, the malingerer flushed, mumbled an apology and held out his hand. The Desert Rat took it, a little sorry that he had not been more temperate in his language.

"All right, we'll bury the hatchet" he said generously. "Maybe I'm a little too exacting and hard to get along with. I've got more on my brain than this prospect hole, and I'm worried. When I left the wife at San Berdoo we were expecting an arrival in camp, and - well, we were right down to bed-rock, and as it was a case of go now or never with you, I had to bring you in here or perhaps lose the opportunity for a fortune. She wanted me to go. She's a mighty brave little woman. You don't happen to be a married man, do you? With kids? I've got - "

The Indian had paused and was pointing with his gad to the south. Miles and miles away a great yellow cloud was gathering on the horizon, shutting out the sunlight and advancing with incredible speed.

"Sandstorm" warned the Desert Rat, and spoke quickly to the mozo in Spanish. The latter at once turned the cavalcade of burros toward the hills, less than a mile distant; shouting and beating the heavily laden little beasts into a trot, the party scurried for the shelter of a rocky draw before the sandstorm should be upon them.

They won. Throughout that day and night they camped up the draw, safe from the sand blast. Early next morning the wind had subsided and with the exception of some slight changes in topography due to the sandstorm, the desert was the same old silent pulseless mystery.

The party resumed its journey. While the Easterner remained with the Indian, the Desert Rat circled out into the open, heading for a little backbone of quartz which rose out of the sand. He had not noticed this exposed ledge during their flight into the draw, and it was evident that the sandstorm had exposed it.

Suddenly the mozo uttered a low "Whoa," and the burros halted. Off in the sage and sand the Desert Rat was standing with upraised arm, as a signal for them to halt and wait for him. For nearly half an hour he circled around, stepping off distances and building monuments. Presently, apparently having completed his investigations, he beckoned the rest of his party to approach.

"What's up?" demanded the Boston man the moment he and the Indian arrived.

"I've just found Jake Revenner's lost claim. It's one of these marvelously rich ledges that have been discovered and located and lost and found and lost again, and cost scores of human lives. The sandstorms expose them and cover them up again, and after a storm - as now - the contour of the desert is so changed that a man, having staked his claim and gone out for grub, can't find the claim when he comes back. It was that way with the Nigger Ben placer. It's been found and lost half a dozen times. There was a claim discovered out here by a man named Jake Revenner, but he lost it and blew out his brains in sheer disgust. I have just stumbled across one of his monuments with his old location notices buried in a can. The late sandstorm uncovered the ledge, and it looks 'fat' enough for yours truly. *Mira?*"

He tossed a sample to the Indian, and another of about the same size to the white man. The latter lifted it, examined it closely and sat down. He was quite excited.

"By thunder!" he managed to say. "We're in luck."

A slight smile flickered across the face of the Desert Rat, but his voice was as calm and grave as usual.

"Yes, it's rich - very rich. There's a comfortable fortune lying exposed on the surface. By the way, I think I shall pay you a liberal fee for your lost time and abandon that prospect I was taking you in to see. Compared with this, it's not worth considering."

"I should say you should abandon it" the other exulted. "You'd have a fine time trying to get me away from this ledge now. Why, there's millions in it, and I suggest we stake it out at once. Let's get busy."

He jumped up eagerly - from force of habit dusting the seat of his riding breeches - and turned peremptorily to the mozo.

"Get those packs off, Joe, or Jim or whatever your name is, and be quick - "

"You forget, old man," interjected the Desert Rat gently. "He doesn't speak English, and if he did he wouldn't obey you. You see," he added naively, "I've told him not to."

"Oh, well, I didn't mean anything. Don't be so touchy. Let's get busy, for heaven's sake, and stake this claim."

Peter B. Kyne

The Desert Rat stretched himself with feline grace. "I'm sorry" he replied with his tantalizing good-natured smile, "to be forced to object to your use of the plural pronoun in conjunction with that certain tract, piece and parcel of land known and described as the Baby Mine claim. The fact of the matter is, I have already staked it. You see, I was thinking of the little one that will be waiting for me in San Berdoo when I get back. See the point? My baby - Baby Mine - rather a neat play on words, don't you think?"

"Do you mean to say that I'm not in on this find?" demanded the man from Boston.

"Your penetration is remarkable. I do."

"But such a course is outrageous. It's opposed - "

"Please do not argue with me. I found it. Naturally I claim it. I could quote you verbatim the section of the mining law under which I am entitled to maintain this high-handed - er - outrage; but why indulge in such a dry subject? I found this claim, and since I don't feel generously disposed this morning, I'm going to keep it."

"But I'm in the party with you. It seems to me that common justice - "

"For goodness' sake, Boston, don't throw up to me the sins of my past. Of course you're in my party. That's my misfortune, not my fault. I observed this little backbone of quartz and asked you to walk over here with me for a look at it. You wouldn't come. You said your foot hurt you. So I came alone. If you had been with me at the time, now, of course that would have been different. But - "

"But I - well, in a measure - why, we're out here together, sort of partners as it were, and - "

"The Lord forgive you, Boston. My partner! You never were and never could be. I'm particular in the matter of partners. All Desert Rats in good standing are. You're the last man on earth I'd have for my partner. A partner shares the expenses of a trip and bears the hardships without letting out a roar every half mile. A partner *sticks,* Boston. He shares his grub and his money and his last drop of water, and when that's gone he'll die with you like a gentleman. That's what a partner does, but you wouldn't do it."

"Well, I'm entitled to a half interest and I'll see that I get it," shrilled the other furiously. "I'll sue you - "

"How about the Indian?"

"Why, he - he's - "

"Only an Indian, eh? Well, you're entitled to your point of view. Only that mozo and I have slept under the same blanket so often - "

"You can't stop me from staking this claim, too" shouted the Boston man, and shook his skinny little fist under the Desert Rat's nose. The latter slapped him across the wrist.

"Pesky fly" he said.

"You can't stop me, I tell you."

"I can. But I won't. I'm not a bully."

"You think you can beat me out of my rights, do you? I'll show you. I'll beat you out of your half before I'm through with you."

"On whose water!"

The bantering smile broadened to a grin - the graceless young desert wanderer threw back his head and laughed.

"You're such a card, Boston" he chortled. "Such exquisite notions of social usage I have never observed outside the peerage. Really, you shouldn't be allowed to go visiting. You're unmannerly enough to ask for a third helping to cake."

"I insist that I am entitled to a half interest in this claim. As you decline to recognize my rights, I must take the matter in my own hands. I, too, shall stake the claim and endeavor to get my location notice filed in the land office before yours. If you haven't any sense of justice and decency, I have."

"Oh, all right, fire away. I'll take you back to civilization and see that you don't starve or die of thirst on the way. I'm not entirely heartless, Boston. In the meantime, however, while you're staking the claim, it occurs to me that I can gather together a very snug fortune in the next day or two. There appears to be more gold than quartz in this rock - some indeed, is the pure quill. All hands, including the jacks, will go on a short ration of water from now on. Of course we're taking chances with our lives, but what's life if a fellow can't take a chance for a fortune like this? I'd sooner die and be done with, it than live my life without a thrill. That's why I've degenerated from a perfectly matriculated mining engineer into a wandering desert rat. Would you believe it, Boston, I lived in your town once. Graduated from the Tech. Why, I once made love to a Boston girl in a conservatory. I remember her very well. She spilled pink lemonade over my dress shirt. I took a long chance that time; but out here, even if the chances are longer, when you win - "

He kissed his grimy paw airily and flung it into space.

"'The Lord is my shepherd,' he quoted, 'I shall not want.' This morning He left the door opened and I wandered into His Treasure House, so I guess I'll get busy and grab what I can before the Night Watchman comes around. Ever see the Night Watchman, Boston? I have. He's a grave old party with a long beard, and he carries a scythe. You see him when you're thirsty, and - well, in the pursuit of my inborn hobby for taking chances, I'll introduce you to him this trip. Permit me to remind you once more of the consequences if you help yourself to the water without consulting me. It'll militate against your chances of getting to the land office first."

The Desert Rat helped the mozo unpack the burros, while the man from Boston tore some pages from his notebook and proceeded to write out his location notices and cache them in monuments which he built beside those of his predecessors. He even copied the exact wording on the Desert Rat's notices. He forgot his blistered heel and worked with prodigious energy and interest, receiving with dogged silent disdain the humorous sallies of the Desert Rat, to whom the other's sudden industry was a source of infinite amusement.

Peter B. Kyne

The Desert Rat and the Indian were busy with pans and prospector's picks gouging out "stringers" and crevices and picking up scattered pieces of "jewelry" rock. When all the "color" in sight had been cleaned up, the Desert Rat produced a drill and a stick of dynamite from the pack, put in a "shot" and uncovered a pocket of such richness that even the stolid Cahuilla could not forbear indulgence in one of his infrequent Spanish expletives. It was a deposit of rotten honeycombed rock that was nine-tenths pure gold - what is known in the parlance of the prospector as a "kidney."

The disgruntled claimant to a half interest in the Baby Mine reached into the hole and seized a nugget worth fully a thousand dollars. The Desert Rat tapped him smartly across the knuckles with the handle of his prospector's pick and made him drop it.

"If you please, Boston" he said gently. "You're welcome to share my grub, and I'll whack up even with you on the water, and I'll cook for you and wait on you, but I'll be doggoned if it isn't up to you to furnish your own dynamite. There was ten thousand in loose stuff lying, on the surface, and you might have been pardoned for helping yourself to as much of it as you could carry personally, but you elected to restake the claim and now all that easy picking belongs to the Indian and me. He's a good Indian and I'm going to let him have some of it. He won't take much because he's fond of me. I saved him from being lynched for killing a white man who deserved it. But for years he's just hungered for a top-buggy, with side bars and piano box and the whole blamed rig painted bright red, so he can take his squaw out in style; and I'm going to see that he gets it. However, that's neither here nor there. You keep your fingers out of the sugar bowl, old sport. It's a lovely sight and hard to resist, I know, but do be careful."

All that day the Desert Rat and his Indian retainer worked through the stringers and pockets of the Baby Mine, while the man from Boston sat looking at them, or, when the spirit moved him, casting about in the adjacent sand for stray "specimens" of which he managed to secure quite a number. The next morning, as soon as it was light enough to see, the work was commenced again, and by noon the last piece of rotten honeycombed rock with its streaks and wens of dull virgin gold had been cleaned up. The Desert Rat used the last of his dynamite in a vain endeavor to unearth another "kidney," and finally decided to call it quits.

"They took eighty-two thousand dollars out of one little carload of ore in the Delhi mine in Nevada county" he announced, "but the Baby Mine makes that record look amateurish. It's the richest strike I have ever heard of, with the exception, possibly, of the big strike at Antelope Peak. They took out nearly three hundred thousand there in less than three days, just scratching it out of stringers and crevices with their jack-knives. Boston, my dear man, I have more than three hundred pounds of gold with, as I said before, some quartz, but not enough to bother. At twelve ounces to the pound, twenty dollars to the ounce, I'm going back to San Bernardino and buy a bath, a new suit of store clothes and a fifty-dollar baby carriage for my expected heir. With my dear little wife and the baby and all this *oro,* I'll manage to be quite happy.

"However, just to show you that there isn't a mean bone in my body, I'm going to withdraw my claim to the Baby Mine. My mozo and I are about to load this magnificent bunch of untainted wealth into the kyacks, and hit for civilization, and while we're getting ready to break camp you run out and destroy my location notices. I leave the whole works to you. I do this for a number of reasons - the first being that you will thus be induced to return to this section of California. Not knowing the country, you will doubtless perish, and thus from the placid bosom of society a thorn will be removed. Secondly, if you should survive long enough to get in, you could never find your way out without me for a guide - and it wouldn't be safe to hire this Indian. He dislikes you. The third reason is that I believe this is just a phenomenally rich pocket and that I have about cleaned it out. The fourth reason is that another sandstorm will probably cover the Baby Mine before long, and the fifth reason is: 'What's the use going desert-ratting until your money's all gone!'"

"Well, I'll see that I get my share of that plunder" snapped the unhappy tenderfoot. "Of course, right now, it may seem perfectly proper from your point of view to take advantage of certain adventitious circumstances, but - "

"Yes, the humble little jackass is really an adventitious circumstance. By jingo, that hadn't occurred to me at all. I guess you're right, Boston. I'll have to give you half the plunder. Now that we've settled that point, let's divide the adventitious circumstances. I have four of them and I'll sell you two for your half of the gold. No? Price too high? All right! I'll agree to freight your share in for you, only I'm afraid transportation rates are so high in the desert that the freight will about eat up all the profit. I'm afraid that the best I can do for you is to give you your half and let you carry it yourself. If you want to tote it out on your back, Boston, help yourself. No! Well, well!"

"We'll not discuss the matter further, if you please. At another time and place, perhaps - "

"Perhaps? Perhaps! Well, I'm stripping down our food supply to the bare necessities in order to make room for this gold, and the water is pretty low. If we don't strike water at Chuckwalla Tanks there'll be real eloquence to that word 'perhaps.' However, that discussion can wait. Everything appears to be propitious for an immediate start, so let's defer the argument and *vamoose*. Giddap, you hairy little desert birds. Crack along out o' this."

But following the dictates of his nature, when Fortune smiled and bade him "take a chance," the Desert Rat had already delayed too long his departure from the Baby Mine. The supply of water still left in the kegs was so meager that with any other man the situation would have given rise to grave concern. As it was, however, all that troubled the Desert Rat was what he was going to do with the man from Boston when that inconsistent and avaricious individual should "peter out." More than once, in his pursuit of the rainbow, the Desert Rat had known what it was to travel until he couldn't travel another yard; then to jump up and travel ten miles more - to water! He did not know the extent of his own strength, but whatever might be its limitations he knew that the Cahuilla was good for an equal demonstration of endurance. But the man from Boston! He was quickly read. The Desert Rat gave him until midnight that night, but he wilted at ten o'clock.

"A sore heel, a mean soul and no spunk have killed more men than whisky" the Desert Rat commented

Peter B. Kyne

whimsically, as he pulled the weak brother out of a cluster of catclaw. "Boston, you're an awful nuisance - you are, for a fact. You've had water three times to our once, and yet you go to work and peter out with Chuckwalla Tanks only five miles away. Why, I've often covered that distance on my hands and knees. Come, now, buck up. Hang on to the rear cross of one of the pack saddles and let the jack snake you along."

"I can't, I'm exhausted. I'll die if I don't have a drink."

"No, you'll not die. No such luck. And there isn't any more water. However, you've been spoiled in the raising, so I suppose we'll have to defer to you - particularly since it's my fault that we're short of water. What can't be cured must be endured, and I can't let you die."

He spoke to the Indian, who took two canteens and departed into the night.

"He's going to hike on ahead to Chuckwalla Tanks and bring back some water for you, Boston" the Desert Rat explained. "He'll return about daylight, and we'll wait here until he arrives. It's dangerous, but the jacks aren't in a bad way yet. They can make it to the Tanks, even after sunrise."

"Thanks" murmured the sufferer.

The Desert Rat grinned. "You're getting on" he commented.

"Where is Chuckwalla Tanks?" The tenderfoot sat up and stared after the figure of the departing Indian, still visible in the dim moonlight.

"In a little gorge between those low hills. You can just make out their outlines."

"Yes, I see them. And after that the closest water is where?"

"The Colorado river - forty miles due south. But we're headed northwest and must depend on tanks and desert water-holes. It's hard to tell how close one is to water on that course. But it doesn't matter. We'll refill the kegs at Chuckwalla Tanks. There's most always water there."

"And you say the Colorado river is forty miles due south."

"Well, between forty and fifty."

"Much obliged for the information, I'm sure."

He straightened suddenly and drew back his arm. The Desert Rat saw that he was about to hurl a large smooth stone, and simultaneously he dodged and reached for his gun. But he was a fifth of a second too slow. The stone struck him on the side of the head, rather high up, and he collapsed into a bloody heap.

On the instant the footsore man from Boston developed an alacrity and definiteness of purpose that would have surprised the Desert Rat, had he been in condition to observe it. He seized the gad which the mozo had dropped, climbed upon the lightest laden burro and, driving the others before him, set off for Chuckwalla Tanks. The Indian had disappeared by this time, and there was little danger of overtaking him; so with the two low hills as his objective point, the

Easterner circled a mile out of the direct course which he knew the Indian would take, and when the dawn commenced to show in the east he herded the pack-animals down into a swale between two sand-dunes. With remarkable cunning he decided to scout the territory before proceeding further; hence, as soon as there was light enough to permit of a good view, he climbed to the crest of a high dune and looked out over the desert. As far as he could see no living thing moved; so he drove the pack train out of the swale and headed for the gorge between the hills. The thirsty burros broke into a run, hee-hawing with joy as they sniffed the water, and within a few minutes man and beasts were drinking in common at Chuckwalla Tanks.

The man permitted them to drink their fill, after which they fell to grazing on the short grass which grew in the draw. While he realized the necessity for haste if he was to succeed in levanting with the gold, the tenderfoot had been too long a slave to his creature comforts to face another day without breakfast. He abstracted some grub from one of the packs and stayed the pangs of hunger. Then he bathed his blistered feet, filled the water kegs, rounded up his pack train and departed up the draw. After traveling a mile the draw broadened out into the desert, and the man from Boston turned south and headed for the Rio Colorado. He was walking now and appeared to have forgotten about his blistered heel, for at times he broke into a run, beating the burros, screaming curses at them with all the venom of his wolfish soul, for he was pursued now by the fragments of his conscience. His attack upon the Desert Rat had been the outgrowth of a sudden murderous impulse, actuated fully as much by his hatred and fear of the man as by his desire to possess the gold. One moment he would shudder at the thought that he had committed murder; the next he was appalled at the thought that after all he had only stunned the man - that even now the Desert Rat and his Indian retainer were tracking him through the waste, bent on wreaking summary vengeance.

He need not have worried so prematurely. A low range of black malpais buttes stretched between him and the man he had despoiled, and as yet the direction of his flight could not be observed. He drifted rapidly south and presently disappeared into one of those long swales which slope gradually to the river.

Here, weaving his way among the ironwood that grow thickly in this section of the desert, for the first time since the commission of his crime he felt safe.

　　　　Peter B. Kyne

CHAPTER II

It was still dark when the Desert Rat regained consciousness. He lay for quite a while thereafter, turning things over in his befuddled brain, striving to gather together the tangled thread of the events of the night. Eventually he succeeded in driving his faculties into line. He rolled over, got to his hands and knees and paused a minute to get a fresh grip on himself. His aching head hung low, like that of a dying horse; in the silence of the night he could hear the drip, drip of his blood into the sand.

Presently he began to move. Round and round in the sage he crawled, like some weary wounded animal, breaking off the rotten dead limbs which, lie close to the base of the shrub. Three piles of sage he gathered, placing the piles in a row twenty feet apart. Then he set fire to them and watched them burst into flame.

It was the desert call for help: three fires in a row by night, three columns of smoke against the horizon by day - and the Cahuilla Indian, coming down the draw from Chuckwalla Tanks five miles away, saw flaming against the dawn this appeal of the white man he loved, for whom he lived and labored. Straight across the desert he ran, with the long tireless stride that was the heritage of his people. His large heavy shoes retarded him; he removed them, tucked them under his arm and with a lofty disdain of tarantulas and side-winders fled barefooted. Three-quarters of an hour from the time he had first seen the signal-fires, the mozo was kneeling beside the stricken Desert Rat, who lay unconscious close to one of the fires. The water from the mozo's canteen revived him, however, and presently he sat up, while the Cahuilla washed the gash in his head and bound it up with his master's bandanna handkerchief.

As the Indian worked, the white man related what had occurred and how. He recalled his conversation with his assailant, and shrewdly surmised that he would head for the Colorado river, after having first secured a supply of water at Chuckwalla Tanks. The Desert Rat's plan of action was quickly outlined.

"You will help me to get to the Tanks, where I'll have water and a chance to rest for a day or two until I'm able to travel; then I'll head for the Rio Colorado and wait for you in Ehrenburg. I'll keep one canteen and you can take the other; I have matches and my six-shooter, and I can live on quail and chuckwallas until I get to the river. You have your knife. Track that man, if you have to follow him into hell, and when you find him - no, don't kill him; he isn't worth it, and besides, that's my work. It's your job to run him down. Bring him to me in Ehrenburg."

It was past noon when they arrived at the Tanks, and the Indian was carrying the Desert Rat on his back. While the man was quite conscious, he was still too weak from the effect of the blow and loss of blood to travel in the heat.

At the Tanks the Indian picked up the trail of four burros and a man. He refilled his canteen, took a long drink from the Tank, grunted an "*Adios, senor,*" and departed up the draw at the swift dog-trot which is typical of the natural long-distance runner.

The Desert Rat gazed after him. "God bless your crude untutored soul, you best of mozos" he murmured. "You have one virtue that most white men lack - you'll stay put and be faithful to your salt. And now, just to be on the safe side, I'll make my will and write out a detailed account of this entire affair - in case."

For half an hour he scribbled haltingly in an old russet-covered note-book. This business attended to, he crawled into the meager shade of a *palo verde* tree and fell asleep. When he awoke an hour or two later and looked down the draw to the open desert, he saw that another sandstorm was raging.

"That settles it" he soliloquized contentedly. "The trail is wiped out and the best Indian on earth can't follow a trail that doesn't exist, But that wretched little bandit is out in this sandstorm, and the jacks will stampede on him and he'll pay *his* bill to society - with interest. When the wind dies down the pack outfit will drift back to this water-hole, and when Old Reliable finds out that the trail is lost, *he'll* drift back too. Anyhow, if the burros don't show we'll trail *them* by the buzzards and find the packs. Ah, you great mysterious wonderful desert, how good you've been to me! I can sleep now - in peace."

He slept. When he awoke again, he discovered to his surprise that he had been walking in his sleep. He had an empty canteen over his shoulder and he was bareheaded. His head ached and throbbed, his tongue and throat felt dry and cottony; he seemed to have been wandering in a weary land for a long time, for no definite reason, and he was thirsty.

He glanced around him for the water-hole beside which he had lain down to sleep and await the mozo and the burros. On all sides the vast undulating sea of sand and sage stretched to the horizon, and then the Desert Rat understood. He had been delirious. With the fever from his wound and the thought of the fortune of which he had been despoiled, uppermost even in his subconscious brain, he had left Chuckwalla Tanks and started in pursuit. How far or in what direction he had wandered he knew not. He only knew that he was lost, that he was weak and thirsty, that the pain and fever had gone out of his head, and that the Night Watchman walked beside him in the silent waste.

It came into his brain to light three fires - to flash the S. O. S. call of the desert in letters of smoke against the sky - and he fumbled in his pocket for matches. There were none; and with a sigh, that was almost a sob the dauntless Argonaut turned his faltering footsteps to the south and lurched away toward the Rio Colorado.

Throughout the long cruel day he staggered on. Night found him close to the mouth of a long black canyon between two ranges of black hills, whose crests marked them as a line of ancient extinct volcanoes.

"I'll camp here to-night," he decided, "and early tomorrow morning I'll go up that canyon and hunt for water. I might find a 'tank.'"

He lay down in the sand, pillowed his sore head on his arm, and, God being merciful and the Desert Rat's luck still holding, he slept.

At daylight he was on his way, stiff and cramped with the chill of the desert night. Slowly he approached the mouth of the canyon, crossing a bare burnt space that looked like an old "wash."

Suddenly he paused, staring. There, before him in the old wash, was the fresh trail of two burros and a man. The trail of the man was not well defined; rather scuffed in fact, as if he had been half dragged along.

"Hanging to the pack-saddle and letting the jack drag him" muttered the lost Desert Rat. "I'll bet it's little Boston, after all, and I'm not yet too late to square accounts with that *hombre.*"

In the prospect of twining his two hands around the rascal's throat there was a certain primitive pleasure that added impetus to the passage of the Desert Rat up the lonely canyon. The thought lent new strength to the man. Dying though he knew himself to be, yet would he square accounts with the man who had murdered him. He would -

He paused. He had found the man with the two burros. There could be no mistake about that, for the canyon ended in a sheer cliff that towered two hundred feet above him, and in this horrible *cul de sac* lay the bleached bones of two burros and a man.

Here was a conundrum. The Desert Rat had followed a fresh trail and found stale bones. Despite his youth, the desert had put something of its own grim haunting mystery into this man who loved it; to him had it been given to understand much that to the layman savored of the occult; at birth, God had been very good to him, in that He had ordained that during all his life the

Desert Rat should be engaged in learning how to die, and meet the issue unafraid. For the Desert Rat was a philosopher, and even at this ghastly spectacle his sense of humor did not desert him. He sat down on the skull of one of the burros and laughed - a dry cackling gobble.

"What a great wonderful genius of a desert it is!" he mumbled. "It's worth dying in after all - a fitting mausoleum for a Desert Rat. Here I come staggering in, with murder in my heart, stultifying my manhood with the excuse that it would be justice in the abstract, and the Lord shows me an example of the vanity and littleness of life. All right, Boston, old man. You win, I guess, but I've got an ace coppered, and even if you do get through, some day you'll pay the price."

He sat there on the bleached skull, his head in his hands, trembling, pondering, yet unafraid in the face of the knowledge that here his wanderings must end. He was right. It was a spot eminently befitting the finish of such a man. It was at least exclusive, for the vulgar and the common would never perish here. In all the centuries since its formation no human feet, save his own and those of the man whose skeleton lay before him, had ever awakened the echoes in its silent halls. Pioneers, dreamers both, men of the Great Outdoors, each had heard the call of the silent places - each had essayed to fight his way into the treasure vaults of the desert; and as they had begun, so had they finished - in the arms of Nature, who had claimed the utmost of their love.

The Desert Rat was a true son of the desert. To him the scowl of the sun-baked land at midday had always turned to a smile of promise at dawn; to him the darkest night was but the forerunner of another day of glorious battle, when he could rise out of the sage, stretch his young legs and watch the sun rise over his empire. He knew the desert - he saw the issue now, but still he did not falter.

"Poor little wife," he mumbled; "poor little unborn baby! You'll hope, through the long years, waiting for me to come back - and you'll never know!"

His faltering gaze wandered down the canyon where his own tracks and those of the dead shone gray against the brown of the sun-swept wash. He had followed a trail that might have been ten years old; perhaps, in the years to come, some other wanderer would see *his* tracks, halting, staggering, uncertain, blazing the ancient call of the desert: "Come to me or I perish." And following the trail, even as the Desert Rat had followed this other, he, too, in his own time, would come at length to the finish - and wonder.

The Desert Rat sighed, but if in that supreme moment he wept it was not for himself. He had many things to think of, he had much of happiness to renounce, but he was of that breed that dares to approach the end.

Like one who wraps the drapery of his couch.
About him, and lies down to pleasant dreams.

For him the trail had ended here, as it had for this other remnant of vanished life that lay before him now with arms outstretched. The Desert Rat stared at the relic. A cross! The body formed a cross! Here again was The Promise -

A thought came to the perishing wanderer. "I'll leave a

message" he gobbled. He could not forbear a joke. "To be delivered when called for" he added. "This other man might have done the same, but perhaps he didn't care - perhaps there wasn't anybody waiting at home for him."

From his shirt pocket he drew the stub of a lead pencil and the note-book in which he had written his will and the record of his betrayal. He added the story of his wanderings since leaving Chuckwalla Tanks, and the postscript:

> The company in which I will be found was not of my own seeking. He was here before me by several years and I found nothing whereby he might be identified.

He tore the leaves out of the note-book, stuffed them inside his empty canteen and screwed the cap on tight; after which he cast about for a prominent place where he might leave his last message to the world.

At the head of the canyon stood an extinct volcano, its precipitous sides forming the barrier at the western end of the canyon. Away back in the years when the world was young, a stream of thin soupy lava, spewed from this ancient crater, had flowed down the canyon out onto the desert. It was this which the Desert Rat had at first taken for an old "wash." Owing to the pitch of the canyon floor, most of the lava had run out, but a thin crust, averaging in thickness from a quarter to three quarters of an inch, still remained. Originally, this thin lava had been a creamy white, but with the passage of centuries the sun had baked it to a dirty brown and the lava had become disintegrated and rotten. As the hot lava had hardened and dried it had cracked, after the fashion of a lake bed when the water has evaporated, but into millions and millions of smaller cracks than in the case where water has evaporated from mud. As a result of this peculiar condition, the entire lava capping in the canyon was split into small fragments, each fragment fitting exactly into its appointed place, the whole forming a marvelous piece of natural mosaic that could only have been designed by the Master Artist.

With the point of his pocket knife the Desert Rat pried loose one of these sections of lava. Where it had been exposed to the sun on top it was brown, but the under side was the original creamy white.

The mystery of the phantom trail was solved at last. In fact, not to state a paradox, there had been no mystery at first - at least to the Desert Rat. The moment he saw the bones he guessed the answer to that weird puzzle.

The tracks were easily explained. When one walked on the surface of this thin lava crust it broke beneath him and crumbled into dust. The brown dust on top mingled with the underlying white, the blend of colors on the whole forming a slate-colored patch with creamy edges, marking the boundaries of the foot-prints; and here, in this horrible canyon, where rains would never erode nor winds obliterate, the tracks would show for years until the magic of the desert had again wrought its spell on the landscape and the ghostly white tracks had faded and blended again into the all-prevailing brown.

The Desert Rat was something of a geologist, and had he not been dying, an extended examination of this weird formation would have interested him greatly.

But he had his message to leave to his loved ones, and time pressed. In the joy and pride of his strength and youth he had dared the desert. He had dreamed of a fortune, and this - this was to be the awakening...

He crawled out into a smooth undisturbed space and fell to work with the point of his knife. Carefully he raised piece after piece of the natural mosaic, inverted it and laid it back in its appointed place. At the end of two hours he finished. There, in inlaid letters of creamy white against the desert brown, his message flared almost imperishable:

Friend, look in my canteen and see that I get justice.

A century must pass before that message faded; as for the coming of the messenger, he would leave that to the Almighty.

The Desert Rat was going fast now. He moved back a few feet, fearful that at the end he might obliterate his message. With his fading gaze fixed on the mouth of the canyon he lay waiting, hoping, praying, brave to the last ... and presently help came.

It was the Night Watchman!

CHAPTER III

Serenely indifferent to the fact that but a few hours' average running time intervenes between it and San Francisco on the north, and Los Angeles on the south, the little desert station of San Pasqual has always insisted upon remaining a frontier town.

One can pardon San Pasqual readily for this apparent apathy. Not to do so would savor strongly of an application of the doctrine of personal responsibility in the matter of a child with a club-foot. San Pasqual isn't responsible. It has nothing to be proud of, nothing to incite even a sporadic outburst of civic pride. It never had.

Here, in this story, occurs a description. In a narrative of human emotions, descriptions are, perhaps, better appreciated when they are dispensed with unless, as in the case of San Pasqual, they are worth the time and space and trouble. Assuming, therefore, that San Pasqual, for all its failings, is distinctive enough to warrant this, we will describe the town as it appeared early in the present decade; and, for that matter, will continue to appear, pending the day when they strike oil in the desert and San Pasqual picks itself together, so to speak, and begins to take an interest in life. Until then, however, as a center of social, scenic, intellectual and commercial activity, San Pasqual will never attract globe-trotters, folks with Pilgrim ancestors or retired bankers from Kansas and Iowa seeking an attractive investment in western real estate.

San Pasqual is such a weather-beaten, sad, abject little town that one might readily experience surprise that the trains even condescend to stop there. It squats in the sand a few miles south of Tehachapi pass, hemmed in by mountain ranges ocher-tinted where near by, mellowed by distance into gorgeous shades of turquoise and deep maroon. They are very far away, these mountains, even though their outlines are so distinct that they appear close at hand. The desert atmosphere has cast a kindly spell upon them, softening their hellish perspective into lines of beauty in certain lights. It is well that this is so, for it helps to dispel an illusion of the imaginative and impressionable when first they visit San Pasqual - the illusion that they are in prison.

The basin that lies between these mountains is the waste known as the Mojave desert. It stretches north and south from San Pasqual, fading away into nothing, into impalpable, unlovely, soul-crushing suggestions of space illimitable; dancing and shimmering in the heat waves, it seems struggling to escape. When the wind blows, the dust-devils play tag among the low sage and greasewood; the Joshua trees, rising in the midst of this desolation, stretch forth their fantastically twisted and withered arms, seeming to invoke a curse on nature herself while warning the traveler that the heritage of this land is death. There is a bearing down of one's spirit in the midst of all this loneliness and desolation that envelops everything; yet, despite the uncanny mystery of it, the sense of repression it imparts, of unconquerable isolation from all that is good and sweet and beautiful, there are those who find it possible to live in San Pasqual without feeling that they are accursed.

At the western boundary of the Mojave desert lies San Pasqual, huddled around the railroad water tank. It is the clearing-house for the Mojave, for entering or leaving the desert men must pass through San Pasqual. From the main-line tracks a branch railroad now extends north across the desert, through the eastern part of Kern county and up the Owens river valley into Inyo, although at the time Donna Corblay enters into this story the railroad had not been built and a stage line bore the brunt of the desert travel as far north as Keeler - constituting the main outlet from that vast but little known section of California that lies east of the Sierra Nevada range.

Hence, people entering or leaving this great basin passed through San Pasqual, which accounted for the town that grew up around the water tank; the little row of so-called "pool parlors," cheap restaurants, saloons and gambling houses, the post-office, a drug store, a tiny school-house with a belfry and no bell and the little row of cottages west of the main-line tracks where all the *good* people lived - which conglomerate mass of inchoate architecture is all that saved San Pasqual from the ignominy of being classed as a flag station.

We are informed that the *good* people lived west of the tracks. East of the tracks it was different. The past tense is used with a full appreciation of the necessity for grammatical construction, for times have changed in San Pasqual, since it is no longer encumbered with the incubus that made this story possible - Harley P.

Hennage, the town gambler and the worst man in San Pasqual.

Close to the main-line tracks and midway between both strata of society stood San Pasqual's limited social and civic center - the railroad hotel and eating-house. Here, between the arrival and departure of all through trains, the San Pasqualians met on neutral ground, experiencing mild mental relaxation watching the waitresses ministering to the gastronomic necessities of the day-coach tourists from the Middle West. At the period in which the action of this story takes place, however, most people preferred to find relief from the aching desolation of San Pasqual and its environs in the calm, restful, spiritual face of Donna Corblay.

Donna was the young lady cashier at the combination news stand, cigar and tobacco emporium and pay-as-you-leave counter in the eating-house. She was more than that. She was an institution. She was the day hotel clerk; the joy and despair of traveling salesmen who made it a point of duty to get off at San Pasqual and eat whether they were hungry or not; information clerk for rates and methods of transportation for all desert points north, south, east and west. She was the recipient of confidences from waitresses engaged in the innocent pastime of across-the-counter flirtations with conductors and brakemen. She was the joy of the men and the envy of the women. In fact, Donna was an exemplified copy of that distinctive personality with which we unconsciously invest any young woman upon whose capable shoulders must fall such multifarious duties as those already described; particularly when, as in Donna's case, they are accepted and disposed of with the gentle, kindly, interested yet impersonal manner of one who loves her little world enough to be a very distinct part of it; yet, seeing it in its true light, manages to hold herself aloof from it; unconsciously conveying to one meeting her for the first time the impression that she was in San Pasqual on her own sufferance - a sort of strayling from another world who had picked upon the lonely little desert town as the scene of her sphere of action for something of the same reason that prompts other people to collect postage stamps or rare butterflies.

It has already been stated that Donna Corblay was an institution. That is quite true. She was the mistress of the Hat Ranch.

This last statement requires elucidation. Just what is a hat ranch? you ask. It is - a hat ranch. There is only one Hat Ranch on earth and it may be found a half mile south of San Pasqual, a hundred yards back from the tracks. Donna Corblay owned it, worked it in her spare moments and made it pay.

You see, San Pasqual lies just south of Tehachapi pass, and about five days in every week, the year round, the north wind comes whistling down the pass. When it strikes the open desert it appears to become possessed of an almost human disposition to spurt and get by San Pasqual as quickly as possible. Hence, when the tourist approaching the station sticks his head out of the window or unwisely remains on the platform of the observation car, this forty-mile "zephyr," as they term it in San Pasqual, sighs joyously past him, snatches his headgear, whirls it down the tracks and deposits it at the western boundary of Donna's "ranch." This boundary happens to be a seven-foot adobe wall - so the hat sticks there.

In the days when Donna lived at the Hat Ranch she would pause at this wall every evening on her way home from work long enough to gather up the orphaned hats. Later, after cleaning and brushing them, she would sell them to the boys up in San Pasqual. There was a wide variety of style, size and color in Donna's stock of hats, and fastidious indeed was he who could not select from the lot a hat to match his peculiar style of masculine beauty. And, furthermore: damned was he who so far forgot tradition and local custom as to purchase his "every-day" hat elsewhere. He might buy his Sunday hat in Bakersfield or Los Angeles and still retain caste, but his every-day hat - never! Such a proceeding would have been construed by Donna's admirers as a direct attack on home industry. In fact, one made money by purchasing his hats of Donna Corblay. If she never accepted less than one dollar for a hat, regardless of age, color, original price and previous condition of servitude, she never charged more. Hence, everybody was satisfied - or, if not satisfied at the time, all they had to do was to await the arrival of the next train. The "zephyrs" were steady and reliable and in San Pasqual it is an ill wind that doesn't blow somebody a hat.

In San Pasqual stray hats were not looked upon as flotsam and jetsam and subject to a too liberal interpretation of the "Losers-weepers-finders-keepers" rule. There was a dead-line for hats beyond which no gentleman would venture, for, after a hat had once blown beyond the town limits it was no longer a maverick and subject to branding, but on the other hand was the absolute, undeniable and legal property of Donna Corblay.

So much for the hats. As for the ranch itself, it wasn't,

properly speaking, a ranch at all. It was a low, four-room adobe house with a lean-to kitchen built of boards. It had a dirt roof and iron-barred windows and in the rear there was a long rectangular patio with a fountain and a flower garden. In fact, the ranch was more of a fortress than a dwelling-place and was surrounded by an adobe wall which enclosed about an acre of the Mojave desert. Originally it had been the habitation of a visionary who wandered into San Pasqual, established the ranch and sunk an artesian well. With irrigation the rich alluvial soil of the desert will grow anything, and the original owner planned to raise garden-truck and cater to the local trade. He prospered, but being of that vast majority of humankind to whom prosperity proves a sort of mental hobble, he made up his mind one day to go prospecting. So he wrote out a notice, advertising the property for sale, and tacked it to a telegraph pole in front of the eating-house.

Alas for the frailty and suspicion of human nature! The self-centered and self-satisfied citizens of San Pasqual had condemned the vegetable venture from the start. It had been too radical a departure from the desert order of things, and the fact that a mere stranger had conceived the idea sufficed to damn the enterprise even with those who gloried in the convenience of fresh vegetables; while the fact that the vegetable culturist was now about to leave branded the experiment a failure and was productive of a chorus of "I told you so's." The announcement of the proprietor of the ranch that he would entertain offers on a property to which he had no title other than that entailed in the God-given right of every American citizen to squat on a piece of land until he is driven off, was received as a rare piece of humor. In disgust the founder of the Hat Ranch abandoned his vegetable business, loaded his worldly effects on two burros and departed, leaving the kitchen door wide open. He never returned.

In the course of time a young woman with a two-months-old daughter came to San Pasqual to accept the position of cashier in the eating-house. The old adobe ranch was still deserted - the kitchen door still wide open. It was the only vacant dwelling in San Pasqual, and the woman with the baby decided to move in. She hired a Mexican woman to clean the house, sent to Bakersfield for some installment furniture and to Los Angeles for some assorted seeds. About a week later a Cahuilla buck with his squaw alighted from a north-bound train and were met by the woman with the baby girl. That night the entire party took possession of the Hat Ranch.

That first mistress of the Hat Ranch was Donna Corblay's mother, so before we plunge into the heart of our story and present to the reader Donna Corblay as she appeared at twenty years of age behind the counter at the eating-house on the night that Bob McGraw rode into her life on his Roman-nosed mustang, Friar Tuck, a short history of those earlier years at the Hat Ranch will be found to repay the time given to its perusal.

For more than sixteen years after her arrival in San Pasqual, Donna's mother had presided behind the eating-house pay counter. She was quiet and uncommunicative - a handsome woman whose chief beauty lay in her eyes - wonderful for their brilliance and color and the shadows that lurked in them, like the ghosts of a sorrow ineffable. Up to the day she died nobody in San Pasqual knew very much about her - where she

Peter B. Kyne

came from or why she came. She gave no confidences and invited none. In a general way it was known that she was a widow. Her husband had gone away and never returned, and it was a moot question in San Pasqual whether the Widow Corblay was grass or natural. Be that as it may, the fact remains that the absent one was missed and that his wife remained faithful to his memory, as several frontier gentlemen, who had sought her hand in marriage, might have testified had they so desired.

Mrs. Corblay lived for her child, and was accused of being wantonly and sinfully extravagant in her manner of dressing this child. She maintained and supported two Indian servants, which fact alone raised her a notch or two socially above the wives, sisters and daughters of the railroad men and local business men who lived in the cottages west of the tracks. A great many of these estimable females disliked her accordingly and charged her with "'puttin' on airs." Indeed, more than one of them had ventured the suggestion that Mrs. Corblay had a past, and that her child was its outward expression. Of course, they couldn't prove anything, but - and there the matter rested, abruptly. That "but" ended it, even as the tracks end at the bumper in a roundhouse. One felt the jar just the same.

Some hint of this provincial interest in her and her affairs must have reached Mrs. Corblay shortly after her arrival, so with true feminine obstinacy she declined to alleviate the abnormal curiosity which gnawed at the heart of the little community. She died as she had lived, considerable of a mystery, and San Pasqual, retaining its resentment of this mystery, visited its resentment upon Donna Corblay when

Donna, in the course of time, gave evidence that she, also, possessed an ultra-feminine, almost heroic capacity for attending strictly to her own business and permitting others to attend to theirs.

Early in her occupation of the adobe ranch house Mrs. Corblay had inaugurated the hat industry, with fresh vegetables as a side line. The garden was presided over by a dolorous squaw who responded to the rather fanciful appellation of Soft Wind. Sam Singer, her buck, was a stolid, stodgy savage, with eyes like the slits in a blackberry pie. Originally the San Pasqualians had christened him "Psalm Singer," because of the fact that once, during a revival held by an itinerant evangelist in a tent next door to the Silver Dollar saloon, the buck had attended regularly, attracted by the melody of a little portable organ, the plaintive strains of which appeared to charm his heathen soul. An unorthodox citizen, in the sheer riot of his imagination, had saddled the buck with his new name. It had stuck to him, and since in the vernacular psalm singer was pronounced "sam singer," the Indian came in time to be known by that name and would answer to none other.

Donna grew up slightly different from the other little girls in San Pasqual. For instance: she was never allowed to play in the dirt of the main street with other children; she wore white dresses that were always clean, new ribbons in her hair; she always carried a handkerchief; she attended the little public school with the belfry but no bell, and her mother trained her in domestic science and the precepts of religion, which, lacking definite direction perhaps by reason of the fact that there was no church in San Pasqual, served, nevertheless, as a bulwark against the assaults of vice and vulgarity which, in a frontier town, are very thinly veiled. As a child she was neither precocious nor shy. From a rather homely, long-legged gangling girl of fourteen she emerged apparently by a series of swift transitions into a young lady at sixteen, giving promise of a beauty which lay, not so much in her physical attractions, which were generous, but in that easily discernible nobility of character which indicates beauty of soul - that superlative beauty which entitles its possessor to be alluded to as "sweet," rather than pretty or handsome. At the dawn of womanhood she was a lovely little girl, kind, affectionate, imaginative, distinctly virginal,

- a flower... born to blush unseen,
And waste its sweetness on the desert air.

When Donna was nearly seventeen years old her mother died. It was the consensus of opinion that heart trouble had something to do with it. In fact, Mrs. Corblay had often complained of pains in her heart and was subject to fainting spells; besides which, there was that in her eyes which seemed to predicate a heartache of many years' standing. At any rate, she fainted at the eating-house one day and they carried her home. She passed away very quietly the same night, leaving an estate which consisted of Donna, the two Indian servants, and a quantity of coin in a teapot in the cupboard at the Hat Ranch which upon investigation was found to total the stupendous sum of two hundred and twenty-eight dollars and ninety-five cents.

There was no one except Donna to attend to the funeral arrangements, and for eight hours following her mother's death she was too distracted to think of anything but her great grief. Soft Wind prepared her mistress for the grave after a well-meant but primitive fashion, while Sam Singer squatted all morning in the sand in front of the compound and smoked innumerable cigarettes. Presently he got up, went to his own little cabin within the enclosure and was invisible for ten minutes. When he emerged he was clad in a new pair of "bull breeches," a white stiff-bosomed shirt without a collar but with a brass collar button doing duty nevertheless, while a red silk handkerchief, with the ends drawn through a ring fashioned from a horseshoe nail, enveloped his swarthy neck. He had rummaged through the stock of hats and appropriated a Grand Army hat with cord and tassels, and arrayed thus Sam Singer walked up the tracks to San Pasqual.

Arrived here Sam's very appearance heralded news of grave importance at the Hat Ranch. Such extraordinary and unwonted attention to dress could portend but one of two things - a journey or a funeral. Inasmuch, however, as Sam was coatless and Mrs. Corblay had been carried home ill the day before, San Pasqual allowed itself one guess and won.

To those who sought to question him, however, Sam Singer had nothing more polite than a tribal grunt. He proceeded directly to the Silver Dollar saloon, where he held converse with a man who seemed much interested in the news which Sam had to impart, for he nodded gravely several times, gave Sam fifty cents and a cigar and then hurried around to the public telephone station in "Doc" Taylor's drug store.

Five minutes later, by some mysterious person, Mrs. Daniel Pennycook, wife of the yardmaster, was informed over the telephone that Donnie Corblay's mother was dead.

"So I understand" replied Mrs. Pennycook volubly. "Poor thing! There was always somethin' so mysterious like about - "

The use of the word "like" was habit with Mrs. Pennycook. She rarely took a decided stand in anything except Mr. Pennycook, and always modified her modifying adjective with the word "like"; an annoying practice which had always rendered her an object of terror to Mrs. Corblay. To the latter it always seemed as if Mrs. Pennycook was desirous of saying something nasty, but lacked the courage to come out flatfooted with it.

Her unknown informant interrupted, or attempted to interrupt, but Mrs. Pennycook was now started on her favorite topic, in such haste that she failed to give the customary telephonic challenge:

"Who's speaking, please?"

She continued. "Yes, she was kinder quiet like any kept to herself like - "

"Well," said the unknown, "she's dead now, and that little daughter o' hers is all alone down there with her Indian woman. If you knew Mrs. Corblay was dead, why in blue blazes didn't you or some other woman in this heartless village go down there and comfort that child? I've asked three of your neighbors already, but they're washin' or dustin' or cookin' or somethin'."

"I was so terrible shocked like when I heard it - "

"Well, if the shock's over, for decency's sake, Mrs. Pennycook, go down to the Hat Ranch and keep that little girl comp'ny till this afternoon."

"Who's talkin'?" demanded Mrs. Pennycook belligerently.

"I am."

"Who are you?"

"Nobody!"

For several seconds Mrs. Pennycook shot questions into the transmitter, but receiving no response she hung up, furious at having been denied the inalienable right of her sex to the last word. Shortly thereafter her worthy spouse, Dan Pennycook, came in for his lunch. To him Mrs. Pennycook imparted the tale of the strange man who had rung her up, demanding that she go down to the Hat Ranch and see Donnie Corblay. Pennycook's stupid good-natured face clouded.

"Then," he demanded, "why don't you do it? I've been workin' with that string of empties below town all mornin', an' if any woman in this charitable community passed me goin' to the Hat Ranch I didn't see her. It's a shame. Put on your other things right after lunch, Arabella, an' go down. I'll go with you."

"But the gall o' the man, askin' me to do this! I intended goin' anyhow, but him ringin' me up so sudden like, I - "

"My dear," said Mr. Pennycook, "he paid you a compliment."

"Humph" responded Mrs. Pennycook. Then she

sniffed. She continued to sniff at intervals during the meal; she was still sniffing when later she joined her husband at the front gate and set off with him down the tracks to the Hat Ranch.

Arrived at the Hat Ranch Mrs. Pennycook saw at once that Donna was "too upset like" to have any of the details of her mother's funeral thrust upon her. Here was a situation which required the supervision of a calm, executive person - Mrs. Daniel Pennycook, for instance. At any rate Mrs. Pennycook decided to take charge. She was first on the scene and naturally the task was hers, not only as a matter of principle but also by right of discovery.

Now, under the combined attentions of Donna, Mrs. Corblay and Soft Wind, the house, while primitive, had, nevertheless, been made comfortable and kept immaculate. But there is a superstition rampant in all provincial communities which dictates that the first line of action to be pursued when there is a death in the family is to scrub the house thoroughly from cellar to garret, and Mrs. Pennycook had been inoculated with the virus of this superstition very early in life. She tucked up her skirts, seized a broom and a mop, rounded up Soft Wind and proceeded to produce chaos where neatness and order had always reigned.

It was at this juncture that Donna Corblay first gave evidence of having a mind of her own. She dried her tears and gently but firmly informed Mrs. Pennycook that the house had been thoroughly cleaned and scrubbed three days previous. She begged Mrs. Pennycook to desist. Mrs. Pennycook desisted, for if Donna couched her request in the language of entreaty, her young eyes flashed a stern command, and Mrs.

Pennycook was not deficient in the intuition of her sex. So she composed herself in a rocking chair and by blunt brutal questioning presently ascertained that Mrs. Corblay had left her daughter two hundred and twenty-eight dollars and ninety-five cents.

This decided Mrs. Pennycook. She dilated upon the importance of having a clergyman come down from Bakersfield for the funeral, and suggested the services (at the metropolitan rates usually accorded such functionaries) of the local alleged quartette, which regularly made night hideous in San Pasqual's lone barber shop.

"It'll be kinder nice like, don't you think, Donna?" she queried.

Donna nodded dubiously.

"An' what was your poor dear mamma's church?" continued Mrs. Pennycook.

"She didn't have any" Donna answered, truthfully enough.

Again Mrs. Pennycook sniffed. "Well, then, I suppose Mr. Tillingham, of the Universal Church - "

Donna interrupted. "Mamma always knew she would be taken from me without warning, and she often told me not to give her an expensive funeral. I think she would have liked some services but I can't afford them."

"But, dearie, that's so barbarous like!" exclaimed the dismayed Samaritan. "There ought to be some one to say some prayers an' sing a hymn or two."

"Mamma always said she wanted to be buried simply. She thought it was sweet and beautiful to have services, but not essential. She was always skimping and saving for me, Mrs. Pennycook. She said I wasn't to wear mourning; that the - living needed more prayers than - the - dead. She - she said that when she was gone God would be good to her and that - I - she said I would need all the money we had."

"A-a-h-h-h!" breathed Mrs. Pennycook. She understood now. What a baggage the girl was! How heartless, begrudging her poor dead mother the poor comfort of a Christian burial, because she wanted the money for herself! Privately Mrs. Pennycook prophesied a bad ending for Donnie Corblay. She winked knowingly at her husband, then with truly feminine sarcasm:

"Well, at *least,* Donna, you'll *have* to buy a coffin an' a *grave* an' have the grave *dug* - "

"Sam Singer will attend to that. I'm going to bury mamma among the flowers at the end of our garden. I'll have a nice plain coffin made in San Pasqual - "

"Oh!" Mrs. Pennycook trembled.

"Mamma always said," Donna continued, "that undertakers preyed on the dead and traded in human grief, and for me not to engage one for her funeral. I'm going to do just what she told me to do, Mrs. Pennycook."

"Quite right, Donnie, quite right" interjected Mr.

Pennycook. He was an impulsive creature and even under the hypnotic eye of Mrs. P. he sometimes broke out of bounds.

"Daniel! Come!"

Daniel! At the mention of his Christian name Mr. Pennycook quivered. He knew he was in for it now, but he didn't care. It occurred to him that he might as well, to quote a homely proverb, "be hanged for a sheep as a lamb." He had visited the Hat Ranch to tender aid and sympathy, and despite the impending visitation of his wife's wrath he resolved to be reckless for once and deliver the goods in bulk.

"Your poor mother was a sensible woman, Donnie girl," he told the orphan, "an' you're a dutiful daughter to follow out her last wishes under these - er - deplorable circumstances - er - er - I mean it's a terrible hard thing to lose your mother, Donnie, an' - damme, Donnie, I'm sorry. 'Pon my word, I'm sorry."

Mrs. Pennycook's lips moved, and while no sound issued therefrom, yet did Dan Pennycook, out of his many years of marital submission, comprehend the unspoken sentence:

"Dan Pennycook, you're a fool!"

"Ya-a-h" growled Mr. Pennycook, thoroughly aroused now and striving to appear belligerent. His wife silenced him with a look; then turned to Donna. She had a duty to perform. She was a great woman for "principle" and the performance of what she conceived to be her duty. She was a well-meaning but misguided person ordinarily, who loved a fight with her own family on the broad general ground that it denoted firmness of character. Mrs. Pennycook was so long on virtue and character herself that half her life was spent disposing of a portion of these attributes to the less fortunate members of her household.

She entered now upon a calm yet stern discussion of the perfectly impossible proceeding of making a private cemetery out of one's back yard; but Mr. Pennycook had recovered his poise and decided that here was one of those rare occasions when it behooved him to declare himself - by the way, a very rare proceeding with Mr. Pennycook, he being known in San Pasqual as the original Mr. Henpeck.

"Mrs. Pennycook," he thundered, "you will please 'tend to your own business, ma'am. Donnie, my dear, I'm goin' to wire Los Angeles an' order up a heap o' big red roses on 25 - damme, Mrs. Pennycook, what the devil are *you* lookin' at, ma'am?"

"Nothing" she retorted, although it is a fact that had she been Medusa a singularly life-like replica of Dan Pennycook in concrete might have been produced, upon which the posterity of San Pasqual might gaze and be warned of the dangers attendant upon mating with the Mrs. Pennycooks of this world.

Donna commenced to cry. Mr. Pennycook's sympathy, albeit checked and moderated to a great extent by the presence of his wife, was, nevertheless, the most genuine sample of that rare commodity which she had received up to that moment. His action had been so - brave - so spontaneous - he knew - he understood; Dan Pennycook had a soul. And besides he was going to wire for some red roses - and O, how scarce were red roses in San Pasqual!

"O Mr. Pennycook, dear Mr. Pennycook" she wailed, and sought instant refuge on his honest breast. She placed her arms around his neck and cried, and Mr. Pennycook cried also, until his single Sunday handkerchief was used up - whereat he pleaded dumbly with his wife for her handkerchief - and was refused. So, like some great blubbering boy, he used his fists, while Mrs. Pennycook looked coldly on, working her lower lip and the tip of her nose, rabbit-fashion, for all the world like one who, having anticipated a sniff of the spices of Araby, has detected instead a shocking aroma of corned beef and cabbage.

It was a queer tableau, indeed; Donna weeping on Mr. Pennycook's breast, when every instinct of her sex, even the vaguest acceptance of tradition and custom, dictated that she should have wept on Mrs. Pennycook's breast. Mrs. Pennycook realized the incongruity of the situation and was shrewd enough to attribute it to a strong aversion to her on the part of Donna Corblay. She resolved to make them both pay for her humiliation - Dan, within the hour, Donna whenever the opportunity should occur.

CHAPTER IV

When Donna and Mr. Pennycook had succeeded eventually in overcoming their emotions, the worthy yardmaster and his wife took their departure. Mr. Pennycook was compelled to return to work and something told him that Donna would be happier alone than with Mrs. Pennycook; hence he made no objection to her leaving the Hat Ranch.

They had scarcely left when the man whom Sam Singer had consulted at the Silver Dollar saloon earlier in the day appeared from the north angle of the adobe wall, where he had been lurking, and dodged into the Hat Ranch enclosure. Donna was seated at the kitchen table, her face in her hands, when he arrived. He could see her through the open half-window of the lean-to, so he came to the window, thrust his head and shoulders in and coughed.

Donna raised her head and gazed into the face of the worst man in San Pasqual!

This peculiarly distinguished individual was Mr. Harley P. Hennage, the proprietor of a faro game in the Silver Dollar saloon. He had an impassive, almost dull, face (accentuated, perhaps, from much playing of poker in early life) which, at times, would light up with the shy smile of a trustful child, revealing three magnificent golden upper teeth. He bore no more resemblance to the popular conception of a western gambler than does a college professor to a coal passer. Mr. Hennage lived in his shirtsleeves, paid cash and hated jewelry. He had never been known to carry a derringer or a small, genteel, silver-plated revolver in his waist-coat pocket. Neither did he appear in public with a bowie knife down his bootleg. Not being a Mexican, he did not carry a knife, and besides he always wore congress gaiters. Owing to the fact that he was a large florid sandy person, with a freckled bristly neck and a singularly direct fearless manner of looking at his man with eyes that were small, sunken, baleful and rather piggy, the exigencies of Mr. Hennage's profession had never even warranted recourse to his two most priceless possessions - his hands. Yet, despite this fact, and the further fact that he had never accomplished anything more reprehensible than staking his coin against that of his neighbor, Mr. Hennage had acquired the reputation of being the worst man in San Pasqual. In the language of the country, he was a hard *hombre,* for he looked it. When one gazed at Mr. Hennage he observed a human bulldog, a man who would finish anything he started. Hence, he was credited with the ability and inclination to do the most impossible things if given half an excuse. It is needless, therefore, to remark that Mr. Hennage's depravity, like Mrs. Pennycook's virtue, partook more or less of the nature of the surrounding country; that is to say, it was susceptible of development.

Most people in this queer world of ours harbor an impression that if you make friends with a dog he will not bite you, and that lion tamers are enabled to accumulate gray hairs merely by the exercise of nerve and the paralyzing influence of the human eye. Hence, when the worst man in San Pasqual confronted Donna, she did not at once scream for Sam Singer, but looked Mr. Hennage in the eye and quavered.

"Good morning, Mr. Hennage."

It was hard work continuing to look Mr. Hennage in the eye. To-day he looked more like a bulldog than ever, for his eyes were red-lidded and watery.

Mr. Hennage nodded. He drew a silk handkerchief from his coat pocket and blew his nose with a report like a pistol shot before he spoke.

"How's the kitty?" he demanded.

Donna glanced toward the store and about the kitchen wearily and replied.

"I don't know, Mr. Hennage. I guess she's around the house somewhere."

"The Lord love you" murmured the gambler. The hard lips lifted, the dull impassive face was lit for an instant by the trustful childish smile, and through the glory of that infrequent facial expression Harley P.'s three gold front teeth flashed like triple searchlights.

"I mean, Miss Corblay, have you any money?"

"Only a little bit, Mr. Hennage" Donna quavered. The question frightened her and she hastened to assure the bad man that it was a very little bit indeed, and all that her mother had been able to save. She trembled lest the monster might take a notion to rob her of even this meager amount.

"I just had a hunch it was that way with you." The worst man in San Pasqual wagged his great head, as if to compliment himself on his penetration. "I just knew it."

This was not strictly the truth. Sam Singer had managed to convey to the gambler some hint of the Corblay fortunes, financial as well as material, and had begged of him to exercise his superior white man intelligence to aid the Indian in wrestling with this white man's problem that confronted the dwellers at the Hat Ranch. Rather a queer source, indeed, for Sam Singer to seek help for his young mistress; but then Sam was not an educated aborigine; he was not given to reflecting upon the ethics of any given line of procedure. The fact of the matter was that Harley P. Hennage was the only white man in San Pasqual who deigned to honor Sam Singer with a greeting and his cast-off shoes. In return Sam had honored Harley P. with his confidence and an appeal to him for further aid.

"I have attended to everything" continued Mr. Hennage. "Preacher, quartette from Bakersfield - they're real good, too. Playin' in a theater up there, but I engaged to get 'em back in time for the evenin' performance on a special train - so they said they'd come. An' I've ordered an elegant coffin, the best they had in stock, with a floral piece from Sam Singer an' his squaw an' a piller o' white carnations with 'Mother' in violets - from you, understand? Everything the best, spick an' span an' no cost to the estate. Compliments o' Harley P. Hennage, Miss Donna." He paused and rubbed his hairy freckled hands together in an embarrassed manner. "I hope you won't think I'm actin' forward, because I ain't one o' the presumin' kind. I just wanted to do somethin' to help out because - your mother was a very lovely lady. Three times a day for ten years she give me my change an' there never was a time when she didn't have a decent, kindly word for me - the only good woman in this town that'd look at me - God bless her! Mum's the word, Miss Donnie. Don't let nobody know I did it, because it'd hurt your reputation. And don't tell Mrs. Pennycook! Pennycook's a clean, decent old sport, but look out for the missus!" Here Mr. Hennage lowered his voice, glanced cautiously around to make certain that he would not be overheard by Mrs. Pennycook, leaned further in the window and improvising a megaphone with his hands, whispered hoarsely the damning words: "She *talks!*"

Donna nodded. For a long time she had suspected Mrs. Pennycook of this very practice.

"I've got to light out now" Mr. Hennage continued. "Folks'll wonder if they see *me* hangin' around here. But before I go I want to tell you somethin'. Your mother was a-countin' out my change yesterday when she got took. She thought she was goin' then on account o' the pain bein' sharper than common, an' she cries out: 'Donnie! Donnie! My baby, whatever is a-goin' to become o' you when I'm gone!' I was the only one that heard her say it. I caught her when she was fallin', an' I told her I'd see that you didn't lack for nothin' while I lived an' that I'd keep an eye on you an' see that nothin' wrong happened to you. Your mother couldn't speak none then, Miss Donnie, but she give my hand a little press to show she was on an' that whatever I did was done with her say-so.

Consequently, Miss Donnie, any time you need a friend you just ring up the Silver Dollar saloon an' tell the barkeep to call Hennage to the 'phone. Remember! I ain't the presumin' kind, but I can be a good friend - "

He dodged back as if somebody had struck at him. Before Donna could quite realize what he had been saying he had disappeared. She ran to the iron-barred gate, looked out and saw him walking up the railroad tracks toward San Pasqual. She called after him. He turned, waved his hand and continued on - a great fat bow-legged commonplace figure of a man, mopping his high bald forehead - a plain, lowly citizen of uncertain morals; a sordid money-snatcher coming forth from his den of iniquity to masquerade for an hour as the Angel of Hope, and returning - hopeless.

For the last tie that bound Harley P. Hennage to San Pasqual was severed. His soul was not mediocre; he could dwell no longer in San Pasqual without feeling himself accursed. Never again could he bear to sit on his high stool at the lunch counter in the railroad eating-house, where he had boarded for ten years, and watch a stranger taking cash. He had watched Donna's mother so long that the vigil had become a part of his being - a sort of religious ceremony - and in this little tragedy of life no understudy could ever star for Harley P. Her beautiful sad eyes were closed forever now and the tri-daily joy of his sordid existence had vanished.

"What little things go to make up the big pleasures of life! Who could guess, for instance, that the simple deceit of presenting a twenty-dollar piece in payment of a fifty-cent meal check had held for Harley P. a greater joy than the promise of ultimate salvation? Yet it had; for during the slight wait at the pay counter while the cashier counted out his change he had been privileged to view her at close quarters, to mark the contour of her nose, to note the winning sweetness of her tender mouth, to hearken to the music of her low voice counting out the dollars, and, perchance, saying something commonplace himself as he gathered up his change! Yet that had been sufficient to make of San Pasqual a paradise for Harley P. He knew his limitations; he had presumed but once, long enough to ask the cashier to marry him. Her refusal had made him worship her the more, only he worshiped thereafter in silence and from afar. She had not laughed at him nor scorned him nor upbraided him, lowly worm that he was, for daring to hope that he might be good enough for her! No. She had told him about her husband, who had gone prospecting and never returned; of Sam Singer who had been rescued on the desert when close to death, of his return with a wild story of much gold and a man, whose name he did not know, who had killed her husband and escaped with the gold. She respected Mr. Hennage, she admired him, she knew he was good and kind - and she did not refer to his method of making a living. She merely laid her soft hand on his, as he reached for his nineteen dollars and a half change, and said:

"Do you understand, Harley?"

Yes, she had called him Harley that day, and he had understood. Her heart was out in the desert. He took the terrible blow with a smile and a flash of his gold teeth, and never referred to his secret again.

He thought of her now, as he waddled back to his neglected game in the Silver Dollar saloon. He wished that he might have been privileged to admittance into that little room off the kitchen where something told him she was lying; he wished that he might see her once again before they buried her - but that would be presuming. He wished he knew of some plan whereby that poor body might be spared the degradation of interment in the lonely, windswept, desert cemetery, side by side with Indians, Mexicans, Greek section hands and the rude forefathers of San Pasqual.

What a profanation! That horrible cemetery, surrounded by a fence of barbed wire and super-annuated railroad ties, to receive that beloved clay. He pictured her as he had seen her every day for ten years, and a rush of vain regret brought the big tears to his buttermilk eyes; the chords of memory twanged in his breast and he paused on the outskirts of San Pasqual with hands upraised, fists clenched in an agony of desperation.

"I can't stand it" he muttered. "I can't. It'll be lonely. I've got to get out. I'll close my game after the funeral an' *vamose.*"

But to return to affairs at the Hat Ranch.

While Harley P. Hennage sat in the Silver Dollar saloon that afternoon dealing faro automatically and pondering the problem of the precise purpose for which he had been created; and while Mrs. Pennycook went from house to house west of the tracks, expounding her personal view of the extraordinary situation at the Hat Ranch, a south-bound train pulled in and discharged a trained nurse, an undertaker, a rectangular redwood box and more floral pieces than San Pasqual had seen in a decade. After instituting some inquiries as to its location, the nurse and the undertaker proceeded to the Hat Ranch, followed by a wagon bearing the box and the flowers.

But why dilate on these mournful details! Suffice the fact that Mrs. Corblay was laid away next morning in conformity with the wishes of the only human being who had any right to express a wish in the matter. The Bakersfield quartette was there and sang "Lead, Kindly Light" and "Nearer My God To Thee"; the Bakersfield minister was there and read: "I am the Resurrection and the Life"; Soft Wind threw ashes on her head and cried in the Cahuilla tongue, "Ai! Ai! Beloved," after the manner of her people, while Sam Singer stood at the head of the grave like a figure done in bronze. Dan Pennycook was there, supporting Donna, and made a spectacle of himself. Mrs. Pennycook was there - and superintended the disposal of the flowers on the grave; in fact, all San Pasqual was there, with the exception of Harley P. Hennage - and nobody wondered why *he* wasn't there. It was well known that he was not one of the presuming kind and had nothing in common with respectable people. And when it was all over, the San Pasqualians went their several ways, assuming - if, indeed, such an assumption did occur to any of them - that the unknown who had provided these expensive obsequies would without doubt provide for Donna also.

That night as Donna lay awake in bed, grieving silently and striving to adjust herself to a philosophical view of the situation, she heard the front gate open and close very softly; then slow, stealthy footsteps passed on the brick walk around the house and down the patio to the end of the garden. It was very late. Donna wondered who could be visiting the Hat Ranch at such an hour, for No. 25, which was due in San Pasqual at midnight, had just gone thundering by. She crept to the window and looked out.

Beside the flower-covered mound at the end of the garden a man was kneeling, with the moonlight casting his grotesque shadow on the blossoms. Presently he stood up, and Donna saw that he had detached one of Dan Pennycook's big red roses and was reverently hiding it away in his breast pocket. Standing hidden in the darkness of her room, Donna could see Harley P.'s face distinctly as he came down the moonlit patio. The terrible mouth was quivering pitifully, tears bedimmed the little, deep-set, piggy eyes to such an extent that Harley P. groped before him with one great, freckled, hairy hand outstretched. He passed her open window.

"My love! My love!" she heard him mutter, and then the slow stealthy footsteps passed around the corner of the house and died away in the distance. Harley P. Hennage had said his farewell to happiness. He was an outcast now, a soul accursed, fleeing from the soul-crushing loneliness and desolation of San Pasqual.

When two weeks had passed, the nurse so thoughtfully provided by the gambler that Donna Corblay might not be obligated even to the slight extent of companionship and comfort during that trying period to the women of San Pasqual, returned to Bakersfield. In the interim Donna had been offered, and had accepted, the position at the railroad hotel and eating-house so long held by her mother. It was a good position. The salary was sixty dollars a month. With this princely stipend and the revenue from the Hat Ranch, and feeling perfectly safe under the watchful eyes of Sam Singer and Soft Wind, Donna faced her little world at seventeen years of age in blissful ignorance of the fact that she was marked in San Pasqual.

She had committed two crimes. In the matter of her mother's funeral she had scorned the advice of her elders and had dared to overthrow ancient custom; and - ridiculous as the statement may appear - she had aroused in Mrs. Pennycook the demon of jealousy! It is a fact. In the bigness of his simple heart the yardmaster had yielded up to Donna a spontaneous portion of tenderness and sympathy, which first amazed Mrs. Pennycook, because she never suspected her husband of being such an "old softy," and then enraged her when she reflected that never since their honeymoon had Dan shown *her* anything more than the prosaic consideration of the unimaginative married man for an unimaginative wife.

It did not occur to Mrs. Pennycook that she had not sought to bring out these qualities in her husband by a display of affection on her part. It never occurred to her that Dan Pennycook was a homely, ordinary, rather dull fellow, in dirty overalls and in perpetual need of a shave; that Donna was a beauty who could afford to pick and choose from a score of eager lovers. She only knew that Donna had aroused in Dan Pennycook the flames of revolt against the lawful domination of his lawful wife; that he was of the masculine gender and would bear watching. Miss Molly Pickett, the postmistress, whose official duties not so onerous as to preclude the perusal of every postal card that passed through her hands (in addition to an occasional letter, for Miss Molly was not above the use of a steam kettle and her own stock of mucilage), was Mrs. Pennycook's dearest friend and her authority for the knowledge that while all men will bear watching, married men will bear a most minute scrutiny. Mrs. Pennycook knew that as a wife she was approaching the unlovely age when fickle husbands tire and cast about for younger and prettier women. Hence she decided to trim her mental lamps and light the dastard Daniel out of temptation.

Her first move was a master-stroke of feminine genius. She issued an order to her husband to buy no more hats of Donna Corblay.

Three loud cheers for Mr. Pennycook! He revolted. He did more. He turned on Mrs. Pennycook - he shook a smutty finger under her nose. He said something. He said he would see her, Mrs. Pennycook, further - in fact, considerably further - than that! All of which was very rude and vulgar of Mr. Pennycook, we must admit, but -

And now our stage is set at last; so assuming three years to have passed, behold the curtain rising, discovering Donna Corblay behind the cashier's counter in the railroad eating-house in the little desert hamlet of San Pasqual.

It is a different Donna that confronts us now, and the first glimpse is almost sufficient to cause us to view with a more complacent eye the mental travail of any married lady whose husband might be exposed to the battery of Donna's eyes.

Such wonderful eyes! Dark blue, wide apart, intelligent, tender, with a trick of peeping up at one from under the long black lashes, and conveying such a medley of profound emotions that it is small wonder that men - and occasionally women - forgot their change in the excitement of gazing upon this superior attraction.

In his old favorite seat down at the end of the lunch counter we see Mr. Harley P. Hennage partaking of his evening meal. He has been away from San Pasqual for three years, and he has just returned. Also he has just decided to remain (for reasons best known to himself), although we may be pardoned for presuming that it may be because he sees an old, tender memory reflected in Donna's eyes. *Quien sabe?* He is older, homelier, sandier than when we saw him last, and he has gambled much. So we can't read anything in his face. Moreover, we do not care to. Instinctively our gaze reverts to Donna, for the day's work is finished, she had proved her cash and is about to go home to the Hat Ranch.

She is a woman now, a glorious, healthy, athletic creature, with wavy hair, very fine and thick and black, and glossy as polished ebony. Her face is tanned and glowing, and the halo of brilliant black hair only serves to accentuate the glow and to remind us of an exquisite cameo set in jet. She is taller by three inches than the average woman, broad-shouldered, full-breasted, slim-waisted, a figure to haunt a sculptor's memory.

She is dressed in a wash frock of light blue material, with a low sailor collar that shows to bewildering effect her strong full throat. She wears a flowing black silk navy reefer and when she puts on her hat prior to leaving we realize that she has not studied male head-gear alone, but has taken advantage of her semi-public position to copy styles and to glean from the women's magazines, on sale at the counter, the latest hints in metropolitan millinery.

This is the Donna Corblay that faces us this September evening. She has developed from a girl into a woman, and we wonder if her mind, her soul, has had equal development, or has it slowly starved in her unlovely and commonplace surroundings?

It has not. Donna has never been away from San Pasqual since the day she entered it a babe in arms, but - she presides over the news counter in addition to her other duties. Here she has access to all the latest "best-sellers," also the big national magazines, and through these means she has kept pace with a world that is continually passing her by in Pullman sleepers. To her has been given the glorious gift of imagination, and dull, sordid, lonely San Pasqual, squatting there in the desert sands, cannot rob her of her dreams. Rather has she grown to tolerate the place, for at her will she can summon up a host of unreal people to throng its dreary single street; she can metamorphose the water tank into a sky-scraper, the long red lines of box cars on the sidings into rows of stately mansions. She reads and dreams much, for only between the arrival and departure of trains is she kept busy. She sends for books that would never find a sale in San Pasqual, and some day - ah! the glory of anticipation! she is going to Los Angeles, where the event of her life is to take place. Going to be married? No? No, indeed. She is going to a theater.

So much for an intimate description of our leading lady as she appears when the curtain rises. But in all plays, whether in real life or on the stage, there must be a leading man. Very well, be patient. In due course he will appear. Donna has been dreaming much of this hero of late. His name is Gerald Van Alstyne, and he is tall, with curly golden hair, piercing blue eyes and a

Peter B. Kyne

cleft chin; in short, a veritable Adonis and different, so different, from the traveling salesmen who leer at her across the counter and the loutish youths of San Pasqual who, despairing of her favor, call her by her first name because they know it annoys her. Donna has not the slightest doubt but that this young fellow will come rushing in to the eating-house some day, discover her when he comes to pay his check, and eventually return and keep on returning until that final happy day when they shall go away together, to walk hand in hand through green fields and listen to the birds and bees, to linger under the shade of green trees, to wander in an Elysium. She does not know what green fields and running water look like, but she has read about them -

The director's whistle is heard in the wings; the play is on at last!

As Donna thrust the last hatpin through her glorious hair and turned to leave the place of her employment, her glance rested upon Mr. Harley P. Hennage, covertly watching her over the edge of his soup spoon. She removed her glove, walked around the end of the lunch counter and held out her hand.

"Well, Mr. Hennage. This *is* a delightful surprise. I'm *so* glad to see you back in San Pasqual. Where have you been these past three years?"

Harley P. scrambled down from his high stool, took her cool hand and blushed.

"I wouldn't like to tell you," he said, "but I've been in some mighty-y-y funn-y-y places, where I didn't meet no beautiful young ladies like you, Miss Donnie. I ain't much of a man at handin' out compliments - I never was one o' the presumin' kind - but you sure do put San Pasqual on the map. Miss Donnie, you do, for a fact."

Donna smiled her appreciation of Harley P.'s gallantry. "You left without saying good-by" she reminded him. "If I had needed you I couldn't have found you. Do you remember? You said if I ever needed a friend - "

The big gambler grinned. "You never needed me, Miss Donnie. You never would need a man like me, but you might have needed money. If you'd a-needed money, now, why, Dan Pennycook he'd a-seen you through."

Mr. Hennage did not judge it necessary to tell Donna that he had left the worthy yardmaster in charge of her destinies, with a thousand dollars on deposit in a bank in Bakersfield, in Dan's name, for Donna's use in case of emergency. Mr. Hennage lived in an atmosphere of money, where everybody fought to get his money away from him and where he fought to get theirs; hence finances were ever his first thought. As for Donna, she did not think it necessary that she should express a contrary opinion regarding Dan Pennycook. She said:

"Why didn't you come to the counter at once and say hello?"

He shook his head, "I wanted to all right, but I hated to appear presumin', an' with my rep in this village you know how people are liable to talk. World treatin' you well, Miss Donnie?"

"I think I get more fun out of San Pasqual than most of the people in it."

"Well, then, you must spend a lot o' time lookin' into a mirror" replied Harley P., and blushed at his effrontery. "That's the only way the San Pasqual folks can get any fun - a-lookin' at your face."

"Mr. Hennage, I fear you're getting to be one of the presuming kind. I declare I haven't had such pretty speeches made me this year. By the way, how's the kitty?"

Harley P.'s russet countenance swelled like the wattles on a Thanksgiving turkey. He leaned over the counter and gazed under it; his glance swept the room; he even, peered under his stool. Finally he looked up at Donna with his three gold teeth flashing through his trustful, childish smile.

"I dunno" he answered. "I guess she's around the house somewheres. I ain't seen her in quite a spell."

"I thought so," she answered gravely, "or you wouldn't have returned to San Pasqual. Small game for a small pocketbook, eh, Mr. Hennage?" She came closer to him. "I don't mind telling you - just between friends, you understand - that I have a couple of hundred to stake you to if you're hard up, but for goodness sake don't tell Mrs. Pennycook. She talks."

"Good Lord" gasped the gambler, and choked on a crouton. "D'ye mean it, Miss Donna?"

"Certainly."

"You're a dead game sport and I'd take you up, because I understand that it's between pals, but you ain't got no notion o' tryin' to square me for - you know!"

"I might - if I didn't understand all about that - you know? As it is I want to show you that I'm grateful, and my experienced eye informs me that you arrived in a box car. An empty furniture car, I should say, judging by that scrap of excelsior in your back hair, although the car might have been loaded with crockery."

Mr. Hennage removed the evidence and gazed at it reflectively.

"I suppose, now, if that'd been a feather, you'd a-swore I flew in."

"Possibly. You've been a high flyer in your day, haven't you?"

Mr. Hennage grinned. "I've flew some, but I've come home to roost now. How's the old savage down at the Hat Ranch?"

"Sam Singer is unchanged. Nothing ever changes in this country, Mr. Hennage."

"Nothin' but money," he corrected, as he fished a bill out of his vest pocket, "an' money sure changes hands, more particular when I'm around."

"Are you going back to the Silver Dollar saloon?"

"Yes, I suppose so."

"Faro, roulette, black jack, coon can or craps?"

"The old game - faro."

"I'll bank you up to five hundred."

"That's not the right thing for a young lady to do, is it?" queried the gambler. "Havin' truck wit' my kind o' people. Me - I'll do anything, but a young lady, now - "

"Please do not compare me with Mrs. Pennycook" Donna pleaded. "I am not the guardian of San Pasqual's morals. I'll stake you because I like you and I don't care who knows it - if you don't."

"You're a brick" the gambler declared. "I don't need your money, you blessed woman. I'm 'fat'" and he waved a thousand-dollar bill at her. "I did ride into San Pasqual on a freight, but I did it from choice, an' not necessity. The brakie was an old friend o' mine an' asked me to ride in wit' him. But all the same it's grand to think that there's women like you in this tough old world. It helps out a heap. You're just like your poor mother - a real lady an' no mistake."

Donna blushed. She was embarrassed, despite the earnest praise of Harley P. She gave him her hand. He took it with inward trembling, lest she might be seen shaking hands with him and dishonored. She said good-night.

"Walkin' home alone?" Harley P. was much concerned. "Not that I'm fishin' for an invitation to see you safe to the Hat Ranch, because that'd start talk, an' anyhow I ain't one o' the presumin' kind an' you know it; but it's dark an' the zephyr's blowin' like sixty, an' if there was one hobo on that freight I come in on there was a dozen."

"Why, I didn't realize it was so late," Donna answered.

"I'll have to wait until the moon comes up. But I never walk home when I'm kept late. The division superintendent lends me the track-walker's velocipede and I whiz home like the limited. There isn't any danger, and if there was I could outrun it. Do you wish to register before I go, Mr. Hennage? I suppose you'll want your old room?"

The gambler nodded and Donna returned to the cashier's counter. After assigning Mr. Hennage to his quarters she telephoned to the baggage room next door where the track-walker for that division stored his velocipede, and asked to have the machine brought out and placed on the tracks.

For perhaps half an hour she conversed with Harley P., much to that careless soul's discomfort, for he was terribly afraid of affording the San Pasqualians grounds for "talk." And as she waited the moon arose, lighting up the half mile of track that led past the Hat Ranch; and Fate, under whose direction all the dramas of life are staged, gave the cue to the Leading Man.

He entered San Pasqual, riding down through the desert from Owens river valley. But he was not in the least such a Leading Man as Donna had pictured in her dreams. He was tall enough but his hair was not crisp and curly and golden. Most people would have called it red. Not, praise be, a carroty red, a dull negative, scrubby red, but a nicer red than that - dark auburn, in fact. And he had an Irish nose and an Irish jaw and Irish eyes of bonny brown. In but one particular did he resemble the dream man. He did have a cleft in his chin. But even that was none of nature's doing. A Mexican with a knife was solely responsible. Yet, worse than all of these disappointments is the fact that his name was *not* Gerald Van Alstyne. No, indeed. The Leading Man owned to the plain, homely, unromantic patronymic of Bob McGraw. The only thing romantic and - er - literary about Bob McGraw was his Roman-nosed mustang, Friar Tuck - so called because he had been foaled and raised on a wooded range near Sherwood in Mendocino county. As a product of Sherwood forest, Mr. McGraw had very properly christened him Friar Tuck, and as Friar Tuck's colthood home lay five hundred miles to the north, it will be seen that Mr. McGraw was a wanderer. Hence, if the reader is at all imaginative or inclined to the science of deduction, he will at one mental bound, so to speak, arrive at the conclusion that Bob McGraw, if not actually an adventurous person, was at least fond of adventure - which amounts to the same thing in the long run. Most people who read Robin Hood are, as witness Mr. Tom Sawyer.

The moon was coming up just as the red-headed young man from Owens river valley rode into San Pasqual. As he approached the railroad hotel and eating-house he saw a girl emerge, and pause for a moment before walking out to climb aboard a track-walker's velocipede. In the light that streamed through the open door he saw her face, framed in a tangle of black wind-blown wisps of hair; so he reined in Friar Tuck and stared, for he - well! Most people looked twice at Donna Corblay, and the red-headed man was young.

So he sat his horse in the dribbling moonlight and watched her seize the handles of the lever and glide silently off into the night. He had been standing in the stirrups, leaning forward to look at her hands as they grasped the lever, and now he sat back in his saddle, much relieved.

"No wedding ring in sight" he mused. "My lady of the velocipede, I'll marry you, or my name's not Bob McGraw."

Just then Mr. Harley P. Hennage appeared in the doorway. He saw Bob McGraw, recognized him, and immediately dodged back and went out another door. He wanted to rush out and shake hands with Mr. McGraw, of whom he was very fond, but we regret to state that Mr. McGraw owed Harley P. Hennage the sum of fifty dollars and had owed it for three years, and Mr. Hennage hesitated to seek Mr. McGraw out for purposes of friendship, fearing that Mr. McGraw might construe his advances as a roundabout dun. Ergo, Mr. Hennage fled.

Bob McGraw watched Donna Corblay, and when she was about three hundred yards distant and beyond the town limits, he saw that a switch had been left open, for the velocipede suddenly left the outside track, cut obliquely across several parallel rows of tracks before she could control it, and shot in behind a string of box cars. As the girl disappeared, three dark figures sprang after her and a scream came very faintly against the wind.

Bob McGraw laughed and drew a gun from under his left armpit.

"I'd ride to hell for you" he muttered joyously, and sank the rowels home in Friar Tuck.

CHAPTER V

As has been intimated elsewhere in this story, San Pasqual has the reputation of being a "tough" town. This is due in a large measure to the fact that it is a division terminal, and at all division terminals train crews must reckon with that element in our leisure class which declines to pay railroad fare and elects to travel on brake-beams rather than in Pullman sleepers. Having been unceremoniously plucked from his precarious perch, the dispossessed hobo, finding himself stranded in a desert town where the streets are not electrically lighted, follows the dumb dictates of his stomach and the trend of his abnormal ambition, and promptly "turns a trick." Occasionally there is an objection on the part of the "trickee" and somebody gets killed. Naturally enough, it follows that the sound of pistol shots is frequently heard in the land, and since it happens nine times out of ten that the argument is between transients, the permanent resident is not nearly so interested in the outcome as one might imagine - particularly when the shooting takes place at night and beyond the town limits.

Harley P. Hennage had crossed from the eating-house, and had just reached the porch of the Silver Dollar saloon, when above the whistling of the "zephyr" he heard the muffled reports of three pistol shots. One "Borax" O'Rourke, a "mule-skinner" from up Keeler way, who had just arrived in San Pasqual to spend his pay-day after the fashion of the country, heard them also.

"Down the tracks," O'Rourke elucidated. "Tramps fightin' with a railroad policeman, I guess. Let's go down."

"What's the use?" objected Mr. Hennage. "A yegg never does any damage unless he's right on top of his man. They all carry little short bulldog guns, an' I never did see one o' them little bar pistols that would score a hit at twenty yards after sundown. They carry high."

At that instant the sound of another shot was heard, but faintly.

"That's the hobo" announced Mr. Hennage with conviction. "Them first three shots came from a life-size gun."

Half a minute passed; then came the report of six shots, following so quickly upon each other that they sounded almost like a volley.

"Nine shots" commented "Borax" O'Rourke. "That's an automatic."

"That's what it is!" Mr. Hennage walked to the end of the porch. He was just a little excited. "It's all off with the hobo" he continued. "I know the man that's using that automatic, and he can shoot your eye out at a hundred yards. I saw him ridin' in just as I left the eatin' house."

"He must have been movin' to get down there in such a hurry. What's a man on horseback doin' chasin' hobos across a web of railroad tracks, an' if he was headed south, seems to me he'd have laid over for supper - "

But Harley P. had a flash of inspiration now. "Come on, O'Rourke" he shouted, and made a flying leap off the saloon porch. Borax followed, and the two raced down the street at top speed - which, in the case of Mr. Hennage, owing to his weight and his bow-legs, was not remarkable. Borax easily outdistanced him.

Meanwhile, a rather spectacular panorama had been unfolding itself back of the string of box-cars. Guided by Donna's screams, Bob McGraw sent his horse away at a tearing gallop, lifting him in great leaps across the maze of railroad tracks, and in a shower of flying cinders brought him up, almost sitting, in the little foot-path between two lines of track. Almost under Friar Tuck's front feet, Donna was struggling in the grasp of three ruffians, one of whom was endeavoring to tie a handkerchief across her mouth. The velocipede had been derailed by means of a car-stake placed across the track.

Bob McGraw's long gun rose and fell three times, and at each deadly drop a streak of flame punctured the moon-light. The three assailants went down, shot through their respective legs - which remarkable coincidence was not a coincidence at all, but merely a touch of kindly consideration on the part of Bob McGraw, who didn't believe in killing his man when wounding him would serve the same purpose.

As the three brutes dropped away from her the man from Owens river valley lowered his weapon, and

Donna, pale, terrorized and disheveled, reeled toward him. He swung his horse a little, leaned outward and downward, and with a sweep of his strong left arm he lifted her off the ground and set her in front of him on Friar Tuck's neck, just as one of the wounded thugs straightened up, cut loose with his bulldog gun and shot Bob McGraw through the right breast.

Donna heard a half-suppressed "Oh!" from her deliverer, and felt him sway forward a little. Then, seeming to summon every atom of grit and strength he possessed, he whirled his horse, scuttled away around the rear of the box-car, out of danger, and set Donna on the ground.

"Wait here" he commanded, through teeth clenched to keep back the blood that welled from within him. "I was too kind - to those hounds."

He rode back and finished his night's work. War-mad, he sat his horse, reeling in the saddle, and emptied his gun into the squirming wretches as they sought to crawl under the car for protection.

Donna was terribly frightened, but she was the last woman in the world to go into hysterics. She realized that she was saved, and accordingly commenced to cry, while waiting for the horseman to reappear. A minute passed and still he did not come, and suddenly, without quite realizing what she was doing or why she did it, the girl went back to the scene of the battle to look for him. She was not so badly frightened now, but rather awed by the silence, Donna was desert-bred, and in all her life she had never fainted. For a girl she was remarkably free from "nerves," and she had lived too long in San Pasqual to faint now at sight of the three still figures huddled between the ties, even had she seen them; which, she had not. All that Donna saw was a roan range pony, standing quietly with drooping head, while his master sprawled in the saddle with his arms around his horse's neck. Donna went quickly to him, and when the moon came out from behind a hurrying cloud she was enabled, with the aid of the ghastly green glare from a switch lantern which shone on his face, to observe that he was quite conscious and looking at her with untroubled boyish eyes.

His hat was lying on the ground, securely anchored by the pony's left fore foot. With rather unnatural calmness and following, subconsciously perhaps, her acquired instinct for salving hats for the men of her little world, Donna stooped, slapped the pony's leg to make him release the hat and picked it up. She stood for a few seconds, with the hat in her hand, looking at him pityingly. The man's brown eyes blazed with admiration.

"What a woman!" he wheezed. "You're brave - like a man. You came back. I'd like - to live - to serve you further - "

He gurgled, a red stain appeared at the corners of his mouth, and he closed his eyes for a moment. When he opened them again his soul was shining through and he smiled a little. He did not again attempt to speak, yet, for all that, Donna heard the man-call to the woman that belonged to him, the mate for whom he had been destined when the world was first created. There are in this world personalities so finely attuned to each other that mere words are unnecessary to express the feelings of each for the other when first they meet. Between certain rare souls the gulf of convention may be bridged by a glance; the divine miracle of a pure and holy love, leaping to life in an instant, can suffer no defilement by a spontaneous and human impulse to grasp the precious gift ere life departs.

Some women love at first sight, but the vast majority, lacking the imagination to perceive, at a glance, the attributes that go toward the making of a Man, only think they love and delay a conventional period before yielding. But Donna Corblay had lived so long in sordid, unimaginative, unromantic San Pasqual that, from much inhibition and introspection, she was different from most women. She had grown to rely on herself, to trust her own judgment and to bank on first impressions. As she faced Bob McGraw now, her first impression was that he was telling her with his eyes that he loved her, that he had ridden in behind this string of box-cars to purchase her honor at the price of his life, because he loved her. And inasmuch as there appeared to be nothing unusual or unconventional in his telling her this - with his eyes, Donna was sensible of but one feeling and one desire; a feeling of gratitude to him for the priceless gift of his love and her honor, a desire to -

She dropped his hat, wiped the blood from his lips and kissed him.

Bob McGraw smiled wistfully.

"It's worth it," he whispered, "and few women are - worth - dying for."

"You must not die," the girl cried passionately. "You're my Dream Man and I've waited so long for you and dreamed of your coming! I'll pray for you, I'll ask God to give you to me - "

An almost fanatical joy beamed in her wonderful eyes, the color had returned to her cheeks; and to Bob McGraw, faltering there on the edge of eternity, her radiant regal presence brought a wondrous peace. For a moment he saw the moonlight reflecting the light in her eyes; a strand of her hair blew across his face - he smelled its perfume; the intoxication of her glorious personality caused him to marvel and doubt his own waning sense of the reality of things. He leaned toward her hungrily and lapsed into unconsciousness, while his big limp body commenced to slide slowly out of the slippery saddle. She caught him in her strong arms, eased him to the ground and knelt there with his red head in her lap, showering his face with her kisses and her tears. It was thus that "Borax" O'Rourke, badly blown after his three-hundred-yard dash, found them.

"Great snakes, young lady, what's happened?" gasped Mr. O'Rourke.

"Three brutes and a man have been killed" she replied.

"What the - who - who's that feller? Are you - "

"Don't ask questions, Borax. I am not hurt, but I have no time to answer questions. Please remove that car-stake and replace the velocipede on the tracks."

Her cool demeanor, despite her tears, her terse commands, indicating a plan for prompt action of some kind, flabbergasted Borax to such an extent that he commenced to swear very fluently, without for a moment realizing that there was a lady present. And just at this juncture Harley P. Hennage arrived.

As might be expected, Harley P. wasted no time catering to the call of curiosity.

"Let me have him, Miss Donna," he ordered. "We'll put him on the velocipede and rush him up to the hotel. I'll - "

"No, Mr. Hennage. He belongs to me. Place him on the velocipede and help me take him home."

"To the Hat Ranch?"

"Yes, of course, I can care for him there, if he lives."

"Why, Miss Donna - "

"Do it, please" she commanded. "I know best. Set him on the little platform and tie his legs to the reach. Then stand behind him to work the lever, and let him rest against your knees. I'll follow with the horse."

"Remarkable! Very remarkable!" soliloquized the big gambler. Without further ado he proceeded to carry out Donna's orders.

"Borax," Donna continued, "you run up to the drug store and tell Doc Taylor what's happened. I'll send Sam Singer back with the velocipede for him."

She gathered the reins in her left hand and swung aboard Friar Tuck. Harley P., having disposed of his gory burden on the limited accommodations of the track velocipede, seized the levers and trundled away, followed by Donna on Friar Tuck, cautiously picking his way between the ties.

Borax O'Rourke stood for a moment, gazing after them.

"She acts like a mother cat with a kitten" he muttered. "Damned if she wasn't kissin' the feller - an' him a stranger in town!"

He walked rapidly back to San Pasqual, and such was his perturbation that he sought to have "Doc" Taylor unravel the puzzle for him.

"Hysterics" was the doctor's explanation.

"Rats" retorted O'Rourke.

"All right, then. It's rats." The doctor grabbed his emergency grip and departed on the run for the Hat Ranch. Sam Singer met him half-way with the velocipede.

O'Rourke returned to the Silver Dollar saloon where, since he was a vulgarian and a numbskull, he retailed his story to the loungers there assembled.

"I'll never git over the sight o' that girl a-kissing that young feller" he concluded. "Why, I'd down a hobo every mornin' before breakfast if I knowed for certain she'd treat *me* that-a-way for doin' it."

The situation was canvassed at considerable length, and only the entrance of the constable with a request, for volunteers to help him remove the "remainders" that were littering up the right of way below town, served to turn the conversation into other channels.

Upon their arrival at the Hat Ranch a shout from

Harley P. Hennage brought Sam Singer and Soft Wind to the front gate. Donna dismounted, tying Friar Tuck to the "zephyr" by the simple process of dropping the reins over his head, and hurried into the house to prepare her mother's old room for the reception of the wounded man. Bob McGraw was very limp and white as Harley P. and the Indian carried him in. The gambler undressed him while Sam Singer sprang aboard the velocipede and sped back toward town to meet the doctor.

When the doctor arrived, he and Harley P. Hennage went into the bedroom, closing the door after them. Donna remained in the kitchen. She had already ordered Soft Wind to light a fire in the range and heat some water, and when presently the gambler came out to the kitchen he nodded his appreciation of her forethought ere he disappeared again with the hot water and a basin.

In about an hour Doctor Taylor emerged, grip in hand.

"I've done all I can for him, Miss Corblay" he told her. "I'm going up town to close the drug store and get a few things I may need, but I'll be back within an hour and spend the balance of the night with him."

"Will he live?"

Donna's voice was calm, her tones hinting of nothing more than a friendly interest and sympathy; yet Harley P., watching her over the doctor's shoulder, guessed the stress of emotion under which she strove, for he, too, had seen her kiss Bob McGraw as he lay unconscious in her arms.

"I fear he will not. The bullet ranged upward, perforating the top of his right lung, and went on clean through. I've seen men recover from wounds in more vital parts, but a .45-caliber bullet did the trick to our young friend, and a .45 tears quite a hole. He's big and strong and has a fighting chance, but I'm afraid - very much afraid - of internal hemorrhage, and traumatic pneumonia is bound to set in."

"He will not die!" said Donna.

The doctor looked at her curiously. "I hope not" he said. "But he'll need a trained nurse and the best of care to pull through. It's long odds."

"That young feller's middle name is Long Odds." Mr. Hennage had arrived at the conclusion that Donna needed a great deal of comforting at that moment. "He's lived on long odds ever since he came into this country."

"How do you know, Hennage?" the doctor demanded. "I tell - "

"Long odds an' long guns, like birds o' feather always flock together" the gambler answered him drily, "This young feller wouldn't feel that he was gettin' any joy out o' life if he didn't tackle the nub end o' the deal. I'm layin' even money he comes up to the young lady's expectations."

Donna thanked him with her eyes, and Harley P. crossed to the door and looked down the long patio to where a small white wooden cross gleamed through the festoons of climbing roses.

"He ought to have a nurse" the doctor advised Donna.

"Very well, doctor. You will telephone to Bakersfield, or Los Angeles, will you not, and engage one?"

"I don't think our patient can afford the expense. Hennage frisked him and all the money - "

"Thank you, I will attend to the financial side of this case, Doctor Taylor."

Mr. Hennage turned from his survey of the patio.

"Doc," he complained, "it's time for you to move out o' San Pasqual. You've stayed too long already. You're gettin' the San Pasqual sperrit, Doc. You ain't got no sympathy for a stranger."

"Well, you don't expect me to put up twenty-five a week and railroad fare - "

"Never mind worryin' about what you've got to put up with, Doc. If you know all the things I put up with - thanks, Doc. Hurry back, and don't forget to 'phone for that nurse."

"Ain't it marvelous how a small camp always narrers the point o' view?" the gambler observed when the doctor had gone. "Always thinkin' o' themselves an' money, A man in my business, Miss Donna, soon learns that mighty few men - an' women, too - will stand the acid. That young feller inside (he jerked a fat thumb over his shoulder) will stand it. I know. I've applied the acid. An' you'll stand the acid, too," he added - "when Mrs. Pennycook hears you kissed Bob McGraw. Ouch! That woman's tongue drips corrosive sublimate."

Donna blushed furiously.

"You - you - won't tell, will you, Mr. Hennage?"

"Of course not. But that chuckleheaded roughneck O'Rourke will. Why did you kiss him? I ain't one o' the presumin' kind, but I'd like to know, Miss Donna."

"I kissed him" - Donna commenced to cry and hid her burning face in her hands. "I kissed him because - because - I thought he was dying - and he was the first man - that looked at - me so different. And he was so brave, Mr. Hennage - "

"That you thought he was a man an' worth the kiss, eh, Miss Donna?"

"I guess that's the explanation" she confessed, the while she marveled inwardly that she should feel such relief at unburdening her secret to the worst man in San Pasqual.

"If some good woman had only done that for me" the gambler murmured a little wistfully. "If she only had! But of course this young Bob, he's different from - what I was at his age - "

"I couldn't help it" Donna sobbed; "he's one of the presuming kind."

Harley P. sat down and laughed until his three gold teeth almost threatened to fall out.

"God bless your sweet soul, Miss Donna," he gasped,

"go in and kiss him again! He needs you worse than he does a nurse. Go in an' kiss the presumin' cuss."

"You're making fun of me" Donna charged.

"I'm not. Can't a low-down, no-account man like me even laugh where there's happiness? Why, if that young feller goes to work an' spoils it all by kickin' the bucket, I'd die o' grief."

"You know him, do you not?"

"I should say so."

"Is he - "

"Yes, he's the nicest kind of a boy."

"How old is he!"

"Twenty-eight."

Donna was thoughtful.

"Nice disparity in ages, don't you think, Miss Donna?"

Donna blushed again. "What is his business!" she asked.

"Well, that's a right hard question to answer, Miss Donna. He was a lawyer once for about a month, after he got out o' college, an' then he worked on a newspaper. After that, just to prove he was a human bein', he got the notion that there was money in the chicken business. Well, he got out o' the chicken business with a couple o' hundred dollars, an' then he come breezin' into a minin' camp one day an' tried bustin' a faro bank. Failed agin. I'm responsible for that failure, though. The next I see of him is a year later, in McKittrick, where he's runnin' a real estate office an' dealin' in oil lands. But somehow there never was no oil on none o' the land that Bob tied up, so he got plumb disgusted an' quit. He was thinkin' o' tourin' the country districts sellin' little pieces o' bluestone to put in the bowls of kerosene lamps to keep 'em from explodin', when I see him next. He borrowed fifty dollars from me - which he ain't paid back yet, come to think on't - an' went to Nevada minin' an' just at present he's about settled into his regular legitimate business. He was headed that way from birth. I could read the signs."

"What is his present profession?"

"He's an Inspector o' Landscapes."

"You're wrong. He's not a Desert Rat."

"He is. I can prove it."

"He's too young. They don't begin to 'rat' until they're close to forty. I could name you a dozen, and the youngest is thirty-eight."

"Oh, you're thinkin' o' the ordinary, garden variety. But I tell you this McGraw man's a Desert Rat. The desert's got him. Generally it don't get 'em so young, but once in a while it does, An' of all the Desert Rats that ever sucked a niggerhead cactus, the feller that goes huntin' lost mines is the worst. They never get over it."

Donna permitted herself a very small smile.

"Sometimes they do" she reminded him.

"I wouldn't be surprised. But not until they've found what they're lookin' for. However, we'll wait an' see if Bob McGraw - like that name, Miss Donna?"

"I love it."

"We'll wait an' see if he pulls through this, an' then we'll find out if he can be cured o' desert-rattin'. In the meantime I'll wait here until Doc gets back. I ain't one of the presumin' kind, but I think I'd better stay. An' you - I think you'd better go in an' have another good look at this Desert Rat o' yours. He's breathin' like the north wind sighin' through a knot-hole."

He watched her disappear.

"For the sight o' a good woman, O Lord, we thank Thee," he murmured, "an' for the sight o' a good woman with grit, we thank Thee some more. Great grief, why wasn't I born good an' good-lookin' 'stead o' fat an' no account?"

At ten o'clock Doc Taylor returned to the Hat Ranch and found the condition of his patient unchanged. He was still unconscious and his loud, stertorous breathing, coupled with the ghastly exhaust of air through the hole on his breast, testified to the seriousness of his condition. Throughout the night Donna sat by the bedside watching him, while the doctor remained in the kitchen with Mr. Hennage.

Toward morning Bob McGraw opened his eyes and looked at Donna very wonderingly. Then his glance wandered around the room and back to the girl. He was plainly puzzled.

"Where's my horse," he whispered, "and my spurs and my gun and hat?"

Donna bent over him and placed two cool fingers on his lips.

"The hemorrhage has stopped," she warned him, "and you mustn't speak or move, or you may bring it on again."

"I remember - now. I fired - low - and he - got me. Where's Friar Tuck?"

"Your horse? He's in the corral at San Pasqual, and your gun is in the kitchen with your spurs, and your hat - why, I guess I forgot to bring your hat with me. But don't worry about it. I'm Donna Corblay of the Hat Ranch, and I'll give you your choice of a hundred hats if you'll only get well."

"Are you - the - girl - that kissed me?"

Donna's voice was very low, her face was very close to his as she answered him. His lean brown hand stole confidingly into hers - for a long time he was silent, content to lie there and know that she was near him.

Presently he looked up at her again, with the same dominating, wistful entreaty in his brown eyes. She lowered her head until her cheek rested against his, and his arm went upward and around her neck.

"God - made you - for me" he whispered. "I love you, and my name is Bob McGraw. I guess - I'll - get well."

"Beloved," she breathed, "of course you'll get well. I want you to." She smoothed the wavy auburn hair back from his forehead. "Go to sleep" she commanded. "You can't talk to me any more. I'm going to go to sleep, too."

She drew a bright Mexican serape over her shoulders, sat down in a rocking-chair by the side of the bed and closed her eyes. For what seemed to her a lapse of hours, although in reality it was less than five minutes, she tried to induce a clever counterfeit of sleep, but unable longer to deprive herself of another look at her prize she opened her eyes and gazed at Bob McGraw. To her almost childish delight he was watching her; and then she noticed his little, cheerful, half-mocking smile.

She flushed hotly. For the first time she permitted the searchlight of reason to play on the events of the night, and it occurred to her now that she had been guilty of a monstrous breach of convention, an unprecedented, unmaidenly action. She felt like crying now, with the thought that she had held herself so cheap. Bob McGraw saw the flush and the pallor that followed it. He read the unspoken thought behind the changing rush of color.

"Don't feel - that way - about it" he whispered haltingly. "It's unusual - but then - you and I are unusual, too. There seems to be - perfect - under-standing, and between a - man and a woman that means - perfect peace. It had to - be. It was preordained - our meeting. What is - your name?"

Donna again told him.

"Nice - name. Like it."

He closed his eyes and dropped off to sleep like a tired boy.

CHAPTER VI

Donna sat there until sunrise, rocking back and forth, striving to weave an orderly pattern of reason out of the tangle of unreason in which she found herself when, confronted by that look in Bob McGraw's brown eyes. She failed. She could not think calmly. She was conscious of but one supreme emotion as she gazed at this man who had ridden into her life, gun in hand. She was happy. Heretofore her life had been quiet, even, unemotional, always the same - and now she was happy, riotously, deliriously happy; and it did not occur to her that Bob McGraw might die. She willed that he should live, for life was love, and love - what was love? Something that surged, a wave of exquisite tenderness, through Donna's lonely heart, something that throbbed in the untouched recesses of her womanhood, arousing in her a fierce, almost primitive desire to possess this man, to fondle his auburn head, to caress him, to work for him, slave for him, to show her gratitude and adoration by living for him, and - if need be - by dying for him!

It occurred to her presently that there was nothing so very unmaidenly in her action, after all. She felt no distinct loss of womanly reserve - no crumbling of the foundations of dignity. She still had those attributes; to-morrow, when she returned to the cashier's counter at the eating-house, she would still have these defensive weapons against the invasions of the sensual, smirking, patronizing male brutes with which every passing train appeared to be filled; the well-dressed, hard-finished city men, who held her cheap because she presided behind an eating-house cash-register. How well she knew their quick, bold stares, their so clumsy subterfuges to enter into conversation with her; and how different was Bob McGraw to such as they!

Here at last was the reason, unseen and unrecognized at first, manifesting itself merely in the spontaneous and unconscious shattering of her maidenly reserve, but distinctly visible now. It was not that Bob McGraw had come to her out of the desert at a time when she needed him most; it was not that he came in all the bravery and generous sacrifice of youth, shedding his blood that she might not shed tears; it was not the service he had rendered her that made her love him, for San Pasqual was "long" on mere animal courage. It was the adoration that gleamed in his eyes - an adoring stare, revealing respect behind his love - that one quality without which love is a dead and withered thing.

She knew him now - the man he was. She saw the priceless pearl of character he possessed. Bob McGraw was a wild, reckless, unthinking, impulsive fellow, perhaps, but for all that he was the sort of man at whose feet women, both good and bad, have laid their hearts since the world began. He was kind. Harley P. Hennage was right. Bob McGraw was a Desert Rat. But a Desert Rat lives close to the great heart of Mother Nature, and his own heart is clean.

The dawn-light came filtering across the desert and lit up the room where she sat. She turned to the bed and saw that Bob McGraw was watching her again, and on his face was that little, cheerful, mocking, inscrutable smile.

Again Donna found herself powerless to resist the appeal in the man's eyes. She was crying a little as she slipped to her knees beside the bed and laid her cheek against his.

"I can't help it" she whispered. "I seem to have loved you always, and oh, Bob, dear, you'll be very, very good to me, won't you? You must be brave and try to get well, for both our sakes. We need each other so."

Bob McGraw did not answer readily. He was too busy thanking God for the great gift of perfect understanding. Moreover, he had a perforated lung and a heart whose duties had suddenly been increased a thousand-fold, if it was to hold inviolate this sacred joy of possession which thrilled him now. He was alert and conscious, despite the shock of his wound, and the reserve strength in his six feet of splendid manhood was coming to his aid. When he could trust himself to speak, he said:

"You're a very wonderful woman."

"But you were laughing at me - a little."

"Not at you, at Fate - the great, big, bugaboo Fate."

"Why?"

"Because I - can afford to. My luck's - turned."

"You dear, big, red-headed philosopher."

"And you - didn't you save my hat?"

"No, dear. Don't worry over such a trifle as a hat. I'll give you a - "

"But this was - a - good hat" he complained. "I paid twenty dollars - "

"Never mind your old hat. Don't talk. I'm selfish. I want to listen to you, but for all that, you must be quiet."

He sighed. Forget all about that big, wide sombrero - genuine beaver - that cost him twenty dollars only a week ago? His horse, his saddle, his hat, his spurs, his gun - he was particular about these possessions, for in his way Mr. McGraw was something of a frontier dandy. His calm contempt of life and death amused Donna when she compared it with his boyish concern for his dashing equipment. Hats, indeed! Worrying over a lost hat while a guest at the Hat Ranch! If Bob McGraw could only have understood Donna Corblay's contempt for hats he would never have mentioned the matter twice.

She gauged the size of his red head with the practiced eye of one who has sold many hats.

"Seven and a quarter" she mused fondly. "Wouldn't he look splendid in that big new Stetson that blew in the day before yesterday! You great big man-baby. I'll save that one for you."

And having decided this momentous question of hats, she kissed him and went out to the kitchen to prepare breakfast for Doctor Taylor and Harley P. Hennage.

After having breakfasted at the Hat Ranch, Harley P. Hennage helped himself to Bob McGraw's automatic gun, reloaded it and walked back to San Pasqual. He had never carried a gun before, but something seemed to tell him that he might need one to-day. Borax O'Rourke generally carried one and if Borax had talked, Mr. Hennage meant to chastise him. In consequence of which decision, Mr. Hennage, like a good gambler, decided to fill his hand and not be caught bluffing.

Arrived outside the Silver Dollar, Harley P. immediately found himself greatly in demand. Borax O'Rourke, having told all he knew, which was little enough, and aching to supply further details, was the first man to accost him.

"Well, Hennage," he began, "what's the latest? Any more kissin' goin' on?"

Mr. Hennage's baleful eyes scouted the mule-skinner's person for evidence of hardware. Observing none, he said fiercely "You mutton-headed duffer!" and for the first time within the memory of the citizens of San Pasqual he had recourse to his hands. He clasped Mr. O'Rourke fondly around the neck and choked him until his eyes threatened to pop out, the while he shook O'Rourke as a terrier shakes a rat. Then, after two prodigious parting kicks, accurately gauged and delivered, the gambler crossed over to the hotel, leaving the garrulous one to pick himself out of the dust, gasping like a chicken with the pip. It is worthy of remark that the discomfiture of Borax O'Rourke was observed by Mrs. Daniel Pennycook, who having noted from afar the approach of Mr. Hennage, had endeavored to intercept him first. Judging from his hasty action that the gambler was not in that state of mind most propitious to the dissemination of the information which she sought, Mrs. Pennycook decided to bide her time and returned to her cottage and her neglected housework.

Mr. Hennage went at once to his room, where he lay down and went to sleep. Late in the afternoon he was awakened by a knocking at his door. He sprang out of bed and unlocked the door, and Dan Pennycook came into the room.

"Hello, Dan" the gambler greeted him. "You look worried."

"You would too, if you knew what I know" replied Pennycook. He sat down. "Harley, old man, you've laid violent hands on a mighty hard character."

"Well," retorted the gambler, "ain't that the kind to lay violent hands on? You wouldn't expect me to choke old Judge Kenny, or that little Jap laundryman, would you?"

"But O'Rourke is dangerous. He's got two guns reachin' down to his hocks an' he's tellin' everybody he'll get you on sight."

"Barkin' dogs never bite, Dan. However, I wish you'd carry a message for me. Will you?"

"Who to?"

"The dangerous Mr. O'Rourke. Tell him from me he'd better go back to the borax works at Keeler, where he got his nickname, an' take up his old job o' skinnin' mules. Tell him I'll loan him that roan pony in the corral, an' he can saddle up an' git. Tell him to send the little horse back with the stage-driver. I want him to ride out tonight, Dan. Tell him it's an order."

Pennycook nodded. "If I was you, though, Harley, I'd heel myself."

The gambler opened a bureau drawer and brought forth McGraw's automatic pistol. He smiled brightly.

"No use givin' orders unless a feller can back 'em up, Dan" he said. "Thanks for the hint, though. Of course you'll tell Borax privately. No use arousin' his pride lettin' the whole town know he had to go. He's a rat, but a rat'll fight when he's cornered - an' I don't want to kill him."

"I will" replied Mr. Pennycook. "I'd hate to see any more trouble in this town."

"Thank you, Dan."

"Donna all right?"

"Yes."

"Who's the feller that interfered?"

"Stranger ridin' through."

"Hard hit?"

"Right lung. He'll pull through."

"Hope so" responded the amiable yardmaster, and left.

Mr. Hennage got back into bed and pulled the sheet over him again. But it was too hot to sleep, so he lay there, rubbing his chin and thinking. Late in the afternoon he heard the sound of a horse loping through the street beneath his window. He sprang up and looked out, just in time to see Borax O'Rourke riding out of town on Bob McGraw's roan bronco.

Mr. Hennage permitted himself a quiet little smile. "Now there goes the star witness for the prosecution" he mused. "But I'll stay an' tell 'em Borax was mistaken. I guess, even if I ain't a gentleman, I can lie like one."

He bathed and dressed and started over to the post-office - not because he expected any mail, for he did not. No one ever wrote to Mr. Hennage. But he had seen Mrs. Pennycook dodging into the post-office, and it was his intention to have a quiet little conversation with the lady.

When he arrived at the post-office, however, Mrs. Pennycook was not in sight. Mr. Hennage stepped lightly inside, and at that moment he heard Miss Molly Pickett, the postmistress, exclaim: "Well, for the land's sake!"

"It's a fact, Miss Pickett. She kissed him!"

The voices came from the inner office, behind the tier of lock boxes. Realizing that he was in a public place, Mr. Hennage did not feel it incumbent upon him to announce his presence by coughing or shuffling his feet. He remained discreetly silent, therefore, and Mrs. Pennycook's voice resumed:

"She had him taken right down to the Hat Ranch, of all places. Of course it wouldn't do to bring him up town, where he could be looked after. Of course not! He might be sent to a hospital and she wouldn't have a chance to look after him herself. I never heard of such carryings-on, Miss Pickett. It's so scandalous like."

Miss Pickett sighed. "Who is he?" she demanded.

"That's what nobody can find out. I told Dan to ask Harley Hennage, but you know how stupid a man is. I don't suppose he even asked."

"Well, all I've got to say, Mrs. Pennycook, is that Donna Corblay's taking a mighty big interest in a man she's never even been introduced to. Still, I'm not surprised at anything she'd do, the stuck-up thing. She just thinks she's it, with her new hats and a different wash-dress every week, and her high an' mighty way of looking at people. She could have been married long ago if she wasn't so stuck-up."

"Oh, nobody's good enough for *her*" sneered Mrs. Pennycook. "If a dook was to ask her she wouldn't have him. She'd sooner make fools of half the married men in town."

"She thinks she's too good for San Pasqual" Miss Pickett supplemented.

"I suppose she imagines her grand airs make her a lady," Mrs. Pennycook deprecated, "but for my part, I think it shows that she's kinder vulgar like."

"Well, what do you think o' last night's performance?" Miss Pickett demanded.

"I can't think, dearie" murmured Mrs. Pennycook weakly. "I'm so shocked like. It's hard to believe. I know the girl for a sly, scheming, hoity-toity flirt, but to think that she'd act so low like! Who told *you* she kissed him?"

"Borax O'Rourke."

"He told everybody."

"Well, then, if it's got around, public like, we can't shield her, Miss Pickett, an' I guess it's no use trying. Water will seek its own level, Miss Pickett. You remember her mother. Nobody ever knew a thing about her, an' you remember the talk that used to be goin' around about *her*."

"The tree grows as the twig is bent" Miss Pickett murmured.

"I'll say this much, though, Miss Pickett" continued Mrs. Pennycook. "You're a woman an' so'm I, an' you know, just as well as I do, that no man or set o' men ever looks twice at any respectable woman that goes right along tendin' to her business. You know that, Miss Pickett. A man's got to have *some* encouragement."

"Well" Miss Pickett was forced to remark. "I've been postmistress an' assistant postmistress here for fifteen years, an' nobody's ever insulted me, or tried to flirt with me. I can take my oath on that."

"I believe you, Miss Pickett" interrupted Harley P. Hennage serenely. "Even in a tough town like San Pasqual human courage has its limitations."

Miss Pickett flew to the delivery window and looked out. Harley P. was looking in.

"Is that so!" sneered Miss Pickett.

"Looks like it" retorted the gambler. "You're Exhibit A to prove it, ain't you, Miss Pickett? I hope I see you well, Mrs. Pennycook" he added.

"So you're back, are you?" Mrs. Pennycook's voice dripped with sarcasm.

"Yes, I've been away three years, but I see time ain't softened the tongues nor sharpened the consciences o' some of my old lady friends. You're out late this afternoon, Mrs. P., with your scandal an' your gossip."

"There ain't no mail for you, Mr. Card Sharp" Miss Pickett informed him acidly.

"I didn't call for any" the gambler replied, and eyed her sternly. She quivered under his glance, and he turned to Mrs. Pennycook. "Would you oblige me, Mrs. Pennycook, with a few minutes of your valuable time - where Miss Pickett can't hear us talk? Miss Pickett, you can go right on readin' the postal cards."

"I'm a respectable woman - " Mrs. Pennycook began.

"Well, it ain't ketchin', I guess" he retorted. "I ain't afraid."

"What do you want? If you've got anything to say to me, speak right out in meeting."

"Not here" the gambler answered. "It'll keep."

He walked out of the post-office and waited until Mrs. Pennycook came by.

"Mrs. Pennycook, ma'am."

She tilted her nose and glanced at him scornfully, but did not stop.

"It's about Joe" the gambler called after her.

If he had struck her she could not have stopped more quickly. She turned, facing him, her chin trembling.

"I thought you'd stop" he assured her. "Nothin' like shakin' the bones of a family skeleton to bring down the mighty from their perch. Bless you, Mrs. Penny-cook, this thing o' bein' respectable must be hard on the constitution. Havin' been low an' worthless all my life, I suppose I can't really appreciate what it means to a respectable lady with a angelic relative like your brother."

The drawling words fell on the gossip like a rain of blows. Her eyelids grew suddenly red and watery.

"It ain't a man's trick to hammer you like this, Mrs. Pennycook," the gambler continued, almost sadly, "but for a lady that's livin' in a glass house, you're too fond o' chuckin' stones, an' it's got to stop. Hereafter, if you've got somethin' to say about Donna Corblay you see that it's somethin' nice. You gabbed about her mother when she was alive, and the minute I saw you streakin' it over to Miss Pickett I knew you were at it again. Now you do any more mud-slingin', Mrs. Pennycook, and I'll tell San Pasqual about that thug of a brother o' yours. He's out o' San Quentin."

"But his time wasn't up, Mr. Hennage," wailed Mrs. Pennycook. "He got fifteen years."

"He served half of it and was paroled."

Mrs. Pennycook bowed her head and quivered. "Then he'll be around here again, blackmailing poor Dan an' me out of our savings." She commenced to cry.

"No, he won't. I'll protect you from him, Mrs. Pennycook. I want to make a bargain with you. Every time you hear any of the long-tongued people in this town takin' a crack at Donna Corblay because they don't understand her and she won't tell 'em all her business, you speak a good word for her. Understand? And the first thing tomorrow mornin' I want you to get out an' nail that lie that Donna Corblay kissed the feller that saved her from them tramps last night. It's a lie, Mrs. Pennycook. I was there, an' I know. I ordered O'Rourke out o' town for circulatin' that yarn. Suppose this town knew your twin brother was a murderer an' a highwayman? Would they keep still about it?"

"No" faltered Mrs. Pennycook.

"I can keep Joe away from you, I have somethin' on him. You'll never see him again. I'll save you from gossip an' blackmail, but you've got to take programme."

"I will" Mrs. Pennycook promised him fervently.

"Then it's a go" said Harley P. and walked away. He returned to the Silver Dollar saloon, smiling a little at the joke in which he had indulged at the expense of Mrs. Pennycook. He had informed her that he had "something on" her brother Joe, but he had neglected to inform her what the "something" was which he had "on" brother Joe. Mr. Hennage could see no profit in telling her that it was a blood-stained tarpaulin, under which Mrs. Pennycook's brother reposed, quite dead, in the back room of the stage stable, to which impromptu morgue Joseph, with his two companions, had been borne by the committee of citizens headed by the constable, shortly after the elimination of the trio by Mr. Bob McGraw.

No, Mr. Hennage, while a man of firmness and resource, was not brutal. He contrived, however, to avoid identification of the body by keeping Dan Pennycook from attending the coroner's inquest, for he was a good gambler and never wasted a trump.

"I never knew there was such fun at funerals" he soliloquized while returning from the cemetery. He bit a large piece out of his "chewing" and gazed around him. "Doggone it" he muttered, "if this ain't the worst town in California for killin's. I never did see such a one-horse camp with such a big potter's field. If I wasn't a inquisitive old hunks I'd get out of such a pesky hole P. D. Q. I wouldn't a' come back in the first place if it hadn't a' been for that Joe person. Dog-gone him!"

This was quite true. For some months Mr. Hennage had been running a game in Bakersfield, which, at that time, was a wide open town, just beginning to boom under the impetus of rich oil strikes. It had been one of his diversions, outside of business hours, to walk down to the freight yards once a week and fraternize with the railroad boys. In this way he managed to keep track of affairs in San Pasqual. Upon the occasion of his last trip to the freight yards he had spied Mrs. Pennycook's brother dodging into an empty box-car. Mr. Hennage had seen this worthy upon the occasion of his (Joe's) last visit to San Pasqual, the object of the said visit having been imparted to him by Dan Pennycook himself. Having no money available for the black-mailer, poor Pennycook had come to Hennage to borrow it. Upon the occasion of the payment of the loan, Pennycook informed Mr. Hennage joyfully that Joe was out of the way for fifteen years and Mr. Hennage had rejoiced with the yardmaster. Hence, when Mr. Hennage observed Joe sneak into the box-car, he at once surmised that Joe was broke and headed for San Pasqual to renew his fortunes. Having a warm spot in his heart for Dan Pennycook, Mr. Hennage instantly decided to follow Joe in another box-car, which, in brief, is the reason why he had returned to San Pasqual.

Presently Mr. Hennage paused and glanced across the blistering half-mile of desert, to where the sun glinted on the dun walls of the Hat Ranch. In the middle distance a dashing girlish figure in a blue dress was walking up the tracks.

Mr. Hennage's three gold teeth flashed like heliographs.

"This world is so full o' a number o' things,
I'm sure we should all be as happy as kings"

he quoted, and walked across to meet her.

CHAPTER VII

Early in the forenoon of the day following Bob McGraw's spectacular advent into San Pasqual, the nurse for whom Doc Taylor had telephoned to Bakersfield arrived at the Hat Ranch. She proved to be a kind middle-aged woman, devoted to her profession and thoroughly competent to do everything for Bob McGraw that could be done. Her arrival released Donna from the care of watching the wounded man, and she rested at last.

It was late in the afternoon before she appeared again in the sick room, when she was overjoyed to learn of the change in Bob's condition. There was no further hemorrhage from the wound, although his pulse was racing at several degrees above normal. He was awake when Donna entered the room and greeted her with a weak smile of welcome. It may be that at the moment Mr. McGraw fondly hoped that he might be further rewarded with another kiss; but if so he was disappointed. Donna favored him with nothing more tangible than a rather sad, wistful, interested scrutiny, and then, satisfied that he was making his fight, she turned to leave the room, whereupon Mr. McGraw, disregarding his nurse's explicit instructions, presumed to enter into conversation.

"Hello, Donna," he whispered, "aren't you going to

speak to a fellow?"

Donna shook her head.

"But I might die" he pleaded piteously. The nurse intervened.

"Nobody's worried over that remote contingency," she retorted, "so do not endeavor to seek sympathy."

He looked at her so tragically that she could not forbear a little laugh, as she ordered Donna to leave the room.

"The right of free speech - and free assemblage," Mr. McGraw protested hoarsely, "is guaranteed to - every American citizen - under the con - "

"Silence!" commanded the nurse.

Mr. McGraw muttered something about gag rule and the horror of being mollycoddled, sighed dismally and predicted his death within the hour. Donna left the room and he was forced to amuse himself, until he fell asleep, watching the antics of an inquisitive lizard which in turn was watching him from a crack in the sun-baked adobe wall. As for Donna, the very fact that Bob was still a fighter and a rebel proved conclusively that within a week he would be absolutely unmanageable. This thought was productive of such joy in Donna's heart that she became a rebel herself. In the bright evening she took her guitar and went out into the patio, where she stood under Bob's window and sang for him a plaintive little Spanish love song. Donna's voice, while untrained, was, nevertheless, well pitched, sweet and true, and to Bob McGraw, who for three years had not heard a woman's voice raised in song, the simple melody was a treat indeed.

The nurse came out, looked at her and laughed, as who would not; for all the world loves a lover, and the nurse was very human.

"That's quite irregular, Miss Corblay," she commented, "but in this particular case I believe it has a soothing effect. Mr. McGraw has promised me that he will be very good if I can induce you to sing for him every evening. He said 'Bravo' three times."

"Then he has decided not to die after all."

"I think he has changed his mind."

"I'll sing him to sleep" Donna answered - and forthwith did so. And that night, when she retired, she could not sleep herself for the happiness that was hers; that excessive happiness which, more poignant than pain, is often productive of tears.

The wounded man slept well that night. If he suffered nobody knew it. In the morning his condition was slightly improved, and after hearing a most cheerful and favorable report from both doctor and nurse, Donna decided not to prejudice her position at the eating-house by staying away another day, and accordingly she set off up the track to the town. She was half-way there when she observed Harley P. Hennage walking toward her from the direction of the cemetery.

"Well, Miss Donna," he began as he approached, "how are you after the battle?"

"Still a little shaky, Mr. Hennage, but not enough to prevent my going to work. I can count change, to-day, I think."

"Good news, good news. If I was governor of this state I'd declare to-day a legal holiday. How's the wounded hero? Able to sit up and take some food?"

"No, no food as yet. Nothing but nutriment. Who ever heard of a sick man getting anything but that?"

Mr. Hennage showed his three gold teeth. "Ain't Mrs. Pennycook been down with a plate o' calf's-foot jelly or somethin' o' that nature?" he asked.

It was Donna's turn to laugh. "I hardly think she'll come. She hasn't given me a friendly look in three years."

"Well, of course, you haven't needed her," the gambler reminded her, "but she'll be droppin' in before long, now - Bob McGraw's a stranger in town, an' entitled to the kindly services o' the community as a whole, so Mrs. P. can show up at the Hat Ranch under those conditions without unbendin' her dignity."

"I suppose she is kind enough in her way," Donna began, "but - "

"You don't like her way, eh?"

"I'm afraid I'm inclined to be uncharitable at times."

"Nonsense!" he corrected. "Ain't you been a' nursin' the sick?"

"Yes. Which reminds me that you, also, have been performing one of the works of mercy. You came from the cemetery, did you no?!"

"Yes, I've been buryin' the dead. They had me as witness on the coroner's jury last night, an' after the jury decided that it was justifiable homicide, there was nothin' to do but plant the three o' 'em - before the sun got too high. But let's take up some live topic - "

Again Donna laughed, for while Harley P.'s humor was rather grim, Donna had lived long enough in San Pasqual to appreciate it. The big gambler loved to see her laugh, and the thought that she was courageous enough to enjoy his jest, considering the terrible experience which she had lately undergone, filled him with manly admiration.

"It's another joke," he began presently, "only this time it's on San Pasqual. I want to put up a job on the town, an' you've got to help me, Miss Donna."

Donna gave him a graceful travesty of a military salute.

"'Onward, Heart of Bruce, and I will follow thee,'" she quoted. "But before you explain your plans, tell me what has poor little San Pasqual been doing of late to earn your enmity?"

"Nothin' much. The town ain't no worse than any other one-horse camp for wantin' to know everybody's business but its own. They never found out any o' mine, though, you can bank on that; and it always hurt 'em because they never found out any of your poor mother's when she was livin'. An' since your trouble the other night, they're all itchin' to learn the name o' the brave that saved you. Some o' the coroner's jury was for callin' you to testify at the inquest, but considerin' the hard looks o' the deceased an' what you told me - an' what Borax O'Rourke told everybody else before he left town yesterday, I prevailed on Doc Taylor to testify that you weren't in no fit frame o' mind to face the music, so they concluded to bring in a verdict *muy pronto,* an' let it go at that. They tell me there's been a plague o' hard characters droppin' off here lately, an' anyway, to make a long story short, the boys rendered a verdict on general principles an' there ain't no news for the rest o' the town - particularly the women. The way some o' them women's been dodgin' back and forth between their own homes and the post-office, you'd think it was the finish of a jack-rabbit drive. They're just plumb *loco,* Miss Donna, to find out the name o' this gallant stranger that saved you. They want to know what he looks like, the color o' his hair an' how he parts it, how he ties his necktie, an' if he votes the Republican ticket straight and believes in damnation for infants."

"I see," said Donna, "and you want to let them suffer, do you?"

"I wouldn't wag my tongue to save 'em" he retorted bitterly. "Now here's the programme. You've got young McGraw bottled up there at the Hat Ranch, and I want you to keep him there until he's able to walk away without any assistance, an' all that time don't you let nobody see him. I've got Doc Taylor fixed already, which was easy, Doc bein' a bachelor - an' now if you stand in we'll have 'em goin' south. On account o' bein' postmistress an' in a position to get all the news, the town's lookin' to Miss Pickett to produce, an' if she can't produce, I'm hopin' she'll go into convulsions."

"Mr. Hennage," said Donna, "this is most unworthy of you. I didn't think you would harbor a grudge."

"Why, you know my reputation, Miss Donna."

"Yes, you're the worst man in San Pasqual. But I'm afraid I can't agree to enter into this conspiracy."

"Why not?"

"It's unlawful."

"Miss Donna, I'm serious - "

"It's cruel and unusual punishment - "

"I'd light a fire under 'em" said Harley P. ferociously. "Better stand in, Miss Donna - to oblige me."

"All right, it's a go, if you put it that way."

"Shake! You'll enjoy it, Miss Donna. You'll find yourself real popular when you get up to the hotel. Some o' the natives was thinkin' o' bringin' their blankets an' three days' rations, an' campin' in front o' the hotel until you arrived. Well, good-by, till supper-time. I'm goin' to breeze along down to the Hat Ranch an' warn the nurse agin spies an' secret emissaries masqueradin' as angels o' mercy."

He waved his big hand at her and waddled down the track toward the Hat Ranch. Arrived there, he introduced himself to the nurse and made a few perfunctory inquiries regarding the condition of her patient, after which, with many premonitory coughs, he ventured to outline his campaign as San Pasqual's official news censor. The nurse was not lacking in a sense of humor, and readily agreed to enlist under the banner of Harley P.

"An' remember," he warned her, as he prepared to leave, "to look sharp if you see a forty-five-year-old damsel, with a little bright red face, all ears an' no chin, like the ace o' hearts. That'll be Miss Pickett. She'll have with her, like as not, a stout married lady, all gab an' gizzard, like a crow, an' a mouth like a new buttonhole. That'll be Mrs. Pennycook. Look out for 'em both. They talk!"

And having played this unworthy trick on the gossips of San Pasqual, Mr. Hennage returned to town in a singularly cheerful state of mind, and devoted the balance of the day to the duties of his profession.

That night, when he went to his dinner at the eating-house, he stopped at the counter to have a little chat with Donna.

"What luck?" he asked.

"I declare I'm almost exhausted. I've been dodging questions and tripping over hints all day long."

"Miss Pickett come over to offer sympathy."

"Yes."

"Hu-u-um! An' after she went away, I suppose Mrs. Pennycook come in as thick as three in a bed?"

Peter B. Kyne

"She was very nice."

"She'd better be" he remarked, and Donna thought that beneath the jocularity of his manner she detected a menace.

"What have you heard?" she queried.

"I've heard," he replied deliberately, "that Donna Corblay is harboring a desperate character in her home."

"I heard something else to-day. While we're gossiping, Mr. Hennage, I'll tell you the latest - the very latest. It's reported that Dan Pennycook is drinking."

"No!" Mr. Hennage was concerned. He was fond of Dan Pennycook. "Who told you!" he inquired.

"He was seen buying a bottle of port wine in the Silver Dollar saloon this afternoon, and you know his wife is strictly temperance."

"Oh, shucks! There's nothin' to that report. I can account for that just as easy as lookin' through a hoop. It's goin' to be wine jelly, after all. I thought maybe it might be calf's-foot, but - " he broke off. "I wish," he said earnestly, "I could get hold of a low-spirited billy goat, Miss Donna, an' tie him to your front gate when Mrs. P. arrives. You want to warn the nurse, Miss Donna. Remember what the old sharp in the big book says: 'Beware o' the Greeks when they come into camp with gifts.' Hey, Josephine!"

He hailed his waitress.

"About twenty-five dollars' worth o' ham an' eggs," he ordered, "with some pig's ear and cauliflower on the side. I ain't had such a big appetite for my grub since I was a boy."

That evening, when Donna left the eating-house for her home, it seemed to her that the Hat Ranch must be situated at least ten miles further from San Pasqual than it had been two days previous. It almost seemed as if she would never reach the gate that pierced the big seven-foot adobe wall which shut Bob McGraw in from the prying eyes of the townspeople; she felt that her heart, over-burdened with its weight of agonized happiness, must break before she found herself once more standing by Bob's bed, gazing down at him with a look of proprietorship and love.

As she stood there, smiling, her face flushed from the exertion of her rapid walk, her jaunty straw hat casting little vagrant shadows across her great, dark, sparkling eyes, he awakened and looked up. She was drawing off her gloves, and one who has ridden in the waste places as much as had Bob McGraw soon learns that simple signs are sometimes pregnant of big things. The big thing, as Bob read it then, was the fact that she had just come home; that she had hurried, for she was breathing hard. Why had she hurried? Why, to see him, Bob McGraw - and in such a hurry was she that she had not waited to remove her hat and gloves. This was all very gratifying; so gratifying that Mr. McGraw would almost, at that moment, have welcomed a .45 through his other lung, if thereby he could only make her understand how deeply gratified he really was - how dearly he loved her and would continue to love her. He was so filled with such thoughts as these that he continued to gaze at her in silence for fully a minute before he spoke.

"It's been a long, hot day" he whispered. "I worried. Thought you might be kept - late - again."

The adorable old muggins! The very thought of having somebody to worry over her was so very new to Donna, and so very sweet withal, that she *called* Mr. McGraw an adorable old muggins, and pinched the lobe of his left ear, and tweaked the sunburned apex of his Irish nose. Then she kissed the places thus pinched and tweaked, and declared that she was happy enough to - to - to *swear!* "I understand - perfectly" said Bob McGraw, and there is no doubt that he did. The idea of a glorious young Woman like Donna swearing was, indeed, perfectly ridiculous. Of course, nerve-racked tired waitresses and be-deviled chefs "cussed each other out" as a regular thing up at the eating-house during a rush, and Donna, having listened to these conversational sparks, off and on, for three years, felt now, for the first time, as she imagined they must feel - that the unusual commotion in one's soul occasionally demands some extraordinary outlet.

"I could beat Soft Wind with the broom, or tip over the stove, or do something equally desperate" she told him. "I feel so deeply - it hurts me - here," and she pressed her hand to her heart.

"Think of me," he whispered, "hurt on - both sides. Bullet - hole in - right lung - key-hole in - my heart."

The blarney of the wretch! Really, this McGraw man was the most forward person! As if he could ever, by any possibility, love her as she loved him!

"You great red angel" she said. Then she ruffled his hair and fled out to the kitchen to investigate the exact nature of the savory concoction which the nurse was preparing for her invalid. No royal chef, safe-guarding the stomach of his monarch against the surreptitious introduction of a deadly poison in the soup, could have evinced a greater interest in the royal appetite than did Donna in Bob McGraw's that night. As the nurse was about to take the bowl of broth which she had prepared, in to her patient, Donna dipped up a small quantity on a teaspoon and tasted it.

"A little more salt, I think" she announced, with all the gravity of her twenty years.

The nurse glanced at her for a moment, before she took her glowing face between her cool palms and kissed the girl on each cheek. Then she reached for the salt cellar, dropped a small pinch into the soup, seized the tray and marched out, smiling. She was one of the women on this earth who can understand without asking - at least Donna thought so, and was grateful to her for it.

The three weeks that followed, while Bob McGraw, having battled his way through the attack of traumatic pneumonia incident to the wound in his lungs, slowly got back his strength, seemed, indeed, the most marvelous period of Donna Corblay's entire existence. On the morning after her conversation with Harley P., Mrs. Pennycook, true to the gambler's prediction, did favor the Hat Ranch with her bustling presence, and wrapped in a snow-white napkin the said Mrs. Pennycook did carry the hereinbefore mentioned glass of wine jelly for the debilitated stranger in their midst. Donna was at the eating-house when Mrs. Pennycook called, but the nurse received her - not, however, without an inward chuckle as she recalled Mr. Hennage's warning and discovered that Mrs. Pennycook's mouth did really resemble a new buttonhole - as the mouth of every respectable, self-righteous, provincial female bigot has had a habit of resembling even as far back as the days of the Salem witchcraft.

For her wine jelly, Mrs. Pennycook received due and courteous thanks from the nurse personally, and also on behalf of Miss Corblay and the patient. To her apparently irrelevant and impersonal queries, regarding the identity of the wounded man, his personal and family history, Mrs. Pennycook received equally irrelevant and impersonal replies, and when she suggested at length that she "would dearly love to see him for a moment - only a moment, mind you - to thank him for what he had done for that dear sweet girl, Donna Corblay," the nurse found instant defense from the invasions by reminding Mrs. Pennycook of the doctor's orders that his patient be permitted to remain undisturbed.

Two days later Mrs. Pennycook, accompanied by Miss Pickett, called again. Miss Pickett carried the limp carcass of a juvenile chicken, and armed with this passport to Bob McGraw's heart and confidence, she too, endeavored to run the guard. Alas! The young man was still in a very precarious condition, and baffled and discouraged, the charitable pair departed in profound disgust.

The next day Dan Pennycook called, at Mrs. Pennycook's orders. The yardmaster, as he bowed to the nurse and ventured a mild inquiry as to the patient's health, presented a remarkable imitation of a heretofore conscientious dog that has just been discovered in the act of killing a sheep. Poor Daniel was easy prey for the efficient nurse. He retired, chop-fallen and ashamed, and the day following, two conductor's wives and the sister of a brakeman, armed respectively with a brace of quail, a bouquet of assorted sweet peas and half a dozen oranges, came, deposited their offerings, were duly thanked and dismissed.

To all these interested ladies, Donna, at the suggestion of Harley P. (who, by the way, fell heir to the brace of quail, which he had prepared by the eating-house chef, and later consumed with great gusto), wrote a polite note of thanks. This, of course merely served to irritate an already irritated community, without affording them an opportunity for what Mr. Hennage termed "a social comeback." He contracted the habit, during that first week, of coming in to his dinner earlier, in order that he might hear from Donna a detailed report of the frantic efforts of her neighbors to get at the bottom of the mystery. Mr. Hennage was enjoying himself immensely.

After the first week had passed without developments, interest in Donna and her affairs began to dwindle, for not infrequently matters move in kaleidoscopic fashion in San Pasqual, and the population, generally speaking, soon finds itself absorbed in other and more important matters. Mrs. Pennycook was quick to note that Donna (to quote Mr. Hennage) was "next to her game," and with the gambler's threat hanging over her she was careful to refrain from expressing any decided opinions in the little circle in which she moved.

At the end of the second week the news that

development work was projected somewhere near the town, doubtless by some syndicate whose operations were so extensive that the work would likely mean a construction camp conveniently near, swept the Bob McGraw-Donna Corblay episode completely aside. Rumor, fanned by the eager desires of the business element of the hamlet, gained headway, despite the fact that false rumor was all too frequent a visitor to San Pasqual, until not more than half a dozen people in the town remembered that Donna Corblay had had an adventure, the details of which they had failed to unearth.

During those three weeks of convalescence, Bob McGraw's splendid condition, due to his clean and hardy life on the range and desert, caused him to rally with surprising rapidity from his dangerous wound. At the end of ten days he was permitted to sit up in bed and talk freely, and a few days later with the assistance of the nurse and Sam Singer he was lifted into a chair and spent a glorious day sitting in the sun in the wind-protected patio. The slight cough which had troubled him at first commenced to disappear, proving that the wound was healing from within, and the doctor announced that at the end of a month Bob would be able to leave the house.

As the reader may have had cause to suspect earlier in this recital, Bob McGraw was not the young man to permit the grass to sprout under his feet in the matter of a courtship. The brief period each evening which he and Donna spent together served to convince each that life without the other would not be worth the living. Their wooing was dignified and purposeful; their love was too pure and deep to be taken lightly or tinged with the frivolity that too often accompanies an ardent love affair between two young people who have not learned, as had Bob and Donna, to view life seriously. Both were graduates of the hard school of practicalities, and early in life each had learned the value of self-reliance and the wisdom of thinking clearly and without self-illusion.

The last week of Bob's stay at the Hat Ranch, under the chaperonage of the nurse, was not spent in planning for the future, for the lovers did not look beyond the reality of their new-found happiness. True, Bob had tried it once or twice, during the long hot days in the patio while waiting for Donna to return from her work, but the knowledge of his inability to support a wife, the present desperate condition of his finances and the unsettled state of his future plans, promptly saturated his soul in a melancholy which only the arrival of Donna could dissipate. As for Donna, like most women, she was content to linger in that delightful state of bliss which precedes marriage. Never having known real happiness before, she was, for the present at least, incapable of imagining a more profound joy than walking arm in arm in the moonlit patio with the man she loved. Without the adobe walls, the zephyr lashed the sage and whirled the sand with fiendish disregard of human happiness, but within the Hat Ranch enclosure Donna Corblay knew that she had found a paradise, and she was content.

CHAPTER VIII

Donna's mail-order library proved a great source of comfort to Bob during the lonely days at the Hat Ranch. At night she sang to him, or sat contentedly at his side while he told her whimsical tales of his wanderings. He was an easy, natural conversationalist, the kind of a man who "listens" well - an optimist, a dreamer. He was, seemingly, possessed of a fund of unfailing good-nature, and despite the fact that the past seven years of his life had been spent far from that civilization in which he had grown to manhood, in unconventional, occasionally sordid surroundings, he had lost none of an innate gentleness with women, that delicate attention to the little, thoughtful, chivalrous things which, to discerning women, are the chief charm in a man. And withal he was a droll rascal, a rollicking, careless fellow who quickly discovered that, next to telling her that he loved her and would continue to love her forever and ever, it pleased Donna most to have him tell her about himself, to listen to his Munchausenian tales of travel and adventure. Did he speak of cities with their cafes, parks, theaters and museums, she was interested, but when he told her of the country that lay just beyond the ranges, east and west, or described the long valley to the north, rolling gradually up to the high Sierra, with their castellated spires, sparkling and snow-encrusted; of little mountain lakes, mirroring the firs of the heights above them, of meadows and running water and birds and blossoms, he could almost see the desert sadness die out in her eyes, as she trailed him in spirit through this marvelous land of her heart's desire.

"When we're married, Donna," he told her, when there came to him for the first time a realization of the hunger in the girl's heart for a change from the drab, lifeless, unchanging vistas of the open desert, "we'll take horses and pack-animals and go up into that wonderful country on our honeymoon."

She turned to him with glistening eyes, seized his hand and pressed it to her cheek.

"How soon?" she murmured.

He was silent, wishing he had not spoken. He was a little subdued as he answered.

"As soon as my ship comes in, Donna. Just at present it seems quite a long way off, although if nothing happens to upset a little scheme of mine, it will not be more than a year. Things are very uncertain right now." He smiled sheepishly as he thought of his profitless wanderings. "You know, Donna, I've been a rolling stone, and I haven't gathered very much moss."

"We can wait. I haven't thought much about the future, either, Bob. I'm just content to know I've got you, and the problem of keeping you hasn't presented itself as yet."

They were silent, listening to the zephyr whistling around the Hat Ranch.

"Do you know," she told him presently, "I haven't stopped to gather up the hats since the night you came. Bob, dear, I'm afraid you're ruining my business."

He stared at her amazed. "I don't understand" he said.

"I don't gather moss," she taunted him; "my specialty is hats," and then she explained for the first time the peculiar side-line in which she was engaged. It was their first discussion of any subject dealing with the practical side of her life, and Bob was keenly interested. He laughed as Donna related some homely little anecdote of the hat trade, and later, after plying her with questions regarding her life, past and present, the mood for a mutual exchange of confidences seized him and he told her something of his own checkered career.

Bob McGraw's father had been a mining engineer who had never accomplished anything more remarkable than proving himself a failure in his profession. He was of a roving, adventurous disposition, the kind of a man to whom the fields just ahead always look greenest, and as a result his life had been a remarkable series of ups and downs - mostly downs. Bob's mother had been an artist of more or less ability - probably less - who, having met and fallen in love with McGraw senior in New York during one of his prosperous periods, had continued to love him when the fortune vanished. Bob had been born in a mining camp in Tuolumne county. He had never seen his mother. She died bringing him into the world. His father had drifted from camp to camp, each successive camp being a little lonelier, less lively and less profitable than its predecessor. He had managed to keep his son by him until Bob was about ten years old, when he sent him to a military academy in southern California. At eighteen, Bob had graduated from the academy, and at his father's desire he entered the state university to study law.

Long before he had waded half-way through the first book of Blackstone, Bob had become fully convinced that he was his father's son, and that mining engineering would be vastly more to his liking. It was a profession, however, upon which his father frowned. Like most men who have made a failure of their vocation, he dreaded to see his son follow in his father's footsteps. He was insistent upon Bob following the law; so to please him young Bob had managed to struggle through the course and by dint of much groaning and burning of midnight oil, eventually he was admitted to practice before the Superior Court. Unknown to his father, however, he had been attending the courses in geology and mining engineering, in which he had made really creditable progress. He was unfortunate enough to pass his law examinations, however, whereupon his father declared that he must make his own way in the world thereafter. He secured for his son a position in the office of an old friend, a corporation lawyer named Henry Dunstan, where Bob while not actively engaged upon some minor detail of Dunstan's large practice had the privilege of going down into the police courts for a little practical experience in the gentle art of pleading.

A month later, McGraw, pere, while ascending the shaft of the mine where he was employed as super-intendent, was met by an ore bucket coming down. Bob closed his office, went up country to the mine and saw to it that his father was decently buried. Fortunately there was sufficient money on hand to do this, Bob's parent having received his pay check only the day before.

There had been no estate for Bob to probate, and his few briefless weeks scouting around the police courts and acting as a messenger boy for Henry Dunstan had given him a thorough disgust for the profession of the law. He left his position with Dunstan and went to work on a morning paper at fifteen dollars a week. At the end of two months he was getting twenty - also he was very shabby and in debt. It was his ambition to gather together sufficient money to enable him to complete his mining course and secure his degree.

He hated the city; it was not in his nature to battle and grub with his fellows for a few paltry dollars, and the call of his father's blood was strong in his veins. Bob was the kind of fellow who likes to make a heap of his winnings, when he has any, and stake it all on the turning of a card; if this metaphor may be employed to designate Bob McGraw's nature without creating the impression that he had, inherited a penchant for the gaming table. It had been born in him to take a chance. And the gold fever, inherited from his father, still burned in his blood. He drifted to Nevada, where he did a number of things - including the assault on Mr. Hennage's faro bank, which, as we have already been informed, also resulted disastrously.

These adventures occupied the first two years of Bob McGraw's wanderings. For the next eighteen months he worked in various mines in various capacities, picking up, in actual experience, much of the mining wisdom which circumstances had denied that he should acquire in college. His Nevada experiences had given him a taste of the desert and he liked it. There was a broad strain of poetry in his make-up, inherited perhaps from his mother, and the desert appealed to that mystical sixth sense in him, arousing his imagination, taunting him with a desire that was almost pre-natal to investigate the formation on the other side of the sky-line. It pandered to the spirit of adventure in him, the purple distances lured him with promise of rich reward, and the day he made the remarkable discovery that he had saved enough money to purchase two burros, an automatic pistol, a box of dynamite and the usual prospector's outfit, he took the trail through Windy Gap and Hell's Bend into Death Valley.

Here Bob McGraw learned the true inwardness of a poem which he had once recited as a boy at school. "Afar In the Desert I Love to Ride." Only Bob walked. And after walking several hundred miles he found nothing. But he had seen lots of country, and the silence pleased him. Also he had met and talked with other desert wanderers, with whom he had shared his water and his grub, and in return they had infected him still further with the microbe of unrest. He heard tales of lost mines, of marvelous strikes, of fortunes made in a day, and that imaginative streak in him, inherited from his mother, fused with the wanderlust of his father, combined to make of him a Desert Rat at twenty-three.

He came out of the desert, on that first trip, at Coso Springs, and doubled north along the western edge of the White mountains up through Inyo county picking, prospecting, starving, thirsting cheerfully as he went. At the town of Bishop, his stomach warned him that it would be a wise move to sell his outfit and seek a job; which he accordingly did. He found employment with a cattle company and went up to Long valley in Mono county. Here he was almost happy. Life on a cow range suited him very well indeed, for it took him away from civilization and carried him through a mineral country. He rode with a prospector's pick on his saddle, and in addition the scenery just suited him. There was just enough of desert and bare volcanic hills, valley and meadow and snow-capped peaks to please the dreamer and lover of nature; there was always the chance that a "cow," scrambling down a hillside, would unearth for him a fortune.

Thus a few more years had slipped by. In the summer and fall Bob McGraw rode range. In the winter he quit his job, invested his savings in two burros and a prospector's outfit and roved until summer came again and the heat drove him back to the range once more. He was very happy, for the future was always rose-tinted and he had definitely located two lost mines. That is to say, he could say almost for a certainty that they lay within five miles of certain points. Somehow, his water had a habit of always giving out just when he got to those certain points, and when he had gone back after more water something had happened - a new strike here, a reported rush elsewhere, to lure him on until he was once more forced to abandon the trail and return to work for his grubstake in the fall.

This was the man who had ridden into San Pasqual and got as far as the Hat Ranch; when as usual, something had happened.

He told Donna his story simply, with boyish frankness, interlarding the narrative with humorous little anecdotes that robbed the tale of the stigma of failure and clothed it in the charm of achievement. She laughed in perfect understanding when he described how some desert wag had placed a sign beside the trail at Hell's Bend at the entrance to Death Valley. "Who enters here leaves hope behind."

"I saw that sign when I came by, Donna," he told her, "and I didn't like it. It sounded too blamed pessimistic for me, so when I broke camp next morning I changed the sign to read 'Soap' instead of 'Hope.'"

Donna's laughter awoke the echoes in the silent patio, and Bob McGraw, certain of his audience, rambled on. Ah, what a dreamer, what a lovable, careless, lazy optimist he was! And how Donna's whole nature went out in sympathy with his! She knew so well what drove him on; she envied him the prerogative of sex which denied to her these joyous, endless wanderings. "I love it" he told her presently. "I can't help it. It appeals to something in me, just like drink appeals to a drunkard. I'm never so happy as when gophering around in a barren prospect hole or coyoting on some rocky hillside. But it's only another form of the gambling fever, and I realize that whether my present plans mature or not I've got to give it up. It was all right a few years ago, but now the idea of wandering all my life over the mountains and desert, and in the end dying under a bush, like a jack-rabbit - no, I've got to give it up and follow something definite."

Again she patted his hand. She knew the resolution cost him a pang; it pleased her to learn that he had made it because he realized that he owed something to himself; not because of the fact of his love for her.

"It won't take you long, once you have made up your mind" she encouraged him.

134   Peter B. Kyne

"I don't want to be rich," he explained. "When I started out, Donna, I had that idea. I wanted money - in great big gobs, so I could throw it around with both hands and enjoy myself. I used to think a good deal about myself in those days, but five years in the desert and riding the range changes one. It takes the little, selfish foolish notions out of one's head and substitutes something bigger and nobler and - and - well, I can't exactly explain, dear, but I know a little verse that covers the subject very thoroughly:

The little cares that fretted me,
I lost them yesterday
Among the fields above the sea,
Among the winds at play,
Among the lowing of the herds,
The rustling of the trees,
Among the singing of the birds,
The humming of the bees;
The foolish fears of what might happen,
I cast them all away
Among the clover-scented grass,
Among the new-mown hay,
Among the hushing of the corn
Where drowsy poppies nod,
Where ill thoughts die and good are born,
Out in the fields with God."

The hint of the desert sadness died out in the girl's eyes as he declaimed his gospel.

"Oh," she cried softly, "that's beautiful - beautiful."

"That's the Litany of a Pagan, Donna," he answered. "One has to believe to understand when he goes to church in a city, but if you're a Pagan like me, you only have to understand in order to believe."

"I am," she interrupted passionately, "I'm a Pagan and the daughter of a Pagan. My father was a Sun Worshiper - like you."

"Tell me about yourself and your people," he said, and Donna told him the story with which the reader is already familiar. He questioned her carefully about Sam Singer and the man who had murdered her father and despoiled him of his fortune.

"Who was this tenderfoot person?" he asked. "Didn't Sam Singer know his name?"

"No. We never knew the man's name. When my father left for the desert he merely told mother that he was going to meet an Eastern capitalist at Salton. Sam says the only name my father called the man was Boston."

"Boston?"

Donna nodded.

"That means he hailed from Boston, and your father called him that in sheer contempt. No wonder they fought."

He was silent, thinking over that strange tale of a lost mine which Sam Singer had told Donna's mother.

"Well, I'm not going to keep on desert ratting until somebody cracks me on the head and stows me on the shelf" he said presently.

He waved his arm toward the north. "Away up there, a

hundred and fifty miles, I've cast my fortune - in the desert of Owens river valley. I've cut out for myself a job that will last me all my life, and win or lose, I'll fight the fight to a finish. I'm going to make thirty-two thousand acres of barren waste bloom and furnish clean, unsullied wealth for a few thousand poor, crushed devils that have been slaughtered and maimed under the Juggernaut of our Christian civilization. I'm going to plant them on ten-acre farms up there under the shadow of old Mt. Kearsarge, and convert them into Pagans. I'm going to create an Eden out of an abandoned Hell. I'm going to lay out a townsite and men will build me a town, so I can light it with my own electricity. It's a big Utopian dream, Donna dear, but what a crowning glory to the dreamer's life if it only comes true! Just think, Donna. A few thousand of the poor and lowly and hopeless brought out of the cities and given land and a chance for life, liberty and the pursuit of happiness; to know that their toil will bring them some return, that they can have a home and a hope for the future. That's what I want to do, and when that job is accomplished I will have lived my life and enjoyed it; when I pass away, I want them to bury me in Donnaville - that's to be the name of my colony - and for an epitaph I'd like Robert Louis Stevenson's "Requiem":

Under the wide and starry sky
Dig the grave and let me lie,

Glad did I live and gladly die
And I laid me down with a will.

This be the verse you grave for me;
Here he lies where he longed to be;
Home is the sailor, home from the sea,

And the hunter home from the hill."

He paused, a little flushed and exalted. Never before had Bob McGraw unburdened his heart of its innermost secrets, its hopes, its fears, its aspirations; for a moment now he almost quivered at the thought that Donna would look upon him as a dreamer, an idealist - perhaps a fool - he, a penniless desert wanderer assuming to hold in his sunburnt palm the destinies of the under dogs of civilization - the cripples too weak and hopeless to be anything more than wretched camp-followers in the Army of Labor.

He glanced down at her now, half expecting, dreading to meet, the look of gentle indulgence so common to the Unbeliever. But there was no patronizing smile, no tolerant note in her voice as she asked simply:

"And this great, beautiful Utopia of yours, Bob - what did you call it?"

"It doesn't exist yet," he explained hastily, "but it - it may. And when it does become a reality, I'm going to call it Donnaville."

"Why?"

"Because it sounds so much better than Bobville or Robertstown, and because it will be beautiful. It will be the green fields of God after centuries upon centuries of purgatory; because it will be the land I've been telling you about, where you'll find all the things your soul is hungry for; where we will own a big farm, you and I, with great fields of alfalfa with purple blossoms; and there'll be long rows of apple and pear trees and corn and - don't you understand, dear? It will be the most beautiful thing in the desert. And yet," he added a little sadly, "I may be beaten into the earth and all my life Donnaville will remain nothing but a dream, a desire, and so I - I - "

"Nobody can despoil you of your dreams," she interrupted, "and hence you'll never be beaten, Bob. The dreamers do the world's work. But tell me. How do you propose to establish Donnaville? Tell me all about it, dear. I want to - help."

He gave her a grateful glance. "I guess I must be wound up to-night," he began, "but it is good to talk it over after hugging it to myself so many years, and suffering and striving as I have suffered and striven since I came into this country.

"When I pulled out of Death Valley on my first trip I came into Inyo from the south and worked up along the base of the White mountains as far as Bishop. The Owens river valley runs north and south, with the White mountains flanking it on the east and the high Sierra on the west. It is from ten to fifteen miles wide, that valley, with the Owens river running down the eastern side most of the way until it empties into Owens lake just above Keeler. The lake is salty, bitter, filled with alkali, boras and soda, and for nearly forty miles above its mouth the river itself is pretty brackish and alkaline. Away up the valley the river water is sweet but as it approaches the lake it gathers alkali and borax from the formation through which it flows. This renders it unfit for irrigating purposes and at first glance the lower end of the valley seemed doomed to remain undeveloped unless somebody led pure water from above down the valley in a big cement-lined canal and the cost of such a canal would thus render the project prohibitive, unless the water company which might tackle the job also owned the land.

"The valley is pure desert, although there are a great many brilliant green streaks in it, where streams of melted snow water flow down from the mountains and either disappear in the sands or just manage to reach the river or the lake. The valley looks harsh and desolate, but once you climb the mountains and look down into it, it's beautiful. I know it looked beautiful to me and I wished that I might have a farm there and settle down. For the next few years, every time I drifted up or down that valley I used to dream about my farm, and finally I picked out a bully stretch of desert below Independence, and made up my mind to file a desert claim of three hundred and twenty acres, provided I could see my way clear to a water-right that would insure sufficient water for irrigation.

"There wasn't any alkali in the land that I imagined would be my farm some day - when I found the water. Of course I didn't want the river water at this point, on account of the alkali in it, and from the formation I judged that I wouldn't have much success putting in artesian wells. Besides, I didn't care to be a lone rancher out in that desert. I've always been a sociable chap, when I could meet the right kind of people, and unless I could have neighbors on that desert I didn't want any farm.

"I scouted for the water all one summer, but didn't find any. However, just at a time when I was getting ready to come out of the mountains and hustle for next year's grubstake, I found a 'freeze-out' in the granite up on the slope of old Kearsarge, and it netted me nineteen hundred dollars.

"That water question always bothered me. I knew the land was rich - a pure marle, with lots of volcanic ash mixed with it, and that it would grow anything - with water. You ought to see that land, Donna. Why, the sage grows six feet tall in spots, and any desert land that will grow big sage will produce more fortunes than most gold mines - if you can only get the water. There the land lay, thousands of acres of it, but good water wasn't available, so the land was worthless.

"However, Donna, I had wandered around in the desert long enough to observe that wherever Nature appears to have created a paradox, there's always a reason. If Nature makes a mistake here, she places a compensating offset over there. Here was a valley that with irrigation could be made marvelously fertile at this point, only the river had to go brackish and alkaline just where it was needed most. I couldn't develop an irrigation system from any of the little streams that flowed down the Sierra, because there wasn't enough water, and there was no place to impound it, even if there had been sufficient water.

"While I was pondering this peculiar situation, a very strange thing occurred. The lower portion of the valley, including the stretch of desert on which I had my eye, was suddenly withdrawn from entry and thrown into a Forest Reserve by the Department of the Interior. It was a queer proceeding that - including a desert timbered with sage-brush and greasewood in a Forest Reserve. Withdrawing from entry lands that would not even remotely interest settlers!

"I thought this over a great deal, and by and by I began to see the light. I had suspected from observation and personal experience that there was a powerful private influence at work in the state land office, and by reason of their seeming control of the office were engaged in looting the state of its school lands which were timbered. In the congressional investigation into certain land frauds in California, it was discovered that the men accused of the frauds had been aided by corrupt minor officials in the General Land Office - clerks and chiefs of certain bureaus, whom the land-grabbers kept on their private pay-rolls. This was a matter of public record. Fortunately for the government, however, it has generally managed to secure for the head of the Land Department able and incorruptible men to whom no taint of suspicion attached - men whom the land-grabbers dare not attempt to corrupt.

"At the outset, I strongly suspected that the corrupt influence, which presumably had been exposed and punished in former investigations, was nevertheless still at work. The suspicion that grossly erroneous reports, intentionally furnished the General Land Office by officials of the Forestry Department in California, was responsible for the inclusion of the desert in the Forest Reserve, strengthened into belief the more I thought it over. I thought I could detect in this hoodwinking of the Department of the Interior, through the agency of some local official, who had been 'reached' by the land ring, the first move in a well-planned raid on the public domain, *through the state land office.*

"I quietly investigated the surveyor-general of the state, who is also ex-officio Registrar of the State Land Office. I discovered that he was a man of unimpeachable public and private life. I discovered also that he was in ill health, and had been during the greater

Peter B. Kyne

portion of his tenure in office; that he rarely spent more than two hours each day in his office; that frequently he was away from his office for a month at a time, ill, and that the office practically was dominated by his deputy. The surveyor-general was a quiet, easy-going man, advanced in years and inclined to take things easy, and the upshot of my investigations confirmed me in the belief that he was taking things easy - too easy - and that his wide-awake deputy was doing business with the land ring, by virtue of his unhampered control of the office and the implicit confidence reposed in him by the surveyor-general.

"There could be but two reasons for this ridiculous action by the Department of the Interior in thus including a desert in a Forest Reserve. Either an error had been made by the local forestry officials in defining the boundaries of the reserve, and thus reporting to the General Land Office, or the job was intentional. If the former, the error would be discovered and the boundaries rectified.

"Well, a year passed and the boundaries were not rectified, despite the fact that I wrote half a dozen complaining letters to the General Land Office. The answer was easy. The land-grabbers had subsidized somebody and my letters never got to headquarters. So I knew a big job was about to be pulled off. I guessed that the land-grabbers had solved the water problem further up the valley and were scheming to get control of the lower valley and lead the water to it, and while developing their water supply they wanted the land denied to the public. There was always the chance that some smart nester would come, file on a half-section and start boring artesian wells. If he struck water, the news would travel and other settlers would come in and take a chance, and before long there might be a hundred settlers in there. There would be no reason to fear that they would stay forever, unless they got a big artesian flow on every forty acres, and knew they could get water in sufficient quantity. But they would have found water and it would have taken say three years for them to discover that their claims could not support them, Nesters are a dogged breed of human. It takes a nester a long time to wake up to the fact that he's licked, and until they woke up, the nesters would be liable to block the water wheels of a private reclamation scheme.

"Then, too, if it should become bruited abroad, while the valley was open for entry, that water for irrigation was being developed up the valley, settlers could have flocked in down the valley - and waited for the water. A nester is patient. His life is spent in waiting. Under the desert land laws one can file on three hundred and twenty acres, or a half-section, pay twenty-five cents per acre down and then wait four years before being compelled to file with the land office the proof of reclamation that will entitle him to final patent to his land. The land ring, of course, knew this, and by their corrupt influence had so maneuvered to hoodwink the General Land Office that the valley had been withdrawn from entry. When they had protected themselves from prospective settlers, it would be safe for them to develop their water away up the valley. When they were ready, it would be easy enough, to suddenly discover that a desert valley had, by some stupid error, been included in a Forest Reserve, the boundaries would be readjusted immediately, the valley once more thrown open for entry and - dummy entrymen, Johnny-on-the-spot, to file on the land for the water company! Within the statutory limit of four years the water company would have had time to extend its canals and laterals, the dummy entrymen would have been able to show proof of reclamation and secure their patents, and after waiting a year, perhaps to preserve appearances, they would, for a consideration, gradually transfer their holdings to the water company, Within five years, the water company would have owned the entire valley, would have reorganized, called themselves a land and irrigation company and gone into the real estate business, selling five to twenty acre farms, with a perpetual water right, at prices ranging from three to five hundred dollars per acre.

"I didn't, of course, know who was behind the game, but I knew the rules by which it would be played. I'm more or less of a mining engineer, Donna, and it's part of a mining engineer's business to know the laws relating to the public domain. I could see that unless I developed water first and filed on the land first, I would never get my farm in the valley without paying dearly to the thieves who had stolen from me my constitutional right to it.

"Hence, for the past two summers, Donna, I've been up in the Sierra looking for water. It seemed to me that with so many mountain lakes up there below the snow-line, I must find one that I could tap and bring the water down into my valley. If Nature made a mistake in the valley, she would compensate for it up in the mountains, and I had an abiding faith that if I searched long enough I'd find the water.

"I circled around mountain lakes where in all probability no human foot but mine had ever trod. I crawled along the brink of a chasm three thousand feet deep, and crossed a glacier crevice on a rawhide riata. I camped three nights on a peak with so much iron ore in it that when an electrical storm came up it attracted the lightning and struck around me for hours. I crawled and crept and climbed; I fell; I was cut and bruised and hungry and cold; but all the time I was up there in the mountains I could look on the valley - my valley - and it was beautiful and I didn't mind.

"A big thought that had been in the back of my brain for a long time came to me with renewed force while I was up there in those Inyo Alps - the thought that if I could find the water it would be riches enough for me. But I wanted the land, too - not merely a half-section for myself, but the whole valley - only I didn't want it for myself. It would only be mine in trust, a sacred heritage that belonged to the lowly of the earth, and I wanted to save it for them. I could see them all at that moment, the roustabouts, the laborers and muckers, the unskilled toilers of the world. It was the hewers of wood and the drawers of water that I wanted that valley to bloom for; the poor, poor devils whose only hope is the land that gave them birth and life and would receive them in its bosom when they perished. Ten acres of that lonely thirsty land, waiting there for me to reclaim it from the ruin of ages - ten acres of my desert valley and some water and an equal chance - that's what I wanted for each of my fellow-Pagans, and I made up my mind to get it for them from the robber-barons that planned to steal it.

"It comforted me a whole lot, that thought. It gave zest to the battle, and made the prize seem worth fighting for. And I guess the God of a Square Deal was with me that day, for I found the water. I discovered a lake a mile wide and nearly five miles long, fed by countless

Peter B. Kyne

streams from the melting snow on the peaks above. I walked around it, but I couldn't find any outlet, and yet the lake never seemed to have risen higher than a certain point. This puzzled me until I discovered a sandstone ledge half-way around its eastern edge, and through a gigantic crevice in this sandstone the water escaped. When the lake rose to the edge of this crevice, during the summer when the snow was melting up on the face of old Mount Kearsarge, the surplus flowed off into some subterranean outlet, probably emerging at the head of some canyon miles away on the other side of the range. This lake was hemmed in by hills, and between two of these hills a canyon dropped away sheer to the desert two thousand feet below. I made careful estimates and discovered that by shooting a tunnel three hundred feet through the country rock at the head of this canyon I would come out on the other side of the place where the two hills met, and pierce the lake below this sandstone crevice. I could drain the lake until the surface of the water gradually came down to the intake, when I could put in a concrete pier with an iron head-gate and regulate the flow. Even in winter when the lake was frozen over I would have a steady flow of water, for my tunnel would tap the lake below the ice.

"Having found the water, my next move was to go down into the valley, into the great, hot, panting hungry heart of Inyo to protect the land for my Pagans. At the land office in Independence I registered my filing and turned to leave, just as a clerk came out and tacked a notice on the bulletin board. I read it. It was the customary notice to settlers that the lower valley had been withdrawn from the Forest Reserve and would be thrown open to entry at the expiration of sixty days from date.

"I went to the feed corral, where I had kept Friar Tuck all summer, while I was up in the mountains. I paid my livery bill, threw the saddle on Friar Tuck and headed south, for I knew that if I was to turn robber baron and steal the valley for my Pagans I'd have to hustle. I got to San Pasqual one night three weeks ago - and here I am."

Donna was silent. For perhaps a minute she gazed into his tense, eager face.

"What will it cost to drive that tunnel?" she queried finally.

"With me superintending the job and swinging a pick and drill myself, I estimate the cost at about five thousand dollars."

"And how long does your right hold good before commencing operations?"

"The law allows me a year."

"And you have five weeks left in which to plan your campaign to acquire the land?"

"Five weeks. And I'm about to attempt an illegal procedure, only I'm going to do it legally. I want to tie up fifty sections on that valley - aggregating 32,000 acres. I have money enough in bank at Bakersfield after paying my expenses here, to accomplish that. If I can tie that land up, my water-right is worth millions. If the other fellows get the land, they will buy my water-right at their own figures, or starve me out and acquire the right when I am forced to abandon it by reason of my inability to develop it; or failing that they will proceed on their original plan and lead their own water down the valley in canals. Without the water the land is worthless, and without the land my water-right is practically worthless - to me. To control that 32,000 acres of desert I will have to put up the purchase price of $40,000 for the men I induce to file on the land, and after paying the filing fee of $5 and the initial payment of $20 on each of the fifty applications for the land, I'll be in luck if I'm not left stranded at the State Land Office."

"But can you accomplish this in opposition to the land ring, if you secure all the money you will require?"

"No" he answered. "The plan I have outlined is a mere contingency. In order to carry it out, I must get my filings into the land office before theirs - and they control the land office."

"Then, how can you hope to succeed?"

Bob smiled. "Hope doesn't cost anything, Donna. It's about the only thing I know of that can't be monopolized. A man can hope till he's licked, at least, and despite the fact that I have neither money nor corrupt influence, I have a long chance to win. I have one grand asset, at least."

"What may that be?" queried Donna.

"All anybody ever needs - a bright idea."

CHAPTER IX

Bob McGraw threw back his red head and chuckled. "A bright idea, sweetheart," he repeated, "and if it works out and I am enabled to file first, the problem of getting back to the desert will be a minor one. The real problem is the acquisition of four or five thousand dollars to drive my tunnel, and after that I must scrape together thirty-nine thousand dollars to advance to my poor Pagans, in order that they may pay for the land on which I shall have induced them to file. In the meantime I do not anticipate any diminution in the appetites of myself and Friar Tuck.

"Well, after I have my tunnel driven and the head-gates in and my Pagans have the land, I have only started. The land must be cleared of sage and greasewood, which in turn must be piled and burned. Then I must build several miles of concrete aqueduct, with laterals to carry the water for irrigation, and I must install a hydro-electric power-plant, purchase telegraph poles, string power lines, build roads, houses, barns and fences. I think I shall even have to build one hundred and fifty miles of railroad into Donnaville and equip it with rolling stock."

He thrust both arms out, as if delving into the treasures of his future. "Whew-w-w!" he sighed. "I'll need oodles of money. I'm going to be as busy as a woodpecker in the acorn season."

Donna drew his arm within hers and they walked slowly - up and down the brick-lined patio.

"It means a fight to the finish, Bobby dear - and you're terribly handicapped. If your suspicions are well founded you will find yourself opposed by men with the power of wealth and political influence behind them."

His whimsical exalted mood passed. In the presence of the girl he loved and whom he hoped to marry he suddenly realized that he stood face to face with a gigantic sacrifice. To carry through to a conclusion, successful or unsuccessful, this great work to which he had set his hand meant that until the finish came he must renounce his hope of marriage with Donna. True, he might win - but it would take years to demonstrate that victory was even in sight; if he lost, he felt that he could never have the heart to ask her to share with him his poverty and his failures.

An intuitive understanding of his thoughts came to Donna at that moment; she realized that under that gay, careless exterior there beat the great warm heart of a man and a master, on whom, for all his youth and strength and optimism, a great load of care was already resting - the destiny of his people. She realized that he needed help; she thought of her insignificant savings (some six hundred dollars) reposing in the strong-box of the eating-house safe, and the first impulse of her generous heart was to offer him these hard-earned dollars. In the task that Bob McGraw had set himself, moral support was a kindly thing to offer, but dollars were the things that counted!

However, to offer him financial aid now, no matter how badly he required money, would not avail. The dictates of his manhood would not permit him to accept, and until God and man had given her the right to make the offer she must remain silent.

"I can wait here until you're ready to come for me, Bob," she said bravely. "It's a big task - a man's work - that you're going to do, and win or lose, I want you to fight the good fight. I know the kind of man I want to marry. If he starts anything that's big and noble and worthy of him, I want him to finish it - if he wants to marry me. Success or failure counts but little with men like you; it is only the fight that matters, and there are some defeats that are more glorious than victories. Remember that little jingle, dearie:

The harder you're hit, the higher you bounce,
Be proud of your blackened eye.
It isn't the fact that you're licked that counts,
But how did you fight - and why?"

"You quoted your Pagan's Litany to me to-night, sweetheart. I want you to be true to it. I don't know a thing about desert land laws and riparian rights, but I do know that if you sold your Pagans into bondage for money to marry me, I'd be ashamed of you - and disappointed. Don't let your love for me weaken your defenses, Bob. If you win I want to live with you in Donnaville, but if you lose - I want you to make me a promise, Bob."

"You wonderful woman! What is it - you wonderful, wonderful woman?"

"I'm asking for a promise, dear."

"I'll grant it."

"If you lose, you'll come to me and we'll be married despite defeat and failure, and you'll live here, with me - at the Hat Ranch until - "

"Oh, Donnie, girl, I couldn't do that!"

"I understand your point of view. Perhaps you think me bold - or unconventional. But a woman has certain rights, Bob. She should be given the right to outline her own ideas of happiness, regardless of tradition and ancient usage, provided she conforms to all of the law, legal and moral. If you go forth to battle and they slaughter you, I claim the right to pick up your poor battered old heart and give it the only comfort - I mean, if I have to wait, I love you enough to work with you - and for you - when further waiting is useless - "

She pressed her face against his great breast and commenced to cry.

"I have never been really happy until you came" she sobbed. "We're young, Bob - and I do not want to wait - for happiness - until the capacity for it - is gone."

He patted the beautiful head, soothing her with tender words, and it was characteristic of the man that in that instant he made his decision.

"Within six weeks I shall know how long the fight is to last, Donna. If I can put through a scheme which I have evolved to secure that land without recourse to the desert land laws - if I can get my applications filed first in the State Land Office - I shall have won the first battle of the war. If I fail to do this I shall have lost the land, and without further ado I shall sell my water-right to the best possible advantage. The enemy may conclude to pay me a reasonable price for it, rather than declare war and delay the development of their land. The power possibilities of my water-right are tremendous and I think I can force a good price, for I can poke away at my tunnel and by doing the assessment work I can keep my title alive for a few years. Of course, in the event that I should, after the lapse of years, be financially unable to develop my water-right, or interest others in it, I should lose it and they would grab it, no doubt. But they will buy me out, I think, rather than brook delay."

She raised her face, transfigured through the tears.

"Then, win or lose - "

"Win or lose, if you desire it and I can scrape together the price of a marriage license, we'll be married in six weeks.

"I'm so tired of the desert, dear. I'm lonely."

"A little like Br'er B'ar, eh, darling! You want to see the other side of the mountain." He pressed her to him lovingly. "Of course" (with masculine inconsistency Bob was beginning to equivocate) "I may not be able to sell my water-right and the enemy may elect to play a waiting game and starve me out. In that case, it would not be fair to you to burden you with a husband whose sole assets are his dreams and his hopes."

"That makes no difference" she exclaimed passionately. "We're young. We'll fight the rest of the battle together."

"Well, there's strength in numbers, at any rate, beloved. You're my mascot and I'm bound to win." He placed his left hand under her chin and tilted her face upward. He was stooping to seal their compact with a true lover's kiss, when the sound of footsteps startled them. Both turned guiltily, to confront Mr. Harley P. Hennage.

"Hah-hah," puffed Mr. Hennage, "at it again, eh?" He stood at the corner of the house, with his three gold teeth flashing in the moonlight.

"Kill-joy!" hissed Bob McGraw. "His Royal Highness, Kill-joy the Thirteenth!"

Harley P. shook a fat forefinger at the lovers. "If I was a young feller, Bob McGraw - "

"Mr. Hennage, you're an old snooper, that's what you are!" cried Donna. "You're all the time snooping."

"Explain this unwarranted intrusion, Harley P. Hennage" Bob demanded, as he advanced with out-stretched hand to greet the gambler. "I'll have you know that in approaching this ranch hereafter, you will be required to halt at the front gate and whistle, cough, stamp your feet, yell or fire six shots from a Colts revolver - "

"You mean a presidential salute o' twenty-one twelve-inch guns" retorted Harley P. "I ain't no snooper. I've wore corns on my hands a-bangin' that there iron gate to announce my approach, an' it wasn't no use; so I just made up my mind you was ready to receive me an' I come ramblin' in. Donnie, you know I ain't one o' the presumin' kind."

He held out a hand to Bob and another to Donna. "How?" he queried, and made swift appraisal of Bob McGraw from heels to hair. "You've filled out a whole lot since the last time I seen you standin' up. How's tricks?"

"Great. I'll be out in a day or two."

The gambler nodded his approval of this cheerful news. Donna brought out another chair and the trio sat in the secluded patio and talked generalities for ten minutes. Donna knew that Mr. Hennage must have some reason for calling other than a mere desire to pay his respects to Bob, and presently he unbosomed himself.

"Our mutual friend, Miss Pickett, has a notice pasted up on the wall o' the post-office, advertisin' a registered letter for one Robert McGraw." The gambler tittered foolishly. "Ain't a soul can tell Miss Pickett who the feller is or where he's at, except me an' Doc Taylor an' Miss Donna - an' we're all swore to secrecy, so I come down to scheme out a way to bell the cat - meanin' Miss Pickett" he added, apparently as an afterthought.

"A letter for me?" Bob was surprised. "Why, it's years since I have received a letter. I wonder who could know that I might be found in San Pasqual I didn't tell anybody I was headed this way, and as a matter of fact I hadn't intended staying here beyond that first night."

"Well, there's a letter there all right," reiterated Mr. Hennage, "an' if I was called on to give a guess who sent it I'd bet a stack o' blue chips I could hit the bull's eye first shot. A dry, purse-proud aristocrat, with gray chin whiskers an' a pair o' bespectacled blue lamps that'd charm a Gila monster, they're that shiny, lined up at the Silver Dollar bar the other day an' bought a drink for himself. Yes, he drank alone - which goes to prove that men with money ain't always got the best manners in the world. Well, after stowin' away his little jolt, he comes fussin' around among the boys, askin' which one of 'em is Mr. Robert McGraw. Of course he didn't get no information, an' wouldn't 'a got it if the boys had it. So he goes down to see Miss Pickett, an' bimeby me an' him meets up in front o' the eatin' house, an' he up an' asked me if I could tell him who owns that little roan cayuse kickin' up his heels over in the feed corral.

"Of course, I seen right off that Miss Pickett had her suspicions an' had sicked this stranger onto me; so when he informed me that he'd been told I knew the name o' the little hoss' owner, I told him I did - that the little roan hoss belonged to a Mexican friend o' mine by the name o' Enrique Maria Jose Sanchez Flavio Domingo Miramontes.

"He give me a sour look at that. 'Well, that don't correspond none with the initials on the saddle' he says.

"'Shucks,' I says,'that don't signify nothin'. Mexicans is the biggest hoss thieves living besides, I ain't feelin' disputatious to-night, so I'll just close up my game an' go get my scoffin's.'

"'But I must find this man' he says, 'It means a great deal to him - an' me.'

"'What do you call a great deal?'

"'Money' he says.

"I says: 'See here, pardner, don't you go givin' no money to no Mexican, because he'll only gamble it away on three-card monte.'

"'I don't mean your Mexican friend,' he says, like a snappin' turtle, 'I'm after a man named Robert McGraw,'

"'Oh,' I says, 'you mean that red-headed outlaw from up country? Why I didn't know he was wanted. What's it this time? He ain't got himself mixed up in more trouble, has he?'

"'I prefer to refrain from discussin' the details,' says this wealthy gent, 'with a perfect stranger.'

"'Oh, very well' I says. 'I didn't seek this interview, but when you mentioned the hoss I could tell by the look in your eye that McGraw's been robbin' you o' somethin'. Well, you might own that hoss, but you've got to prove property. McGraw sold the hoss to Enrique an' lit out for Bakersfield, an' I won the hoss from Enrique at faro. I been keepin' him in the corral in order to give the Mexican a chance to buy him back. But McGraw's not in town. He won't be here for a week or two yet.'

"'Thank you, my man,' says he, an' pulls a card, just about the time I was gettin' ready to pull his nose. 'If you should see Mr. McGraw, you might be good enough, to tell him he can learn of somethin' to his advantage by communicatin' with me right away.'

"'Well, my man,' I says, 'I do hope it's an alibi,' an' I took the card an' he went back to Miss Pickett. I want to tell you, children, that any time Miss Molly thinks she can spring a secret out o' me she's got to go some."

Peter B. Kyne

Mr. Hennage chuckled, produced a white square of cardboard and handed it to Bob. Donna, leaning over his shoulder, read:

MR. T. MORGAN CAREY PRESIDENT INYO LAND & IRRIGATION COMPANY, 414-422 SOUTHERN TRUST BUILDING, LOS ANGELES, CALIFORNIA

"I've heard of that fellow before," mused Bob, "and it strikes me his name is associated with some unpleasant memory, but I can't recall just what it is. However, I can hazard a good guess as to what he desires to see me about. I'm glad you didn't tell him where I might be found, Hennage. It was thoughtful of you. I do not care to meet T. Morgan Carey - yet."

"Well," said Mr. Hennage, "he's a smart man an' smells o' ready money. However, I wasn't goin' to give him no information until I'd talked with you first, although my main idea was to throw Miss Pickett off the scent. I'm goin' up to Bakersfield to-night, Bob, and just to keep up appearances, you give me an order for that registered letter, datin' the order from Bakersfield, to-morrow, an' I'll mail that order from Bakersfield to myself in San Pasqual. Then to-morrow night when I get back I'll go to the post-office for my mail. I ain't had a letter come to me in ten years. Miss Pickett'll give me the letter, I'll open it right in front o' her an' flash the order for the registered letter, an' the old gossip'll be annoyed to death to think she's lost the trail."

When presently Bob went into the house to write the desired order for Harley P., Donna and the gambler were left alone for a few minutes. Instantly Mr.

Hennage became serious.

"Looky here. Miss Donnie," he said, "Bob McGraw's free, white an' twenty-one an' he can play his own hand. I ain't one of the presumin' kind an' I hate to tell any man his own business, but if twenty years o' gamblin' an' meetin' all kinds an' conditions o' men ain't made me as fly as a road-runner, then that there artesian well is spoutin' mint juleps. Say, Miss Donnie, if ever I see a cold-blooded, fishy, snaky, ornery man, it's this T. Morgan Carey - an' at that he's a dead ringer for a church deacon. That Carey man would steal a hot stove without burnin' himself. Now, this young Bob is an impulsive cuss, an' if he has any dealin's of a money nature with this sweet-scented porch-climber that's on his trail, you take a tip from Harley P. Hennage, Miss Donnie, an' act as lookout on Bob's game. Miss Donnie, I can tell a crook in the dark. Let a crook try to buck my game an' I have him spotted in a minute. I just *feel* 'em."

"Thank you, Mr. Hennage. I have great faith in your judgment."

"Well, generally speakin', I call the turn, if I do say so myself."

He sat there, his bow-legs spread apart, his hands folded across his ample abdomen, staring thoughtfully at the little white cross down at the end of the garden.

"You're a heap like your mother" he said presently, and sighed.

When Bob returned with the order for the registered letter, Mr. Hennage tucked it carefully in his side coat pocket; then from his rear hip pocket he produced Bob McGraw's automatic gun.

"I took charge o' this the night o' the mix-up" he explained as he returned it. He looked hard at Bob. "When you're ready to toddle about" he added, with a lightning wink and a slight movement of his fat thumb and forefinger, as if counting a stack of imaginary bills, "send Sam Singer up to let me know. *Comprende, amigo?"*

Bob smiled at this sinful philanthropist. "Not necessary, old man - if you'll drop in at the Kern County Bank and Trust Company in Bakersfield to-morrow and get me a check-book. I have owed you fifty for three years and I'd like to square up."

"Sure you ain't bluffin' on no pair?"

"Thank you, Harley. I have a small stake."

"Well, holler when you're hit." He waved his hand and departed with a "*Buenas noches,* children."

Scarcely had the gate slammed behind him when Bob turned to Donna with beaming face.

"They're after my water-right, sweetheart - they're after it already!" His exultant laugh rang through the patio, "I knew I was treading on somebody's toes when I filed on that water, Donna. By George, I must investigate T. Morgan Carey and ascertain the kind of man I have to fight."

"He came here looking for you a week after you arrived. Doesn't that seem strange? How did he discover you had a water-right, investigate it, ascertain its value and then, come seeking you, all in the course of one week?"

"That is very easily explained, Donna. It merely verifies my suspicions that there is a ring of land-grabbers operating in this state, which ring controls some official of the State Land Office and keeps on its pay-roll an employee in every United States land office in California. The moment I filed on that water, T. Morgan Carey was notified by his tool in the State Land Office that Robert McGraw (I gave my address as Independence, Inyo county) had filed on one hundred thousand miners' inches of water for power and irrigation. Now, there isn't that much non-alkaline water available anywhere in the valley - at least under the control of one man or one corporation, and of course it frightened Carey. He wired his field engineer, who was probably in Inyo county at the time, to investigate. The engineer found my location notices tacked to a cottonwood tree right where I'm going to drive my tunnel, and he immediately reported to Carey that the location was very valuable. Also he wired my name and general description and probably stated that the last seen of me I was headed south for the railroad on a roan bronco. They've traced me by my horse to San Pasqual, and now they're trying to find me with a registered letter; very probably acting under the advice of Miss Pickett, who, apparently, is an elderly bird and not to be caught with Harley P. Hennage's chaff.

"It's absurdly simple, dear. They want my water, for they must eliminate competition, and they want to tie me up before I have an opportunity to sell to somebody who realizes the value of my holdings. Up Inyo way they know me for a range rider, a desert rat, a ne'er-do-well, and it may be they are under the impression that I am like most of my kind - that I can be mesmerized by the sight of four or five thousand dollars."

"Harley P. will give me your letter to-morrow night and I'll bring it home with me. We'll know definitely, then, what to expect. In the meantime, Bob, I think you've dreamed enough for one night. You've been up all day and you've talked and it's time you went to bed."

"'Talk'" he echoed, "talk! That's what. I've been talking - talk. But when I clash with T. Morgan Carey's company I'll talk - turkey. If you'll kiss me good-night, Donna, I think I can manage to last until morning."

Late the following afternoon Harley P. Hennage returned from Bakersfield and at once went to the post-office and secured Bob's registered letter. He brought it over to Donna at the eating-house, delivering with it a pantomime of the inquisitive Miss Pickett when she discovered that the order for delivery of the registered letter to the gambler was dated and mailed from Bakersfield.

At dinner Bob read the letter and silently handed it over to Donna. It was from T. Morgan Carey. On behalf of the Inyo Land & Irrigation Company Carey requested the favor of an interview at an early date to take up with Bob the matter of purchasing his newly acquired water-right on Cottonwood lake, or submitting a proposition for consolidation with, certain rights held by his company. He begged for an early reply.

"Will you reply to his letter?" Donna queried.

"Yes. I shall write him that my location is not for sale."

"Then write it from Bakersfield" Donna suggested. "Harley P.'s reputation is bad enough, but you mustn't convict him of lying."

Three days later Bob's strength had so far returned that Doc Taylor told him he might leave San Pasqual whenever he pleased. Bob realized that a longer stay at the Hat Ranch, while inviting enough, would nevertheless prove expensive, by reason of the retention of his nurse, for Donna could not continue to entertain him unchaperoned, even in such a free-and-easy town as San Pasqual, and he was fearful that a longer stay, even under the prevailing conditions, might prove embarrassing to Donna, in case interest in his affairs should revive; hence he announced his determination of going up to San Francisco to recuperate and complete his plans for the acquisition of thirty-two thousand acres of the public domain in the desert of Owens river valley.

Donna did not endeavor to dissuade him. She realized that a longer stay was impossible, much as both desired it, and Bob had his work to do and not a great deal of time in which to do it. Accordingly Bob issued a check to Doc Taylor that evening in payment of his fee, dismissed his nurse and paid her off, and left with Donna another check, to be cashed by Harley P. Hennage and the proceeds applied to the care and maintenance of Friar Tuck until Bob's return to San Pasqual.

During the afternoon Bob dispatched Sam Singer to

Harley P. Hennage with a request for a shaving outfit, a shirt, underwear, a necktie and a new suit of khaki. Armed with information respecting the physical dimensions of Mr. McGraw, the gambler had attended to Bob's shopping, and upon Donna's return to the Hat Ranch that night she discovered that during her absence a transformation had taken place. Bob was arrayed in his new habiliments, and paraded up and down the patio for the inspection of Donna and the nurse.

"Well, Donna" he called to her, "how do I look? Presentable? I know I'm feeling clean and respectable again, at any rate, and I've asked Sam Singer to bury that ruin of rags I wore into town."

"Your gun hangs below the tail of your khaki coat."

"Then I'll tuck it up under my arm."

Donna helped him remove the coat, after which he buckled the belt over his right shoulder, permitting the gun to hang securely in the holster under his left arm.

"Now, I don't look so confoundedly woolly and western" he said. "I do hate to go about looking like the hero of a dime novel. I suppose if a tourist saw that gun hanging down he'd think I was bloodthirsty. It would never occur to him that a gun comes in handy in the wilderness."

"Why not leave it here until your return?"

Bob grinned. "It's a good gun, Donna. I might be able to pawn it for enough to help out on my return trip. Of course I have a watch, but its hockable value is negative. When I was very young I was foolish enough to have my initials engraved on the case, but of course I know better now - by George, Donna girl, I haven't any hat!"

She flashed him one of her rare wonderful smiles. "I was waiting for you to make that discovery" she said. "You lost your hat the night you arrived in San Pasqual, but I haven't worried about it. I've been saving a splendid big sombrero for you, Bob."

She went to her room, returning presently with a "cowboy" hat that must have been the joy and pride of the tourist who sacrificed it to the San Pasqual zephyr. She pinched it to a peak and set it jauntily on his auburn head, then stood off and surveyed him critically.

"It's a dear" she announced.

"Looks dear, too" he replied whimsically. "Must have cost the original owner a month's board. Whew! That's a bird of a hat, Donna girl. Thank you. It's as good a hat as I'll ever own."

He sat down forthwith, turned back the sweat-band, moistened it slightly and with the stub of an indelible pencil wrote his name in full. He had ridden range long enough to acquire the habit of branding his property, and in that land of breeze and sunshine he knew the dangers that beset a maverick hat.

That night they walked together in the patio for the last time. Neither felt inclined to conversation, for the thoughts of each were occupied with dreams of the future, and the tragedy of that farewell lay heavy upon them. Lover-like, each exacted from the other a promise to write every day, and that important detail finally settled, Donna found it easy enough to be brave and let him go.

At eleven o'clock Sam Singer appeared in the patio to announce his willingness to trundle Bob up to San Pasqual on the same trackwalker's velocipede upon which Bob had arrived at the Hat Ranch. The nurse was not to leave until the next day, and being a discreet woman, and kindly withal, she had had the delicacy to bid her patient farewell in the patio. Donna accompanied him to the front gate, and there Bob with many a fervent promise to take good care of himself - and not to forget to write every day, took her in his arms, kissed her quickly before the tears should have a chance to rise, and was gone.

She watched him stride slowly through the gloom to the velocipede waiting on the tracks; she saw him climb aboard. Then the Indian's body bent over the levers and the machine glided away into the night. She stood at the gate and watched it until it vanished; she waited until Twenty-six came thundering by at eleven-thirty-five and heard the grind of the brakes as the long train pulled up at the station. Five minutes later she heard it pull out of San Pasqual, with many a short and labored gasp, casting a lurid gleam across the desert as it sped northward into Tehachapi Pass, carrying Bob McGraw forth to battle, to fight for his land and his Pagans.

When the last dim flicker of the green tail lights had disappeared Donna retired to her room and cried herself to sleep. Once more she was left to battle alone with the world, and the days would be long until Bob

McGraw came back.

Three hours after leaving Donna Corblay at the Hat Ranch, Bob McGraw alighted from the train at Bakersfield and went at once to a hotel. He arose late the next morning, breakfasted in the most appalling loneliness and later wended his way weakly to the bank where his meager funds were on deposit. Here he had his account balanced and discovered that his total fortune amounted to a trifle over sixteen hundred dollars, so he closed out his account and purchased a draft on San Francisco for the amount of his balance, less sufficient money to pay his current expenses.

This detail attended to, Mr. McGraw next proceeded to do what he had always done when in a civilized community - spend his money recklessly. He went back to the hotel, called Donna on the long-distance phone and frittered away two dollars in inconsequential conversation. However, he felt amply rewarded for the extravagance when Donna's voice - deep, throaty, almost a baritone - came to him over the wire; the delighted, almost childish cry of amazement which greeted his "Hello, Donna girl" was music to his soul.

Bob was the kind of man who always thinks of the little things. He knew Donna had gone to work that morning feeling blue and lonely, and the substitution of that mood for one of genuine happiness for the rest of the day Mr. McGraw would have considered cheap at the price of his great toe or a hastily plucked handful of his auburn locks. As for money - bah! Had it been his last two dollars it would have made no difference. He would have telephoned just the same and trusted to heaven to rain manna for his next meal.

But Bob McGraw was nothing if not an impetuous lover. Even in the case of one who, like himself, had plans afoot where every dollar counted, we might pardon readily the expenditure of two dollars on conversation, in view of the extraordinary circumstances; but Mr. McGraw's next move savors so strongly of the veal period of his existence that no amount of extenuating circumstances may be adduced in defense of it. While the promoter of Donnaville was a true son of the desert, he was college-bred, and with the sight now, for the first time in several years, of trolley cars, automobiles and people wearing clean linen, old memories surged up in Mr. McGraw's damaged breast, and despite the fact that his long legs were now weak and wobbly from the premature strain of his journey from the hotel to the bank and back again, he fared forth once more and pursued the uneven tenor of his way until he found himself in a florist's shop.

Here no less than six dozen red carnations caught Mr. McGraw's fancy, the purchase price of which, in addition to the express charges prepaid to San Pasqual, further denuded him of ten dollars. Into the heart of this cluster of fragrance he caused to be secreted a tiny envelope enclosing a card, upon which he had drawn a heart with a feathered arrow sticking through it; and for fear this symbolic declaration of undying devotion might not be sufficient, he scrawled beneath it: "Love from Bob."

Ah, if he could only have seen Donna's face when the express messenger next door brought that votive offering in to her! Red carnations were not frequent in San Pasqual. It was the first lover's bouquet Donna had ever received and she bent low behind the cash register and kissed the foolish little card, for the hand of her Bob had touched it! The carnations she bore home to the Hat Ranch in triumph, and two weeks later when Soft Wind, a stranger to romance, threw them out, Donna wept.

His mission of love finally accomplished, Bob returned to his hotel and went to bed. Late that afternoon he arose, much refreshed, dined and waited around the lobby until it was time for the bus to leave for the north-bound train.

By nine o'clock next morning he was in San Francisco. He found frugal lodgings in a third-class hotel, and after writing a letter to Donna, he went down town, purchased a suit of "store" clothes, and spent the balance of the day in the public law library.

By nightfall Bob had saturated his brain with legal lore bearing on every feature of the laws governing the acquisition of lands in the public domain, and was satisfied that the hazy plan which he had outlined was not only within the law, but really did have some vague elements of feasibility. The beauty of Bob's plan, however - the part that appealed to the sporting instinct in his ultra-sporty soul - lay in the fact that it would cost him only fifteen hundred dollars to try! Twelve hundred and seventy-five in preliminary payments, filing fees and notary's fees, and the balance in hotel bills, traveling expenses, etc.; but as an offset to his comparatively brilliant prospects of going hungry and ragged there was the dim, long chance that he *might* win millions, provided his venture should be attended with a fair percentage of supernatural luck. That was all Bob McGraw had to cheer him on to victory - a million-to-one chance; yet, such was his peculiar mental make-up, the terrific odds only proved an added attraction.

CHAPTER X

Now; in order to insure even perfunctory understanding of the procedure under which Bob McGraw
planned to acquire his lands, and to give an inkling of
the difficulties confronting him, it is necessary that the
reader take a five-minute course in land law. This is
regrettable, for it is a dry subject, even in the matter of
swamp and overflow lands, so we shall endeavor to
make the course as brief as possible.

Section sixteen and thirty-six in each township
throughout the United States are commonly designated
as "school lands," for the reason that the Federal
government has ceded them to the various states, to be
sold by the states for the use and benefit of their public
school funds. School lands are open to purchase by any
citizen of the United States, and in the case of
California school lands the statutory price is one dollar
and twenty-five cents per acre.

Now, frequently it happens that by reason of the
inclusion of certain of these "school lands" in a Forest
Reserve, a Reclamation District, an Indian Reservation, a National Park, a Government Military
Reservation or an old Mexican grant (which latter
condition obtains very frequently in California, where
the titles to many huge grants still hold since the days
of the Mexican occupation) they are lost to the state. In

such cases, the Federal government reimburses the state suffering such loss of school lands, by extending to the state the privilege of selecting from the public lands within its borders an acreage corresponding to the acreage thus lost by reason of inclusion in a restricted area.

The lands thus selected from the public domain in exchange for school lands lost to the state, having been taken in lieu, thereof, are known as "state lieu lands," and the lands which were originally state school lands and which have been lost to the state by reason of their inclusion in some restricted area, are spoken of as the "basis" for the exchange.

If a citizen of the United States, duly qualified, desires to purchase state school lands at the statutory price of one dollar and twenty-five cents per acre, he must file his application for a section, or such fraction thereof as he may desire, or be entitled to purchase, with the surveyor-general of the state, who is also ex-officio registrar of the State Land Office. If there are no school lands open for purchase at the time, naturally they cannot be purchased; but if, on the contrary, the state owns many sections of school lands which have been included in restricted areas, the surveyor-general will select for the applicant from the public domain such state lieu lands as the purchaser may desire. However, no such selection of lieu lands can be made by the surveyor-general unless there is a corresponding loss of school lands *as the basis for the selection.*

Now, this basis constituted the horns of a dilemma upon which Bob McGraw had once found himself impaled in an attempt to purchase three hundred and twenty acres of timbered land in the public domain -

land which he knew would, in the course of a few years, become very valuable. Bob's restless nature would not permit of his taking up the claim under the homestead law, for that would entail residence on the property for more years than Bob could afford to remain away from his beloved desert; hence he decided to acquire it by purchase as state lieu land at a time when he knew there were no available school lands lying outside restricted areas. Mr. McGraw saw an attractive profit in purchasing at one dollar and twenty-five cents per acre three hundred and twenty acres of timber worth fully fifty dollars per acre.

Thrilled, therefore, with most pleasurable anticipations, Mr. McGraw had duly filed his application for purchase of this particular half-section, under Section 3495 of the Political Code of the State of California. He knew that, owing to the recent extension of the Forest Reserve policy, thousands of acres of school lands had recently been lost to the state, and that therefore, under the law, there could be no legal hindrance to his purchase of lieu lands - particularly in view of the fact that there were several hundred thousand acres of government lands within the state from which to make his selection!

To Bob's surprise, his application for the purchase of lieu lands had been denied, under a ruling of the State Land Office - a ruling having absolutely no foundation under any section of legislative procedure - which stipulated that before the State Land Office could receive or grant an application for the purchase of lieu lands, the intending purchaser *must first designate the basis of corresponding loss to the state of school lands.*

"Bless my innocent soul," Mr. McGraw had murmured

at the time, "what a curious rule! I had a notion that that was the surveyor-general's business, not mine. I had a notion that he was paid for compiling that information for the people, and not forcing them to compile it for themselves."

However, in no whit daunted by the prospect of a little research work, Bob had had recourse to the land maps in the office. To his surprise and chagrin he discovered that as fast as he brought to light a "basis" for his selection, he was informed, after some perfunctory investigation by the employees of the State Land Office that these bases *had already been used!* Eventually the light of reason began to sift through the fog of despair and suddenly Bob had a very brilliant idea.

"Euchred!" he muttered to himself. "I do not happen to possess the requisite amount of inside information and I have no means of obtaining it until I ascertain where it is for sale! The purpose of this ridiculous rule is to keep the rabble out of the public domain until some middleman gets a profit out of his information. I'll just give up for the time being and await results."

Bob did not have long to wait. Within a week he received a letter from an alleged land attorney, offering to locate him on state lieu lands worth fifty dollars per acre, in return for the trifling payment of one dollar and twenty-five cents per acre to the state and the further trifling payment of ten dollars per acre to the purveyor of information respecting the necessary basis for the exchange!

At the time this procedure had struck Bob as rather humorous. He was anardent admirer of genius wherever lie saw it, and even this exhibition of evil genius, which so adroitly deprived him of his constitutional right to the public domain without the payment of a middleman's profit, rather aroused his admiration. At the time he was not financially equipped to argue the matter calmly, clearly - and judicially, and he had no money to pay for "inside information." He only knew that the rule requiring applicants to designate the basis was an office-made rule and had no place in Mr. McGraw's copy of the Political Code of the State of California.

And the star-spangled banner in triumph doth wave,
O'er the land of the free and the home of the knave

caroled Bob, and charged the matter up to experience, not, however, without first storing the incident away in his nimble brain for future reference.

Now, while recovering from his wound at the Hat Ranch, Bob had brooded much over the difficulties which would without doubt assail him in his attempt to acquire his lands in Owens river valley; also he had figured out to his own satisfaction the exact method by which the land-grabber was enabled to grab; or, provided the grabber did not care to retain his grab, how he could nevertheless derive tremendous profits from his control of certain officials in the State Land Office. Therefore, after his day spent in the public law library in San Francisco, Bob's brain was primed with every detail of the land laws, and had confirmed his original interpretation of the land-grabbers' clever schemes to defraud. However, not satisfied with his own opinion, he decided to seek a little expert advice on the subject, and to that end he went the following morning to his father's old friend and his own former employer, Homer Dunstan, the corporation attorney, whom he knew to be an authority on land law.

He sent in his name by Dunstan's stenographer, and presently Dunstan appeared in the reception room. He welcomed his old friend's failure of a son in a manner which bespoke forced heartiness, for old sake's sake, and a preconceived impression that the ill-dressed, pale Bob McGraw had come to him to borrow money. They shook hands and stood for a moment looking at each other.

"Glad to see you again, Bobby, after all these years. You've grown. Where in the world have you been ranging since I saw you last?" Homer Dunstan was forcing an interest in Bob McGraw which he was far from feeling, and Bob was not insensible to this.

He grinned. "Drifting, Mr. Dunstan - just drifting. Mines and mining - mostly the latter; there's a difference, you know. It's my inheritance, Mr. Dunstan, despite all poor old dad did to make me follow in your footsteps. So I've quit bucking the inevitable and turned wanderer. Do you happen to be engaged with a client just now?"

"Well - no, not just this minute. Perhaps if you'll call - "

"No, I will not call later. My motto is 'Do it now.' Seeing that you're regularly in the business of dispensing legal advice, I'd like to take advantage of the ever-active present." He pulled from his hip pocket a tattered wallet and produced a hundred-dollar bill. "Mr. Dunstan, how much expert legal advice can you give me for that?"

Dunstan's manner underwent a swift metamorphosis. "Oh, put back your money, boy. I have an hour to spare this morning, and for your father's sake my advice to you will always be given gratis on Mondays and Fridays."

"Glad I called on Friday, even if it is an unlucky day. Your generosity knocks that superstition galley-west, so I'll take you at your word. Also I will gladly retain this century. To tell the truth I have urgent need of it for other things," and he followed Dunstan into the latter's private office. Dunstan indicated an easy chair and presented his ex-assistant with a fifty-cent cigar.

"Well, Bobby, my boy, what's on your soul this morning?"

"A very heavy weight, Mr. Dunstan. Desert land. Acres and acres of it."

"Any water?"

"Not yet."

"Any prospect?!"

"I have it bottled up, and it's all mine. Now I want the land."

"Well?"

"I want to acquire thirty-two thousand acres of state lieu land in Owens river valley, Mr. Dunstan."

"You cannot do it."

"Well, suppose there was a rule in the State Land Office which forced prospective purchasers of state lieu lands to first designate the basis of exchange before their applications would be received and filed. Suppose also that you wanted to turn crook and steal thirty-two thousand acres of lieu land, despite this rule. How would you go about it?"

The lawyer glanced at him keenly. "See here, son, I don't give that kind of advice to young fellows - or old fellows for that matter - even for money. I'm an honest corporation attorney, and stealing the public domain is illegal - and very, very risky."

"Don't worry, sir. When I have your advice, I will not follow it. Tell me how you would steal this land. It's a hypothetical question."

Dunstan smiled. "That's unfair - attacking a lawyer with a hypothetical question. It's rather hoisting him on his own petard, as it were. However, I'll answer it. In the first place, if I planned to go into the business of looting the public domain I would conspire with some prominent official of the State Land Office to institute such a rule."

"Good. Somebody conspired with a surveyor-general forty years ago and had such a rule instituted in the State Land Office. The state legislature, however, has never been asked to confirm that rule and spread it in black and white on the statute books."

"Well, having had such a rule instituted" continued Dunstan, "I would then have the public at a disadvantage. Through my friend in the land office I would have primary access to the field notes of the chief of staff in the field, and I would have advance information of where losses of school lands were soon to occur. In other words I would be in position to designate every basis of exchange of lost school lands for lieu lands, and the public would not. I'd give some weak brother say one hundred dollars to file on some lieu lands and use the basis which I would designate, and in the meantime I would hustle around, secure in the knowledge that I had the basis tied up. It would appear of record as used in the state land office. When I had secured a customer for the lieu land I had tied up with my dummy applicant, the dummy would abandon his filing in favor of my client, I would collect the difference between the statutory cost of the land and the price my client paid me for it, whack up with my friends in the land office and consider myself a smart business man."

Bob nodded. "I figured it out that way also. Now, suppose an outsider - myself, for instance - succeeded in getting his application filed without designating the basis for the exchange of lands, and the surveyor-general has issued me a receipt for my preliminary payment of twenty dollars on account of the purchase of the lieu land - what then? When he discovered I was an outsider, could he reject my application?"

"Well, he might try, Bob. But with his receipt in your possession, that would be bona-fide evidence of an implied contract of bargain and sale between you and the State of California. You could institute a mandamus suit and force him to make the selection of lieu lands for you."

"I figured it out that way" said Bob musingly. "The only rift in the surveyor-general's lute is the fact that while he has never yet bumped up against the right man, he is due to so bump in the very near future. However, Mr. Dunstan, I do not think our present surveyor-general is doing business with the land ring. I think the guilty man is one of his deputies through whom ninety-nine per cent of the office routine is transacted, and the land-grabbers have him under their thumbs."

"Then why not go direct to the surveyor-general with your troubles?" queried Dunstan.

Bob shook his head. "No hope in that direction. The office records show all bases used, and the deputy - the surveyor-general, in fact - can find defense for their arbitrary ruling in the matter of designation of the basis - by claiming that their office force is not large enough to permit of such extended search of the records; hence they turn their records over to the applicant of lieu lands and let him search for himself. The surveyor-general, being honest, will be hard to convince that his deputy is not - particularly since the deputy is probably an old friend."

"It's a peculiar condition" said Dunstan. "The worst that can happen to the deputy is to lose his job, the dummy entryman can abandon his filing at any time he may elect, and there is no law making it a felony to accept money in exchange for information - if you do not state where you acquired it. How are you going to stop this looting?"

"I'm not quite certain that I want it stopped - right away" said Bob, and grinned his lazy inscrutable smile. "I want to do a little grabbing myself, only I want to do it legally. I have a scheme worked out to do this, but I want you to confirm it. Just now you schemed out a plan to get public lands illegally, and you ought to be able to scheme a plan to get them legally, operating on the state lieu land basis. I want thirty-two thousand acres of desert land and the law only allows me a selection of six hundred and forty. I want to get this thirty-two thousand acres without corrupting any weakling in the employ of the state, without paying money to dummy entrymen, without designating the basis for the selection of my fifty sections, without antagonizing the land ring and without disturbing that rule of the State Land Office, can it be done?"

Dunstan frowned at his visitor. "Of course it cannot be done" he retorted sharply. "Why do you ask me such fool questions?"

"Because it might be done - with a little luck and some money."

Dunstan shook his head. "There is only one way for you to acquire desert land, Bob, without disturbing the rule in that land office. You'll have to file on a half-section only, under the Desert Land Law of the United States of America, paying twenty-five cents per acre down at the time of filing your application. Then you must place one-eighth of it under cultivation and produce a reasonably profitable crop. You must spend not less than, three dollars per acre in improvements, and convince the government that the entire tract, if not actually under irrigation, is at least susceptible to it. That accomplished, you can pay the balance of one dollar per acre due on the land, prove up and secure a patent. That's the only way you can secure desert lands without doing some of the things you wish to avoid doing."

Bob shook his head. "Too slow, too expensive and generally irritating. Why, I'd have to live on the land until I could prove up!"

"Well, then, Bobby boy, put your scruples behind you and pay somebody to live on it and prove up for you." "No use" mourned Bob. "I can see myself at the head of a long procession of desert-land enthusiasts, bound for McNeill's Island, and I'm too young to waste my youth making little rocks out of big ones. Even if the attorney-general didn't have me on the carpet, I'd have to ride herd on one hundred dummy entrymen with a Gatling gun, or else equip each one with an Oregon boot. My land lies in a devil's country and I don't think they'd stay. You see, Mr. Dunstan, were it not for that confounded rule I mentioned, I could purchase a full section of desert land in the public domain, under the provisions of the state lieu land law. Under that law the land would only cost me one dollar and twenty-five cents per acre, while under the United Slates Desert Land Laws it would cost me not less than four dollars and a quarter per acre. Too much money for Bob McGraw. Now, Owens river valley is pure desert, Mr. Dunstan, and it lies, or will lie, very shortly, in the public domain. It is not agricultural land, neither is it coal-bearing nor timbered, so I can purchase it by the full section, which will only require fifty entrymen. Besides, there have never been any entries made heretofore in the section of the valley that I have my eye on, and I'd like to get my land in one strip without having it checker-boarded with adverse holdings."

Dunstan smiled a little wearily. "But we're not getting anywhere, Bob, my boy. You're simply wasting your breath. Just what nebulous idea for the acquisition of this desert land have you floating around in that red head of yours? Now, then, proposition Number One."

"I cannot oppose that rule. I must sneak my applications in and get them filed and secure a receipt, when I will be in position to force the attorney-general to make the selections for my clients."

"Oh, they're clients, eh?" said Dunstan. "I thought they were to be dummy entrymen."

"They are - but they don't know it - and not knowing it, they will not be committing a crime."

"Ignorance of the law excuses nobody, Robert. But proceed with proposition Number Two."

"My clients are to be paupers - so I must pay for the land which they will file upon. Hence I shall need money."

Homer Dunstan figured rapidly on a desk pad.

Notarial fees on fifty applications	@	$ .50	$ 25.00
Filing fees	"	"	"	@	5.00	250.00
First payment	"	"	"	@	20.00	1000.00

Total, $1275.00

"It will take $1275 to start you off, Bob, presuming, for the sake of argument, that your filings are accepted - which, of course, they will not be."

"Oh, I have the twelve seventy-five, all right" said Bob confidently.

"Well, after your applications are passed to patent, you

will have to put up $780 more for each section, or $39,000 in all. Have you provided for this additional sum?"

"Why, no sir. I was going to ask you to lend it to me."

"Indeed! Well, assume that I'm that soft-headed, Bobby, and proceed to proposition Number Three."

"Well, under the law, my applications must be acted upon within six months after filing. The surveyor-general must approve or disapprove them within six months, and if he approves them - "

"Which he will not" promptly interjected Dunstan.

"I'll sue him and make him. Well, when the applications are sent on to the Commissioner of the General Land Office at Washington for his ratification of the exchange of the lieu lands, they may be hung up there a long time - years, perhaps - "

"Certainly. The land ring will see to that."

"Then, don't you see, Mr. Dunstan" said Bob, brightening, "I'll have lots of time to get that balance of $39,000 together."

"I'm so glad" said Homer Dunstan. "Then I won't have to lend you the money after all. Well, when you're an old man, Bobby, and that red head of yours is snowy white, your lands will be passed to patent and - "

"But the peculiar thing about this operation, Mr. Dunstan, lies in the fact that the land ring will readily ascertain my financial condition, and that of my clients - "

"In which event, my dear boy, your lands will be rushed to patent right away, you will be notified that they are waiting for you to pay the balance due on them within, thirty days, and if at the end of thirty days you do not pay that $39,000, your applications lapse automatically and your initial payment will be forfeited to the state as liquidated damages."

"I fear that is just what will happen. That is why I want to know if you are prepared to lend me $39,000 to call their bluff. I will assign you a half interest in a certain water-right which I possess, as security for the advance. My water-right is worth millions."

"It will have to be, if I am to consider your suggestion seriously. Get your fifty applications passed to patent first, however. Then see me, and I'll lend you the money you require, provided I find upon investigation that the security is ample. Is your water-right developed?"

"No, sir. I've just filed on it."

Dunstan permitted himself a very thin smile. "You're your father's son, Bob. You see visions and you'll die poor. I am firmly convinced that you're honest, but as firmly convinced that you're chasing a will-o'-the-wisp - so I hold out very little hope for you in the matter of that loan."

"But my water-right is good for ten times the amount" pleaded Bob desperately, and produced T. Morgan Carey's letter to bolster up his argument. "All I need is money to develop it."

"And in the meantime it's worth ten cents. Bob, you weary me."

"I'm sorry, sir. You're the only human being in this world that I can come to for help; and I never ask help of any man, unless I can pay him well for his trouble, And I think I can pay you well - I know I can."

Dunstan eyed him more kindly. "Your father was a visionary, Bob, only he looked the part. You do not. I have difficulty in convincing myself that you're insane; but surely, Bob, you must admit that no sane man would seriously consider your proposition. Tell me how you expect to induce fifty paupers to apply for land for you, to do it in good faith and be within the law, and yet hand the land over to you. Dang it, boy, the thing's impossible. You can't do it."

"I can" replied Bob McGraw doggedly. "I can."

"All right then, you do it. Put that trick over, Bob, and I'll take off my hat to you."

"You may keep your hat on your head. I want $39,000."

"Do the impossible and I'll give it to you - without security."

"Taken" said Bob McGraw. "I'll hold you to that, Mr. Dunstan. I'll simply round up fifty paupers, or their equivalent, with a constitutional right to purchase state lieu land and permit me to pay for it for them. Then after I have secured the land for them I will buy it back from them - "

Homer Dunstan roared with laughter. He pointed a
bony finger at Bob McGraw.

"Young man, the right to purchase state lieu land is a
strictly personal one and it is unlawful for one person
to purchase for another. Of course you can buy it back,
Bob, but the attorney-general will have a leg-iron on
you before the ink is dry on your check. Transfer of
title under such circumstances would be looked upon
as bona-fide evidence of fraud, unless your clients
could prove conclusively that they had parted with
their lands for a valuable consideration - "

Bob McGraw in turn pointed *his* finger at Dunstan.
"Ah, that's the weak point in the law, Mr. Dunstan" he
exulted. "A valuable consideration. I can beat that. I'll
give my clients ten dollars per acre for lands which
cost them one dollar and a quarter, and there isn't a
lawyer in the land - yourself included - who wouldn't
consider that a valuable consideration."

"McGraw," said Dunstan rising impatiently, "you're a
consummate ass! Where the devil do you expect to get
$320,000 to buy their land from them? I suppose you
think I'll help you with that, also. Your stupidity
annoys me, Robert. Damme, sir, you're light in the
upper story."

Bob McGraw laughed aloud. "I won't need it. All I
shall ever ask of you is that first $39,000. The water I
have bottled up in the Sierra will make the land worth
three hundred dollars an acre. Don't you see where I
can afford to pay ten dollars per acre for it?"

"You can't do business on gab, McGraw. Money makes the mare go, and you cannot induce fifty men to waste their constitutional right to lieu land on your bare word that your water-right will make a desert valuable. You'll have to take 'em down there, at your own expense, and show 'em - "

"Old maids in New England buy stocks in wild-cat prospect holes in Nevada. Do the promoters have to bring them out to see the holes?"

"Nobody but a fool or an idiot would listen to your crazy proposition, and fools and idiots are not qualified under the law to do anything except just live and try to avoid being run over by automobiles. But granted that you can do all these things, what are you going to do with your land when you get it?"

Bob McGraw stood up and leaned both brown hands on the edge of Homer Dunstan's desk. The genial mocking little smile was gone from his face now, for Dunstan's query had brought him back from the land of improbabilities into the realm of his most ardent day-dream. He raised his hand in unconscious imitation of every zealot that had preceded him down the ages; the light of the visionary who already sees the fulfillment of his dreams blazed in his big kind brown eyes.

"I'm going to give it to the lowly of the earth" he said. "I'm going to subdivide it into ten-acre farms, with a perpetual water-right with every farm. I'm going to build a town with a business block up each side of the main street. I'm going to install a hydro-electric plant that will carry a load of juice sufficient to light a city of a million inhabitants. I'm going to reclaim the desert and make it beautiful, and I'm going to have free light and free fuel and free local telephone service and free water and, by God! free people to live in my free country. I'm going to gather up a few thousand of the lowly and the hopeless in the sweat-shops of the big cities and bring them back to the land! Back to *my* land and *my* water that I'm going to hold in trust for them, the poor devils! Back where there won't be any poverty - where ten acres of Inyo desert with Inyo water on it will mean a fortune to every poor family I plant in my desert."

"Why?" demanded Homer Dunstan smiling.

"Why?" Bob McGraw echoed the attorney's query. He gazed at Dunstan stupidly. "Why, what a damn-fool question for you to ask, Mr. Dunstan! Isn't it right that we should look to the comfort of our helpless fellow-man? Isn't it right that we strong men should give of our strength to the weak? What in blue blazes are we living for in this enlightened day and generation if it isn't to do something that's worth while, and to leave behind us at the last something that hasn't got the American eagle stamped on it with the motto 'In God We Trust.' Ugh! How the good Lord must hate us for that copyrighted chunk of sophistry I It's a wonder He doesn't send His angels down to make us tend to business."

"Well, I'm not going to worry about it" retorted Dunstan crisply. "I'm too busy, and you're Johnny McGraw's boy Bob, so we won't quarrel about it. Good luck to you, old man. Get all the fun out of life that you possibly can - in your own way - and when you get your land and can show me, I'll take a $39,000 mortgage on it, at eight per cent. Now, good-by and get out. I'm a busy man."

Bob McGraw took up his big wide hat, shook hands with his father's old friend, and with heightened color withdrew. Out in the hall he paused long enough to swear; then, as suddenly, the old mocking cheerful inscrutable smile came sneaking back to his sun-tanned face, and he was at peace again. He had suddenly remembered that he was Bob McGraw, and he had faith in himself. He thought of Donna, waiting for him in lonely San Pasqual; he raised his hard brown fist, and in unconscious imitation of Paul Jones he cried aloud:

"I have not yet begun to fight!"

CHAPTER XI

It must have been a sublime faith in that homely adage that there are more ways of killing a cat than by choking him with butter which moved Bob McGraw to cudgel his nimble brain until he had discovered exactly how it would be possible for him to accomplish legally what every freebooter with an appraising eye on the public domain is troubled to accomplish illegally. The sole difference between Bob's projected course and that of his competitors' would be a slightly lessened profit; but after inventorying a free and easy conscience and posting it to the credit side of his profit and loss account, Bob knew that this apparent difference would dwindle until it would be scarcely perceptible.

Immediately after breakfast on the morning of the day following his interview with Homer Dunstan, Bob set to work to draw up the circular letter and contract form, to be submitted later to his prospective clients. In about fifteen minutes he had outlined the following:

THE PROPOSITION IS THIS

I have information of some state lieu lands which I believe can be taken up under the State laws at $1.25 per acre. The right to buy them will very probably have to be established and enforced by legal proceedings.

Now, this right to purchase state lieu lands is a limited personal right. (See Political Code, Section 3495, et seq.) I am willing to try to make YOUR right good to a tract of this land, under the conditions of the contract herewith. I am willing to stand the expenses of suit to enforce your right, and to advance for you the legal fees and the first preliminary payment to the state, on the chance of being able to secure you something sufficiently valuable to justify you in paying me the fee provided for in the contract. Read the contract carefully and note that you retain the right to cancel it and relieve yourself of all obligation in the matter *by abandoning your claim to the land.*

READ THE CONTRACT CAREFULLY BEFORE YOU SIGN IT. BE SURE YOU UNDERSTAND JUST WHAT YOU ARE DOING.

ROBERT MCGRAW.

"That looks like fair warning" mused Mr. McGraw, as he reread this document. "I defy any man to look between the lines and scent my hocus- pocus game."

Bob next proceeded to draw up the contract. It was a simple contract, framed in language that could not fail of comprehension by the dullest mind. For and in consideration of the sum of one dollar, the receipt whereof was duly acknowledged, Bob McGraw agreed to furnish, his applicants for land with certain valuable information, whereby the applicant would be enabled to file, or tender his application for, certain state lieu lands, "bounded and particularly described as follows:" (Here he left a space sufficient for the insertion, at a later date, of the exact description of the lands he desired; the descriptions he would glean from maps of the valley on sale in the United States Land Office in San Francisco.)

He agreed to tender the application of his client to the State Land Office and to conduct, at his own expense, any litigation that might arise or become necessary to establish the right of his client to purchase the land from the state; stipulating, however, that he (McGraw) should be the sole judge of the necessity for such litigation. He agreed to pay the filing fees and the first payment on the land, required at the time of filing the application, and to represent the applicant before the state land office; also to notify his client, by registered letter, at the address given him, whenever the application should be approved; and it was distinctly stipulated that the applicant should not be required to elect whether or not he would abandon the application until served with this written notice!

In consideration, also, of the services, fees and costs provided for in the contract, *Mr. McGraw would make a charge of Three Dollars per acre for all, or any part, of the land which the applicant might be awarded the opportunity to purchase;* this fee to be payable to him, his heirs or assigns, *if and whenever the application of his client* should be duly approved by the Registrar of the State Land Office.

In consideration of these covenants, the applicant was to bind himself to pay Mr. Robert McGraw the stipulated fee of Three Dollars per acre, in addition to the One Dollar and Twenty-five Cents per acre demanded by the state, *reserving, however, the right to abandon his filing at any time prior to its approval by the Registrar of the State Land Office, but pledging himself not to abandon without first furnishing his attorney (Robert McGraw) with a proper instrument of abandonment, in order that some other person might be located on the land.* In addition the applicant was required to state that he was duly qualified, under the law, to make the application *and that he had read both the application form and the contract and was familiar with the section of the code under which he made it.*

A critical perusal of the terms of this shrewd contract will readily convince even a layman that it was perfectly legal. Bob hurled mental defiance at every legal light in the country to prove collusion and conspiracy to defraud under that contract. It proved merely that Bob McGraw was acting in his capacity as a duly authorized attorney-at-law, seeking to turn an honest penny.

Now, in the first place, the abandonment clause in the contract, while not holding his client to the contract, nevertheless held the land to Bob McGraw! He anticipated that, in the event of his success in forcing the registrar of the state land office to accept and approve the applications, the land ring would immediately seek out each applicant, charge the applicant with being a party to a gigantic land fraud conspiracy and threaten him with a Federal Grand Jury investigation in case he did not at once abandon his filing! The poor and the ignorant are easily intimidated, and Bob McGraw had figured on this. In the event of "cold feet" on the part of his applicant, the applicant would come to *him,* to abandon, as per the terms of the contract, but by that time Bob would have a man with nerve to take his place, and his scheme would still be impervious to "leaks!" While the land was "tied up" by a McGraw applicant, Bob knew the enemy could not get it.

When Bob's clients signed that contract, it meant nothing! But the moment the applications were approved for patent, and the State Land Office had so notified him, and he, in turn, had so notified his clients, his clients were no longer his clients. They were his victims! His contract then constituted a promissory note, and Mr. McGraw knew enough law to realize that failure to pay a promissory note or perform a contract is actionable. Should his client repudiate the contract *prior* to the approval of the application, he was safe; but to repudiate it *after* approval and after Bob McGraw had advanced him the money to pay for the land - ah, that was a different matter. Bob McGraw knew he could secure a judgment against his unfortunate client in any court of law in the country - and the land was good for the judgment! Having advanced the cash to purchase the land for his clients, Bob McGraw would hold that deadly contract over their heads as security for the advance!

Under the terms of the contract, when fulfilled, each client would owe Bob his three dollars per acre on six hundred and forty acres, or a total of one thousand nine hundred and forty dollars as a legal attorney's fee, and to the clients that Bob McGraw intended to select, a debt of such magnitude would loom up in all the pristine horror of the end of the world at hand and salvation not yet in sight. With, malice aforethought the promoter of Donnaville was trading on the credulity of the very people he planned to benefit! He knew with what ease the poor rush into debt where the creditor requires nothing down; he knew also the avidity with which they grasp the first means of escape from the burden, once it becomes onerous; and at the thought the villain McGraw chuckled pleasurably.

Peter B. Kyne

"Once under the McGraw thumb, and I have them! I'll demand cash on the nail for my services. They will be unable to pay me. I'll harass them and threaten to sue them, and then, when I have them thoroughly cowed, I'll send a secret agent around to buy their land from them at ten dollars an acre. After using their constitutional right to purchase lieu lands, they are entitled to a profit on the investment, and besides, I must show a 'valuable consideration' or have a secret service operative trailing me.

"However, I will not have sufficient funds on hand to pay them ten dollars per acre spot cash, so I shall turn over to them their signed contracts and thus relieve them of that bugbear, and for these three-dollar contracts they shall credit me with a payment of four dollars and twenty-five cents per acre on the land! I will secure them for the balance by a first mortgage on the property! And with that accomplished, I court an official investigation. Come on, you secret service operatives, and prove Bob McGraw a crook. I am a crook, and I know it, but nobody else shall know it and I have never been accused of talking in my sleep. I'm a crook, but I'm an honest crook, and the ends justify the means. Besides, I'm going to present every one of my clients with a cheek for three thousand six hundred and seventy dollars for the mere scratch of a pen and the use of their constitutional right to purchase lieu land. Why, I'm a philanthropist! I'm going to make fifty men happy by giving them a lot of money for something they never knew they had. Three thousand six hundred and seventy dollars for the use of one constitutional right, when the market price is a hundred! McGraw, my boy, this must never leak out. If it does, your sanity will be questioned, in addition to your morality."

Thus figured Bob McGraw, the sage of Donnaville. Let him but get his applications past the land ring's tool in the state land office, and a receipt issued for his first payment, and Donnaville would be no longer a dream. Should the applications be rejected later on some flimsy pretext, he would commence a mandamus suit to enforce the selection of his lands, and force action of the pending applications of the land ring, whereby they so artfully "tied up the basis" of exchange. If he should find himself opposed by a corrupt judge who should rule against him, he would not be daunted. If beaten in the Superior Court he would appeal the case to the United States Circuit Court, for Bob McGraw had a sublime faith in the ability of Truth, crushed to earth, to rise again and kick the underpinning from crooked-ness and graft, provided one never acknowledged defeat. And he could go into court with clean hands, for he broke no law himself and he would induce no one else to break it, in thought, spirit or action!

The road to Donnaville stretched ahead of him now, smooth and white and free from ruts, and with but one bridge to cross. For the successful crossing of that bridge Bob McGraw had not evolved a plan, for he was merely a human being, and human cunning has its limitations. It was a bridge which he must cross when he came to it. He only knew that he must make the effort on a certain day - the day that Owens river valley should be thrown open to entry. He must be first at the window of the land office, and once before that window, the future of Donnaville, the future of Bob McGraw and his sweetheart in San Pasqual, lay in the laps of the gods. He must manage somehow to get his applications filed that day, without designating the basis of the exchange of school lands for the lieu lands which he sought; for that was information which Bob

McGraw did not possess, and should it come into his possession the day after the valley was opened for entry, it would be worthless; for the land ring, in the parlance of the present day, would have "beaten him to it."

To get those precious filings accepted! That was all that worried him now. Prior to his visit to Homer Dunstan, this task had seemed to Bob the least of his worries compared with the titanic task of accumulating the money necessary to pay for the land when the filings should be approved. Yesterday everything had revolved around the necessity for thirty-nine thousand dollars, until the contemplation of this monetary axis had threatened to set his reason tottering on its throne. But that worry no longer existed. Homer Dunstan had indicated very clearly to Bob that he considered him insane, but Homer Dunstan had pledged him the thirty-nine thousand dollars when he could come to him with the notification from the Registrar of the State Land Office that the lands had been passed to patent, and Bob knew that Dunstan would keep his word, provided his death did not occur prior to the granting of the patents.

The rough draft of the contract having been drawn up to his satisfaction, Bob sallied forth in search of a public stenographer. He knew that he had evolved rather a clever scheme, and he was averse to permitting the details of his plan to fall under the comprehending eye of some boss printer, whose enterprise might perchance soar beyond the boundaries of his vocation. So Bob sought, instead, a public stenographer and had his copy multigraphed by a young lady whose interest could never, by any possibility, center in anything more than her fee.

The job was delivered two days later, and with the knowledge that he had thirty days in which to make the acquaintance of his fifty prospective clients, Bob resolved to devote one more week to the problem of still further recruiting his shattered vitality before getting down to active work.

He spent that week wandering through Golden Gate Park, along the romantic and picturesque San Francisco water-front, and in moving-picture shows. Each morning, before starting for the day's wanderings, he wrote a long letter to Donna and then waited for the first mail delivery for her letter to him. Those letters came with unfailing regularity, and in that city where Bob McGraw prowled through the day, unknown and unnoticed, there was no man so free from the curse of loneliness as he. The very opening line in Donna's matutinal greeting - "My Dear Sweetheart" - routed the blue devils that camped nightly on his worried and harassed soul, as he lay abed and wrestled with the mighty problems that confronted him. To Bob McGraw those three words held the open-sesame of life; they gave him strength to cling to his high, resolve; they whispered to him of the prize of the conflict which awaited him at the end of his long road to Donnaville, and sent him forth to face the world with a smile on his dauntless face and a lilt in his great kind heart.

Time glided by on weary wings, but eventually the day arrived for Bob to open his campaign. He must clear for action. It was imperative that he must have his fifty applications filled out and the signatures of his clients attested before a notary public on the very date upon which the desert of Owens river valley would be opened for entry, for to have them dated the day before would nullify them - to arrive with them at the land office the day after would be too late. Bob was obsessed with a suspicion that amounted almost to a conviction that the land ring would endeavor to acquire the desert valley by practically the same method which he was pursuing, *only for every section of lieu land upon which they filed, they would be enabled to show a corresponding loss of school lands.* His line of reasoning had convinced him that they had caused dummy entrymen to file on worthless lands in some other part of the state, in order that these bases might appear of record in the land office as already used, in case of an investigation; he was equally convinced that these dummy applications had never been acted upon in the land office, but were being held up there until the land ring was ready to act, when their dummy entrymen would abandon their filings on the worthless land, thus throwing the original basis open for use once more and permitting the land ring to step in with other dummy entrymen and use the basis for the acquisition of *valuable* lands. It was absurdly simple when one understood it and took the time to reason it out.

Of one thing Bob was morally certain. The representative of the land ring would be on hand, bright and early, to file the dummy applications. Bob decided, therefore, that the field of his operations until that eventful day must be confined to the state capital, Sacramento, where the state land office was located. He must recruit his little army of applicants from the capital itself, attest their applications before a notary public after midnight of the day preceding the opening of the valley for entry, and be first at the filing window when the land office opened.

Accordingly Bob proceeded to Sacramento. Immediately upon his arrival he rented a cheap back office, a desk and some chairs, and for the time being announced himself to the world, through the medium of a modest sign on his office door, as The Desert Development Company. The following day he set to work.

He interviewed street sweepers, hotel porters, cab drivers newspaper reporters, milk-wagon drivers, barkeepers and laborers along the river docks - in fact every follower of an occupation which Bob judged might be sufficiently unremunerative to keep its votaries in poverty as long as they persisted in sticking to it. By discreet questioning he learned whether the prospective client had money in bank, or was involved in debt. If the former, Bob terminated his interview and neglected to return; if the latter, Bob would present the victim with a good cigar and proceed to unfold a tale of wealth in desert lands.

To these men Bob explained every detail of his proposition and gave them a copy of his contract form and his explanatory circular attached. He answered all their questions patiently - and satisfactorily, and he was particularly insistent upon calling to their attention the fact that they were not required to put up a single dollar in order to acquire the land. Naturally, this seeming philanthropy immediately inspired suspicion and a request for information as to what was in the deal for Mr. McGraw; whereupon Mr. McGraw would point proudly to that clause in the contract which stipulated a three-dollar-per-acre fee and inform them that he had private and reliable information of not less than two irrigation schemes which were being projected in the valley - schemes which would give their apparently worthless land a value of at least ten dollars per acre and enable both Mr. McGraw and his client to turn a nice little profit together. He showed them where he was helpless without them and where they were profitless without him, and to make a profit of three dollars per acre for himself he was willing to buy the land for them and take their promissory notes in payment. More: he would agree to carry them for the land until they had an opportunity to sell out at a profit of at least three thousand dollars! Mr. McGraw demanded to know if anything could possibly be fairer than that.

It could not, and the clients were forced to admit it. Win, lose or draw, it cost them nothing to play the game with Bob McGraw. After all is said and done the average human being is a gambler and likes long odds, and Bob's prospective clients were not so deficient in intelligence as in ready cash. They knew that desert land without irrigation is worthless; that no man would advance them money to purchase it at $1.25 per acre unless he saw a profit in the deal for himself. Consequently, irrigation was the only solution of that problematic increase in value, and if Mr. McGraw could afford a flyer so could they.

Bob had foreseen this line of reasoning, for he knew that spot cash is the bugbear of life and that a good salesman can sell anything provided he sells it on time. Long before the expiration of the period he had set himself to accomplish this task, he had signed up fifty eager applicants for desert land, procured their addresses and then retired to his little back office to write letters to Donna and await the rising of the sun on his day of destiny.

The day preceding the one on which the valley would be opened for entry was a busy one for Bob McGraw. His cash reserve was beginning to run so low that he decided to save the dollar postage necessary to remind his clients that they were to meet him in his office at midnight of that day; consequently, and in view of the fact that his old-time strength practically had been restored to him, he walked several miles in order to call upon his clients at their places of employment and secure from their lips a solemn promise to be on hand at the appointed hour. His apparent anxiety made them all the more eager to sign up with him, and not a single client failed him.

This matter attended to, Bob engaged a notary public, with instructions to meet him at his office at midnight. By eleven-thirty the corridors of the silent office building were thronged with the eager fifty; at eleven-forty-five the notary arrived and at exactly one minute past midnight Bob commenced to sign his clients up. The notarial blanks had already been filled out and, together with the notary's seal, had been attached to each contract. In addition to the contract Bob took a power-of-attorney in duplicate from each applicant; the notary swore each of the fifty applicants in as many minutes, Bob paid him twenty-five dollars and he departed; after which Bob made a short speech to his clients and exhorted them to stand by their guns in the event of influence being brought to bear upon them to abandon their filings; whereupon the fifty gave him their promises, collectively and individually, shook the hand of their benefactor and departed to their homes.

Nothing now remained for Bob to do except present his fifty applications for filing at the land office in the morning, and realizing the truth of that ancient saw anent the early bird and the resulting breakfast he decided to wait in the office until it should be time for him to go to the land office. In the meantime, he decided to while away the lonely hours by a review of his financial status, so he locked the door and devoted the succeeding five minutes to the comparatively trifling task of counting his money and figuring on the outlay necessary to carry him back to San Pasqual. He was horrified to discover that after providing twelve hundred and fifty dollars for the registrar of the state land office (in the event that the day of miracles was not yet past and his filings should be accepted), his return journey by rail would terminate somewhere in the heart of the San Joaquin valley. Even after pawning his gun, Mr. McGraw could still see, in his mind's eye, at least one hundred miles of dusty county road stretching between him and San Pasqual, and he was not so conceited as to imagine that he was strong enough to walk a hundred miles with nothing more tangible than the scenery to sustain him en route. Moreover, he had promised Donna that they should be married immediately upon his return. The situation was truly embarrassing, and Mr. McGraw cast about him for a means to extricate himself from his terrible predicament. In his agony he saw a flash of light - and smiled as he realized that it radiated from Mr. Harley P. Hennage's three gold teeth.

"Saved!" quavered Mr. McGraw. "Good old Harley P! I'll just touch the old boy for that fifty again, in case I need it. If they accept my applications, I'll have to assault Harley, and if they decline the applications I will still have my twelve hundred and fifty. But in the meantime I'll write to Hennage and tell him frankly just how I'm fixed, and if it comes to a show-down I'll drop the letter in the mail, return to San Francisco and wait for him to send me a postal money order."

He turned to his desk, drew a blank sheet of paper toward him and indited a brief note to Mr. Hennage.

Dear Harley P.:

I have just made the discovery that I was too precipitate in paying you that fifty I owed you for three years. I am a financial wreck on a lee shore, but with millions in sight, and I will be very grateful if you will strain your good nature long enough to send me a P. O. order for the aforesaid fifty, addressing me General Delivery, San Francisco. I will explain the transaction to you when I get back to San Pasqual, merely mentioning in passing that until you send me the fifty the prospects for my immediate return are, to say the least, somewhat vague. I never could walk very far in my Sunday shoes.

Thanking you, my dear Harley, until you are better paid, believe me to be

Your sincere friend, ROBERT MCGRAW.

This communication Bob folded and sealed in an envelope. He was too preoccupied in the folding to notice that he had folded two sheets of paper instead of one. The second sheet was a spare copy of his marvelous contract for the acquisition of desert lands, which through some accident had become mixed, with the printed side up, among some loose sheets of blank legal-size typewriter paper which the unconventional Robert had purchased in the pursuit of his correspondence with Donna. His choice of letter paper was characteristic of Bob. He was a man who required room in which to operate.

His letter sealed and stamped, Bob slipped it into his pocket, lifted his long legs to the top of his rented desk, tilted back his chair, lit a cigar and gave himself up to the contemplation of his future. Providentially, his future, as he viewed it there in that lonely office, waiting to see what the dawn would bring to him of wealth or woe, was sufficiently indefinite to keep his fertile brain actively employed until, far off in the city, he heard a clock booming the hour of six; when he yawned, closed down his desk, picked up his suit-case which stood, packed with, his few poor possessions in one corner, and departed.

In an all-night restaurant he ate a hurried breakfast; then, suit-case in hand, walked over to the capitol building. The capitol grounds were deserted as he strolled through, entered the State House and passed down a dim deserted corridor until he came to the door of the state land office. He had definitely located the office, the previous day, in order to provide against possible fatal delay in finding it this morning. Apparently he was the sole applicant for desert lands that morning, and anticipating that there would be no great rush to file entries he set his suit-case down in the corridor, sat himself on the suit-case and waited for the office to open for business. In order to make certain that he would not be usurped in line, however, when the office opened for business, he had placed his suitcase directly in front of the door, against which he leaned his weary back. The door, he noticed, opened from within. In case it opened secretly, Mr. McGraw would thus fall into the surveyor-general's office, and hardy, indeed, would be he who could dispute his claim to priority in the line. In fact, so satisfied was he

with this strategic position, and so tired and drowsy
was he withal, that presently he relaxed his
determination to remain wide awake.

Peter B. Kyne

CHAPTER XII

The first intimation that Bob received of this laxity came in the shape of a sharp dig in the ribs from the index finger of a young man who demanded to know why Mr. McGraw didn't wake up and pay for his lodging. Bob turned his startled sleepy eyes up at the stranger. He had expected to confront a janitor, but his first glance informed him that he was mistaken. The individual before him evidently was a state employee; but for all that Bob could advance no excuse for his free and easy action in assaulting him with his index finger. No one except the janitor or the night watchman had a right to such familiarity with Mr. McGraw's ribs and he resented being told to wake up before he was ready.

"You'll have to get out of my way, friend" the stranger informed him.

"Not if I know it, old-timer" replied Bob. "I'm first in line, with orders to stick here and maintain my position at all hazards. I'll share the suit-case with you, but you mustn't try to crush in in advance of me."

The stranger eyed him curiously. "I'm an employee of the state land office" he said coolly. "Please permit me to get into the office."

Bob looked at his watch. It was just eight o'clock, and he knew that the land office did not open until nine. He wondered who this industrious individual might be and what reason he had for getting down to work an hour beforehand; and then; like a bolt from the blue, The Big Idea flashed into Bob McGraw's brain.

He yawned sleepily. "Great snakes!" he said, "I've been waiting here an hour for you. I beg your pardon, old-timer. I didn't recognize you at first, although I should have known you right off by that little mole on your left cheek."

He scrambled to his feet and picked up his suit-case, while the stranger looked at him sharply.

"Why are you here so early?" he demanded. Bob McGraw would have liked to ask him the same question but he refrained.

"There's been an inquisitive stranger investigating the old man and - well, you know what a fox Carey is? At the last moment it didn't seem wise to come through on the original programme, so I came up instead. I'm used to taking chances and I'm going to be well paid for this."

Was it fancy, or did Bob really detect a more friendly light in the man's eyes? He decided that he had not overplayed his hand, so, fearful that he might, he remained discreetly silent and waited for the door to be opened. The stranger inserted the key in the lock and stepped into the room. Bob followed him uninvited, turned carefully and sprung the lock on the door. The deputy (for such Bob guessed him to be) passed through a gate in the counter and on into an inner office. He returned a moment later, pulling on his office coat. At the counter he paused and faced Bob. There was still a suspicious look in his alert intelligent eyes.

Bob drew the fifty applications from his suit-case and passed them over the counter. "Hurry with them" he said. "There isn't any time to lose. Did Carey tell you anything about that fellow McGraw, who filed on the Cottonwood lake water?"

The deputy nodded.

"He's dangerous" warned Mr. McGraw. "He's tumbled to the little combination and he'll upset the apple-cart if you don't beat him to it. He may attempt to bully the old man into a consolidation by threatening to mandamus your chief and force him to accept the filings. McGraw's dangerous and he's got big influence behind him. The old man's worried."

The deputy arched his eyebrows cynically. "Where do you come in?" he queried.

Bob drew back the lapel of his coat and showed the butt of his automatic gun nestling under his left arm.

"I'm playing a purely professional engagement, my friend. If McGraw should show up here this morning it is my business to take care of him."

The deputy's suspicions were allayed at last. He smiled in friendly fashion.

"Keep him away until nine-thirty and there's no danger" he said. He scooped up Bob's applications and skimmed through them. "Did you bring the coin?"

Bob placed twelve hundred and fifty dollars on the counter and shoved it toward the deputy.

"I won't wait for the receipts. It's too risky. Make them out as fast as you can and I'll call for them after the office opens." He grinned knowingly. "I'm going out in the corridor to keep inquisitive people away and give you time to work."

"You didn't bring the instruments of abandonment for the old filings - "

"I know it. Carey has them. He'll probably bring them over himself later in the day. Too risky - getting over here so early. There's a gumshoe man on his trail."

"All right" said the deputy, and hastened to his desk with the bundle of applications. Bob unlatched the door, peered cautiously up and down the deserted corridor, and apparently finding the coast clear stepped out into the hall.

For fifteen minutes he walked up and down the corridor without meeting any one more formidable than the janitor, and presently the janitor, having completed the sweeping of the corridor, betook himself and his brooms elsewhere. He came back a few minutes later, however, and disappeared in a small room at the end of the corridor, only to reappear again with a bucket of wet sawdust in his hand.

Bob McGraw walked to the main entrance of the State House and back again to the door of the land office. Still nobody came. He was approaching the main entrance to the State House a second time when he heard an automobile chugging through the capitol grounds and pause outside the main entrance. Half a minute later a man appeared at the head of the corridor and approached rapidly. As he came nearer Bob saw that he was about fifty years old. He wore a carefully trimmed imperial and a gold pince-nez and seemed to exude a general air of pomposity and power. He had glittering cold gray eyes and they snapped now with anger and apprehension as he half walked, half ran, down the corridor. Bob's keen glance, roving over the man for details, observed that he carried a small Gladstone bag in his right hand, but inasmuch as the front end of the bag carried no initials, Bob waited until the man had passed him and then cast a sidelong glance at the other end of it. In small gold letters across its base he read the initials: T. M. C.

"T. Morgan Carey!"

In a bound Bob was at the stranger's side and laid a firm detaining grip on the latter's arm. The man turned angrily and glared at Bob.

"Mr. T. Morgan Carey?" said Bob McGraw quietly, "you're wanted!"

The man trembled. Bob could feel a distinct quiver pass up the arm he was holding.

"Wha - what - who wants me?" he said.

"Your dear old Uncle Samuel. He'd like to have you explain a delicate matter in connection with the public domain. Give me the little grip and come along quietly. I think that would be the better way. If you make a row about it, of course I'll have to put the bracelets on you; and I'm sure neither of us wishes that to happen, Mr. Carey."

Bob spoke kindly, almost regretfully, but there was no mistaking the fact that he meant business. T. Morgan Carey's face was ghastly. He surrendered the grip without protest, the while he gazed at Bob like a trapped animal. Presently he managed to pull himself together sufficiently to demand in a trembling voice:

"But - why - I don't understand. Where's your authority? Have you a warrant for - this - this outrageous procedure?"

"I have no warrant for you, Mr. Carey. I - "

"Then let me pass about my business, sir. How dare - "

"Easy, easy! You are not arrested in the commonly accepted sense of that term, but if you play horse with me you will be. I came here this morning to find you and ask you to come quietly with me and answer a few questions; also to let me see what you're carrying in this grip. Come along now, Carey. You only make out a case against yourself by resisting. I suppose you are aware of the fact that a secret service agent requires no warrant to make an arrest. (Bob did not know that such was the case, but he made the statement at any rate.) You are temporarily - apprehended - upon information and belief. If you are worried about the publicity that may attach, I give you my word the newspapers shall not hear of this unless a formal charge is entered against you. Come with me if you please, Mr. Carey."

He drew Carey's right arm through his own strong left

and marched him down the corridor. It had been his first intention to escort T. Morgan Carey to the office of the now defunct Desert Development Company and lock him up there for the good of his soul - but a more convenient means of marooning his enemy now presented itself. The door to the janitor's room was open; an electric light burned within, and from the keyhole of the half open door a bunch of keys was suspended.

Bob's brain worked with the rapidity of a camera-shutter. He threw Carey's bag into the room, whirled and clamped his right hand over Carey's mouth, while with his powerful left arm around the land-grabber's body he gently steered his victim into the room. Carey struggled desperately, but Bob held him powerless. Finding himself as helpless as a child in that grizzly-bear grip, he ceased his struggles. Instantly he was tripped up and laid gently on the floor, on his back, with Bob McGraw's one hundred and eighty pounds of bone and muscle camped on his torso, holding him down. With his right hand effectually silencing Carey's gurgling cries for help, and a knee on each arm to hold Carey still, with his left hand Bob drew a bandanna handkerchief from his pocket and gagged his man with as much ease as he would have muzzled a little dog. Then he searched through his victim's pockets until he found the land-grabber's handkerchief; whereupon he flopped Carey on his face and bound his hands behind him. It was but the work of an instant for Bob to tear off his own suspenders and bind Carey's ankles together. Next he rooted through a bin of waste paper and found some stout cord with which he bound Carey at the knees. Then, leaving his victim helpless on the floor, he picked up the little bag, turned off the light, stepped softly out, closed and locked the door behind him, slipped the bunch of keys into his pocket, and returned to the land office. He knocked, and presently the door of the private office further down the hall opened gently and the deputy glanced warily out. Seeing Bob at the main entrance he went around and let him in.

"I took a chance" Bob explained, "and went out after the balance of the dope. Any sign of the other gang around?"

"Not a soul."

"Good news. I had an idea Carey put those abandonment papers in this little bag" and he held up the bag in such a manner that the deputy could not fail to see the initials T. M. C. on one end. This had the effect of allaying any lingering suspicion which the deputy may have been entertaining, and without waiting to see the contents of the bag he hurried back to his desk to complete the work of filing Bob's fifty applications.

In the meantime Bob had opened the bag. It contained applications for seventy-odd sections of land in Owens River Valley, together with an equal number of instruments of abandonment of filings on land throughout the state.

It was as Bob had suspected. The corrupt deputy had informed Carey where the loss of school land would occur. Carey's dummy entrymen had tied up for him these bases of exchange for lieu lands by instantly applying for *worthless* lieu lands, and these applications had been held up in the land office unacted upon, in order that the bases might show of record as used; then, at the word from Carey, these filings on worthless land had been abandoned, in order that Carey might use the bases for the acquisition of the lands he really desired.

"I'm a fool for luck" murmured Bob McGraw, as he counted off fifty of these instruments of abandonment, closed the bag and set it in the corner with his suitcase. He approached the counter and tossed the lot over to the deputy.

"Here are the instruments of abandonment, old-timer," he said casually. "I had a notion Carey put them in that grip. Better get 'em on record right away and let those receipts for the filings slide until the office opens for business. I'll go outside and lean up against the door. Don't worry. I'll be first in line, and if the other gang should be at my heels I'll slip you over a bunch of dummies, to throw 'em off the scent, and you can hand me back the receipts for the real thing." He winked comically and went out into the corridor again.

Slowly the minutes dragged by. Bob looked at his watch. It was a quarter of nine. Five minutes passed and still the corridor was deserted. Two minutes more flitted by and then the janitor came around the corner from the next corridor, a bucket in one hand and a mop in the other. Bob grinned as he saw the man try the door of the room where T. Morgan Carey lay trussed up. He rattled the knob several times, then searched his pockets for his keys. Not finding them, he went away grumbling.

It was just nine o'clock when the janitor returned. Bob McGraw was close enough, to him now to see that he carried a key, which he slipped into the lock, opened the door and passed into the gloom of the room beyond. Bob trembled lest he step on T. Morgan Carey's face. While the janitor was fumbling for the electric switch, Bob stepped softly in after him, and as softly closed the door behind him, just as the janitor switched on the light. He turned at the slight sound of the closing door and found himself gazing down the long blue barrel of an automatic gun.

"No unnecessary noise, if you please" said Bob McGraw gently. "This is one of those rare occasions where silence is golden. Observe that man on the floor, my friend? He tried to make a noise and just see what happened to him."

The janitor's mouth had opened to emit a yell. He closed it now, slowly, and licked his lips.

"What do you want?" he demanded, and Bob McGraw realized instantly that in the janitor he had not met a poltroon.

"The pleasure of your society for half an hour" murmured Bob, and smiled. "I'm not going to hurt you if I can avoid it, but if you make a row I'll tap you back of the ear with the butt of this gun. The individual on the floor has been poking his nose into my business and I had to put him in storage for a while. Unfortunately you discovered him, so, much to our mutual displeasure, I must ask you to bear him company until nine-thirty, after which you may return to your janitorial labors. Don't worry. I'm not a hold-up man. Have a cigar. Also a five-spot to pay you in advance for the inconvenience I am subjecting you to."

The janitor's face became normal at once. He accepted

the cigar and the five-dollar piece, seated himself on an upturned bucket and set himself patiently to await the moment of his liberation. He sat there grinning and blowing smoke at Bob McGraw.

At nine-thirty, Bob, judging that the deputy had had ample time in which to place his affairs in shape, decided to raise the siege. He put up his gun, unlatched the door and backed out, motioning to the janitor to accompany him. The latter obeyed with alacrity.

"Come on into the land office with me, old man" Bob invited him. "When my business is finished there I'll give you back your keys and ask you to unwrap the gentleman we just left."

They entered the land office together.

"Did that friend o' mine leave something with you for me?" Bob queried of the deputy, and flashed him a lightning wink.

"Waiting for you" responded the deputy, and handed Bob McGraw a large manila envelope. "All O. K." he added, and returned the wink.

"Sure you recorded those abandonments?" he queried. The deputy nodded.

"Then we're all O. K. on the matter of designating the basis, are we?"

Again the deputy nodded. Bob turned and handed the keys to the janitor.

"That being the case" he announced cheerfully but in a

low tone of voice, "our friend, the janitor, will immediately proceed to release Mr. T. Morgan Carey and bring him into court. Permit me to introduce myself. I am Mr. Robert McGraw, and I have you by the short hair, you crooked little sneak. You should have looked up and down the corridor and noticed all the witnesses I had posted to observe you letting me into your office before it was officially opened. Oh, I'm not worried about what you can do now. It's only nine-thirty and I can easily prove that it is a physical impossibility for one man to do the work you've done this morning, and do it in one short half hour. You have entered fifty instruments of abandonment, so there are that number of bases open to permit of the exchange of fifty sections of lieu land, the filing receipts for which I hold in my hand. Old-timer, I dare you to attempt the job of falsifying a public record, even at the command of our esteemed old friend, T. Morgan Carey. By the way, here he is. Gracious, what a hurry we're in! Howdy, T. Morgan?"

T. Morgan Carey had fairly leaped into the room.

"You - you scoundrel!" he cried, and shook his fist at Bob McGraw. "I'll get you for this" he said in low trembling tones, "if it takes my last dollar."

"No, you won't" retorted the smiling Bob, "at least, not after you've had a heart-to-heart talk with your obliging friend here. I've waited here to square him with you, Carey. He isn't to blame. I just bluffed him out of his boots. You mustn't be hard on him, T. Morgan. You know how easily I bluffed you. Be reasonable. Charity covers a multitude of sins, and there's a lot of land still left in the lower part of Owens Valley, although my friends have had their pick of it.

There's your little old bag with your applications still untouched, although I will admit that I was mean enough to help you file some of those instruments of abandonment from your dummy entrymen. I must hurry along now. Thank you so much - "

The janitor entered. In his hand he held Mr. McGraw's suspenders.

"You might need these" he interrupted, "more particular if you're goin' to do any runnin', an' I'll bet you are."

"Thank you" murmured Mr. McGraw. "You're very thoughtful," and quite calmly he proceeded to remove his coat and vest and replace the suspenders. When he was once more arrayed for the street he thrust his sun-tanned hand through the grilled window to the trembling deputy; he smiled his gay lazy whimsical inscrutable smile.

"*Buenos dias,* amigo" he said; and so astounded was the unhappy deputy that he actually accepted the proffered hand and shook it limply.

"You scoundrel!" hissed T. Morgan Carey, "you - " and then he applied to Bob the unpardonable epithet.

The devil leaped to life in Bob McGraw. His right arm shot out, his open palm landed with a resounding thwack on the side of Carey's head. As the land-grabber lurched from the impact of that terrific slap, McGraw's left palm straightened him up on the other ear, and he subsided incontinently into a corner.

But his natural lust for a fight had now reached

high-water mark in Bob McGraw's soul. He whirled, reached that terrible right arm through the window and grasped the deputy by the collar. Right over the counter, through the window, he snaked him, landing him in a heap on the floor outside. He jerked the frightened official to his feet, cuffed him across the room and back again to the window.

"That," he said, "for your broken oath of office, and that! for your cheap office rule that has no foundation in law but serves to frighten away the weaklings that want to file on lieu land. I must designate the basis, must I? All right, you little crook. Watch me designate it."

He landed a remarkably accurate kick under the official coat-tails, picked the deputy up bodily and hurled him in a heap in the same corner where T. Morgan Carey sprawled, blinking (for his glasses had been shaken off in the melee) and weeping with fear and impotent rage.

For a moment Bob towered above them like a great avenging red angel. Then his anger left him as suddenly as it had come. Carey and the deputy presented such a pitiable sight, although ludicrous withal, that he was moved to shame to think that he had pitted his strength against such puny adversaries. He picked T. Morgan Carey out of the corner, set him on his feet, dusted him off, gave him his hat and restored to him his gold pince-nez. The deputy needed no aid from Bob McGraw, but hastened to the protection of his sanctuary back of the counter. Bob stood looking at Carey, smiling his old bantering debonair smile. He waited until Carey had recovered his composure.

"Carey," he said, "you will remember hereafter, I trust, that it is the early bird that gets the worm, that promptness is a virtue and lying in bed mornings a heinous crime. Now, the next time you run up against a Reuben like me you want to remember the old saying that a stump-tailed yellow dog is always the best for coons. An easy conscience is to be preferred to great riches, Carey. Be honest and you will stay out of jail. Before I go, permit me to introduce myself. I'm Bob McGraw, of No Place In Particular, and a lunatic by nature, breed and inclination. Mr. Man-who-flies-through-the-window, here are duplicate copies of my power of attorney from my fifty clients, authorizing and instructing the surveyor-general to transact all of his official business with them through me. Before I go I want to say that as a usual thing I try to be a gentleman; which, fact induces the utmost regret that I was forced to gag you and truss you up in that filthy little room. If I hurt you physically then I am sorry. I tried to do the unpleasant job gently. However, this is no parlor game that you and I are playing, and desperate circumstances sometimes necessitate desperate measures. As for the blows I struck you - that is too bad, because you're old enough to be my father, but you displayed excessively bad taste in your choice of expletive. Even then I merely slapped you. But I'm sorry it had to come to that."

He paused and gazed calmly about him for a moment.

"I guess that's all" he added innocently. "Good morning."

With a chuckle that mingled triumph, deviltry and the sheer joy of living, Mr. McGraw picked up his suitcase, backed to the door, opened it and fled along the corridor. On the driveway in front of the capitol he saw an automobile standing, throbbing. He ran to it and leaped into the tonneau.

"This is Carey's car, isn't it?" he demanded.

The chauffeur nodded. He would have saluted any one not so distinctly rural as Bob McGraw.

"You're to take me over to Stockton right away. Turn her wide open and fly. Great Scott, we're all in a hurry this morning. Git! *Vamoose,* and scorch the gravel."

Now, it is a curious psychological fact that when a robust authoritative-looking man gives an order with the air of one used to commanding, ninety-nine per cent of the people to whom he gives his orders will hasten to obey without pausing to question his authority. The chauffeur threw in his clutch and the car glided away, while Bob McGraw, glancing back, saw T. Morgan Carey and a uniformed, watchman dashing down the capitol steps.

They were too late. T. Morgan Carey shouted to his chauffeur, but it was not a day of silent motors, and legislation affecting muffler cut-outs was still in the dim and distant Not-Yet.

The car sped out of the capitol grounds and away into the heart of the city. Presently the houses grew more scattered, the traffic dwindled and the car leaped forward at a forty-mile-an-hour clip. They swung down a wide road that stretched south into the sunny San Joaquin, and the mellow piping of meadow larks and linnets came pleasantly in Mr. McGraw's ears; the pungent aroma of tar-weed, the thousand and one little smells of the wide free spaces that he loved floated across to him from the fields on each side of the road, as he sat erect in the tonneau and sniffed the air of freedom.

He had had his fill of cities and he was glad to leave them behind.

CHAPTER XIII

The second event in Donna Corblay's life was about to be consummated. For the first time since her arrival in San Pasqual, a babe in arms, she was about to leave it!

All of her uneventful colorless mediocre life Donna had felt a passionate longing to go up into the country on the other side of the range. To her, the long strings of passenger coaches came to San Pasqual as the heralds of another world - poignant pulsations of the greater life beyond the sky-line, and not as the tools of a whimsical circumstance, bringing to Donna a daily consignment of hats. From earliest childhood she had watched the trains disappearing into Tehachapi Pass, tracing their progress northward long after they had disappeared by the smoke wafted over the crest of the bare volcanic range; until with the passage of many trains and many years the desire to see what lay beyond that grim barrier had developed into an obsession. Because of the purple distances that mocked her, the land of sunshine, fruit and flowers was doubly alluring; her desire was as that of a soul that dwells in limbo and longs for the smile of God.

And to-day she was going out into the world, for this was her wedding day. She had received Bob's telegram, asking her to meet him in Bakersfield, and she was going to meet him; alternately she laughed and wept, for the transcendent joy of two Events in one short day had filled her heart to overflowing, leaving no room for vague forebodings of the future.

Donna dressed herself that morning with painstaking detail. Too late she had discovered that she didn't possess a dress fit to wear at any one's wedding, not to mention her own. From time to time she had dreamed of a swagger tailored suit, but the paradox of a swagger tailored suit in San Pasqual had been so apparent always that Donna could not bring herself to the point of submitting to a measurement in the local dry-goods emporium, having the suit made in Chicago and sent out by express. Instead she had resolutely stuck to wash-dresses, which were more suited to the climate and environs of San Pasqual, and added the tailored suit money to her sinking fund in the strong box of the eating-house safe.

No, Donna was not prepared to obey Bob McGraw's summons. She wept a little as she reflected how provincial and plebeian she must appear, stepping down from the train at Bakersfield, clad in a white duck walking suit, white shoes and stockings and a white sailor hat. She wanted Bob to be proud of her, and her heart swelled to bursting at the thought that she must deny him such a simple pleasure. Poor Donna! Once she had thought that suit so beautiful. It was a drummer's sample which she had purchased from a commercial traveler who, claiming to own his own samples, had been prevailed upon to accept a price for the suit when at length he became convinced that under no circumstances would Donna permit him to make her a present of it. He had informed her at the time that it was the very latest Parisian creation and she had believed him.

If Donna had only known how ravishing that simple costume made her appear and what a vision she would be to the hungry eyes of Bob McGraw! Yet, she was ashamed to let even the San Pasqualians see her leaving town in such a dowdy costume, and as she walked up the tracks from the Hat Ranch that momentous morning, bearing aloft a parasol that but the day before had been the joy of her girlish existence, she was fully convinced that a more commonplace addendum to a feminine wardrobe had never been devised.

She was certain that all San Pasqual must know her secret - that this was her wedding day. She shuddered lest the telegraph operator had suspected something, despite Bob's commendable caution, and had incited the townspeople to line up at the depot, there to shower her with rice and hurl antiquated footgear after the train that bore her north. Such horrible rites were preserved and enacted with religious exactitude in San Pasqual.

Until that morning Donna never had really known how ardently she longed to escape from the sordid commonplace lonely little town. With its inhabitants she had nothing in common, although she noted a mental exception to this condition as, from afar, she observed Harley P. Hennage standing in front of the eating-house door, picking his teeth with his gold toothpick. She felt a sudden desire to go to the worst man in San Pasqual and pour out to him the whole wonderful story; then to await his quizzical congratulations and bask for a moment in his infrequent honest childish smile, for Donna had a very great longing to-day to permit some human being to bear with her the burden of her joy.

She was still a block from the center of the town when the train pulled in from the south, the last car coming to a stop close to where she was standing. Donna observed that the male entities of her little world had assembled to see that the train pulled in and out again safely, and had their attention centered upon the new arrivals who were rushing into the eating-house for a hurried snack. She saw her opportunity. There was no necessity for her to brave the crowd at the window in order to purchase a ticket. Decidedly luck was with her this morning. She took her suitcase from Sam Singer, the faithful, climbed aboard the last car, walked through into the next car, which happened to be a sleeper, found a vacant state-room, entered, pulled down the window shade and waited until the train started. As her car rolled past the depot she peered out and saw Harley P. Hennage scratching his head with one hand, while in the other he held a letter which he was reading. Donna could not help wondering who had written a letter to the worst man in San Pasqual.

She was glad of the seclusion of the state-room until the train was a mile outside San Pasqual, when she went out on the observation car. Donna knew she ran little risk of meeting a San Pasqualian in first-class accommodations, and as she sat there, watching the shiny rails unwinding behind her, her luxurious surroundings imparted a sense of charm and comfort which she had never felt before. The scenery in the pass proving uninteresting, she forgot about it and gave herself up to a day-dream which had become a favorite with her of late - a dream which had to do with a little Spanish house surrounded by weeping willows and Lombardy poplars (Donna had once seen a picture of a house so surrounded); of a piano, which she would learn to play, of a perfectly appointed table at which she sat with Bob across the way, smiling at her and assuring her (with his eyes) that he loved her, while his glib tongue informed her that the soup was by far the best he had ever tasted.

As Donna dreamed she smiled - unconsciously - a smile intended for Bob McGraw, and a drummer who sold lace goods for a St. Louis house appropriated that smile to himself. He leered across the aisle familiarly and with a vacuous smile inquired:

"Say, sister! Ain't you the little girl that takes cash in the eatin' house at San Pasqual? I thought your face looked kinder familiar."

Donna suddenly ceased dreaming. She glanced across at her interlocutor, and by reason of long obedience to the unwritten rule of eating-houses which requires that one must be pleasant to customers always, she forgot for a moment that she was on her way to be married. She nodded.

"Goin' up to Bakersfield?"

Again Donna nodded.

"Well, if you ain't got anything on, what's the matter with some lunch and an automobile ride afterward, sister? What're you goin' to do in Bakersfield?"

"I am going to meet a young man at the station" replied Donna sweetly. "A tall young man with a forty-four-inch chest and a pair of hands that will look as big as picnic hams to you when I tell him that you've been impertinent to me."

The face of the impertinent one crimsoned with embarrassment. He mumbled something about not meaning any offense, fussed with his watch-charm for a minute, coughed and finally fled to the day-coach.

Donna smiled after his retreating figure. How good it was, after three years of subjection to the vulgar advances of just such fellows as he, to reflect that at last she was to have a protector! An almost unholy desire possessed her to see Bob climb aboard at the next station, twine his lean hands around that drummer's trachea and shake some manhood into him. This thought suggested reflections upon the present state of Bob's health, so she took his last letter from her hand-bag and read it for the forty-second time. But it was unsatisfactory - it dealt entirely with Donna and his experiences with applicants for lieu land, so she abstracted, one by one, every letter she had ever received from him and read them all. So absorbed was she in their perusal that the other side of the range, which had always been such a matter of primary importance, was now relegated to oblivion.

The brakeman came through the car shouting: "Bakersfield! The next station is Bakersfield!" but Donna did not hear him. She was dreaming of Bob McGraw.

The train came to a stop. Donna dreamed on - and presently a familiar voice spoke at her side.

"Well - sweetheart! The train pulls out again in two minutes and I've been looking for you in every car - "

"Bob!"

It was he, looking perfectly splendid in a marvelous blue suit that must have cost at least eighteen dollars. He held out his hands, drew her to him and, in the sight of all mankind, he kissed her, and whispered to her endearing little names. She could not reply to them; she could only take his hand, like a little lost child, and follow him through the car, down the steps and into the hotel bus which was to take them up town. And on the way up town neither spoke to the other, for it seemed to each that even their most commonplace remarks to-day must be freighted with something sacred, in which the inquisitive world at large would be bound to manifest a stupendous interest. And inasmuch as it was plainly none of the world's business -

The bus had stopped in front of a tremendous hotel. It was four stories high! All along the front of the first story it was *glass* and Donna could look right through it and see everything that was going on inside! She paused on the top step of the bus to view the marvels of this town of less than twenty thousand inhabitants, and then a skeezicks of a boy, very gay in brass buttons, and with a darling little round cap on her perky head, came and took forcible possession of her suitcase. He tore it right out of Bob's hand and ran away with it. Donna was on the point of crying out at the theft, when Bob reached up and lifted her bodily to the ground.

"Reuben! Reuben!" he breathed tenderly in her ear, "don't stare so at the great round world. You're so beautiful," he added, "and I'm so proud of you! Where *did* you get that marvelous dress?"

She glanced up at him, radiant. He was proud of her! He liked her dress! It was sufficient. Bob McGraw, man of the world, had set the stamp of his approval on his bride, and nothing else mattered any more. She followed him into the hotel, where he checked her suitcase with the skeezicks who had stolen it, and then led her into the dining-room.

"Let's have lunch, Donna" he said, "or at least pretend to. I couldn't eat now. I want to talk. The man who can eat on his wedding day is a vulgarian, and dead to the finer feelings."

They found a secluded table and ordered something, and when the waitress had taken the order and departed, Bob leaned across the table.

"You're so beautiful!" he repeated. "I love you in that white suit."

"I hadn't anything but this old thing, dear. I hated to come up looking like a frump - "

"Listen to the girl! Why, you old sweetheart-"

"Do you love me, Bob?"

"More than ever. In the matter of love, Donna, absence really makes the heart - "

"How much?" She lifted her face toward him adoringly.

"Ten hundred thousand million dollars' worth" he declared, and they both laughed.

"I don't know whether you're a man or just a big boy" Donna told him.

She sighed. "But then I don't know anything to-day, except that if I am ever happier than I am this minute I shall die. I shall not be able to stand it. But, dearie! You haven't told me a word about Donnaville!"

So Bob related to her a minute history of himself from the moment he had left her until he had leaned over her in the observation car. He described, with inimitable wit and enjoyment, his experience in the land office, and together they examined the fifty receipts.

"I'm sorry you had to lock Mr. Carey in the room and gag him and tie him up" said Donna regretfully. "Maybe he'll have you arrested!"

"I'm sorry, too, dear. But then it was the only thing I could do and I had to keep him quiet. Oh, I don't care" he added defiantly. "I'd muss up an old crook like Carey every hour for your sake. But he won't have me arrested. That would be too dangerous for him."

"Then you can get the land right away?" she queried.

He shook his head. "The cards haven't even been dealt, sweetheart. My applications will almost certainly be held up six months in the state land office before they are approved by the surveyor-general and forwarded to the Commissioner of the General Land Office at Washington to be passed to patent by the United States. And I shall be very greatly surprised if Carey hasn't a friend in Washington who will see that the granting of the patents is delayed for several years. Then, when the matter cannot be delayed any longer, Carey will induce one of his dummies to protest the applications, alleging that they are part of a gigantic land fraud scheme, and a few more years will go by while this protest is being investigated."

"But you'll win in the long run, will you not?"

He shrugged expressively. "I may. I anticipate that Carey will give me all the time he can to get my water-right developed and earn thirty-nine thousand dollars to pay for the land for my Pagans."

"But I thought Mr. Dunstan had promised to loan you that money?"

"Homer Dunstan is an old man, Donna girl. If he should die in the interim, my name is in the lion's mouth."

"But what are we to do, Bobby?" she quavered, suddenly frightened, as the enormousness of the man's task loomed before her.

"*Quien sabe*" he said ruefully. "We'll marry first and think of it afterward - that is, if you still think you want to marry a chap whose cash assets represent less than thirty dollars of borrowed money."

She thought swiftly of the boor who had spoken to her on the train that morning; of her dull lonely changeless life in San Pasqual; and the longing for protection was very great indeed. She wanted some one on whom she might lean in the hour of stress and woe, and she had selected him for that signal honor. Why, then, should they not marry? They would not always be poor. He had his work to do and she had hers, and their marriage need not interfere. She wanted to help him, and with her woman's intuition she realized that his was the nature that yearns for the accomplishment of great things when spurred to action by the praise and comfort of a mate in sympathy with his dreams and his ideals. She almost shuddered to think of what might happen to him should he marry a girl who did not understand him! It seemed to her that for his sake, if for no other, she must marry him, and when she raised her brilliant eyes to his he read her answer in their limpid depths.

"Do you need me?" she queried.

"Very much" he answered humbly, "but not enough to insist upon you sharing my poverty with me. You're self-supporting and it isn't fair to you, but rather selfish on my part. And you must realize, Donna dear, that I cannot remain in San Pasqual. I have my work to do; I must make money, and I cannot take you to the place where I hope to make it."

"I expect to be left alone, Bob. But I do not mind that. I've lived alone at the Hat Ranch a long time, dear, and I can stand it a little longer. I do not wish to tie you to my apron-strings and hamper you. What are your plans?"

"Well," he said a little sheepishly, "I thought I'd like to make one more trip into the desert. I have some claims over by Old Woman mountain, in San Bernardino county, and they're pockety. I might clean up a stake in there this winter. It's about the only chance I have to raise the wind, but even then it's a gambler's chance."

He was a Desert Rat! The lure of the waste places was calling to him again, tormenting him with the promise of rich reward in the country just beyond. Donna thought of her own father who had left his bride on a similar errand, and the thought that Bob, too, might not come back stabbed her with sudden anguish. But he was a man, and he knew best; in a desert country some one must do the desert work; he loved it and she would not say him nay. Yet the big tears trembled on her long lashes as she thought of what lay before him and her heart ached that it must be so. He watched her keenly, waiting for the protest which he thought must come. Presently she spoke.

"We must figure on an outfit for you."

His brown eyes lit with admiration, for he realized the grief that lay behind that apparently careless acceptance of his plan, and loved her the more for her courage.

"Yes, I'll need two burros, with packs, and some drills, tools, dynamite and grub - two hundred dollars will outfit me nicely. I'll have to scout around and borrow the money somewhere, and to be quite candid, Donna, I have designs on our gambler friend, Hennage."

She smiled. "Dear, good old Harley P.! He'd grubstake you if it broke the bank."

"Well, I'm going to figure along that line at any rate. So, if you're quite ready, Donna, we'll go down to the court-house, procure the license, hunt up a preacher and take each other for better or for worse."

"I think it will be for better, dear."

"Well, it can't be for worse, I'm sure, than it is to-day. Nevertheless I'm a frightened man."

She ignored this subtle hint of procrastination. "I'm ready, Bob. But before we start, there's one matter that I haven't explained to you. I do not care to have our marriage known. Those talkative people in San Pasqual would - talk, under the circumstances - that is, dear, I want to keep right on at the eating-house until you're ready to take me away from San Pasqual forever. Now, I know that's going to hurt you - that thought of your wife working - but nobody need ever know it, and when you're ready we'll leave the horrible old place and never go back any more. We have so much to do, Bob, and - "

"You do hurt me, Donna" he protested. "You have exacted from me a promise and you are forcing me to fulfill it under circumstances which render it mighty hard. Of course we love each other and I do want to marry you, but ah, Donna, I don't feel like a man to-day, but a mendicant. What can I do, sweetheart? If you marry me to-day you'll have to work if you want to live." There was misery in his glance. "However, all my life I've been doing things differently - or rather indifferently - so why should I stop now? It will at least comfort me out there alone in the desert to know that I have a wife waiting at home for me. I think the joy of that will outweigh the sting of shame that a married pauper must feel - "

"No, no, Bob, you mustn't say that. You mustn't feel that way about it. You are not a pauper." She stood up and he helped her into her coat, and after paying the waitress they departed together for the city hall.

But Bob was a sad bridegroom. Donna had wired him that she had arranged for a two-weeks' vacation, and he had been at pains to acquaint her with the extreme low ebb of his finances, in the hope that she would voluntarily suggest a delay of their marriage, but to his great distress she had not seen fit to take his pathetic hint - she who ordinarily was so quick of comprehension; so, rather than refer to the matter again, he decided to step into a telegraph station immediately after the ceremony and send a hurried call for help to Harley P. Hennage - the gambler being the only man of his acquaintance whom he knew to be sufficiently good-natured and careless with money to respond to his appeal.

When at length they reached the city hall Donna waited, blushing, outside the door of the marriage bureau while Bob entered and parted with two dollars and fifty cents for the parchment which gave him a legal right to commit what he called a social and economic crime. Later he came out and insisted that Donna should return with him to Cupid's window, there to receive the customary congratulations and handshake from Bob's acquaintance who had issued him the license, and who, following the practice of such individuals, felt it incumbent upon him to offer his felicitations to every customer.

Leaving the court-house Bob and Donna wandered about town until they came to a church. A gentleman of color, engaged in washing the church windows, directed them to the pastor's residence in the next block. They accordingly; proceeded to the rectory and Bob rang the front door bell. The pastor answered the bell in person. The bridegroom grinned at him sheepishly while the bride, very much embarrassed, shrunk to the bridegroom's side and gazed timidly at the reverend gentleman rubbing his hands so expectantly in the doorway.

"Won't you come in?" he said, in tones most kindly and hospitable. "Just step right into the parlor and I'll be with you as soon as I can get my spectacles."

"Thank you" said Bob. They entered. The rector went into his study while Bob wagged a knowing head at his broad retreating back.

"He knows what we want, you bet" he whispered. "No flies on that preacher. I like him. I like any man who can do things without a diagram and directions for using."

Donna nodded. She was quite impressed at the clergyman's perspicacity. She was quite self-possessed when he returned with his spectacles, a little black book, his wife and the gardener for witnesses, and a "here-is-the-job-I-love" expression on his amiable features. He examined the license, satisfied himself, apparently, that it was not a forgery, and after standing Bob and Donna up in a corner close to a terra-cotta umbrella-holder filled with pampas plumes, he proceeded with the ceremony.

CHAPTER XIV

Now, to the man in whose nature there is a broad streak of sentiment and who looks upon his marriage as a very sacred, solemn and lasting ceremony, no speech in life is so provocative of profound emotion as the beautiful interchange of vows which links him to the woman he loves. As Bob McGraw stood there, holding Donna's soft warm hand in his, so hard and tanned, and repeated: "I, Robert, take thee, Donna, for my lawful wife; to have and to hold, from this day forward, for better, for worse, for richer, for poorer (Here Bob's voice trembled a little. Why should this question of finance arise to smite him in the midst of the marriage ceremony?), in sickness; and in health, until death us do part," his breast swelled and a mist came into his eyes. His voice was very low and husky as he took that sacred oath, and it seemed that he stood swaying in a great fog, while from a great distance, yet wonderfully clear and firm and sweet, Donna's voice reached him:

"I, Donna, take thee, Robert, for my lawful husband - " and the minister was asking him for a ring.

For a ring!

Bob started. The perspiration stood out on his forehead! - there was agony in his brown eyes. In the sudden reaction caused by that awful request, he blurted out:

"Oh, Great Grief, Donna! I forgot all about the ring!"

"I didn't" she replied softly. From her hand-bag she produced a worn old wedding ring (it had been her mother's) and handed it to Bob. At this he commenced to regain his composure, and by the time he had slipped the ring on Donna's finger and plighted his troth for aye, all of his troubles and worries vanished. The minister and his gardener shook hands with them, and the minister's wife kissed Donna and gave her a motherly hug - primarily because she looked so sweet and again on general feminine principles. Bob, not desiring to appear cheap on this, the greatest day in history, gave the minister a fee of twenty dollars, and five minutes later found himself on the sidewalk with his wife, rejoicing in the knowledge that he had at least justified his existence and joined the ranks o' canny married men - the while he strove to appear as scornful of the future as he had been fearful of it five minutes before. He jingled less than three dollars in small change in his vest pocket, and while he strove to appear jaunty, away inside of him he was a worried man. He could not help it.

"Mrs. McGraw" he said finally, "on the word of no less a personage than your husband, you're some bride."

"Mr. McGraw" she retorted, "on the word of no less a personage than your wife, you are *some* bridegroom. Why *did* you forget the ring?"

Why did he forget the ring? Really, it did seem likely that he must quarrel with his wife before they had been married ten minutes. How strangely obtuse she was to-day!

"Why, Donna" he protested, "how should I know? I never was married before, and besides I was thinking of something else all day." He slapped his vest pocket and cupped a hand to an ear, in a listening attitude.

"Did you hear a faint jingle?" he queried solemnly.

She pinched his arm, interrupting his flow of nonsense. Women who dearly love their husbands delight in teasing them, and as Donna turned her radiant face to his Bob fancied he could detect a secret jest peeping at him from the ceiled shelter of her drowsy-lidded eyes. Yes, without a doubt she was laughing at him - and he as poor as a church-mouse. He frowned.

"This is no laughing matter, Mrs. McGraw."

The roguish look deepened.

"Now, what else have I done?" he demanded.

"Nothing - yet. But you're contemplating it."

"Contemplating what?"

"Telegraphing Harley P. Hennage."

"Friend wife" said Bob McGraw, "you should hang out your shingle as a seeress. You forecast coming events so cleverly that perhaps you can inform me whether or not we are to walk back to San Pasqual, living like gypsies en route."

"Why, no, stupid. I have money enough for our honeymoon."

"Donna" he began sternly, "if I had thought - "

"You wouldn't have consented to such a hasty marriage. Of course. I knew that - so I contrived to have my way about it. And I'm going to have my way about this honeymoon, too. Five minutes ago I couldn't have offered you money, but I have the right to do so now. But I would not hurt your feelings for the world. I'll loan you six hundred dollars on approved security."

He shook his head. "You can't mix sentiment and business, Donna, and I have no security. Besides, I'm not quite a cad."

"Oh, very well, dear. I know your code and I wouldn't run counter to it for a - well for a water right in Owens Valley - notwithstanding the fact that I took you for richer or for poorer. And I did figure on a honeymoon, Bob."

He threw up his hands in token of submission. "I'll accept" he said, although he was painfully embarrassed. She was making the happiest day of his life a little miserable, and for the first time he experienced a fleeting regret that Donna's ideals were not formed on a more masculine basis. By the exercise of her compelling power over him she had him in her toils and he was helpless. Nothing remained for him to do save make the best of a situation, the acceptance of which filled him with chagrin.

"Don't pull such a dolorous countenance, Bob. Why, your face is as long as Friar Tuck's. I promise I will not harass you with the taunt that you married me for my money. In fact, my husband, it's the other way around. I might accord you that privilege."

She drew his arm through hers. "I have a little wedding present for you, Bobby dear" she began. "I'm going to tell you a little story, and now please don't interrupt. You know all summer you were up in the mountains, and after that you were rather in jail at the Hat Ranch, where I didn't bring you any newspapers. Consequently, from being out of the world so long, you haven't heard the latest news about Owens Valley. I heard it before you left San Pasqual, but I wouldn't tell you. I wanted to keep the news for a wedding present.

"For several months something very mysterious has been going on in our part of the world. There has been a force of surveyors and engineers in the valley searching for a permanent water supply for some great purpose, though nobody can guess what it is. But it's a fact that a pile of money has been spent in Long Valley, above Owens Valley, and more is to be spent if it can buy water. The chief engineer of the outfit read in the paper at Independence the account of your filing at Cottonwood Lake and he has had men searching for you ever since. One of them called to interview you at San Pasqual, for, like T. Morgan Carey, they had traced you that far. He came into the eating-house and asked me if I knew anybody in town by the name of Robert McGraw. I told him I did not - which wasn't a fib because you weren't in town at the time. You were in bed at the Hat Ranch. An engineer was with him and while they were at luncheon I overheard them discussing your water-right. The engineer declared that the known feature alone made the location worth a million dollars. Do you like my wedding present, dear?"

He pressed her arm but did not answer. She continued.

"I talked over the matter of water and power rights with Harley P. and he says they will pay a big price for anything like you have. I didn't tell him you owned a power and water-right - just mentioned that I knew a man who owned one. Since then I've been reading up on the subject and I discovered that you have enough water to develop three times the acreage you plan to acquire. One miner's inch to the acre will be sufficient in that country. So you see, Bob, you're a rich man. That explains why Carey was so anxious to find you. He wanted to buy from you cheap and sell to those people dear. Why, you're the queerest kind of a rich man. Bob. You're water poor. Don't you see, now, why you can take my money? You have three times more water than you need; you can sell some of it - "

Bob paused, facing his bride. "And you knew all this a month ago and didn't write me!"

"I was saving it for to-day. I wanted this to be the happiest day of our lives,"

"Ah, how happy you've made me!" he said. His voice trembled just a little and Donna, glancing quickly up at him, detected a suspicious moisture in his eyes.

Until that moment she had never fully realized the intensity of the man's nature - the extent of worry and suffering that could lie behind those smiling eyes and never show! She saw that a great burden had suddenly been lifted from him, and with the necessity for further dissembling removed, his strong face was for the moment glorified. She realized now the torture to which she had subjected him by her own tenderness and repression; while their marriage had been a marvelous - a wonderful - event to her, to him it had been fraught with terror, despite his great love, and her thoughts harked back to the night she and Harley P. Hennage had carried him home to the Hat Ranch. Harley P. had told her that night that Bob would "stand the acid." How well he could stand it, only she, who had applied it, would ever know.

"Forgive me, dear" she faltered. "If I had only realized - "

"Isn't it great to be married?" he queried. "And to think I was afraid to face it without the price of a honeymoon!"

"You won't have to worry any more. You're rich. You can sell half the water and we will never go back to San Pasqual any more."

His face clouded. "I can't do that" he said doggedly.

"Why not?" she asked, frightened.

"Because I'll need every drop of it. I've started a fight and I'm going to finish it. You told me once that if I sold out my Pagans for money to marry you, you'd be disappointed in me - that if I should start something that was big and noble and worthy of me, I'd have to go through to the finish. Donna, I'm going through. I may lose on a foul, but I'm not fighting for a draw decision. I schemed for thirty-two thousand acres, and if I get that I have the land ring blocked. But there are hundreds - thousands - of acres further south that I can reach with my canals, and I cannot rest content with a half-way job. The land ring cannot grab the desert south of Donnaville, because they haven't sufficient water, and if they had I wouldn't give them a right of way through my land for their canals, and I wouldn't sell water to their dummy entrymen. I want that valley for the men who have never had a chance. I've got the water and it's mine in trust for posterity. It belongs to Inyo and I'm going to keep it there."

She did not reply. When they reached the hotel, instead of registering, as Donna expected he would, Bob went to the baggage-room and secured her suit-case which he had checked there two hours before. She watched him with brimming eyes, but with never a word of complaint. He was right, and if the two weeks' honeymoon that she had planned was not to be, it was she who had prevented it. She had set her husband a mighty task and bade him finish it, and despite the pain and disappointment of a return to San Pasqual the same day she had left it, a secret joy mingled with her bitterness.

Poor Donna! She was proud and happy in the knowledge that her husband had proved himself equal to the task, but she found it hard, very hard, to be a Pagan on her wedding day.

Bob brought their baggage and set it by her side. "Watch it for a few minutes, Donna, please" he said. "I forgot something."

He found a seat for her and she waited until his return.

"Have you got that six hundred with you, Donna?" he asked gravely.

She opened her hand-bag and showed him a roll of

twenty dollar pieces.

"Good," he replied, in the same grave, even tones. "Here is my promissory note, at seven per cent, for the amount, payable one day after date, and this other document is an assignment of a one-half interest in my water-right, to secure the payment of my note."

He handed them to her. In silence she gave him the money.

"Are you quite ready, Donna? I think we had better start now" he said.

She nodded. She could not trust herself to speak for the sobs that crowded in her throat. He observed the tears and stooped over her tenderly.

"Why, what's the matter, little wife?"

"It's - it's - a little hard - to have to give up - our honey-moon" she quavered.

"Why, Mrs. Donna Corblay Robert McGraw! Is that the trouble? Well, you're a model Pagan and I'm proud of you, but you don't know the Big Chief Pagan after all! Why, we're not going back to San Pasqual for a week or ten days. I was so busy thinking of all I have to do that I must have forgotten to tell you that we're going up to the Yosemite Valley on our honeymoon. I want to show my wife some mountains with grass and trees on them - the meadows and the Merced river and the wonderful waterfalls, the birds and the bees and all the other wonderful sights she's been dreaming of all her life."

She carefully tore the promissory note and the assignment of interest into little bits and let them flutter to the floor. The tears were still quivering on her beautiful lashes, but they were tears of joy, now, and her sense of humor had come to her rescue.

"Foolish man" she retorted, "don't you realize that one cannot mix sentiment and business? Be sensible, my tall husband. You're so impulsive. Please register and have that baggage sent up to our room, and then let me have a hundred dollars. I want to spend it on a dandy tailored suit and some other things that I shall require on our honeymoon. In all my life I have never been shopping, and I want to be happy to-day - all day."

"Tell you what we'll do" he suggested. "Let's not think of the future at all. I'm tired of this to-morrow bugaboo."

"I'm not. We're going honeymooning to-morrow."

Harley P. Hennage had at length fallen a victim to the most virulent disease in San Pasqual. For two days he had been consumed with curiosity; on the third day he realized that unless the mystery of Donna Corblay's absence from her job could be satisfactorily explained by the end of the week, he would furnish a description of Donna to a host of private detectives, with instructions to spare no expense in locating her, dead or alive.

Donna's absence from the eating-house the first day had aroused no suspicion in Mr. Hennage's mind. It was her day off, and he knew this. But when Mr. Hennage appeared in the eating-house for his meals the day following, Donna's absence from the cashier's desk impelled him to mild speculation, and when on the third morning he came in to breakfast purposely late only to find Donna's substitute still on duty, he realized that the time for action had arrived.

"That settles it" he murmured into his second cup of coffee. "That poor girl is sick and nobody in town gives three whoops in a holler. I'll just run down to the Hat Ranch to-night an' see if I can't do somethin' for her."

Which, safe under cover of darkness, he accordingly did. At the Hat Ranch Mr. Hennage was informed by Sam Singer that his young mistress had boarded the train for Bakersfield three days previous, after informing Sam and his squaw that she would not return for two weeks. Under Mr. Hennage's critical cross-examination Soft Wind furnished the information that Donna had taken her white suit and all of her best clothes.

"Ah," murmured Mr. Hennage, "as the feller says, I apprehend."

He did, indeed. A great light had suddenly burst upon Mr. Hennage. Both by nature and training he was possessed of the ability to assimilate a hint without the accompaniment of a kick, and in the twinkling of an eye the situation was as plain to him as four aces and a king, with the entire company standing pat.

He smote his thigh, "Well I'll be ding-swizzled and everlastingly flabbergasted. Lit out to get married an' never said a word to nobody. Pulls out o' town, dressed in her best suit o' clothes, like old man McGinty, an' heads north. Uh-huh! Bob McGraw's at the bottom o' this. He started south the day before, an' he ain't arrived in San Pasqual yet."

He sat down at Donna's kitchen table and drew a letter and a telegram from his pocket.

"Huh! Huh - hum - m - m! Writes me on Monday from Sacramento that he's busted, an' to send him a money order to San Francisco, General Delivery. Letter postmarked ten thirty A. M. Then he wires me from Stockton, the same day, to disregard letter an' telegraph him fifty at Stockton. Telegram received about one P. M. Well, sir, that tells the story. The young feller flopped by the wayside an' spent his last blue chip on this telegram. I wire him the fifty, he wires her to meet him in Bakersfield, most likely, an' they're goin' to get married on my fifty dollars. *On my fifty dollars!*"

Mr. Hennage looked up from the telegram and fastened upon Sam Singer an inquiring look, as if he expected the Indian to inform him what good reason, if any, existed, why Bob McGraw should not immediately be apprehended by the proper authorities and confined forthwith in a padded cell.

"I do wish that dog-gone boy'd took me into his confidence," mourned the gambler, "but that's always the way. Nobody ever trusts me with nuthin'. Damn it! *Fifty dollars!* I'll give that Bob hell for this - a-marryin' that fine girl on a shoestring an' me a-hangin' around town with upward o' six thousand iron men in the kitty. It ain't fair. If they was married in San Pasqual I wouldn't butt in nohow, but bein' married some place else, where none of us is known, I'd a took a chance an' butted in. I ain't one o' the presumin' kind, but if I'd a-been asked I'd a-butted in! You can bet your scalp,

Sam, if I'd a-had the givin' away o' that blushin' bride, I'd 'a shoved across a stack o' blue chips with her that'd 'a set them young folks on their feet. Oh, hell's bells! If that ain't plumb removin' the limit! Sam, you'd orter be right thankful you're only an Injun. If you was a human bein' you'd know what it is to have your feelin's hurt."

He smote the table with his fist. "Serves me right," he growled. "There ain't no fun in life for a man that lives off the weaknesses of other people," and with this self-accusing remark Mr. Hennage, feeling slighted and neglected, returned to his game in the Silver Dollar saloon. He was preoccupied and unhappy, and that night he lost five hundred dollars.

Bright and early next morning, however, the gambler went to the public telephone station and called up the principal hotel in Bakersfield. He requested speech with either Mr. or Mrs. Robert McGraw. After some delay he was informed that Mr. and Mrs. McGraw had left the day before, without leaving a forwarding address.

"Well, I won't say nothin' about it until they do" was the conclusion at which Mr. Hennage finally arrived. "Of course it's just possible I happened across the trail of another family o' McGraws, but I'm layin' two to one I didn't."

And having thus ferreted out Donna's secret, Harley P., like a true sport, proceeded to forget it. He moused around the post-office a little and put forth a few discreet feelers here and there, in order to discover whether San Pasqual, generally speaking, was at all interested. He discovered that it was not. In fact, in all San Pasqual the only interested person was Mrs.

Pennycook, who heaved a sigh of relief at the thought that her Dan was, for the nonce, outside the sphere of Donna's influence.

In the meantime Donna and Bob, in the beautiful Yosemite, rode and tramped through ten glorious, blissful days. It would be impossible to attempt to describe in adequate fashion the delights of that honeymoon. To Donna, so suddenly transported from the glaring drab lifeless desert to this great natural park, the first sight of the valley had been a glimpse into Paradise. She was awed by the sublimity of nature, and all that first day she hardly spoke, even to Bob. Such happiness was unbelievable. She was almost afraid to speak, lest she awaken and find herself back in San Pasqual. As for Bob, he had resolutely set himself to the task of forgetting the future - at least during their honeymoon. He forgot about the thirty-nine thousand dollars he required, he forgot about Donnaville; and had even the most lowly of his Pagans interfered with his happiness for one single fleeting second, Mr. McGraw would assuredly have slain him instanter and then laughed at the tragedy.

It was very late in the season and the vivid green which, comes with spring had departed from the valley. But if it had, so also had the majority of tourists, and Bob and Donna had the hotel largely to themselves. Each day they journeyed to some distant portion of the valley, carrying their luncheon, and returning at nightfall to the hotel. After dinner they would sit together on the veranda, watching the moon rise over the rim of that wonderful valley, listening to the tree-toads in noisy convention or hearkening to the "plunk" of a trout leaping in the river below. Hardly a breath of air stirred in the valley. All was peace. It was an Eden.

On the last night of their stay, Bob broached for the first time the subject of their future.

"We must start for - for home to-morrow, Donna" he said. "At least you must. You have a home to go to. As for me, I've got to go into the desert and strike one final blow for Donnaville. I've got to take one more long chance for a quick little fortune before I give up and sell my Pagans into bondage."

"Yes" she replied heedlessly. She had him with her now; the shadow of impending separation had not yet fallen upon her.

"What are your plans, Donna?" he asked.

"My plans?"

"Yes. Is it still your intention to keep on working?"

"Why not? I must do something. I must await you somewhere, so why not at San Pasqual? It is cheaper there and it will help if I can be self-supporting until you come back. Besides, I'd rather work than sit idle around the Hat Ranch."

He made no reply to this. He had already threshed the matter over in his mind and there was no answer.

"I'll accompany you as far as San Pasqual, Donna. We'll go south to-morrow and arrive at San Pasqual, shortly after dark. I'll escort you to the Hat Ranch, change into my desert togs, saddle Friar Tuck and light out. I'll ride to Keeler and sell horse and saddle and spurs there. At Keeler I'll buy two burros and outfit for my trip; then strike east, via Darwin or Coso Springs."

"How long will you be in the desert?"

"About six months, I think. I'll come out late in the spring when it begins to get real hot. Do you think you can wait that long?"

"I think so. Will it be possible for me to write to you in the meantime?"

"Perhaps. I'll leave word in the miners' outfitting store at Danby and you can address me there. Then, if some prospector should be heading out my way they'll send out my letters. My claims are forty miles from Danby, over near Old Woman mountain. If I meet any prospectors going out toward the railroad, I'll write you."

"The days will be very long until you come back, dear, but I'll be patient. I realize what it means to you, and Donnaville is worth the sacrifice. You know I told you I wanted to help."

"You are helping - more than you realize. You'll be safe until I get back?"

"I've always been safe at the Hat Ranch, but if I should need a friend I can call on Harley P. He isn't one of the presuming kind" - Donna smiled - "but he will stand the acid."

"And you will not worry if you do not receive any letters from me all the time I am away?"

"I shall know what to expect, Bob, so I shall not worry

- very much."

They left the Yosemite early next morning, staging down to El Portal, and shortly after dusk the same evening they arrived at San Pasqual. There were few people at the station when the train pulled in, and none that Donna knew, except the station agent and his assistants; and as these worthies were busy up at the baggage car, Bob and Donna alighted at the rear end and under the friendly cover of darkness made their way down to the Hat Ranch.

Sam Singer and Soft Wind had not yet retired, and after seeing his bride safe in her home once more, Bob McGraw prepared to leave her.

She was sorely tempted, at that final test of separation, to plead with him to abandon his journey, to stay with her and their new-found happiness and leave to another the gigantic task of reclaiming the valley. It was such a forlorn hope, after all; she began to question his right to stake their future against that of persons to whom he owed no allegiance, until she remembered that a great work must ever require great sacrifice; that her share in this sacrifice was little, indeed, compared with his. Moreover, he had set his face to this task before he had met her - she would not be worthy of him if she asked him to abandon it now.

"I must go" he said huskily. "The moon will be up by ten o'clock and I can make better time traveling by moonlight than I can after sun-up."

She clung to him for one breathless second; then, with a final caress she sent him forth to battle for his Pagans.

She was back at the cashier's counter in the eating-house the next morning when Harley P. Hennage came in for his breakfast.

"Hello, Miss Donna" the unassuming one greeted her cordially. "Where've you been an' when did you get back to San Pasqual? Why, I like to 'a died o' grief. Thought you'd run away an' got married an' left us for good."

He watched her narrowly and noted the little blush that marked the landing of his apparently random shot.

"I've been away on my first vacation, went up to Yosemite Valley. I got back last night."

"Glad of it" replied Mr. Hennage heartily. "Enjoy yourself?"

"It was glorious."

He talked with her for a few minutes, then waddled to his favorite seat and ordered his ham and eggs.

"Well, she didn't fib to me, at any rate, even if she didn't tell the whole truth" he soliloquized. "But what's chewin' the soul out o' me is this: 'How in Sam Hill did they make fifty dollars go that far?' If I was gettin' married, fifty dollars wouldn't begin to pay for the first round o' drinks."

It had not escaped the gambler's observing eye that Donna had been crying, so immediately after breakfast Mr. Hennage strolled over to the feed corral, leaned his arms on the top rail and carefully scanned the herd of horses within.

Bob McGraw's little roan cayuse was gone!

"Well, if that don't beat the Dutch!" exclaimed Mr. Hennage disgustedly. "If that young feller ain't one fool of a bridegroom, a-runnin' away from his bride like this! For quick moves that feller's got the California flea faded to a whisper. Two weeks ago he was a-practicin' law in Sacramento, a-puttin' through a deal in lieu lands; then he jumps to Stockton an' wires me for fifty dollars; then he hops to Bakersfield an' gits married, after which he lands in the Yosemite Valley on his honeymoon. From there he jumps to San Pasqual, an' from San Pasqual he fades away into the desert an' leaves his bride at home a-weepin' an' a-cryin'. I don't understand this business nohow, an' I'll be dog-goned if I'm a-goin' to try. It's too big an order."

Three days later Harley P. Hennage wished that he had not been so inquisitive. That glance into the feed corral was to cost him many a pang and many a dollar; for, with rare exceptions, there is no saying so true as this: that a little knowledge is a dangerous thing.

CHAPTER XV

The once prosperous mining camp of Garlock is a name and a memory now. Were it not that the railroad has been built in from San Pasqual a hundred and fifty miles up country through the Mojave, Garlock would be a memory only. But some official of the road, imbued, perhaps, with a remnant of sentimental regret for the fast-vanishing glories of the past, has caused to be erected beside the track a white sign carrying the word Garlock in black letters; otherwise one would scarcely realize that once a thriving camp stood in the sands back of this sign-board of the past. Even in the days when the stage line operated between San Pasqual and Keeler, Garlock had run its race and the Argonauts had moved on, leaving the rusty wreck of an old stamp-mill, the decayed fragments of half a dozen pine shanties and a few adobe *casas* with the sod roofs fallen in.

There are a few deep uncovered wells in this deserted camp, filthy with the rotting carcasses of desert animals which have crawled down these wells for life - and remained for death. But no human being resides in Garlock. It is a sad and lonely place. The hills that rise back of the ruins are scarlet with oxide of iron; in the sheen of the westering sun they loom harsh and repellent, provocative of the thought that from the very inception of Garlock their crests have been the arena of murder - spattered with the blood of the hardy men who made the camp and then deserted it.

Therefore, one would not be surprised at anything happening in Garlock - where it would seem a wanton waste of imagination to look forward to anything happening - yet at about noon of the day that Harley P. Hennage looked over the rail fence into the feed corral at San Pasqual and discovered that Bob McGraw's horse was gone, a man on a tired horse rode up from the south, turned in through the ruined doorway of one of the roofless tumble-down adobe houses, and concealed himself and his horse in the area formed by the four crumbling walls.

He dismounted, unsaddled and rubbed down his dripping horse with handfuls of the withered grasses that grew within the ruins. Next, the man hunted through Garlock until he found an old rusty kerosene can with a wire handle fitted through it, and to this he fastened a long horsehair hitching rope and drew water from one of the filthy wells. The horse drank greedily and nickered reproachfully when the man informed him that he must cool off before being allowed to drink his fill.

For an hour the man sat on his saddle and smoked; then, after drawing several cans of water for the horse, he spread the saddle-blanket on the ground and poured thereon a feed of oats from a meager supply cached on the saddle. From the saddle-bags he produced a small can of roast beef and some dry bread, which he "washed down" with water from his canteen while the horse munched at the oats.

Late in the afternoon the man stepped to the ruined

doorway and looked south. Three miles away a splotch of dust hung high in the still atmosphere; beneath it a black object was crawling steadily toward Garlock. It was the up stage from San Pasqual for Keeler, and the stranger in Garlock had evidently been awaiting its arrival, for he dodged back into the enclosure, saddled his horse, gathered up his few belongings and seemed prepared to evacuate at a moment's notice. He peered out, as the old Concord coach lurched through the sand past the bones of Garlock, and observed the express messenger nodding a little wearily, his eyes half closed in protest against the glare of earth and sky.

Suddenly the express messenger started, and looked up. He had a haunting impression that somebody was watching him - and he was not mistaken. Over the crest of an adobe wall he saw the head and shoulders of a man. Also he saw one of the man's hands. It contained a long blue-barreled automatic pistol, which was pointed at him. From behind a mask fashioned from a blue bandanna handkerchief came the expected summons:

"Hands up!"

The driver pulled up his horses and jammed down the brake. The express messenger, surprised, hesitated a moment between an impulse to obey the stern command and a desire to argue the matter with his sawed-off shotgun. The man behind the wall, instantly realizing that he must be impressive at all cost, promptly fired and lifted the pipe out of the messenger's mouth. The latter swore, and his arms went over his head in a twinkling.

"Don't do that again" he growled. "I know when a

man's got the drop on me."

"I was afraid your education had been neglected" the hold-up man retorted pleasantly. "Throw out the box! No, not you. The driver will throw it out. You keep your hands up."

The express box dropped into the greasewood beside the trail with a heavy metallic thud that augured a neat profit for the man behind the wall.

"The passengers will please alight on this side of the stage, turn their pockets inside out and deposit their coin on top of the box" continued the road agent. "My friend with the spike beard and the gold eye-glasses! You dropped something on the bed of the stage. Pick it up, if you're anxious to retain a whole hide. Thank you! That pocketbook looks fat. Now, one at a time and no crowding. Omit the jewelry. I want cash."

The highwayman continued to discourse affably with his victims while the little pile of coin and bills on top of the box grew steadily. When it was evident that the job was complete he ordered the passengers back into the stage and addressed the driver.

"Drive right along now and remember that it's a sure sign of bad luck to look back. I have a rifle with me and I'm considered a very fair shot up to five hundred yards. Remember that - you with the sawed-off shotgun!"

"Good-by" replied the messenger. "See you later, I hope."

The horses sprang to the crack of the driver's whip, and

the stage rolled north on its journey. When it was a quarter of a mile away the man behind the wall came out into the road and shot the padlock off the express box, transferred the fruits of his industry to his saddle-bags, mounted and rode out of Garlock across the desert valley, headed northeast for Johannesburg.

As he rode out into the open a rifle cracked and a bullet whined over him. He glanced in the direction whence the sound of the shot came and observed a man on a white horse riding rapidly toward him. The bandit suddenly remembered that the off leader on the stage team was white.

"Old man, you're as clever as you are brave" muttered the bandit admiringly. "You unhook the off leader while I'm monkeying with the box, dig up a rifle and come for me riding bareback. Well, I'm not out to kill anybody if I can help it, and my horse has had a nice rest. I'll run for it."

He did. The rifle cracked again and the bandit's wide-brimmed hat rose from his head and sailed away into the sage. He looked back at it a trifle dubiously, but he knew better than to stop to recover that hat, in the face of such close snap-shooting. That express messenger was too deadly - and too game; so the bandit merely spurred his horse, lay low on his neck and swept across the desert. When he came to a little swale between some sandhills he dipped into it, pulled up, dismounted and waited. The sun was setting behind the gory hills now, and glinted on a rifle which the bandit drew from a gun-boot which a broad sweat leather half concealed. It was better shooting-light now; distances were not quite so deceptive.

Suddenly the man on the white horse appeared on the crest of a distant sand-hill. The outlaw, leaning his rifle across his horse's back, sighted carefully and fired; the white horse went to his knees and his rider leaped clear. Instantly the pursued man vaulted into his saddle and rode furiously away. A dozen shots whipped the sage around him; one of them notched the ear of his straining mount, but in the end the bullets dropped short, the sun set, and through the gathering gloom the outlaw jogged easily up the long sandy slope toward Johannesburg. It was quite dark when he rode around the town to the north, circled through the range back of Fremont's Peak and headed out across Miller's Dry Lake, bound for Barstow.

As for the express messenger, he removed the bridle from his dead horse and trudged back to the waiting coach. On the way he back-tracked the outlaw's trail until he came to the man's hat, which he appropriated.

Donna Corblay was at the eating-house when the first down stage from Keeler came into San Pasqual with the news of the hold-up at Garlock the day before. The town was abuzz with excitement for an hour, when the news became stale. After all, stage hold-ups were not infrequent in that country, and Donna paid no particular heed to the commonplace occurrence until the return to San Pasqual two days later of the stage which had been robbed.

The express messenger told her the story when he came to the counter to pay for his rib steak and coffee. He had with him at the time a broad-brimmed gray sombrero, pinched to a peak, with a ragged hole close to the apex of the peak.

"I wanted to show you this, Miss Corblay" he said, as he exhibited this battered relic of the fray. "You do a pretty good trade in hats, and it's just possible you might have handled this sombrero in the line o' business. Ever recollect sellin' a hat to this fellow - his name's - lemme see - his name's Robert McGraw? It's written inside the sweat-band."

He drew the band back and displayed the name in indelible pencil.

"I lifted it off'n his head with my second shot" the messenger explained. "He was goin' like a streak an' it was snap-shootin', or he'd never 'a got away from me. As it was, I sent him on his way bareheaded, and a bareheaded man is easily traced in the desert. We sent word over to Johannesburg and Randsburg, an' somebody reported seein' a bareheaded man ridin' around the town after dark. We have him headed off at Barstow, and if he can't get through there, he'll have to head up into the Virginia Dale district - and he'll last about a day up there, unless he knows the waterholes. We'll get him, sooner or later, dead or alive. Remember sellin' anybody by that name a hat? It might help if you had an' could describe him. All I could see was his eyes. He was behind a wall when he stuck us up." "No" said Donna quietly, "I - " She paused. She could not articulate another word. Had the express messenger been watching her instead of the hat, he might have noticed her agitation. Her eyes were closed in sudden, violent pain, and she leaned forward heavily against the counter.

"Don't remember him, eh? Well, perhaps he wasn't from San Pasqual. But I thought I'd ask you, anyhow, because if he was from this town it was a good chance he bought this hat from you. Much obliged, just the same," and gathering up his change the express messenger departed to make room for Harley P. Hennage, who was standing next in line to pay his meal-check.

Donna opened her eyes and sighed - a little gasping sob, and turned her quivering face to the gambler. He smiled at her, striving pathetically to do it naturally. Instead, it was a grimace, and there was the look of a thousand devils In his baleful eyes. For an instant their glances met - and there were no secrets between them now. Donna moaned in her wretchedness; she placed her arm on the cash register and bowed her head on it, while the other little trembling hand stole across the counter, seeking for his and the comfort which the strong seem able to impart ito the weak by the mere sense of touch.

"Oh, Harley, Harley" she whispered brokenly, "the light's - gone out - of the world - and I can't - cry. I - I - I can't. I can - only - suffer."

Harley P.'s great freckled hand closed over hers and held it fast, while with his other hand he touched her beautiful head with paternal tenderness.

"Donnie" he said hoarsely. She did not look up. "I'm sorry you're not feelin' well, Donnie. You're all upset about somethin', an' you ought to go home an' take a good rest. You don't - you don't look well. I noticed it last night. You looked a mite peaked."

"Yes, yes" she whispered, clutching at this straw which he held out to her, "I'm ill. I want to go home - oh, Mr. Hennage, please - take me - home."

Mr. Hennage turned and beckoned to one of the waitresses whose duty it was, on Donna's days off, to take her place at the cash counter. As the waitress started to obey his summons, the gambler turned and spoke to Donna.

"Buck up and beat it. I can't take you home, an' neither can anybody else. You've got to make it alone. When you get to the Hat Ranch, send Sam Singer up to me. Remember, Donnie. Send Sam Singer up."

He turned again to the waitress. "You'd better take charge here" he said. "Miss Corblay's been took sick an' the pain's somethin' terrible. I've been a-tellin' her she ought to have Doc Taylor in to look at her. If I had the pain that girl's a-sufferin' right now I'd be in bed, that's what I would. I'll bet a stack o' blues she got this here potomaine poisonin'. Better run right along, Miss Donnie, before the pain gets worse, an' I'll see Doc Taylor an' tell him to bring you down some medicine or somethin'."

Donna replied in monosyllables to the excited queries of the waitress, pinned on her hat and left the eating-house as quickly as she could. She was dry-eyed, white-lipped, sunk in an abyss of misery; for there are agonies of grief and terror so profound that their very intensity dams the fount of tears, and it was thus with Donna. Harley P. accompanied her to the door of the eating-house, but he would go no further. He realized that Donna wanted to talk with him; in a vague way he gathered that she looked to him for some words of comfort in her terrible predicament. Not for worlds, however, would he be seen walking with her in public, thereby laying the foundation for "talk"; and under the circumstances he realized the danger to her, should he even be seen conversing with her from now on. She pleaded with him with her eyes, but he shook his head resolutely. He had heard the news. Inadvertently he had stumbled upon her secret, and she knew this. But she knew also that never by word or sign or deed would Harley P. Hennage indicate that he had heard it. It was like him to ascribe her agitation to illness, and as she turned her heavy footsteps toward the Hat Ranch the memory of that loving lie brought the laggard tears at last, and she wept aloud. In her agony she was conscious of a feeling of gratitude to the Almighty for His perfect workmanship in fashioning a man who was not one of the presuming kind.

It seemed to Donna that she must have wandered long in the border-lands of hell before eventually she reached the shelter of the adobe walls of the Hat Ranch. Soft Wind heard her sobbing and fumbling with the recalcitrant lock on the iron gate, and hurried toward her.

"My little one! My nestling!" she said in the Cahuilla tongue, and forthwith Donna collapsed in the old squaw's arms. It was the first time she had ever fainted.

When she recovered consciousness she found that she was lying fully dressed, on her bed, at the foot of which Soft Wind and Sam Singer were standing, gazing at her owlishly. She commenced to sob immediately, and Sam Singer pussy-footed out of the room and fled up town to lay the matter before Harley P. Hennage. For the second time there was a crisis at the Hat Ranch, and Sam yielded to his first impulse, which was to seek help where something told him help would never be withheld.

In the meantime, Harley P. Hennage had fled to the seclusion of his room in the eating-house hotel. The disclosure of the identity of the stage-robber had overwhelmed the gambler with anguish, and he wanted to be alone to think the terrible affair over calmly. In the language of his profession, the buck was clearly up to Mr. Hennage.

Twice during his eventful career the gambler had sat in poker games where an opponent had held the dead man's hand and paid the penalty. He recalled now the quick look of terror that had flitted across the face of each of these men when it came to the show-down and the pot was lost in the smoke; he endeavored to compare it with the sudden despair and suffering that came into Donna's eyes when the express messenger drew back the sweat-band of the outlaw's hat and showed her Bob McGraw's private brand of ownership.

"No," moaned Mr. Hennage, "there ain't no comparison. Them two tin-horns was frightened o' death, but poor little Donnie is plumb fearful o' life, an' there ain't a soul in the world can help her but me. She's got hers, just like her mother did, an' there ain't never goin' to be no joy in them eyes no more, unless I act, an' act lively."

He sat down on his bed and bowed his bald head in his trembling hands, for once more Harley P. Hennage was face to face with a great issue. He, too, was experiencing some of the agony of a grief that could find no outlet in tears - a three-year-old grief that could have no ending until the end should come for Harley P.

Presently he roused and looked at his watch. He was horrified to discover that he had just forty minutes left in which to arrange his affairs and leave San Pasqual.

He went to the window, parted the curtains cautiously and looked out. At the door of the post-office, a half a block down on the other side of the street, the express messenger, with the hat still in his hand, stood conversing with Miss Molly Pickett.

"You - miserable - old - mischief-maker" he muttered slowly, and with hate and emphasis in every word. "You're tellin' him to see me for information concernin' Bob McGraw, ain't you? You're tellin' him this road agent's a friend o' mine, because I called for a registered letter for him once, ain't you? An' now you're takin' him inside to show him the written order Bob McGraw give me for that registered letter, ain't you? You're quite a nice little old maid detective, ain't you, Miss Molly? You're tellin' him that I knew the man that saved Donnie Corblay, an' that *he* was a friend o' mine, too, because I led his roan horse up into the feed corral an' guaranteed the feed bill. An' everybody knows, or if they don't they soon will, that the initials 'R. McG.' was on that fool boy's saddle. All right, Miss Pickett! Let 'er flicker. Only them Wells Fargo detectives don't get to ask me no questions regardin' that girl's husband. Not a dog-gone question! If I stay in this town they'll subpeeny me an' make me testify under oath, an' then I'll perjure myself an' get caught at it, an' I'm too old a gambler to get caught bluffin' on no pair. No, indeed, folks, I can't afford it, so I'm just a-goin' to fold my tent like the Arab an' silently fade away."

Thus reasoned Mr. Hennage. Both by nature and professional training he was more adept in the science of deduction than most men, and while he had never seen Donna's marriage license he firmly believed that she had been married. He had looked for the publication of the license in the Bakersfield papers. Not having seen it, Mr. Hennage was not disturbed. He understood that Donna, planning to keep on at the eating-house, desired her marriage to remain a secret for the present, and Bob had doubtless arranged to have the record of the issuance of the license "buried." The fact that Friar Tuck had disappeared from the feed corral on the very night of Donna's return to San Pasqual was to Mr. Hennage prima facie evidence that Bob McGraw had returned with her. Donna had gone to the Hat Ranch while Bob had saddled and ridden north. At least, since he had come from the north, Mr. Hennage deduced that to the north he would return. Garlock lay a hard thirty-five miles from San Pasqual, and it seemed reasonable to presume that Bob had stopped there for water, rested until the stage came along and then robbed it.

However, there was one weak link in this apparently powerful chain of evidence. The stage driver and the express messenger both reported the bandit to be mounted on a bay mustang. At close quarters the horse had been, concealed behind the wall with the upper half of his face showing. Well, Bob McGraw's horse was a light roan - a very light roan, with almost bay ears and head, and at a distance, and in certain lights and in the excitement of the hold-up, he might very easily have been mistaken for a bay. Many a bay horse, when covered with alkali dust and dried sweat, has been mistaken for a roan.

In addition there was the evidence of the automatic pistol! Few men in that country carried automatics, for an automatic was a weapon too new in those days to be popular, and the residents of the Mojave still clung to tradition and a Colt's.45. The bandit had shown himself peculiarly expert in the use of his weapon, having shot the pipe out of the messenger's mouth, merely to impress that unimpressionable functionary. It would have been like Bob McGraw, who carried an automatic and was a dead shot, to show off a little!

However, an alibi might very easily discount all this circumstantial evidence, were it not for the fact that there could be no alibi for Bob McGraw, for beyond doubt he must have been in the neighborhood of Garlock that very day. Then there was the hat, with his name in it; also the report that one of the passengers who knew him had recognized the bandit as Bob McGraw.

"Alibi or no alibi, he'll get twenty years in San Quentin on that evidence" mourned Harley P. "Oh, Bob, you infernal young rip, if you was as hard up as all that, why didn't you come to me? Why didn't you trust old Harley P. Hennage with your worries! I'd 'a seen you through. But you wouldn't trust me - just went to work an' married that good girl, an' then pulled off a job o' road work to support her. Oh, Bob, you dog, you've broke her heart an' she'll go like her mother went."

He clenched his big fists and punched the air viciously, in unconscious exemplification of the chastisement he would mete to Bob McGraw when he met him again.

"It ain't often I make a mistake judgin' a man" he muttered piteously, "but I've sure been taken in on this feller. I thought he'd stand the acid - by God! I thought he'd stand it. An' at that there's heaps o' good in the boy! He must 'a been just desperate for money, an' the notion to rob the stage come on him all in a heap an' downed him before he knew. Great Grief! That misfortunate girl! He'll never come back, an' if they trace him to her she'll die o' shame. Whiskered bob-cats, I never thought o' that. She'll have to get out too!"

The gambler had a sudden thought. Donna could do two things. She could leave San Pasqual, or she could stand pat! If she said nothing, not a soul could befoul her by linking her name to that of a stage-robber, She *must* stand pat! There was but one channel through which the news that Bob McGraw had been harbored at the Hat Ranch could possibly filter. People might *think* what they pleased, but they could never *prove,* provided Doc Taylor remained discreet. Therefore it behooved Mr. Hennage to see Doc Taylor immediately. That possible leak must be plugged at once.

Three minutes later the gambler strolled into the drugstore.

"How" he saluted.

"Hello, Hennage."

"What's new?"

"Nothing much. What do you think about that hold-up at Garlock?"

"Pretty bold piece o' work, Doc. Do they know who did it?"

"Fellow named McGraw. And as near as I can make out, Hennage, it's the same fellow I attended that time down at the Hat Ranch."

"It is" Mr. Hennage agreed quietly. "At least, I believe it is. That's what I called to see you about, Doc. Have you said anything to anybody?"

"No - not yet. I wasn't quite certain, and I figured on talking it over with you before I gave Wells Fargo & Company the quiet tip to watch the Hat Ranch for their man."

"Good enough! But they'll be around asking you questions, Doc. Don't worry about that. They won't wait for you to come to them. Ah' when they come to you, Doc, you don't know nothin'. *Comprende?*"

"But McGraw robbed the stage - "

"He didn't kill nobody, Doc. He wasn't blood-thirsty. He shot the horse when he might have shot the messenger. Now, let's be sensible, Doc. Sometimes a feller can accomplish more in this world by keepin' his mouth shut than he can by tellin' every durned thing he knows. Now, as near as I can learn, this outlaw gets away with about four thousand dollars. If the passengers an' the express company get their money back, they'll be glad to let it go at that, an' I'll buy 'em a new padlock for the express box. This is the young feller's first job, Doc - I'm certain o' that. He ain't *bad* - an' besides, I've got a special interest in him. Now, listen here, Doc; I've got a pretty good idea where he's gone to hole up until the noise dies down, an' I'm goin' after him myself. I'll make him give up the swag an' send it back; then I'll get him out of the country an' let him start life all over again somewhere else. He's a young feller, Doc, an' it ain't right to kick him when he's down. He oughter be lifted up an' given a chance to make good."

Doc Taylor shook his head dubiously. He realized that Harley P.'s plan was best, and in his innermost soul he commended it as a proper Christian course. But he also remembered to have heard somewhere that godless men like Harley P. Hennage and the outlaw McGraw had a habit of being friendly and faithful to each other in just such emergencies - a sort of "honor among thieves" arrangement, and despite Mr. Hennage's kindly words, Doc Taylor doubted their sincerity. In fact, the whole thing was irregular, for even after the return of the stolen money the bandit would still owe a debt to society - and moreover, the worthy doctor was the joint possessor, with Harley P. Hennage, of an astounding secret, the disclosure of which would make him the hero of San Pasqual for a day at least.

"I can't agree to that, Hennage" he began soberly.

"It doesn't look right to me to let a stage-robber go scot-free - "

"Well, I tell you, Doc," drawled Mr. Hennage serenely, "it'd better look right to you, an' damned quick at that. You seem to think I'm here a-askin' a favor o' you. Not much. I never ask favors o' no man. I'm just as independent as a hog on ice; if I don't stand up I can set down. I run a square game myself an' I want a square game from the other fellow. Now, Doc, you just so much as say 'Boo' about this thing, an' by the Nine Gods o' War I'll kill you. D'ye understand, Doc? I'll kill you like I would a tarantula. An' when they come to ask you the name o' the man you 'tended at the Hat Ranch you tell 'em his name is - lemme see, now - yes, his name is Roland McGuire. That's a nice name, an' it corresponds to the initials on the saddle."

Doc Taylor looked into the gambler's hard face, which was thrust close to his. The mouth of the worst man in San Pasqual was drawn back in a half snarl that was almost coyote-like; his small deep-set eyes bespoke only too truly the firmness of purpose that lay behind their blazing menace. For fully thirty seconds those terrible eyes flamed, unblinking, on Doc Taylor; then Mr. Hennage spoke.

"Now, what is his name goin' to be, Doc?"

"Roland McGuire" said Doc Taylor, and swallowed his Adam's apple twice.

"Bright boy. Go to the head o' the class an' don't forget to remember to stick there."

CHAPTER XVI

Mr. Hennage turned slowly and walked out of the drug-store, for he had accomplished his mission. Once again, without recourse to violence, he had maintained his reputation as the worst man in San Pasqual, for his power lay, not in a clever bluff, but in his all-too-evident downright honesty of purpose. Had Doc Taylor presumed to fly in the face of Providence, after that warning, Mr. Hennage felt that the responsibility must very properly rest on the doctor, for the gambler would have killed him as surely as he had the strength to work his trigger finger.

"Well, *that's* over" he muttered as he returned to his room. "She's woman enough to cover the rest o' the trail herself now, poor girl, an' in about a week I'll pull the big sting that's hurtin' her most."

Hastily he packed a suit-case with his few simple belongings, for in his haste he was forced to abandon his old rawhide trunk that had accompanied him in his wanderings for twenty years. But one article did Mr. Hennage remove from his trunk. It was an old magazine. He opened it tenderly, satisfied himself that the faded old rose that lay between the leaves was still intact, and packed this treasure into the suit-case; then, while waiting for the north-bound train to whistle for San Pasqual, he sat down at a little table and wrote a note to Donna:

Dear Miss Donnie:

I am sending you a thousand by Sam Singer. You might need it. Am in trouble and must get out quick. Will stay away until things blow over. Hoping these few lines will find you feeling well, as they leave me at present, I am,

Respect. yrs.

H. P. HENNAGE.

P. S. I came to say good-by a little while ago and was sorry you wasn't feeling well.

This note Mr. Hennage sealed carefully in an envelope, together with a compact little roll of bills, just as the train whistled for San Pasqual. He seized his suit-case and hurried down stairs, and on the way down he met Sam Singer coming up.

"Give this to Miss Donna" said Mr. Hennage, and thrust the envelope into the Indian's hand. "Ain't got no time to talk to you, Sam. This is my busy day," and then, for the last time, he gave Sam Singer the inevitable half dollar and a cigar.

"Good-by, Sam" he called as he descended the stairs. "Be a good Injun till I see you again."

He went to the ticket window, purchased a ticket to San Francisco and climbed aboard the train. Two minutes later it pulled out. As it plunged into Tehachapi Pass, Mr. Hennage, standing on the platform of the rear car, glanced back across the desert at San Pasqual.

"Nothin' like mystery to keep that rotten little camp up on its toes" he muttered. "I'll just leave that mess to stew in its own juices for a while."

He went into the smoker and lit a cigar. His plans were well matured now and he was content; in this comfortable frame of mind he glanced idly around at his fellow-passengers.

Seated two seats in front of him and on the opposite side of the coach, Mr. Hennage observed a gray-haired man reading a newspaper. The gambler decided that there was something vaguely familiar about the back of this passenger's head, and on the pretense of going to the front of the car for a drink of water he contrived, on his way back to his seat, to catch a glimpse of the stranger's face. At the same instant the man glanced up from his paper and nodded to Mr. Hennage.

"How" said Harley P., and paused beside the other's seat. "Mr. T. Morgan Carey, if I ain't mistaken?"

"The same" replied Carey in his dry, precise tones. "And you are - Mr. - Mr. - Mr. Hammage."

"Hennage" corrected the gambler.

"I beg your pardon. Mr. Hennage. Quite so. Pray be seated, Mr. Hennage. You're the very man I wanted to see."

He moved over and made room for Mr. Hennage beside him. The gambler sat down and sighed.

"Hot, ain't it?" he remarked, rather inanely.

"Rather. By the way, Mr. Hennage, have you, by any chance, seen that young man for whom I was inquiring on the day I first had the pleasure of making your acquaintance? His name is McGraw - Robert McGraw. You will recollect that I left with you one of my cards, with the request that you give it to McGraw, should you meet him, and inform him that I desired to communicate with him."

"Yes" replied Mr. Hennage calmly. "I met him one day in San Pasqual an' gave him your card."

"You gave him my registered letter, also?"

So Carey had been talking with Miss Pickett again! Mr. Hennage nodded.

"Tell me, Mr. Hennage" purred Carey. "Why did the man, McGraw, send you to the post-office with an order for that registered letter?"

"Oh, he was in a little trouble at the time an' didn't care to show in public" lied Mr. Hennage glibly.

"I perceive. I believe you mentioned something about his reputation as a hard citizen when I first spoke to you about him."

"Tougher'n a bob-cat" Mr. Hennage assured him, for no earthly reason except a desire to be perverse and not contradict his former statements.

"Hu-u-m-m! I presume you know where Mr. McGraw may be found at present. Is he liable to communicate with you?"

Mr. Hennage was on guard. "Well, I ain't sayin' nothin'" he replied evasively. It was in his mind to discover, if possible, the details of the business which this man of vast emprise could have with a penniless desert rat like Bob McGraw.

"Is this McGraw a friend of yours, Mr. Hennage?" pursued Carey.

"Well," the gambler fenced, "I've loaned him money."

"Ever get it back?" Carey smiled a thin sword-fish smile.

"Certainly. Why do you ask?"

"You consider McGraw honest?"

"Sure shot - between friends. Yes."

Carey turned his head slowly and gazed at the gambler in mean triumph. "Well, I'm sorry I can't agree with you" he said. "Your friend McGraw robbed me of fifteen hundred dollars on the San Pasqual-Keeler stage a few days ago."

The fact that Carey had been a victim of Bob McGraw's felonious activities was news to Mr. Hennage, but he would not permit Carey to suspect it.

"Yes" he replied calmly, "I heard he'd taken to road work."

"He held up the stage" Carey repeated, in the flat tone

of finality which the foreman of a jury might have employed when repeating the verbal formula: "We, the jury, find the defendant guilty, as charged."

"Then you recognized McGraw" ventured the gambler.

"The moment I saw him."

"That's funny" echoed Harley P. "I gathered from what you told me in San Pasqual that you two'd never met up, an' they tell me that durin' the hold-up McGraw was behind a wall an' wearin' a mask. You're sure some recognizer, Mr. Carey."

"We had met prior to the hold-up and subsequent to my conversation with you in San Pasqual."

"Still the bet goes as she lays" repeated Mr. Hennage. "For a near-sighted gent you're sure some recognizer."

"I recognized his voice."

Mr. Hennage was silent for a minute. Carey continued.

"If the sheriff gets him, I'll see to it that McGraw doesn't rob another stage for some time to come."

Still Mr. Hennage was silent. He was digesting the conversation, and this much he gathered:

There was some mysterious business afoot wherein Carey and Bob McGraw were jointly interested, and they had met and quarreled over it, as evidenced by T. Morgan Carey's all too apparent animosity. Mr. Hennage had a haunting suspicion that Carey's animus did not arise from the fact that McGraw had robbed him of fifteen hundred dollars. He felt that there was a deeper, more vital reason than that. All of his days Mr. Hennage had lived close to the primitive; he was a shrewd judge of human impulses and it had been his experience that men quarrel over two things - women and money. The possible hypothesis of a woman, in the suspected quarrel between Bob McGraw and T. Morgan Carey, Harley P. dismissed as untenable. Remained then, only money - and Bob McGraw had no money. His finances were at so low an ebb as to be beneath the notice of such a palpable commercial wolf as T. Morgan Carey; consequently, and in the final analysis, Mr. Hennage concluded that Bob McGraw possessed something which Carey coveted. Whether his spiteful attitude toward the unfortunate Bob arose from this, or the loss of the fifteen hundred dollars, Mr. Hennage now purposed discovering. He leaned toward Carey confidentially and lowered his voice.

"Say, looky-here, Mr. Carey. This boy, McGraw, is a friend o' mine. A little wild? Yes. But what young feller now-a-days ain't? I know he's robbed you o' fifteen hundred dollars, an' I'm sorry for that, but I can fix you up all right. I'm goin' to get into communication with our young friend before long, if he ain't beefed by the sheriff first, or captured alive - but it's ten to one they get him, an' he'll be brought to trial. Well, now, here's what I'm drivin' at. If the boy's nabbed, an' you'll agree to sorter, as the feller says, tangle the woof o' memory an' refuse to swear that you recognize the said defendant as the hereinbefore mentioned stage-robber, I'll see that you get your fifteen hundred back. This is his first serious job, Mr. Carey, an' I wish you'd go easy on him. He ain't really bad."

T. Morgan Carey pounded the back of the seat in front of him.

"Not for fifty thousand dollars" he said. "The suggestion is preposterous. The man is a menace to society and it is my duty to testify against him if he is apprehended."

"Then it ain't a question with you o' money back an' no questions asked?"

Carey shook his head emphatically. "It's principle" he said.

Mr. Hennage appeared chopfallen. In reality he was amused. Never before had Mr. Hennage met a man to whom the abandonment of such "principle" would have been impossible under the terms suggested. Clearly there was something wrong here. Mr. Hennage had met men to whom vengeance would have been cheap at fifty thousand, but principle - the gambler shook his head. He had lived long enough to learn that principle is a marketable commodity, and he was not deceived in T. Morgan Carey's attitude of civic righteousness.

"Well, it's too bad you won't listen to reason, Mr. Carey" he said regretfully. "I thought you might be willin' to go easy on the young feller. It's too durned bad," and he rose abruptly and returned to his own seat. Carey resumed the perusal of his newspaper. He was not anxious to continue the conversation, and he believed he had Mr. Hennage intimidated, and for reasons of his own he was desirous of permitting the gambler to think matters over.

Mr. Hennage proceeded at once to think matters over. "Now, I wonder what that kid-glove crook has against the boy!" he mused. "I can see right off that Bob has an ace coppered, an' this sweet-scented burglar would like to see Bob tucked away in the calaboose while he goes huntin' for the ace. What in Sam Hill can them two fellers have between them? Here's Bob, just a plain young desert rat, a-dreamin' an' a-romancin' over the country, while this Carey is a solid citizen. He's president o' the Inyo Land & Irrigation Company, according to his card. Bob ain't got no money - Carey has a carload of it. Bob ain't got no water - Carey's in the irrigation business. Bob ain't got no real estate, 'ceptin' what he accumulates on his person wanderin' around, and Carey's got land - "

Mr. Hennage emitted a low soft whistle through the slit between two of his gold teeth.

Land! That was it. Land! And government land at that!

Mr. Hennage suddenly recollected the letter which Bob McGraw had written him from Sacramento, requesting a loan of fifty dollars, and enclosing, without comment, a typewritten contract form for the acquisition of state lieu lands. Mr. Hennage had read this contract at the time of its receipt, little thinking that Bob was wholly unconscious of the fact that he had enclosed it with his letter. Mr. Hennage had marveled at the time that Bob should have made no reference to it in his letter.

He took Bob's letter from his breast pocket now, and carefully perused once more this typewritten contract form. To him it conveyed little information, save that Bob had been endeavoring to induce Tom, Dick and

Harry to acquire state lieu lands by engaging him as their attorney, and without the disagreeable necessity putting up any money. A very queer proceeding, concluded Mr. Hennage, in view of the fact that Bob apprehended litigation in order to establish the rights of his clients. At the first reading of this document two weeks previous, the gambler had merely looked upon it as evidence of another of Bob McGraw's harebrained schemes for acquiring a quick fortune - a scheme founded on optimism and predestined to failure; but in the light of recent events the meager information gleaned from the contract form had now a deeper, a more significant meaning.

Here was a conundrum. Carey (according to his card, at any rate) had the water, while Bob McGraw (according to this contract form) was endeavoring to acquire the land. Both were operating in Owens valley. Mr. Hennage smiled. No wonder they had quarreled, for without the land, of what use was the water to Carey? and without the water, of what value could the land be to Bob McGraw?

"I wouldn't give a white chip for a hull county o' such land" mused the gambler, "unless I could set in the game with the chap that had the water, an' Carey bein' a human hog, it stands to reason Bob's a chump to tie up with Him, unless - unless - *he's got water of his own!*"

Mr. Hennage slapped his fat thigh. "By Jupiter," he murmured, "he's got the water! He must have it. He might be fool enough to hold up a stage, but he ain't fool enough to face a lawsuit, without a dollar in the world, tryin' to make people take up land so he can sell 'em water for irrigation, unless he has the water. The boy ain't plumb crazy by no means. *That's the ace he's got coppered!* He's got the water, and if Carey can put him across for that hold-up job, who's to protect the boy's bet? Not a soul, unless it's me, an' I'm only shootin' at the moon. Bob ain't the man to put up a fight for worthless land, an' besides, wasn't Donnie askin' me a lot o' questions about water an' water rights, an' showin' a whole lot of interest, now that I come to think on't? By the Nine Gods o' War! I smell a rat as big as a kangaroo. Bob's been buttin' in on Carey's game; Carey's been tryin' to buy him out, but Bob has Carey on the floor with his shoulders touchin', so he won't sell an' he won't consolidate. If she don't 'tack up that-a-way, I'm an Injun. Carey wouldn't compromise with me an' take back his fifteen hundred. Why! There's a reason. He'd sooner see young Bob in the penitentiary because it'd mean more money to him. He wants Bob out o' the way, so he won't be on hand to draw cards, an' then this Carey person 'll just reach out his soft little mitt and rake in the jack-pot. All right, T. Morgan Carey! Bob's out of it, but even if he is a crook I'll string a bet with him, for Donnie's sake, an' I'll deal you a brace game an' you'll never know that the deck's been sanded."

And having thus, to his entire satisfaction, solved the mystery of the hitherto unaccountable actions of T. Morgan Carey and Bob McGraw, Mr. Hennage dismissed the matter from his mind, lit a fresh cigar and permitted the peanut butcher to inveigle him into a friendly little game of whist with three traveling salesmen.

Harley P. Hennage had purchased a ticket for San Francisco, but when the train reached Bakersfield and he observed T. Morgan Carey leaving the car, bag in hand, the gambler suddenly decided that he, also, would honor Bakersfield with his presence. He excused himself, hastily quitted his innocent game of whist, seized his suit-case and rode up town in the same hotel bus with Carey.

Carey registered first, sent his bag and overcoat up to his room, and then walked over to the telegraph desk. Harley P. Hennage, standing in line to register, noticed that Carey had filed a telegram; consequently, when he had registered and T. Morgan Carey had disappeared into the barber shop, Mr. Hennage, follwing up a strong winning "hunch," walked over to the telegraph desk and laid a ten-dollar piece on the railing.

"I'm goin' to open a book, young lady" he announced. "I'm willin' to bet ten dollars that the respectable old party that just give you a telegram signed Carey is wirin' about a friend o' mine. If I don't guess right, you get the ten bucks. Fair?"

The young lady operator dimpled and admitted that it was eminently fair. She had no illusions (although her position required her to have them) regarding the sacredness of privacy in a telegram, and Mr. Hennage had not as yet asked her to violate a confidence.

"I'm a-bettin' ten bucks" repeated Mr. Hennage, "that the name McGraw occurs in that telegram."

"You win" the operator replied. "How did you guess it?"

"I was born with a veil" he replied. "I got the gift o' second sight, an' I'm just a-tryin' it out. The ten is yours for a copy o' that telegram."

The operator seized a scratch-pad, copied the telegram and cautiously "slipped" it to Mr. Hennage, who as cautiously "slipped" her the ten-dollar bill. He was rewarded for his prodigality by the following:

R. P. McKeon, Mills Building, Sacramento, Calif.

Advise our friend approve McGraw applications at once. Letter follows.

CAREY.

The gambler smiled his thanks and walked across the hotel lobby to the public-telephone operator. On this young lady's desk he laid a five-dollar bill.

"I want you to call up Sacramento on the long distance an' ask the central there to find out who Mr. R. P. McKeon is an' what he does for a livin'."

"We have copies of the telephone directories of the principal cities in the state" came the quick reply. "It makes it easier if we ask for the number direct."

"Five bucks for a look in the book" announced Mr. Hennage. He got the book, with the information that he might have his look for nothing, but being a generous soul he declined. He ascertained that R. P. McKeon was an attorney-at-law.

"As the feller says, I believe I see the light" murmured the gambler. "Now please get me the agent for Wells Fargo & Company at San Pasqual."

When the operator informed him that San Pasqual was on the line, Mr. Hennage went into a sound-proof

Peter B. Kyne

booth and told a lie. He informed the agent at San Pasqual that he was the Bakersfield representative of the Associated Press, and demanded the latest information regarding the hunt for the Garlock bandit. He was informed that there was no news.

"I gotta get some news" he bellowed into the receiver. "What's the exact loss o' your company?"

"Twenty-one hundred eighty-three forty."

"Serves you right. How about the passengers? Got their names an' addresses an' the amounts they lost?"

"No, but the express messenger has and he's in town. Hold the line a minute and I'll go call him."

So Mr. Hennage waited. Five minutes later, when he hung up, he had secured the information and made careful note of it, after which he sought an arm-chair in the hotel window, planted his feet on the window sill and gave himself up to reflection. He was occupied thus when T. Morgan Carey came out of the barber shop, and seeing Mr. Hennage, came over and sat down beside him. Mr. Hennage decided that the financier must have something on his mind, and he was not wrong.

"Mr. Hennage" said Carey unctuously, "I have been thinking over the proposition which you made me coming up from San Pasqual this afternoon, and if you still feel inclined to act as intermediary in this unfortunate affair, I will submit a proposition. Mr. McGraw may retain the fifteen hundred dollars which he stole from me, and I will agree to give him, say, five thousand more, through you, for a relinquishment to me of a water right which he has filed upon in the Sierra overlooking Owens valley. There is also another matter of which McGraw has cognizance, and he must agree to drop that too. His money will be delivered to you, for delivery to him. In return, I will agree to be absent when his case comes to trial, should he be captured. I will agree not to recognize him."

"But suppose he refuses this programme, Mr. Carey. Then what?"

"In that event, my dear Mr. Hennage" replied Carey coldly, "you may tell him from me that I will spend a hundred thousand dollars to run him down. I will have this state combed by Pinkertons, and when I land Mr. Robert McGraw I'll land him high and dry and it will be too late for him to make *me* a proposition then. I have the power and the money necessary to get him - and I know how."

"Well, what a long tail our cat's developing!" drawled Mr. Hennage. "Carey, you give me a pain where I never knew it to ache me before. Now, you just sit still while I submit *you* a little proposition. An' remember I ain't pleadin' with you to accept it. No, indeed. I'm just a-orderin' you to. Bob McGraw can't prove that he didn't rob that stage, but a child could make a monkey out o' you on the witness stand. Talked to him once an' recognized his voice, eh? Pooh! Met him once an' recognized him masked. Rats! I happen to know, Carey, that you didn't recognize the stage robber *until after the messenger returned to the stage with his hat an' showed you his name on the sweat-band.* Then you remembered, because the wish was father to the thought, an' you wanted the boy in jail. Now, looky here. I happen to be mighty heavily interested in this here water right you're plannin' to blackmail McGraw out of. But you ain't got nothin' on me, an' you can't buy me out for a million dollars, an' you ain't got money enough - there ain't money enough in the world - to make me double-cross Bob McGraw just because he's a outlaw from justice."

He tapped Carey on the knee with his fat forefinger. "I'm playin' look-out on this game, an' it's hands off for you. You can't make a bet. You don't get that water right an' you won't get the land; if Bob McGraw ain't on hand to sue for his rights, by the Nine Gods o' War, I'll sue for him, an' I'll put up the money, an' I'll match you an' your gang for your shoe-strings, and you're whipped to a frazzle, an' get that into your head - understand? You're figurin' now on gettin' them applications approved, eh? Well, you just cut it out. If them applications are approved before I'm ready to have 'em approved, you know what I'll do to you, Carey. I'll cut your heart out. Don't you figure for a minute that there ain't somebody protectin' that boy's bet. You scatter his chips an' see what happens to you. Understand? You try upsettin' the Hennage apple-cart one o' these bright days, an' there'll be a rush order for a new tombstone. The motto o' the Hennage family has allers been 'Hands Off Or Take The Consequences.' Of course, if you insist, you can go to it with your private detectives, but you won't get far. You're up against a double-jointed play, Carey. Look out for snags."

T. Morgan Carey stared hard at Harley P. Hennage while the worst man in San Pasqual was delivering his ultimatum. He continued to stare when Mr. Hennage had finished, smiling, for to Carey that golden smile was more deadly than a scowl. Carey knew too well the kind of eyes that were gazing into his; they were the eyes of an honest man, and by the cut of Mr. Hennage's jaw Carey knew that here was a man who would "stay put."

Mr. Hennage laughed boldly, as he realized on what a slender foundation his gigantic bluff was resting, and what an impression his words had made upon Carey. The latter pulled himself together and favored the gambler with a wintry grin.

"Kinder game little pup, after all" thought Mr. Hennage. "He thinks he's licked, but he's goin' to bluff it out to the finish. I believe if this feller was on the level I'd like him. He's no slouch at whatever he tackles, you bet."

"Very well, Mr. Hennage" said Carey quietly, "I think I understand you. See that you understand me, in order that we may both understand each other. You've declared war, on behalf of your felon of a partner. Very well, I accept. It's war."

In turn, T. Morgan Carey tapped Mr. Hennage on the knee with *his* forefinger.

"I'll keep my hands off your business in the state land office. Your applications can pass through for approval, for all I care, but I'll enter a contest, alleging fraud, against you in the General Land Office at Washington, and I'll hold you up for ten years in a mass of red tape. Hennage, you and McGraw have brains, I'll admit, but you can't play my game and beat me at it. If I'm not in on this melon-cutting, I'll spend a million dollars to delay the banquet. Let me tell *you* something. The day will come when you'll come scraping your feet at my office door, begging for a compromise. I'm a business man, and I tell you before you're half through with this fight, you'll come to the conclusion that half a loaf is better than none at all - particularly in the matter of extra large loaves. You'll come to me and compromise."

"Gosh, I'm dry with argument" taunted Mr. Hennage. "Now that we understand each other, let's be friends. We *can* be friends out o' business hours, can't we, Carey? Come an' have a drink."

"With all my heart" Carey retorted, with genuine pleasure. "I must confess to a liking for you, Mr. Hennage. I could kill you and then weep at your funeral, for upon my word you are the most amusing and philosophical opponent I have ever met. I really have hopes that ultimately you will listen to reason."

"There is no hope" said Mr. Hennage, as he took T. Morgan Carey by the arm - almost, as Mrs. Dan Pennycook would have expressed it, "friendly like," and escorted him to the hotel bar. Here Mr. Hennage produced a thousand-dollar bill from his vest pocket (he had carried that bill for ten years and always used it as a flash during his peregrinations outside San Pasqual) and calmly laid it on the bar.

"Wine" he said. Mr. Hennage's order, when doing the handsome thing, was always "wine." The barkeeper set out a pint of champagne and filled both glasses. The gambler raised his to the light, eyed it critically and then flashed his three gold teeth at T. Morgan Carey.

"Here's damnation to you, Mr. Carey" he said. "May you live unhappily and die in jail."

"The sentiment, my dear Hennage, is entirely reciprocal" Carey flashed back at him. They drank, gazing at each other over the rims of their glasses.

Despite the knock-out which Harley P. had given him, T. Morgan Carey was enjoying the gambler's society. Mr. Hennage was a new note in life. Carey had never met his kind before, and he was irresistibly attracted toward the man from San Pasqual.

"Upon my word, Hennage" he said, as he set down his glass, "if your liquor could only be metamorphosed into prussic acid, I'd gladly shoulder your funeral expenses. You're a thorn in my side."

"We understand each other, Carey. Any time you're meditatin' suicide drop around to San Pasqual an' I'll buy you a pistol."

Carey laughed long and loud. "Hennage" he said, "do you know I think I should grow to like you? By George, I think I should. If you should ever come to Los Angeles, look me up," and he presented the gambler with his card.

Mr. Hennage smiled, tore the card into little bits and dropped them to the floor.

"Do I look like a tin-horn?" he queried.

A momentary frown crossed Carey's face; then he, too, smiled. He was finding it hard to take offense at the gambler's bluntness.

"I think you're a dead-game sport, Hennage" he said, and there was no doubt that he meant it. "But I shall not despair. You have brains. Some day, I feel assured, we shall sit down together like sensible men and do business."

"And in the meantime" replied Mr. Hennage, raising an admonitory forefinger, "our motto is 'Keep off the grass.'"

"Oh, I won't walk on your darned old grass" Carey retorted. "I'll just step between it."

They shook hands in friendly fashion, and Carey hurried away. Mr. Hennage stared after him.

"Sassy as a badger" he murmured. "I can't bluff that *hombre*. He'll go as far as he can, an' be ready to jump in the first chance he sees. Bob, my boy, you're up against it."

Mr. Hennage's business in Bakersfield was now completed. He felt certain that a battle between Bob McGraw and T. Morgan Carey was inevitable, should Bob decide to remain in the background and send an ally out to fight for him. However, despite his horror of Bob's crime, the gambler unconsciously extended him his sympathy, and if there was to be a battle, either its commencement had been delayed or its duration prolonged by the little bluff which he had just worked on T. Morgan Carey, and that was all Mr. Hennage was striving for.

"I must find Bob" mused the gambler, "an' I must have time to find him before these people euchre him out o' that valuable water right o' his. An' when I find that young man, I'll bet six-bits he sells that water right to me; then I'll sell it to my friend Carey an' the proceeds o' that sale 'll go to Donnie. A woman can get along without a man, if she's got the price to get along on."

The gambler's line of reasoning was a wise one. In the chain of powerful circumstantial evidence that linked Donna Corblay to Bob McGraw, Mr. Hennage was the most powerful link, and if he was to remove himself beyond the jurisdiction of a subpoena from the Superior Court of Kern county, and thus evade answering embarrassing questions when Bob should be brought to trial (as the gambler felt certain he would be), it behooved Mr. Hennage to travel far and fast.

He went down to the station and purchased a ticket for Goldfield, Nevada. Goldfield was in the zenith of her glory about that time and Harley P. felt certain of a plethora of easy money in any booming mining camp. Indeed, it behooved him to seek pastures where the grass was long and green, for in the removal from Donna's heart of what he termed "the big sting," Harley P. planned to play havoc with his bank-roll.

He proceeded about this delicate task as befits one who has a horror of appearing presumptuous. A week after his arrival in Goldfield he rented a typewriter for a day, took it to his room in the Goldfield hotel and battled manfully with it for several hours. After much toil he evolved the following form letter:

Dear Friend:

A short time ago I robbed the San Pasqual stage at Garlock. I took --- dollars of your money, which I return to you now; with many thanks, for the reason that I don't need it no more and am sorry I took it.

I notice by the papers that they found my hat with my name in it, which serves me right. I did not have no business doing that job in the first place. It was my first and it will be my last. I am going to start fresh again and hope you won't bear me no grudge for what I done.

Trusting that the same has not caused you any inconvenience, and with best wishes I am

Respectfully,

ROBERT MCGRAW.

In the blank space left for the purpose Mr. Hennage inserted in lead-pencil the figures representing the exact amount of coin which he had been informed by the express agent had been taken from each passenger. Next he inserted the exact amount in paper money, together with his letters, in envelopes which he also addressed on the typewriter, stamped them and walked down to the post-office.

"Now, that fixes everything up lovely" he soliloquized, as he watched the envelopes disappear down the main chute. "Wells Fargo & Co. get theirs back, so they'll pull off their detective force an' withdraw the reward; every passenger gets his back, an' if he's called to testify it's a cinch he'll ask the judge to be merciful on the defendant, because he made restitution an' showed sorrer for what he went an' done. Everybody gets fixed up except T. Morgan Carey, an' I work too dog-gone hard for my money to throw it away on *him.* When folks find Bob has sent back the money he stole he won't be anything like the evil cuss he is now an' the whole thing 'll simmer down to a big joke. When that poor broken-hearted little wife o' his hears about it she'll think it ain't so bad after all. She'll figure that they can go somewhere else an' live it down an' that'll ease the ache a heap. Suppose she does meet some o' them San Pasqual cattle in the years to come? What's the odds? Nobody in San Pasqual knows him or ever seen him, 'ceptin' Doc Taylor - an' what's in a name? Nothin'. There's hundreds o' McGraws in California right now, an' more arrivin' on every train."

Thus reasoned the artful Harley P. When his task was completed he stood outside the door of the post-office whimsically surveying the ruin of his fortune. Less than two thousand dollars was all he had to show for a life-time of endeavor, and one thousand of that was contained in a single bill and was Mr. Hennage's pocket-piece. He must never change that bill. It was his little nest-egg against a rainy day, and hereafter he would have to carry it where it could not readily be reached when under the spell of sudden temptation.

He returned to his room, wrapped the bill into a compact little wad and tucked it far into the toe of one of his congress gaiters.

"It's a blessin'" he muttered plaintively, as he replaced his shoe, "that the lives us gamblers leads generally tends to choke off our wind around the fifty-mark at the latest. I'm forty-five an' here in the mere shank o' old age, after runnin' my own game for twenty years, I got to go to work for somebody else."

Peter B. Kyne

CHAPTER XVII

It is one of the compensating laws of existence that the crisis of human despair and grief is reached on the instant that the reason for it becomes apparent; thereafter it occupies itself for a season in the gradual process of wearing itself out. Time is the great healer of human woe, and if in the darkness of despair one tiny ray of hope can filter through, an automatic rebound to the normal conditions of life quickly follows. The death of a loved one would not be endurable, were it not that Hope dares to reach beyond the grave.

For three days following her discovery of Bob McGraw's name written beneath the sweat-band of the outlaw's hat, Donna Corblay lay on her bed at the Hat Ranch, battling with herself in an effort to refrain from thinking the terrible thoughts that persisted in obtruding themselves upon her tortured brain. For three days, and the greater portion of two nights, she had cried aloud to the four dumb walls of the Hat Ranch:

"He didn't do it. He couldn't do it. My Bob couldn't do such a thing. It's some terrible mistake. Oh, my husband! My dear, thoughtless, impulsive husband! Oh, Bob! Bob! Come back and face them and tell them you didn't do it. Only tell me, and I'll believe you and stick by you through everything."

And then the horrible thought that he was guilty; that even now he was being hunted, hatless, hungry, weary and thirsty - a pariah with every honest man's hand raised against him - reminded her that the limit of her wretchedness lay, not in the fact that her faith in him had been shattered, but in the more appalling consciousness that he would not come back to her! Wild herald of woe and death, he had flitted into her life - as carelessly as he came he had departed, and she knew he would not come back.

Yes, Bob was too shrewd a man not to realize that in abandoning his hat he had left behind him the evidence that must send him to the penitentiary should he ever return to his old haunts in Inyo and Mono counties. He loved his liberty too well to sacrifice it, and he knew her code. It did not seem possible to Donna that he would have the audacity to face her again; so, man-like, he would not try.

And then she would think of him as she had seen him that first night, leaning on Friar Tuck's neck and gazing at her in the dim ghostly light of a green switch-lantern - telling her with his eyes that he loved her. She recalled his little mocking inscrutable smile, the manhood that had won her to him when first they met, and against all this she remembered that she had presented him with the hat which the express messenger had showed her - she had seen him write his name in indelible pencil under the leathern sweat-band!

She knew he had ridden north from San Pasqual the night before the hold-up - and thirty-five miles was as much as one small tough horse could do in the desert between the hour at which Bob had left her and his presumable arrival at Garlock, where he lay in wait for the stage. The automatic gun, the hat, the khaki clothing, the blue bandanna handkerchief which the bandit had used for a mask, the fact that he was mounted - all had pointed to her husband as the bandit. But the description of the horse was at variance with the facts, and moreover - Donna thought of this on the third day - where had Bob gotten that rifle with which he killed the express messenger's horse?

He had no rifle when he entered San Pasqual that first night, and he had had none when he left. The hardware store always closed at eight o'clock, and it had been ten o'clock when Bob left the Hat Ranch - so he could not have purchased a rifle in San Pasqual. He could not have gotten it in the desert between San Pasqual and Garlock, for in the desert men do not sell their guns, and if Bob had taken the gun by force from some lone prospector, news of his act would have drifted into San Pasqual next day.

It was then that Donna ceased sobbing and commenced to think, for even if her head inclined her to weigh the evidence and render a verdict, her heart was too loyal to accept it. The memory of Bob McGraw was always with her - his humorous brown eyes, the swing to his big body as he walked beside her, big gentleness, his unfailing courtesy, his almost bombastic belief in himself - no, it was not possible that he could be a hypocrite. That perverse streak in him, the heritage of his Irish forebears, would not have permitted him to run from the messenger. The man with courage enough to turn outlaw and rob a stage had courage enough to kill his man, and Bob McGraw would have fought it out in the open, He would never have taken to the shelter of a sand-dune and fired from ambush. *Bob McGraw, having brains, would have killed the messenger and gone back for his hat!* He was too cunning a frontiersman to leave a trail like that behind him and it was no part of his nature to do a half-way job. Still, the man who had robbed that stage had had no hobbles on his courage. Why, if he - he must have had a reason for not caring to recover that hat - When the desert-bred think, they think quickly; their conclusions are logical. They always search for the reason. The man whose desperate courage had been equal to that robbery - who had accomplished his task with the calm ease and urbanity which proclaimed him a finished product of his profession, should have argued the question with the messenger at greater length! *He should have disputed with him possession of the hat,* for in the desert a hat is more than a hat. It is a matter of life and death, and when the outlaw had abandoned his hat it must have been because he knew where he could secure another before day should dawn and find him bareheaded in the open. Had Bob been the robber he would have remembered that his name was in the hat, and rescued it, even at the price of the express messenger's life, for self-preservation is ever the first law of nature. On the other hand, if the bandit had known that the name was in the hat -

The mistress of the Hat Ranch rose from her bed, while a wild hope beat in her breast and beamed in her tear-dimmed eyes. She went into the room where she kept her stock of hats and began a careful examination of each hat. Nearly all bore some insignia of ownership. Derby hats invariably carried the owner's initials in fancy gilt letters pasted inside the crown, while others had the initials neatly punched in the sweat-band by a perforating machine. Half a dozen hats, apparently unbranded, had initials or names in full written in indelible pencil inside their sweat-bands.

Donna, considered an authority on male headgear, was for the first time learning something of the habits of men - the too frequent necessity for quickly identifying one's hat from a row of similar hats from the hat-hooks in crowded restaurants. Outwardly the hats of all mankind resemble each other, and for the first time Donna realized that it was the habit of men to mark them. She pondered.

"Now, here is a hat bearing the name of James Purdy. Suppose I should sell this hat to Dan Pennycook (unconsciously she mentioned Mr. Pennycook, who dared not buy a hat from her) and he should hold up the stage and have the hat shot off his head. The express messenger who picked it up would go looking for a man named James Purdy. Perhaps - "

Donna sat down and commenced to laugh hysterically. She had just remembered that Bob McGraw had lost a hat the night he came to San Pasqual!

Donna ceased laughing presently and commenced to cry again - with bitterness and shame at the thought of her disloyalty to her husband. Why, she hadn't sold a hat like Bob's for a year. He had lost his hat the night he saved her from the attack of the hoboes, and somebody had picked it up. She remembered Bob's complaint at the loss of his hat, because it was new and had cost him twenty dollars! Some one in San Pasqual had found it, realized its value and decided to keep it. It followed, then, that the man who had found that hat the night Bob lost it had held up the stage at Garlock.

And knowing of the name under the sweat-band (for evidently it was Bob's habit to brand all of his hats thus) and realizing that the finding of the hat would divert suspicion from him, the outlaw had abandoned the hat without a fight!

As Harley P. Hennage would have put it, the entire situation was now as clear as mud!

"And to think that I even suspected him for a moment!" Donna wailed. "Oh, Bob, what will you think of me! I'm a bad, worthless, disloyal wife. Oh, Bob, I'm so sorry and ashamed!"

She was, indeed. But sorrow and shame under such circumstances may exist, at the outset, for about ten minutes. The resurgent wave of joy which her discovery induced quickly routed the last vestige of her distress, and womanlike her first impulse, as a wife, was to wreak summary vengeance on the man who had asserted that her husband had robbed the stage! The idea! She would ascertain the name of this passenger who declared that he had recognized the bandit as Bob McGraw, and force him to make a public apology -

No, she would not do that. To do so would be to presume that her Bob was not, like Caesar's wife, above suspicion, and besides, it would spoil Harley P.'s little joke on San Pasqual. And there was really no danger of Bob's arrest. The sheriff's posse was trailing the other man out across the San Bernardino desert, while Bob, serenely unconscious of the furor created by the finding of his lost hat, was trudging through the range, miles to the north, headed east from Coso Springs with his two burros, circling across country to the Colorado desert and prospecting as he went. Her defense of him when he needed none would merely serve to invite the query: "Why are you so interested in him!" and until the day of Bob's return, she did not wish to answer "Because he is my husband."

No, it would be far better to sit calmly by and enjoy the industry of the man-hunters; then, when Bob returned, he would defend himself in his own vigorous fashion, much to the chagrin of his accusers and the consequent delight of Harley P. Hennage.

Thinking of Mr. Hennage reminded her that he had sent a note by Sam Singer. In her distress she had forgotten about it until now; so, after bathing her eyes, she opened the envelope and acquainted herself with its remarkable contents.

Poor old Harley P.! She read the distress between the lines of that kindly lie that he was in trouble and had to get out of San Pasqual - and as she fingered the little roll of bills she discovered no paradox in Harley P.'s hard face and still harder reputation and the oft-repeated biblical quotation that God makes man to His own image and likeness.

A thousand dollars! How well she knew why he had sent it! He feared that she, like him, would have to leave San Pasqual to avoid answering questions, and fearing that she was but indifferently equipped to face the world, he had refrained from asking questions. Instead he had equipped her, and in his unassuming way had departed without waiting for her thanks or leaving an address - infallible evidence that he desired neither her gratitude nor the return of the money.

"Poor fellow!" she murmured. "How terrible he'll feel

when he discovers it's all a mistake. He'll be ashamed to speak to me. Still, why should he feel chagrined at all? He hasn't said a word."

Foxy Mr. Hennage! It was quite true. He hadn't said a word! Ah, money talks; despite his precautions, Harley P.'s thousand dollars were very eloquent.

The next day Donna took up her life where it had left off. She had scarcely cached Harley P.'s thousand dollars in her private compartment in the eating-house safe when the irrepressible Miss Molly Pickett dropped in to express her sympathy at Donna's three-day illness, casually mentioned the stage robbery, the name in the hat and the sudden exit from San Pasqual of Harley P. Hennage. Incidentally she mentioned the fact that Mr. Hennage had once presented her with an order for a registered letter for a man by the name of Robert McGraw, and taking into consideration this fact and the further fact that birds of a feather always flock together, Miss Pickett opined that the hold-up man was doubtless a bosom friend of Mr. Hennage.

A hearty dinner the evening before, and twelve hours of uninterrupted slumber, had driven from Donna's face every trace of her three days of purgatory. She was alert, smiling and happy; and able to cross swords with Miss Pickett with something more than a gossamer hope of foiling her. She discussed the affair so calmly and with such apparent interest that Miss Pickett was completely mystified, and in a last desperate effort to satiate her curiosity she cast aside all pretense and came boldly into the open.

"Folks do say, Donna, that the man who was shot saving you from those tramps and was nursed at the

Hat Ranch is the same man that held up the stage."

"Indeed! Miss Pickett, folks don't know what they are talking about. Have you asked Doctor Taylor?"

Miss Pickett commenced to spar. As a matter of fact she *had* asked Doc Taylor, and been informed that his late patient responded to the name of Roland McGuire. But there was a hang-dog look in the doctor's eyes which had not escaped Miss Pickett, and intuitively she knew that the worthy *medico* had lied. Donna's question convinced her that she was not mistaken. Her bright little eyes gleamed archly.

"Why, we never did learn who it was that saved you, Donna. Is it a secret?"

"Why, no."

Miss Pickett waited in agony for ten seconds, but Donna, having replied fully to her query, volunteered no further information. In desperation the post-mistress demanded:

"Well, then, why do you keep it to yourself?"

"Is that any of your business, Miss Pickett?"

"No, of course not. But then - "

"Well?"

Miss Pickett was non-plussed, but only for an instant. Like all old maids when bested in a battle of wits by an opponent of their own sex, younger, more attractive and known to be popular with the males of their acquaintance, Miss Pickett was quick to take the high ground of a tactful consideration of circumstances which Donna apparently had overlooked; circumstances which, while savoring slightly of girlish indiscretion, might, nevertheless, be construed as a distinct slip from virtue. An attack, whether by innuendo or direct assertion, on a sister's virtue is ever the first weapon of a mean and disappointed woman, and having no other charms to speak of, Miss Pickett chose to assume that of superior virtue; so, with the subtle sting of her species, she sunk her poison home.

"Well, Donna, if you won't protect your own good name, I'm sure you shouldn't be surprised if your friends endeavor to protect it for you. Everybody in town knows you kept that man at your home for a month - "

"I haven't denied it, or attempted to conceal the fact. In what manner does that reflect on my good name, Miss Pickett?"

"Well, folks *will* talk - you know that."

"Of course I know they will. That's their privilege, Miss Pickett, and I'm not at all interested, I assure you." She smiled patronizingly at the postmistress. "When I want somebody to protect my good name, Miss Pickett, I'll send for a man. Until then you may consider yourself relieved of the task."

"Well, when people know you've kept a desperate character - "

"Who knows it, Miss Pickett? Do you?"

Miss Pickett was forced to acknowledge that she did not, and under a hot volley of questions from Donna admitted further that not a soul in San Pasqual had even hinted to her of such a contingency. Too late the spinster realized that she had, figuratively speaking, placed all of her eggs in one bucket and scrambled them.

Donna realized it too. For the first time in her life she was angry, although not for worlds would she permit Miss Pickett to realize it. She had the postmistress on the defensive now, and she was determined to keep her there; so, in calm gentle commiserating tones Donna read the riot act to the embarrassed gossip. Mentally, morally, physically and socially, she was Miss Pickett's superior and Miss Pickett knew this; her instinctive knowledge of it placed her at a disadvantage and forced her to listen to a few elegantly worded remarks on charity, the folly of playing the part of guardian of a sister's morals and the innate nastiness of throwing mud. It was a rare grueling that Donna gave Miss Pickett; the pity of it was that Mr. Hennage could not have been there to listen to it.

The postmistress was confounded. She could think of nothing to say in reply until the right moment for saying it had fled; and her pride forbade her acknowledging defeat by tossing her head and walking out with a grand air of injured innocence. In the end she lost her composure entirely, for while Donna's remarks had seemed designed for the "folks" whom Miss Pickett seemed to fear might "talk," the latter knew that in reality they were directed at her.

To be forced to listen to an almost motherly castigation from Donna Corblay was too great a tax upon Miss

Pickett's limited powers of endurance. She flew into a rage, all the more pitiful because it was impotent, murmured something about the ingratitude of some people - "not mentionin' any names, but not exceptin' present company," and swept out of the eating-house; not, however, until she had commenced to cry, thus acknowledging her defeat and humiliation and presenting to San Pasqual that meanest of all mean sights, a mean old maid, in a rage, weeping until her eyes and nose are red.

In the afternoon Donna had a visit from a Wells Fargo & Company detective. He was a large fatherly person, who might have had girls of his own as old as Donna, and he stated his mission without embarrassment of preliminary verbal skirmishing. "From various sources around town, Miss Corblay, I gather that it is quite possible you are acquainted with the man McGraw who is suspected of the recent stage robbery at Garlock."

Donna admitted, smiling, that it was quite possible.

"Have you any objection to telling me all you know about him?"

"Not the slightest. It is your business to investigate this matter, and I have refrained from telling others whose business it is not. If I have your word of honor that what I tell you is for the company you represent and not for the gossips of San Pasqual, I can save you time and trouble and expense."

"Thank you. It is a rare pleasure, I assure you, Miss Corblay, for a man in my line of work to receive such a prompt, courteous and businesslike answer from a woman. You have my word that anything you tell me is in confidence."

"Did Miss Pickett send you here?"

"Indirectly. She gave some information to our express messenger who in turn gave it to me. I might add that the interest of our messenger ceased when I took up this case."

"Very well" replied Donna, and proceeded to tell him with infinite detail, everything she knew concerning Bob McGraw, excepting the fact that he was her husband. In five minutes she had tightened the web of circumstantial evidence around him, and then unloosened it, and at the finish of her recital the detective had no questions to ask. He held out his hand and shook hers warmly.

"I think you have solved this case for me, Miss Corblay. However, there is one matter that will be hard to overcome, and that is the identification of McGraw by the passenger, Carey."

"Who?"

"A passenger. His name is T. Morgan Carey, of Los Angeles. He is rather prominent in business circles - a pretty sane, careful man, and his testimony would have considerable evidence with a jury."

"Find out from the messenger if Carey identified Bob - I mean Mr. McGraw (the detective smiled slightly) before the messenger gave chase to the hold-up man, or after he returned with the hat. If the latter, I can explode his testimony. I happen to know that Mr.

Carey is a business rival of Mr. McGraw's and very unfriendly to him. It would be to Carey's great financial advantage to see Bob (again the detective smiled) in jail. Then ask your agent at Keeler to make inquiry and learn if a tall young man with auburn hair didn't ride into town the day following the hold-up, mounted on a roan horse. If he sold the horse, saddle and spurs, purchased two burros and outfitted in Keeler for a prospecting trip, that man was Mr. Robert McGraw and he didn't arrive bareheaded. I think you'll discover that you're following a false lead."

The detective could guess a thing or two; otherwise he would not have been a detective. He guessed something of Donna's more than friendly interest in the man he was after; an interest which he felt to be greater than a mere feeling of gratitude for what McGraw had saved her from, and his sympathies wore with her. She had been "open and above board with him" and he appreciated the embarrassment that might attend should the matter be given publicity.

"Whatever I discover will not be made public, Miss Corblay. Thank you."

He lifted his hat and walked out, while Donna, selecting one of the late magazines from the news-stand, sat down and read for the rest of the afternoon.

Eight days passed before the detective appeared again at the counter.

"Miss Corblay," he reported smiling, "you're a better detective than I. McGraw didn't do the job - that is, your - Bob. But some other McGraw did. The fact is, he's sent back the money he lifted from the company and the passengers. At least, a number of them have reported the return of their cash. Here's a note the agent here received a little while ago."

He passed a type-written sheet across the counter to her. Donna read it carefully.

"The plot thickens. However, this is only added proof that my line of reasoning is correct. This line, 'I didn't have no business to do it in the first place,' clinches the testimony. The Robert McGraw of my acquaintance never uses double negatives."

"And he couldn't have arrived in Goldfield with a burro train in less than six weeks. You say this man uses double negatives. There's a clew. Who, among your acquaintances, Miss Corblay, uses double negatives?"

"Every soul with the exception of Mr. McGraw" replied Donna. "Following a clew like that in San Pasqual would be like looking for a needle in a haystack. But I think I could name the man who wrote that note."

"Who is he?"

Donna favored the detective with a mocking little smile.

"He's a friend of mine" she said, "and I never go back on a friend."

"Well," he replied jokingly, "I can't imagine a friend going back on you. However, I'll not be curious about this chap. He appears contrite, and the incident is closed. But all the same, this is one of the queerest cases I've had in all my experience," and he went out, still puzzled.

Peter B. Kyne

CHAPTER XVIII

Thanksgiving came and went, and with, the approach of Christmas came the knowledge to Donna that her tour of duty behind the cash-counter of the eating-house was rapidly drawing to a close - for the very sweetest reason in all this sad old world; a reason as yet apparent to no one in San Pasqual but Donna herself; a very tiny reason against whose coming Donna had commenced to plan and sew in the lonely hours of her vigil at the Hat Ranch, waiting for Bob to come back, that she might impart to him the secret. Yes, indeed, a most valid reason. Donna hoped it would be a man-baby, with wavy auburn hair like Bob's.

On the first of February she gave notice of her intention to resign her position on the first of the following month. Bob had left with her a hundred and fifty dollars, the balance of her little capital having been expended during their honeymoon trip and in outfitting Bob for his trip into the desert, and but for the fact that the thousand dollars so thoughtfully provided by Harley P. was still in the eating-house safe, Donna would have been placed in a most embarrassing position. With the knowledge that she had ample funds with which to maintain herself and her dependents at the Hat Ranch until the birth of her child, however, Donna decided to remove herself from the prying gaze of the San Pasqualians by resigning her position. The fact that her marriage to Bob was not known in the little town was now an added embarrassment, and the necessity of conveying to the world the news that she had been married since October was imperative. She decided to go up to Bakersfield, visit the city hall and request the clerk who had issued the license to Bob and herself to give the news of its issuance to the papers. She was aware that Bob knew this clerk and for that reason they had been enabled to keep the matter secret.

But the news that Donna Corblay had resigned the best position obtainable for a woman in San Pasqual - and that, without assigning any reason for her extraordinary action - spread quickly, and Mrs. Pennycook, with envious eyes on the position for her eldest daughter, visited the hotel manager and tried her persuasive personality to that end.

After that visit, there was no need for explanation. Mrs. Pennycook, with horrified mien and many repetitions of "But for heaven's sake don't mention my name," furnished the explanation - and to a lady of Mrs. Pennycook's large experience in matters of maternity, there was no heretic in San Pasqual who doubted the authenticity of her verdict.

Of the whisperings, the interchange of gossip and eager speculation as to the identity of the man in the case, the haughty stare of the women and the covert smiles of the men. Donna was not long kept in ignorance. On the fifteenth of the month the manager came to her, announced that he had already been fortunate enough to secure her successor, paid her a full month's salary, and with a few perfunctory remarks touching on his regret at losing her services, indicated that she might forthwith retire to that seclusion which awaited her at the Hat Ranch. Donna, proud, scornful, unafraid in the knowledge that she was an honorable wife, deemed it beneath her dignity to reply. She removed her little capital from the safe, balanced her cash and walked out of the eating-house forever.

She had come to the parting of the ways. Her condition demanded the immediate presence of her husband, notwithstanding the fact that to call him in from his wanderings now might mean the abandonment of his great dreams of Donnaville. All her life she had needed a protector; more than ever she needed one now, and she was torn between a desire for the comfort of his presence and an equal desire to sacrifice that comfort to his great work, by refraining from sending Sam Singer into the desert with a message to him. She knew she could send Sam over the Santa Fe to Danby, and in the miner's outfitting store there Sam would be directed to the country where Bob's claims lay. For two days she wrestled with this problem, deciding finally to prove herself worthy of him and face the issue alone.

But the time had come when San Pasqual, representing Society, must be accorded the right which Society very justly demands - the right to know whether its members are conforming to all of the law, moral and legal. Donna realized that her silence in the matter of her marriage had placed her in an unenviable light, and while she was striving to formulate a plan to make the announcement gracefully. Mrs. Pennycook, emboldened by the absence of Harley P. Hennage, gathered about her a committee of five other ladies and swooped down on the Hat Ranch.

Donna was standing at her front gate when this purity squad approached. She guessed their mission instantly, and welcomed it. Whether gracefully or ungracefully, the matter would soon be over now, and it pleased her a little to note that all six ladies were leading matrons of the little town. Each member of Mrs. Pennycook's committee reflected in her face mingled sadness, embarrassment and curiosity. For three of them Donna felt a genuine regard; she realized that their visit was actuated by a desire to help her, if she required help, to lend her their moral support in the face of suspicion, whether just or otherwise. The other three, including Mrs. Pennycook, Donna knew for that detestable type of womankind best known and described as "catty." Some one of these three who knew would fire the first gun in this most embarrassing campaign, and in order to nullify their fire as much as possible, Donna decided not to wait for that opening broadside, but to sweep them off their feet by a wave of candor and frankness, leaving them stunned with surprise and ashamed of their own suspicions.

Upon its arrival, therefore, Donna greeted the delegation cordially, receiving an equally cordial return of the greeting from all except Mrs. Pennycook, who swept into the Hat Ranch in dignified silence, head up and nose in the air, after the manner of one who scents a moral stench and is resolved to eradicate it at all hazard.

"This *is* an unexpected pleasure" Donna said hospitably. "Do come in out of this dreadful heat. I've just finished baking a lovely layer cake and you're all just in time to sample my cooking. I'll have Soft Wind make some lemonade. We scarcely require ice here, the water from my artesian well is so remarkably cool."

Graciously she herded them all into the shady patio, brought out chairs and ordered Soft Wind to prepare a huge pitcher of lemonade, while she herself carried out a small table, spread a tablecloth over it and crowned it with a layer cake, seven plates, and the accessories.

The delegation squirmed uneasily. The cordiality of this reception and Donna's apparent pleasure at the visit, together with her total lack of embarrassment, placed the ladies at a decided disadvantage. Even Mrs. Pennycook found it a tax on her ingenuity to solve tactfully the problem of accepting Donna's layer cake and cool lemonade in one breath and questioning her morals in the other - if this phraseology may be employed to designate the problem without casting opprobrium on Mrs. Pennycook's table manners.

There was a silence as Donna poured the lemonade and helped each visitor to a section of the layer cake. When she had finished, however, she leaned her elbows on the little table, gazed calmly and a little roguishly at each guest in turn, and stole their thunder with a single question:

"How did you all discover that I am married?"

The silence was painful, until Mrs. Pennycook choked on a cake crumb. It was a question none of them could answer, and this very fact made the silence more appalling! Even Mrs. Pennycook, who had organized the expedition, blushed. Finally she stammered:

"We - we - well, to tell the truth, we hadn't heard."

Donna's eyes were wide with simulated amazement.

"You hadn't heard!"

"No" snapped Mrs. Pennycook, quick to see her opening, "but we were all hoping to hear - for your sake."

"But you guessed something when I resigned my position at the eating-house?"

Donna could scarce restrain a smile as she saw the eagerness with which Mrs. Pennycook showed in her true colors by walking blindly into this verbal trap. A slight sardonic smile flickered across her stern features.

"We didn't suspect. Everybody in town *knew*. And, not to beat about the bush, Miss Corblay, we came here to-day to find out. We're old enough to be your mother and we have daughters of our own, and in a certain sense, havin' known you from a baby, we felt sort o' responsible-like."

"Ah, I see" Donna almost breathed. "You were suspicious-like."

Two of the committee showed signs of inward disturbance, but, having fixed bayonets, Mrs. Penny-cook was now prepared to charge.

"We came to find out if you're an honorable married woman, or - "

"Quite right, Mrs. Pennycook. That is information which you, and in fact every person in San Pasqual, is entitled to know. I am an honorable married woman. I was married in Bakersfield on the seventeenth day of last October."

"Well, then, where's your husband?"

"That is a question which you are not privileged to ask, Mrs. Pennycook. However, I will answer it. My husband is about his lawful business somewhere in the Colorado desert."

"Who is this man?"

"My husband's name is Robert McGraw."

Six separate and distinct gasps greeted this announcement extraordinary. A tear trembled on the eyelid of one of the ladies of whom Donna was really fond and whom she had reason to believe was fond of her.

"Well, dearie" replied Mrs. Pennycook unctuously, "it's kind o' hard-like to tell whether, in your present - er - delicate condition, you're better off unmarried-like, or the wife of a man accused of holdin' up a stage at Garlock."

"It is embarrassing, isn't it?" Donna laughed. She was not in the least angry with Mrs. Pennycook. In fact, the gossip amused her very much, and in the knowledge of the day of reckoning coming to Mrs. Pennycook she could afford to laugh. "What does Dan think about it?"

"Mr. Pennycook, *if* you please" corrected his wife. "We will not mention his name in this matter."

"Well, then, what do you think of it, Mrs. Pennycook?"

"To be perfectly frank-like, an' not meanin' any offense, I think, Miss Corblay, that you drove your pigs to a mighty poor market."

"It does look that way" Donna acquiesced good-naturedly. "I'll admit that appearances are against my husband. However, since I know that the charge is ridiculous, I shall not dishonor him by making a defense where none is necessary. He will be in San Pasqual about the first of April, Mrs. Pennycook, and if at that time you desire to learn the circumstances, he will be charmed, I know, to relate them to you."

"I am not interested" retorted the gossip.

"Judging by this unexpected visit and your pointed remarks, dear Mrs. Pennycook, I think I might be pardoned for presuming that you were."

Mrs. Pennycook made no reply, for obvious reasons. The sortie for information had been too successful to please her, and in Donna's present mood the elder woman knew that she would fare but poorly in a battle of wits. Indeed, she already stood in a most unenviable position in San Pasqual society, as the leader of an unwarranted attack against a virtuous woman, and her busy brain was already at work, mending her fences. In the interview with Donna she had expected tears and anguish. Instead she had been met with smiles and good-natured raillery; and she had an uncomfortable feeling that her fellow committeewomen were already enraged at her and preparing to turn against her. She drank her lemonade hastily and explained that their visit had been for the purpose of setting at rest certain unpleasant rumors in San Pasqual, wherein Donna's reputation had suffered. If the rumors had proved to be without foundation they would have felt it their business to nip the scandal in the bud. If, on the contrary, the rumors were based on truth, they had planned to give her a Christian helping hand toward regeneration.

"I am very glad you did me the honor to call" Donna told the committee. "I had kept my marriage secret, for reason of my own, and I am glad now that my friends will brand these rumors as malicious and untrue."

The committee left in almost as deep sorrow as it had come. Donna walked with them to the front gate, and at parting two of the women kissed her, whispering hurried words of faith in her, and from the bottom of their truly generous womanly souls they meant it. Donna knew they did, and was deeply grateful. In the case of Mrs. Pennycook, however, she had no such illusion. She knew that disappointed vengeance had served to sharpen Mrs. Pennycook's unaccountable and unnatural dislike for her, and it was with secret relief that she watched the members of the committee on social purity return to their respective homes.

The following morning Mrs. Pennycook departed on a journey to Bakersfield, the county-seat. Here she invaded the marriage license bureau and requested an inspection of the record of the marriage license issued to Robert McGraw and Donna Corblay on October seventeenth.

To Mrs. Pennycook's profound satisfaction there was no record of such a license available. Business in the marriage bureau was dull that day, and the license clerk turned over to Mrs. Pennycook the bound book of affidavit blanks, which constitutes the record of the county clerk's office and from which the deputy clerk fills in the marriage license when he issues it. She searched through the records from August up to that very day - searched painstakingly and thrice in succession, while the deputy looked on covertly from a nearby desk and smiled at her activities. He might have informed Mrs. Pennycook that the record of the issuance of a license to his friend Bob McGraw and Donna Corblay could be found in the back of the book, where it would not be discovered by the newspaper reporters who came each day to make notations of the licenses issued. It is an old trick, this; to fill in the affidavit blank toward the back of the book, where the record will not be reached in the regular course of business until a year or more shall have elapsed. The deputy county clerk was a friend of Bob McGraw's and as he had promised not to give him away, he would keep his word; so he snickered to himself and wondered if this acidulous lady could, by any chance, be McGraw's mother-in-law. If so, he felt sorry for McGraw. He sniffed a quick divorce.

Mrs. Pennycook could not find the record she sought, and demanded further information. The clerk informed her gravely that, aside from personal experience, all the information on marriages in Kern county was contained in the book before her; so Mrs. Pennycook returned to San Pasqual, vindicated in the eyes of the committee on individual morals.

The following day Mrs. Pennycook called a meeting in her front parlor, and to the credit of San Pasqual's womanhood be it said that two of the committee failed to respond. However, Miss Molly Pickett volunteered to enlist for the cause, and a quorum being present Mrs. Pennycook announced that Donna Corblay's statement that she was a wife had not been substantiated by the records of the county clerk's office. Having examined the records personally, Mrs. Pennycook felt safe in assuming responsibility for the statement that Donna Corblay was not married, despite her claims to the contrary.

"Then," murmured Miss Pickett sadly, "she is not an honest woman!"

"*Decidedly* not."

"I expected this - for years" Miss Pickett continued, and wiped away a furtive tear. "Poor girl. After all, we shouldn't be surprised. I'm afraid she comes by it naturally. There was a mystery about her mother."

"Well, there's no mystery about Donna" retorted Mrs. Pennycook triumphantly. "She's a disgrace to the community."

"What can be done about it?" one of the committee inquired.

"I believe," another volunteered, "that in San Francisco and Los Angeles they have homes for unfortunate girls. If we can induce her to go to one of these institutions, it seems to me it is our duty to do so."

"I wash my hands of the whole affair" protested Mrs. Pennycook. "I went down there, as you all know, an' did all the talking and acted sympathetic-like, an' got insulted for my pains. I'll not go again."

"Perhaps you didn't approach the subject just right, Mrs. Pennycook - not meanin' any offense - but you know Donna's one of the high an' mighty kind, an' you an' her ain't been any too friendly. I think, maybe, if *I* was to talk to her, now - "

"I'm sure you're welcome, Miss Pickett. Somebody ought to reason with her like before the thing gets too public, an' I don't seem to have the right influence with the girl."

"I'll go call on her, if one or two others will go with me" Miss Pickett volunteered. She omitted to mention the fact that company or no company, she would not have missed the opportunity of taunting Donna for a farm. However, two other ladies decided to go with Miss Pickett, and forthwith the three set out for the Hat Ranch.

There was no layer cake and lemonade reception awaiting *them* at the Hat Ranch. Donna, upon being informed by Soft Wind that three ladies desired to interview her, met the delegation in her kitchen, which they had entered uninvited. She surveyed the nervous trio coldly.

"Is this another investigating committee?" she demanded bluntly.

"Well, in view o' the fact that there never was any marriage license issued to you an' that - that stage-robber - "

"Miss Pickett - and you other two shining examples of Christian charity! Please leave my home at once. Do you hear? At once! I have no explanations or apologies to make, and if I had I would not make them to a soul in San Pasqual. Leave my home instantly."

The three ladies stood up. Two of them scurried toward the door, but Miss Pickett lingered, showing a disposition to argue the question. She had "walled" her eyes and pulled her mouth down in the most approved facial expression of one who, proffering help to the unfortunate, realizes that ingratitude is to be her portion.

Through the aboriginal brain of Soft Wind, however, some hint of the situation had by this time managed to sift. The presence of two delegations of female visitors in one week was unprecedented; and in her slow dumb way she realized that the condition of her mistress was probably being questioned by these white women.

Now, Soft Wind had been Donna's nurse, and since the squaw was untroubled by the finer question of morality in a lady (the mere trifle of a marriage license had been no bar to her own primitive alliance with Sam Singer) it irked her to stand idly by while these white women offered insult to her adored one. She could not understand what was being said (Donna always spoke to her in the language of her tribe, a language learned in her babyhood from Soft Wind herself) but she did know by the pale face and flashing eyes that Donna was angry.

"I came to tell - " began Miss Pickett.

Donna pointed toward the door. "Go" she commanded.

Still Miss Pickett lingered; so Soft Wind, whose forty years of life had been spent in arduous toil that had made her muscles as hard and firm as those of most men, picked Miss Pickett up in her arms, carried her out kicking and screaming and tossed the spinster incontinently over the gate. Sam Singer saw the exit and favored his squaw with the first grunt of approval in many years. Donna, after first ascertaining that Miss Pickett had lit in the sand and was uninjured, leaned over the gate and almost laughed herself into hysterics.

That was the last effort made to reform Donna Corblay. In a covert way Miss Pickett and Mrs. Pennycook conspired to publicly disgrace her and, branded as a scarlet woman, drive her out of San Pasqual, if possible. Donna had declared war, and they were prepared to accept the challenge.

Borax O'Rourke, with six months' wages coming to him from his chosen occupation of skinning mules up Keeler way, had been sighing for the delights of San Pasqual and an opportunity to spend his money after the fashion of the country. This was not possible in Keeler - at least not on the extravagant scale which obtained regularly in San Pasqual; hence, when he learned quite by chance that Harley P. Hennage was no longer in that thriving hive of desert iniquity, Borax commenced to pine for some society more ameliorating than that of twelve mules driven with a jerk-line. In a word, Mr. O'Rourke decided to quit his job, go down to San Pasqual and enter upon a butterfly existence until his six months' pay should be dissipated.

Accordingly Borax O'Rourke descended, via the stage line, on San Pasqual. He heralded his arrival and his intentions by inviting San Pasqual to drink with him, and after visiting each of its many saloons and spending impartially the while, he decided, along toward dusk, that he had partaken of sufficient squirrel whisky to give him an appetite for his dinner, and forthwith shaped his somewhat faltering course for the eating-house.

Here he discovered that Donna Corblay was no longer employed at the cashier's counter - which disappointed him. He ate his dinner in silence, and upon his return to the Silver Dollar saloon he was informed, with many a low jest and rude guffaw, the reason for his disappointment. Whereat he laughed himself.

Now, Borax O'Rourke, while a low, vulgar, border ruffian, had what even the lowest of his kind generally appear to possess: a lingering sense of respect for a good woman. Until the night of the attack upon her by the hoboes in the railroad yard, he had never dared to presume to the extent of speaking to Donna Corblay, even when paying for his meals, although the democracy of San Pasqual would not have construed speech at such a time as a breach of convention. For there were no angels in San Pasqual; the town was merely sunk in a moral lethargy, and the line of demarcation in matters of rectitude was drawn between those who stole and had killed their man, and those who had not. All the lesser sins were looked upon tolerantly as indigenous to the soil, and as Borax O'Rourke had never been accused of theft and had never killed his man (he had been in two arguments, however, and had winged his man both times, the winger and the wingee subsequently shaking hands and declaring a truce), he was not considered beyond the pale. Had he spoken to Donna she readily would have comprehended that he merely desired to be neighborly; she would have inquired the latest news from the borax works at Keeler and doubtless would have sold him a hat.

Nevertheless, for a long time, Borax O'Rourke had nursed a secret passion for the eating-house cashier, a passion, that never could have been dignified by the term "love" (Borax was not equal to that) but rather an animal-like desire for possession. There was considerable of the abysmal brute in Borax. He would have been voted quite a Lochinvar in the days when men procured their wives by right of discovery and the ability to retain possession, and had he dared, he would have made love to Donna in his bearlike way. Hence, as in the case of all pure women in frontier towns, where rough men foregather, Donna's easily discernible purity had been her most salient protection, and beyond such bulwarks Borax O'Rourke had never dared to venture.

It had been a shock, therefore, to Mr. O'Rourke, when he discovered her that August night, crying over a stranger and kissing him. Borax himself was not a bad-looking fellow, in a rough out-o'-doors sort of way, and while he had not been privileged to a close scrutiny of the man whom Donna had kissed, still he believed him to be a rough-and- ready individual like himself, and quite naturally the thought occurred to Borax that he, too, might not have been unwelcome, had he but possessed sufficient courage to make a cautious advance.

He was confirmed in this thought now at the news which he heard upon the first night of his return to San Pasqual, and with the thought that he had been worshiping an idol with feet of clay, Mr. O'Rourke cursed himself for an unmitigated jackass in thus leaving to some other roving rascal the prize which he had so earnestly desired for himself. With the receipt of the information about Donna, Mr. O'Rourke unconsciously felt himself instantly on the same social level with her, and since convention was something alien to his soul, and possession his sole inspiration, he decided that he could make his advances now in full confidence that he might be successful; and if not, there would be no necessity for feeling sheepish over his rebuff.

"I'll ask her to marry me, an' damn the odds" he decided. "There's worse places than the Hat Ranch to live in, with a few dollars always comin' in. She'll be glad enough of the offer, like as not - considerin' the circumstances, an' she can send the kid to an orphan asylum."

By morning this crafty idea had taken full possession of Borax, so after fortifying himself with a half dozen drinks, he set forth for the Hat Ranch. Also, under the influence of the liquor and his overweening pride in his bright idea, he had taken pains to announce his destination and the object of his visit. A crowd of male observers stood on the porch of the Silver Dollar saloon and watched him depart, the while they spurred him on his way with many a jeer and jibe.

Sam Singer was seated in the kitchen at the Hat Ranch, enjoying an after-breakfast cigarette, when O'Rourke came to the kitchen door, hiccoughed and made rough demand for the mistress of the house. Donna, from an adjoining room, heard him and came into the kitchen.

"Well, Borax" she demanded, "what do you want? A hat?"

She saw that he had been drinking, and a sudden fear took possession of her. With the exception of her Indian retainer, Bob McGraw, Harley P. Hennage and Doc Taylor, no male foot had profaned the Hat Ranch in twenty years, and the presence of O'Rourke was a distinct menace.

"Not on your life, sweetheart" he began pertly, "I want you."

Donna spoke to the Indian in the Cahuilla tongue, and Sam Singer sprang at the mule-skinner like a panther on an unsuspecting deer. The lean mahogany-colored hands closed around the ruffian's throat, and the two bodies crashed to the floor together. O'Rourke, taken unaware by the suddenness and ferocity of the attack, was no match. for the Indian. He endeavored to free his arm and reach for his gun, but Sam Singer had anticipated him. Already the big blue gun was in the Indian's possession; he raised it, brought the butt down on O'Rourke's head, and the battle was over, almost before it had fairly started.

"Drag him outside" Donna commanded. The Indian grasped O'Rourke by his legs and dragged him outside the compound. Then he returned to the kitchen, secured a bucket, filled it at the artesian well, and returning, dashed it over the still dazed enemy.

The water did its work, and presently O'Rourke sat up.

"I'll kill you for this" he said; whereat Sam Singer struck him in the face and rolled him over in the dirt. Incidentally, he retained Mr. O'Rourke's big blue gun as a souvenir of the fray.

Peter B. Kyne

Half an hour later a very dejected, bedraggled mule-skinner, bruised, bleeding and covered with sand which clung to his dripping person, returned to San Pasqual, to be heartily jeered at for the result of his pilgrimage; for the San Pasqualians noticed that not only had Mr. O'Rourke suffered defeat, but in the melee his gun had been taken from him, and to suffer such humiliation at the hands of a mere Indian was considered in San Pasqual the very dregs and drainings of downright disgrace.

For two days Borax O'Rourke drowned his chagrin in the lethal waters of the Silver Dollar saloon, and presently to him here there came an anonymous letter, containing, by some devil's devising, a unique scheme for revenge on Donna, and on Sam Singer, who depended on her bounty. At one stroke he could destroy them both, and cast them forth into the wide reaches of the Mojave desert, homeless.

The unknown writer of this anonymous note desired to advise Borax O'Rourke that Donna Corblay had no title to the lands on which the Hat Ranch stood; that the desert was still part of the public domain and subject to entry; that he, Borax O'Rourke, might file on forty acres surrounding the Hat Ranch, and by demonstrating that he had an artesian well on the forty, which would irrigate one-eighth of his entry, he could obtain title to the land. In any event, after filing his application, he would then be in a position to evict his enemies.

This seemed to the brute O'Rourke such a very novel idea that he decided to follow it out immediately. He spent that day sobering up, and the next few days in a trip to the land office one hundred and fifty miles up the valley; at Independence. Upon his return to San Pasqual he had old Judge Kenny, the local justice of the peace, serve formal written notice upon Donna Corblay to evacuate immediately; otherwise he would commence suit.

The news was over San Pasqual in an hour, and formed the basis of much discussion in the Silver Dollar when Borax Somebody hailed him.

"Well, Borax, I see you're goin' to play even. D'ye think you'll be able to oust the girl from the Hat Ranch? The boys have been discussin' it, and it looks like she might put up a fight on squatter's rights."

"I'll git her out all right" rumbled O'Rourke, "an' when I do, I'll chuck the old lady's bones after her. I'll teach her an' that Indian o' hers - "

Borax O'Rourke paused. His tongue clicked drily against the roof of his mouth.

Seated at a card-table across the room, idly shuffling a deck of cards, sat Harley P. Hennage, and he was staring at Borax O'Rourke. At the latter's sudden pause, a silence fell upon the Silver Dollar, and every man lined up at the long bar turned and followed O'Rourke's glance.

For fully a minute Mr. Hennage's small baleful eyes flicked murder lights as their glance burned into O'Rourke's wolfish soul. Then, quite calmly, he comm- enced placing his cards for a game of solitaire, and when he had carefully disposed of them he spoke:

"O'Rourke!"

The word was deep, throaty, almost a growl. Simultaneously the men nearest O'Rourke drifted quickly away from him.

"Well?"

"I don't like your game. Stop it. Hand me an assignment o' that desert entry o' yours by three o'clock, an' get out o' town by four o'clock. Hear me?"

"An' if I don't?" demanded O'Rourke.

"If you don't," repeated Mr. Hennage calmly, "I shall cancel the entry at one minute after four o'clock."

"You can't bluff me."

"I'm not bluffin' this time, you dog. Do I get that assignment of entry?"

Borax O'Rourke knew that his life might be the price of a refusal, but in the presence of that crowd where men were measured by their courage the remnants of his manhood forbade him to answer "yes." He was not a coward.

"I'll be in the middle o' the street at four o'clock" he answered.

"Got a gun?"

"No."

The gambler threw him over a twenty-dollar piece.

"Go get one."

Borax O'Rourke picked the coin off the floor and shuffled out of the Silver Dollar saloon.

Until one minute past four o'clock, then, the incident was closed, and Mr. Hennage returned to his interrupted game of solitaire.

CHAPTER XIX

Why Harley P. Hennage should elect to return to San Pasqual on the very day that Borax O'Rourke issued formal written notice through old Judge Kenny for Donna to vacate the Hat Ranch, which stood upon the desert land whereon he had filed, is one of the mysteries of retributive justice with which this story has nothing to do. Suffice the fact that Mr. Hennage had stayed away from San Pasqual six months, and six months is a sufficient lapse of time for any ordinary public excitement to wear off, particularly in the desert. He had not intended returning so soon, but a letter from Dan Pennycook, to whom Mr. Hennage had communicated his whereabouts, charging the yardmaster to keep him in touch with affairs at the Hat Ranch, had precipitated his descent upon San Pasqual. He had dropped off the Limited at daylight that very morning, and by nine o'clock was in possession of all the facts regarding the mistress of the Hat Ranch.

"It's a nasty mix-up, Harley" Dan Pennycook informed him, when Mr. Hennage sought the yardmaster out in his desire for explicit information touching the hint of trouble to Donna conveyed in the letter which Pennycook had sent him. "Her husband ain't never showed up, an' there ain't no record of her marriage license in the county clerk's office."

"How d'ye know there ain't?" the gambler demanded.

"Ee - er - well, the fact is, Harley, Mrs. Pennycook - "

"She went an' looked, eh?"

"Well, she was concerned about the girl's reputation - "

"Huh-huh. I see. Dan, do *you* believe this scandal?"

"Not a damned word of it" said honest Dan firmly. "There's some mistake. The girl's good. I've seen her grow up in this town since she was a baby, an' girls like Donna Corblay don't go wrong."

Mr. Hennage extended his freckled, hairy hand. "Dan" he said, "I thank you for that. But your missus ain't playin' fair."

Pennycook threw up his hands deprecatingly. "I know it" he said, "an' I can't help it."

Harley P. laid his hand on the yardmaster's shoulder. "Dan" he said, "me an' you've been good friends, man to man, an' there's just a chance that after to-day we ain't a-goin' to meet no more. You take my compliments to Mrs. Pennycook, Dan, an' tell her that I've kept my word, even if she didn't keep hers. That worthless convict brother-in-law o' yours is dead, Dan. You can quit worryin'. He'll never blackmail you again. He's as dead as a mackerel an' I seen him buried. Dan, old friend, *adios.*"

He shook hands warmly with the yardmaster and walked over to the Silver Dollar saloon, where, in order to smother his distress, he played game after game of solitaire. Here, shortly after his arrival, he had learned of Borax O'Rourke's latest move, and when the latter entered the saloon an hour later, Harley P. had delivered his ultimatum.

For an hour after O'Rourke had left the Silver Dollar for the ostensible purpose of purchasing a gun, the gambler continued to play solitaire. At three o'clock he arose, kicked back his chair, sighed, and glanced at the crowd which had been hanging around, watching him.

"Twenty games to-day an' never beat it once" he complained. "No use talkin', boys, my luck's changed." He walked to the bar, laid a handful of gold thereon and gave his order.

"Wine."

He turned to the crowd. "It happens that there ain't no officer o' the law in San Pasqual to-day to interfere in the forthcoming festivities between me an' O'Rourke. I do hope that none o' you boys'll feel called on to interfere. I take it for granted you won't, out o' compliment to me, an' as a further compliment I'd be obliged if you-all'd honor me to the extent o' havin' a little nip."

The crowd shuffled to the bar, and a lanky prospector in from the dry diggings at Coolgardie spoke up.

"I'm a stranger here, but I'll help pull a rope tight around that mule-skinner's neck. It looks to me like a community job, an' if you say the word, friend, I'll head a movement to relieve you o' the resk o' cancelin' that entry."

"Thank you, old-timer" replied Mr. Hennage kindly,

"but this is a personal matter, an' it's been the custom in this town to let every man kill his own skunks. All set, boys. Smoke up!"

Each of his guests half turned, facing the gambler. As one man they spoke.

"How."

"How" replied Harley P., and tossed off his wine with evident relish. He pocketed his change and left the saloon; five minutes later he was bending over a show-case in the hardware department of the general store, and when his purchase was completed he sat down on a keg of nails, laid his watch on the counter before him, lit a cigar and smoked until four o 'clock; then he arose.

He handed his watch to the proprietor.

"I'd be obliged if you was to give that watch to Dan Pennycook" he said, and walked out.

On the threshold he paused. A train, brown with the dust of the hundreds of miles of desert across which it had traveled, was just pulling in to the depot, and while Mr. Hennage realized that any delay in his programme would be a distinct strain on the idlers who had gathered in the porch of the Silver Dollar and adjacent deadfalls to watch the worst man in San Pasqual finally make good on his reputation, still he was not one of the presuming kind, and he declined to make a spectacle of himself for the edification of the travelers peering curiously from the windows of the train.

So he waited until the train pulled out before stepping

briskly into the middle of the street, gun in hand. He crossed diagonally toward the eating-house, watching for O'Rourke.

Suddenly a man appeared around the corner of the eating-house, a long-barreled Colt's in his hand. Mr. Hennage raised his gun, but lowered it again instantly, for the man was Sam Singer. The Indian ran to Mr. Hennage's side.

"*Vamose, amigo mio*" he said in mingled Spanish and English, "me fixum plenty good."

"Sam" said Mr. Hennage, "get out. You're interferin'. This is the white man's burden." With a sudden sweep of his arm he tore the gun from the Indian's hand, and waved him imperiously away, just as the crowd on the porch of the Silver Dollar parted and Borax O'Rourke leaped into the street.

"Git - you Injun" yelled Mr. Hennage. "If he beefs me first you take a hack at him."

Sam Singer, weaponless, sprang around the corner of the eating-house, just as O'Rourke, having gained the center of the street, turned, drew his gun down on Harley P. and fired. A suppressed "A-a-h-h" went up from the crowd as the worst man in San Pasqual sprawled forward on his hands and knees.

O'Rourke brought his gun up, swiftly, dropped it again. Mr. Hennage's left arm buckled under him suddenly and he slid forward on his face, while two more bullets from the mule-skinner's gun threw the sand in his eyes, blinding him, before ricochetting against the eating-house wall.

Sam Singer, peering around the corner of the eating-house, saw the gambler pick himself up slowly. There was a surprised look on his face. He was staggering in circles and as yet he had not fired a shot.

"No luck" he muttered thickly, "no luck," and reeled toward the eating-house. A fifth bullet scored his shoulder and crashed through the wall; the sixth - and last - was a clean miss, and in the middle of San Pasqual's single street Borax O'Rourke stood wonderingly, an empty smoking gun in his hand, staring at the man reeling blindly along the eating-house wall.

Mr. Hennage paused with his broad back against the wall. "The sand" he muttered, blinking, and brushed his eyes with the back of his good right hand, as Sam Singer made a quick scuttering rush around the corner and retrieved the loaded gun which the gambler had taken from him and which Harley P. had dropped when O'Rourke's second bullet had shattered his left arm.

Mr. Hennage saw the Indian stooping, and flapped his broken arm in feeble protest. Then he raised his gun.

"Borax" he said aloud, "I've got a full house," and pulled away, O'Rourke pitched forward, and Harley P. advanced uncertainly toward him, firing as he came, and when the gun was empty and Borax O'Rourke as dead as Cheops, the gambler stood over his man and hurled the gun at the still twitching body.

"Well, I've canceled that entry" he said. He stood there, swaying a little, and a strong arm came around his fat waist. He half turned and gazed into the sun-scorched, red-bearded face of a tall young man clad in a ruin of weather-beaten rags.

It was Bob McGraw. He had come back. Sam Singer, reaching Mr. Hennage's side at that moment, recognized the stranger, and realizing that Mr. Hennage was in safe hands, the Indian dropped his gun (the one he had taken from O'Rourke at the Hat Ranch) and fled to Donna with the news.

Mr. Hennage fixed his fading glance upon the wanderer. He wanted to say something severe, but for the life of him - even the little he had left - he could not; there was a puzzled look in his sand-clogged eyes as he whispered.

"Bob, they've got the goods - on you. There's a warrant - out; you - know - that stage hold-up - at Garlock - "

He lurched forward into Bob McGraw's arms.

"Oh, Harley, Harley, old man" said Bob McGraw in a choking voice.

"Vamose" panted Mr. Hennage. "I'm dyin', son. You can't do no good here."

"My friend, my friend" whispered the wanderer, "don't die believing I'm an outlaw. I didn't do it. On my word of honor, I didn't."

"I'm dyin', Bob. Give me the straight of it."

"I can't. I don't know what you're driving at, Harley. It's a mistake - "

"Everything's a mistake - I'm a mistake" muttered the gambler. "Son, take me - to my - room - in the hotel. I'm a dog with a bad - name, but I - don't want to - die in - the street."

Dan Pennycook, at his work among the strings of empty box-cars across the track, had heard the shooting; had seen the crowd leave the porch of the Silver Dollar saloon and surge out into the street. He came running now, and upon hearing the details of the duel he pressed through the circle of curious men who had gathered to see Harley P. Hennage die. He found Mr. Hennage seated in the sand with his head and shoulders supported by a stranger.

Mr. Hennage smiled his rare, trustful, childish smile as the yardmaster approached.

"Good old Dan!" he mumbled. "He can only - think of one - thing at a - time - like a horse - but - by God - he thinks - straight. Hello, Dan. I'm beefed. Help Bob - carry me in - Dan. I'm so - damned - heavy an' I don't want - any but real friends - to touch me - now."

They picked him up and carried him into the hotel, up the narrow heat-warped stairs and down the corridor to his room. On the way down the corridor, Mr. Hennage sniffed curiously.

"They got - new mattin' in the rooms" he gasped. "Business - must be - lookin' up."

The crowd followed into the room, and watched Bob McGraw and Dan Pennycook lay Mr. Hennage on his old bed. Dan Pennycook hurried for Doc Taylor, while Bob cleared the room of the curious and locked the door. Mr. Hennage beckoned him to his bedside.

"I ain't paid - for this bed yet" he said, "but there's money - in my pants pocket - an' you square up - for the damage - an' the annoyance - "

The tears came into Bob McGraw's eyes as he knelt beside the bed and took the hand of the worst man in San Pasqual in his. He could not speak. The simplicity, the honesty of this dying stray dog had filled his heart to overflowing; for he was young and he could weep at the passing of a man.

"Sho," said Mr. Hennage softly, "sho, Bob. It was low down - o' me to figure you - a crook, but the evidence - man, it was awful - but you - when did you - marry Donnie"

"Last October - in Bakersfield."

"I know - wisht you'd invited me - give the bride away, Bob. This wouldn't - have happened. Damn dogs! They - say - little Donnie – belongs - east o' the tracks. I killed - O'Rourke for - thinkin' it."

A knock sounded on the door, and Bob opened it, to admit Dan Pennycook.

"Doc Taylor's in Bakersfield" he said.

Mr. Hennage grinned. "I knew it - no luck to-day" he said. "Just wipe the - sand out - o' my eyes, Bob - an' let me kick the bucket - without disturbin' nobody. Dan'l, good-by. As the feller says - we shall meet - on that beautiful - shore."

Pennycook wet a towel in the wash-bowl and wiped Mr. Hennage's eyes. Then he wiped his own, squeezed his friend's hand and departed. He had taken Mr. Hennage's gentle hint to leave him alone with Bob McGraw.

For nearly half an hour Bob and Mr. Hennage talked, and when the gambler had learned all he wished to know he closed his eyes and was silent until another knock came on the door. Again Bob opened it. Donna stood on the threshold.

"Oh, sweetheart!" she cried, and her arms went around his neck, while Sam Singer softly closed the door and stood guard outside. At the sound of her voice Mr. Hennage opened his eyes, but since he was not one of the presuming kind he quickly closed them again and feigned unconsciousness until he felt Donna's soft hand resting on his cold forehead.

"You oughtn't to a-come here, Donnie" he said, making a brave show to speak easily despite his terrible wounds. "There ain't - no fun in this - visit - for nobody - but me - "

He turned wearily to hide his face from her, and looked thoughtfully out the window, across the level reaches of the Mojave desert, to where the sun hung low over the Tehachapis. In the fading light the little dust-devils were beginning to caper and obscure the landscape, much as the dark shadows were already trooping athwart the horizon of Mr. Hennage's wasted life. The night - the eternal night - was coming on apace, and it came to Mr. Hennage that he, too, would depart with the sunset, and he had no regrets.

"Don't cry" he said gently. "I ain't worth it. Just hold - my hand. I want you - near - when I can't see you - no more - an' it's gettin' dark - already. You're so much - like your mother - an' she - she trusted me. I was born with - a hard - face - an' nobody ever - trusted me - but you an' - your mother - an' I - wanted to be trusted - all my worthless life - I wanted it - "

He sighed and held out his hands to them. Thereafter for an hour he did not speak. He was thinking of many things now, and the time was short. Presently he opened his eyes and looked out the window again.

"It's - dark" he whispered. "The sun ain't set, has it?"

"It's just setting" Donna answered him. He nodded slightly, and a flush of embarrassment lit up his pale features. For the first and last time in life, Harley P. Hennage was going to appear presumptuous.

"If it's - a boy" he whispered, "would you - you wouldn't mind - would you - callin' him - Harley? Just - his middle name, Donnie - an' he could - sign it - Robert H. - McGraw."

Donna's hot tears fell fast on his face as she leaned over and kissed the death-damp from his brow.

"Oh-thank you" he gasped. "Bob - take off my - shoes - I don't - want - to - die - with - my boots - on. New - gaiters - too - give 'em - to Sam - Singer. Good - Injun - that."

The sun had set behind the Tehachapis now, and twilight was stealing over San Pasqual. It was time for Mr. Hennage to be on his way. He clung to the hands of his friends convulsively, and whatever thoughts came to him in that supreme moment were for the first time reflected in his face. Indeed, one tiny hint of the desolation in his big heart - the agony of a lifetime of misunderstanding and repression, trickled across his hard face; then something seemed to strike him very funny, for the infrequent, trustful, childish smile flickered across his face, the three gold teeth flashed for an instant ere the worst man in San Pasqual slipped off into the shadows.

And whatever the joke was, he took it with him.

In his unassuming way Harley P. Hennage had been sufficient of a personage, and the manner of his death sufficiently spectacular, to entitle him to one hundred and fifty words of posthumous publicity. Within an hour after the street duel the local representative of the Associated Press had his story on the wire, and at eight-thirty next morning T. Morgan Carey, in his club at Los Angeles, read the glad tidings. By nine o'clock a cipher telegram from Carey was being clicked off to his tool in the General Land Office at Washington, instructing him to expedite the listing of the applications of Bob McGraw's clients for lieu land in Owens Valley.

To T. Morgan Carey's way of thinking that inconspicuous paragraph in the morning paper meant as much to him as the receipt of a certified check for a million dollars. Under his instructions, the applications of McGraw's clients had, with the judicious aid of the deputy in the State Land Office, been approved by the surveyor-general and forwarded to Washington for the approval of the Commissioner of the General Land Office. Here, Carey's long arm, reaching out, had stayed their progress until now. Within a week after Mr. Hennage's death the lands would be passed to patent, under the interested attentions of Carey's man in the General Land Office, the State Land Office would notify Bob McGraw at his address furnished them that the lands were ready for him, and to call and pay the balance due. It would then be incumbent upon McGraw to visit the State Land Office, pay the balance of thirty-nine thousand dollars due on the lands and close the transaction.

The way had been nicely smoothed for Carey by the death of Mr. Hennage, who had warned him so earnestly to "keep off the grass." Of course, McGraw, being to Carey's way of thinking an outlaw from justice, would not dare to appear to claim the lands, and if he did, T. Morgan Carey planned to have a hale and hearty gentleman in a blue uniform with brass buttons, waiting at the Land Office to receive him *before he paid for the lands.* With the providential removal of McGraw's queer partner, Carey saw very clearly that, after waiting a reasonable period after due notice of the approval of the applications had been mailed to McGraw, the filings would eventually lapse, the state would claim the forfeit of the preliminary payment of one thousand dollars and the lands would be reopened for entry - whereupon Carey would step in with his own dummy entrymen. He could then proceed with his own system of irrigation, in the meanwhile keeping a watchful eye on McGraw's water right, ready to grab it when the title should lapse through McGraw's failure to develop it.

Harley P. Hennage died on the fifth day of March. On the seventh there were two funerals in San Pasqual. The coroner and two Mexican laborers tucked Borax

O'Rourke away in the potter's field in the morning. In the afternoon every business establishment in San Pasqual closed, every male citizen in San Pasqual arrayed himself in his "other" clothes and attended the funeral of Harley P. Hennage, testifying, by his presence at least, his masculine appreciation of a dead-game sport.

That was a historic day in San Pasqual. Harley P. lay in state in the long gambling hall of the Silver Dollar which, for so many years, he had ruled by the mystic power of his terrible eyes. Dan Pennycook had made all of the funeral arrangements, and when the crowd had passed slowly around the casket, viewing Harley P.'s placid face for the last time, a strange young man, clad in the garb of a prospector, mounted the little dais, so long occupied by the lookout for Harley P.'s faro game, and delivered a funeral oration. It was not a panegyric of hope, and it dwelt not with the promise of a haven for the gambler's soul in one of his Father's many mansions. He told them merely the story of one who had dwelt amongst them - the story of a man they had never known - and he told it in such simple, eloquent words that the men of San Pasqual wondered what dark tragedy underlay his own life, that he must needs descend to mingle with such as they. And wondering, they wept.

They asked each other who this red stranger might be, but none could answer. But when Harley P. Hennage was finally consigned to the desert they watched the stranger and saw him walk down the tracks to the Hat Ranch. Then they understood, and the word was passed that the man was Bob McGraw, the father of Donna Corblay's unborn child.

Peter B. Kyne

Strange to relate, nobody considered it worth while to telephone the sheriff of Kern county. Even Miss Pickett, who since the shooting had been strangely subdued, was not attracted by the recollection of the offer of a reward of five hundred dollars for Bob McGraw, dead or alive; and ten days after the funeral, when a registered letter came to Robert McGraw, she sent for Dan Pennycook, gave him the letter and the registry receipt and asked him to take it down to the Hat Ranch.

Pennycook leaned his greasy elbows on the delivery window and gazed long and sternly at Miss Pickett.

"Miss Pickett" he said presently, "we found a 'nononymous letter on Borax O'Rourke after he was killed. There's folks in San Pasqual that says the letter's in your handwritin'."

"'Tain't so!" shrilled the spinster.

"Well, this man McGraw says it is so, an' he's goin' to get an expert to prove it. He says it's a felony to send a 'nonymous letter through the United States mails. I'm just a-tellin' you to give you fair warnin'."

Miss Pickett, although greatly agitated, pursed her mouth contemptuously and closed the delivery window. Mr. Pennycook left for the Hat Ranch.

"Donna," said Bob McGraw, when Dan Pennycook had departed, after delivering the letter from the State Land Office, "the applications of my clients are approved and ready to be passed to patent. I have been called upon to pay the balance of thirty-nine thousand dollars due on the land, and if there are thirty-nine cents real money in this world, I do act possess them. Will you loan me a hundred dollars, dear, from that thousand Harley P. gave you? I must go to San Francisco on business."

He smiled his old bantering smile. "I'm always broke, sweetheart. I'm an unfortunate cuss, am I not? Those claims of mine didn't yield wages and I was forced to sell my outfit at Danby to get railroad fare back to San Pasqual. And if the train hadn't been ten minutes late - if I hadn't gone into the eating-house looking for you - I would, have arrived in time to have saved poor Hennage. It was my fight, after all, and poor Harley wasn't used to firearms."

They were sitting together in the patio. Donna leaned her head on his broad shoulder. She had suffered much of late. She had fought the good fight for his sake, for the sake of his great dream of Donnaville, and she had fought alone. She was weary of it all and she longed to leave San Pasqual as quickly as possible.

"Are you going to ask Mr. Dunstan for the thirty-nine thousand dollars he promised to loan you, when the lands were ready for you?" she asked dully.

"No" he answered. "It's no use. I need more money, and Dunstan's check wouldn't even get me started. If I'm whipped, there is no sense in dragging my friends down with me. I'm going to Los Angeles and compromise with Carey."

She drew his rough cheek down to hers and patted his brown hands. She knew then the bitterness of his defeat, and she made no comment. She was tired of the fight. A compromise with Carey or a sale of the water right was their only hope, and when Bob spoke of compromise she was too listless to dissuade him. Since that eventful night when he had first ridden into San Pasqual she had been more or less of a stormy petrel; woe and death and suffering had followed his coming, and if Donnaville was to be purchased at such a price, the land was dear, indeed.

She gave him gladly of her slender hoard and that night Bob McGraw went up to San Francisco. Two days later he returned, stopping off at Bakersfield, and the following morning he returned to San Pasqual.

He went at once to the post-office, and after receiving permission from Miss Pickett, screwed into the wall of the post-office lobby what appeared to Miss Pickett to be two pictures, framed. When he had left, she came out of her sanctum and discovered that one of the frames contained a certified copy of a marriage license issued to Robert McGraw and Donna Corblay on October 17th, - , together with a neat typewritten statement of the reasons why interested parties had not been able to discover the record of the issuance of the license at the county seat. It appeared that the minister who had performed the ceremony, after forwarding the license to the State Board of Health for registration, had neglected to return it thereafter to the two most interested parties, which, coupled with Mrs. McGraw's ignorance of the procedure to be followed under the circumstances, had resulted in more or less embarrassment.

The other frame contained a typewritten invitation to the public to earn five hundred dollars by convicting the undersigned of stage robbery. The "undersigned" was Robert McGraw, who would remain in San

Pasqual all day long and would be delighted to answer questions.

From the post-office Bob went to the public telephone station and called up T. Morgan Carey in Los Angeles. He requested an interview at ten o'clock the following morning for the purpose of adjusting a compromise with him.

Needless to state, Mr. T. Morgan Carey granted the request with cheerful alacrity.

"I'm coming to do business" Bob warned him. "No third parties around - understand!"

"Certainly, certainly" responded Carey. "And in order to save time, Mr. McGraw, I'll have the assignment of your water right made out, ready for your signature. I'll have a notary within hailing distance."

Bob could hear him chuckling as he hung up, for to Carey the thought of his revenge on the man who had cuffed him in the State Land Office was very sweet, indeed. His amiable smile had not yet worn off when his office boy ushered Bob McGraw into his private office at ten o'clock next morning. He waved Bob to a chair and looked him over curiously.

"Been too busy lately to dress up, eh?" he queried, as he noted Bob's corduroy trousers tucked into his miner's boots.

"Pretty busy" assented Bob, and smiled.

"Rather spectacular removal - that of our friend Hennage" Carey continued. "From what I learn he was a little slow on the draw."

"O'Rourke beat him to it."

"If I may judge by the single exhibition of your proficiency with a gun which I was privileged to observe, Mr. McGraw, the issue would have been different had you been in Hennage's boots."

"Possibly. But I didn't come here to gossip with you, Carey. I don't like you well enough for that. I want to finish my business and get back to San Pasqual to-night."

"Certainly, certainly. But you're such an extraordinary young man, McGraw, that in spite of our former differences I must own to a desire to know more about you. I could use a man with your brains and ability, McGraw. You're the kind of a fellow I've been looking for - for a great many years, in fact. If you think you could manage to divorce yourself from your ambitions to supersede me in the State Land Office, I could afford to pay you a fat salary to attend to my land matters. I would have to be the boss, however. It has been a rule of my life, McGraw, to gather about me men with more brains than I possess myself. That is the secret of my - er - rather modest success."

Bob smiled. "No use" he answered. "I couldn't wear your collar, Carey. I Ve been a white man all my life and I'm too old to change."

"It's a pity" Carey replied with genuine sincerity. "I can see remarkable possibilities in you, McGraw. I can, indeed. It's a shame to see you waste your opportunities."

"Play ball" commanded Bob sharply.

"Very well, since you desire it. In the matter of those applications for fifty sections of Owens Valley: you have received a notification from the Registrar of the State Land Office, advising you to call and pay thirty-nine thousand dollars. You cannot pay it; neither can your clients. What are you going to do about it?"

Bob shrugged. "*Quien sabe?*" he said.

"Well, Mr. McGraw, I'll tell you. Your applications are going to lapse through non-payment, and I'm going to get the land. So enough of that. You own a valuable water right. I'm going to get that also. Do you wish me to explain why?"

"No, it is not necessary. I think I follow your line of reasoning."

"I am not disappointed in my estimate of your common sense" Carey retorted, and favored his visitor with a cold, quizzical smile. "Here is the assignment of that water right to me. In return I will give you - let me see. I will give you just fifteen hundred dollars for that water right, McGraw, and I am surprised at myself for exhibiting such generosity. And inasmuch as you collected that sum in advance last autumn at Garlock, your signature to the assignment, before a notary who is waiting in the next room, is all that we require to terminate this interview."

"But I told you I came here to compromise."

"I understand fully. Those are my terms. Your water right on Cottonwood lake in return for your freedom.

Stage-robbers cannot be choosers, Mr. McGraw. I recognized you that day at Garlock and I am prepared to so testify."

The land-grabber rose from his swivel chair. His polished suave manner had disappeared now and his cold eyes flashed with anger and hatred.

"I haven't forgotten that day in the State Land Office, McGraw. A slight pressure on this button" - he placed his manicured finger on an ivory push button - "and two plain-clothes men in my outer office will attend to your case, McGraw."

"So those are your final terms, Carey?"

"Absolutely."

Bob crossed his right leg over his left knee, pulled out a five-cent cigar and thoughtfully bit off the end.

"Press the button, old man" he murmured presently. "Confound this cigar, I've busted the blamed wrapper. Got another cigar handy, Carey? Thanks. By George, that's a two-bitter, isn't it? Well, it's none too good for the last of the McGraw family. I'll be in the two-bit class; myself in half an hour. But proceed, Carey. Press the button and call in your plain-clothes men."

He pulled back the lapel of his coat, and the land-grabber saw the butt of a gun nestling under his left arm. From his inner coat pocket Bob drew a cylindrical roll of paper about eight inches long.

Carey eyed him scornfully. "This is the city of Los Angeles, my friend, not the open desert at Garlock. A gunplay would be most ill-advised, I assure you."

"Oh, that's just part of my wardrobe" Bob retorted. "I wouldn't think of using that on a man unless he was real dangerous - and men like you are beneath my notice. Come now, Carey. Which is it to be? Compromise or the penitentiary?"

"Certainly not compromise - on any terms but mine."

"Well, press the button and call them in - _Boston!_"

Carey whirled in his chair, jerked open a drawer in his desk and reached his hand inside. Before he could withdraw it Bob McGraw's big automatic was covering him.

"Take your hand out of that drawer - *Boston.* Out, you dog, or I'll drill you!"

Carey's hand came out of the drawer slowly, very slowly, grasping a small pearl-handled revolver.

"This is the city of Los Angeles, my friend, and not the open desert. A gun-play would be most ill-advised, I assure you" Bob mocked the land-grabber. "You'd better let me have that pop-gun."

He gently removed the little weapon from Carey's trembling hand.

"Now, go over in that corner and sit down - no, not on the floor. Take a chair with you. I'll occupy the arsenal. You might have all kinds of push buttons, burglar alarms and deadly weapons around this desk."

He ran his hands lightly over Carey's person in search of weapons, shoved him into the corner indicated, then turned and snapped the spring lock on the door leading out to the general office; after which he laid his gun on Carey's desk, sat down in Carey's swivel chair, tilted himself back and lifted his hob-nailed miner's boots to the top of Carey's rosewood table close by. And as he gazed, almost sorrowfully, at the land-grabber, he puffed enjoyably at Carey's cigar. Evidently he foresaw a lengthy argument and meant to make himself comfortable before proceeding.

"Well, now, Boston, since we have definitely located you as the murderer of Oliver Corblay in the Colorado desert on the night of May 17th, 188-, I'll give you five minutes to get your nerve back and then we'll get down to business. You will recall that I came here to compromise."

He reached over and placed a brown calloused finger on the push button, and waited.

"Well" he said presently, "what's the answer!"

"Compromise" Carey managed to articulate. Bob removed his finger.

"The court will now listen to any new testimony that may be adduced in the case of The People versus Carey. Fire away, Boston."

"What are you?" panted Carey. "A man or a devil?"

"Just a plain human being, so flat busted, Boston, that I rattle when I walk. What would you suggest to cure me of that horrible ailment?"

"Silence - on both sides - and a hundred thousand for your water right."

"Well, from your point of view, that offer is truly generous. It is now my turn to be surprised at your generosity. But you're shy on imagination, Boston - and I'm - a greedy rascal. You'll have to raise the ante."

"Two hundred thousand."

"Still too low. The power rights alone are worth a million."

"A million, then - you to leave the United States and not return during my lifetime."

Bob laughed. "You don't understand, Boston. Why should I sell you my water right? You must have water on the brain."

"Then, why have you called to see me? Is it blackmail? Why, this interview is degenerating into a ease of the pot calling the kettle black! I'm a fool, McGraw. I shall offer you nothing at all. You can be convicted of stage robbery and you haven't a dollar in the world to make your defense - while I - it takes *evidence* to convict a man like me"

"Yes, I know your kind. You think you're above the law. I notice, however, that you fear it a little. I sprung a good one on you that time, didn't I, Boston? Imagine the self-possessed T. Morgan Carey practically confessing to a murder on a mere accusation."

He wagged his head at Carey sorrowfully, and continued. "You said a minute ago, Carey, that I had brains. You did not underestimate me. I have. I would not have come to you this morning if I did not have the goods on you. Not much. I don't hold you that cheap, Boston - "

"Don't call me that name" snarled Carey.

"All right, Boston, I won't, since you object. Sit quiet, now, and I'll tell you a very wonderful story - profusely illustrated, as the book agents say. It's rather a long story, so please do not interrupt me."

He unrolled the paper which he had taken from his pocket and held it up before his cringing victim. It was an enlargement from a kodak picture of a desert scene. In the foreground lay two human skeletons. Bob picked a pencil off Carey's desk and lightly indicated one of these skeletons.

"That bundle of bones was once Oliver Corblay. Notice those footprints over to the right! See how plainly they loom up in the picture? And over there - see that little message, Bos - I mean, Mr. Carey. It says:

'Friend, look in my canteen and see that I get justice.'

"Behold the friend who looked in the canteen, and who is now here for justice for that skeleton. He's waited twenty years for it, Carey, but he's going to get it to-day. Don't squirm so. You distract my mind from my story.

"Two months ago I was heading up from the Colorado river toward Chuckwalla Tanks. Passing the mouth of a box canyon I observed the footprints of a man in some old rotten lava formation. I could tell that the man who made those footprints was dying of thirst when he made them. He was traveling in circles, every twenty yards, and they always do that toward the finish.

"Well, I hustled up that box canyon with my canteen, hoping I'd arrive in time. Judge of my surprise when I found this heap of bones. I investigated and discovered that owing to the peculiar formation in the box canyon the footprints were practically imperishable. A detailed explanation of the reason why they loom up so white would be interesting, but technical - so let it pass. Suffice the fact that Oliver Corblay made the same discovery when he drifted into that box canyon twenty years ago, and it gave him an idea. He had a message to leave to posterity and he left it in his empty canteen. However, unless attention could be called to the canteen, the man who found the skeleton would merely bury it and never think of looking in the canteen. So Oliver Corblay wrote that message in the lava; really the most ingenious piece of inlaid work I have ever seen.

"I was the first man to travel that way in twenty years. I read the message in the lava and I looked in the canteen. Here is a copy of the story I found there. The original is in a safe deposit box in San Francisco. It is a diary of a trip which you made with Oliver Corblay and his *mozo* when you first came out to this country from - well, never mind the name. It seems to annoy you. This diary tells all about the discovery of the Baby Mine, your attack upon him with a stone and your flight with the gold - in fact, a condensed history of that trip right down to the very day he died in that box canyon.

Peter B. Kyne

"I was so tremendously interested in that remarkable story, Carey, that as soon as I had refilled my water kegs at Chuckwalla Tanks, I headed south again for Ehrenburg. Here, after much inquiry, I learned from two of the oldest inhabitants that a tenderfoot with a train of four burros had arrived there twenty years ago. They remembered you quite well, because you were so new to the country and so frightened after your experience in the desert. You told a tale of a sandstorm and of having been separated from two Indians you had employed. It seems you lay over in Ehrenburg for a week and put in your time working up a lot of rich ore. You gave a deputy United States marshal five hundred dollars to act as your bodyguard that week, and when your bullion was ready you shipped it by express to the mint in San Francisco. In the express office at Ehrenburg I found a record of that shipment. You shipped it under the name 'T. C. Morgan,' a reversal of your real name.

"From Ehrenburg I made my way back up through Riverside county and across San Bernardino county, to the box canyon. I had purchased a little camera in Ehrenburg, and I fizzled a lot of my films owing to the strong light and the fact that I had to stand on one of my jacks when I took the picture, and the little rascal wouldn't stand still. However, I managed to get one good picture out of the lot, and as you will observe, it all shows up very well in the enlargement.

"I left everything in that box canyon just as I found it. It occurred to me that you might fight and ask to be shown; so might a coroner's jury. They could get out there in three days with an automobile now. Leaving the box canyon I pushed north to Danby, where I sold my outfit and bought a ticket for San Pasqual, where I arrived just in time to see my friend, Harley P. Hennage, lay down his life in defense of Oliver Corblay's daughter, who, by the way, happens to be my wife.

"If you are not too frightened, Carey, you will readily diagnose my extreme interest in this case. Oliver Corblay left a will, which I shall not bother to file for probate, for the reason that his entire estate consisted of the gold that you stole from him, and it is my intention to secure his estate for his heir without recourse to law. Oliver Corblay's wife is dead, and his daughter, Donna, is my wife and next in succession.

"By consulting the old records of the United States Mint at San Francisco, I discover that on June 2, 18 - , a cashier's check was issued to a man named T. C. Morgan, in the sum of $157,432.55, in payment of bullion received. This check was endorsed by T. C. Morgan to Thomas M. Carey, and deposited by Thomas M. Carey in the Traders National Bank.

"Now, Carey, $157,432.55, at seven per cent per annum, compounded annually for twenty annums, aggregates a heap of money. I wore myself out trying to figure the exact sum, and finally concluded to call it square at half a million. That original sum that you stole from Oliver Corblay gave you your start in the west, and as you are reputed to be worth five or six millions now, I am going to assess you half a million dollars for my wife - money which justly belongs to her - and another half million for my services as your attorney, wherein I agree to prevail upon my wife not to prosecute you for murder and highway robbery, but to permit you to live on and await the retributive justice that is bound to overtake you. I think this is perfectly fair and square. You have used your money and your power for evil. I am going to use mine for good. Have the kindness, my dear T. Morgan Carey, to dig me up a million dollars, P. D. Q."

CHAPTER XX

Carey sat huddled dejectedly in his chair. Old age seemed to have descended upon him within the hour; with sagging shoulders, mouth half open in terror, and the wrinkled skin around his thin jaws and the corners of his eyes hanging in greenish-white folds, he looked very tired and very pitiful. Despite his terror, however, he was not yet daunted; for with the picture of *two skeletons* before him he saw a gleam of hope and tried to fight back.

"Twenty years is a long time, McGraw," he quavered, "and it's hard to trace a man by a mere similarity of names."

"You can be traced through the Traders National, where you banked that check, and your identity established beyond a doubt. I can trace your career in this state, step by step, from the day you arrived in it."

Carey smiled - a very weak sickly smile, but bespeaking awakened confidence.

"In the face of which, McGraw, your knowledge of our United States' law will convince you that you cannot convict a man with money enough to fight indefinitely, on such flimsy twenty-year-old evidence found in an abandoned canteen. You cannot identify that skeleton, and you will have to prove that - that - well, you'll have to produce oral testimony, or I'll be given the benefit of the doubt."

"I must prove that the man who killed and robbed Oliver Corblay is T. Morgan Carey, and not a stranger masquerading under your name, eh? All right, T. Morgan. I told you I had this story profusely illustrated."

Bob stepped to the door of the private office which led into the hall. He opened it and Sam Singer stepped inside. Bob turned to Carey.

"Permit me to present Oliver Corblay's Indian servant, Mr. Carey. He is a little older and more stolid since you saw him last, but his memory - "

Sam Singer moved forward a few feet and glanced sharply at Carey.

"I think he recognizes you in spite of your beard" said Bob sorrowfully, "and I see no reason - "

"Take him away" panted Carey, on the instant that Sam Singer, with a peculiar low guttural cry, sprang upon the land-grabber. Bob came behind the Indian, grasped him by the chin, and with his knee in the small of the Cahuilla's back as a fulcrum, gently pried him away from his victim and held him fast. Carey lay quivering on the floor, and Bob looked down at him.

"Are you satisfied?" he asked.

Carey nodded feebly, and Bob marched Sam Singer to the door, opened it and gently propelled him out into the hall. He locked the door and returned to the desk.

"I knew the sight of two skeletons would hearten you up, Carey, until you'd be as saucy as a badger. But you're as tame as a pet fox now, so let's get down to business. Don't argue with me. I've got you where the hair is short; I want a million dollars, and if I do not get it within half an hour I won't take it at all and I will no longer protect you from that Indian."

Carey climbed back into his chair. "If I accept your terms" he said huskily, "how am I to know that you will keep your word?"

"You will not know it. You'll just have to guess. When you do what I want you to do I will surrender to you the original document found in the canteen. Is that satisfactory?"

"I guess so. But I cannot give you a million dollars on five minutes' notice, McGraw."

"It's quite a chunk of cash to have on hand, I'll admit. How much can you give me?"

"Five hundred thousand, and even then I'll have to overdraw my accounts with three banks."

"I wish my credit was as good as yours, Carey. Your banks will stand for the overdraft, of course. You'll have to arrange it some other way if they will not."

"I can't give you a cent over half a million to-day, no matter what you do" pleaded Carey piteously, and Bob realized that he was speaking the truth.

"Do not worry, Carey," he replied, "we're going to do business without getting nasty with each other. I'll take your promissory note, at seven per cent, and you can secure me with a little mortgage on your Spring-street-business block. It's worth a million and a half. I am not so unreasonable as to imagine even a rich man like you can produce a million dollars cash on such notice, so during the past week I took the liberty of having the title searched and an instrument of first mortgage drawn up by myself. All we have to do is to insert the figures and then you can sign it. I understand you have a notary within hailing distance. Your own thoughtfulness in having this transfer of my water right ready for my signature suggested this course to me. It occurred to me that I could sell this mortgage to any Los Angeles bank."

Carey covered his face with his hands and quivered.

"What bank do you anticipate selling it to?" he mumbled presently.

"I didn't have any particular choice. If you have enemies I will not sell you into their hands, and you can make the mortgage for as long a period as you please, up to three years. Give me a list of banks to keep away from. I don't want to hurt you unnecessarily, I assure you."

"Thank you, McGraw" quavered his victim. "If you'll let me sit at my desk I'll draw those checks."

"Certainly. Only I want the checks certified, Carey. You understand, of course, that I shall not surrender the evidence I have against you until those checks are paid. I will not risk your telephoning the banks, the moment I leave your office, telling them the checks were secured by force and threats of bodily harm, and for them to decline payment."

Carey wrote the checks, called in a clerk and instructed him to take them to the various banks and arrange for the overdraft and certification - a comparatively easy task, since Carey was a heavy stockholder in all three banks. Within half an hour, while Bob and Carey sat glaring at each other, the checks were returned, and Carey handed them to Bob, who examined them and found them correct. The mortgage was next filled out, the notary called in, and Carey signed and swore to his signature.

"Now, in order to be perfectly legal about this matter, Carey," began Bob, when the notary had departed, "we should show some consideration for all this money. I have here the papers showing I have filed on twenty acres of a mining claim. It's just twenty acres of the Mojave desert, near San Pasqual, and I do not know that it contains a speck of valuable mineral, but that is neither here nor there. I staked it as a mining claim and christened it the Baby Mine."

Here a slight smile flickered across the young Desert Rat's face, as if some very pleasant thought had preceded it. He continued:

"I have had my signature to this deed to the Baby Mine attested before a notary a few minutes prior to my arrival in your office." He handed the document to T. Morgan Carey. "Here's your mine, Carey. I've sold it to you for a million dollars, and unless you spend one hundred dollars a year in assessment work, the title to this million-dollar property will lapse. I wish you luck with your bargain. I shall expect you to record this deed within three days, and that will block any comeback you may start figuring on. If you fail to record this deed I shall construe your act as a breach of faith, return to you all but the five hundred thousand dollars which belongs to my wife, and then proceed to make things disagreeable for you. Remember, Carey, I'm your attorney and you should be guided by my advice."

Carey's face was livid with rage and hatred. "And in addition, I suppose I'm to forget that you're a stage robber, eh?" He reached for the telephone. "By the gods, McGraw, I'll take a chance with you after all. I'm going to fight you."

Bob McGraw drew a large envelope from his pocket. "You may read what this envelope contains while waiting for central to answer your call" he said gently. "I snipped the wires while you were hiding your face in your hands, wondering what you were going to do. These papers are merely a few affidavits, proving an absolute alibi in the matter of that Garlock robbery. I was eating frijoles and flapjacks with three prospectors about fifteen miles south of Olancho at the time this stage was held up, and I was in Keeler the following morning. This document contains a statement of the most amazing case of circumstantial evidence you ever heard of. Its author is the chief of Wells Fargo and besides, I have queer ideas on the subject of punishment for crime. Crime, Mr. Carey, is a great deal like our other human ailments, such as the chicken-pox and tonsilitis. We must bear with it and try to cure it by gentle care and scientific treatment. Prison cells have never cured a criminal, and it would only pain me to see you behind the bars in your old age. And I am certain that my wife would not rejoice at the news of your hanging."

"I suppose money has nothing to do with the celerity with which you hasten to compound a felony, eh?" sneered Carey.

"You unfortunate man! Carey, my late friend, Mr. Hennage, used to say that it was good policy to overlook a losing bet once in a while, rather than copper everything in sight. Your crime was a terrible mistake, Carey. For twenty years you've realized that and you've suffered for it. I'm sorry for you - so sorry that I'm going to use your ill-gotten gains for a good purpose. Come up into Owens valley three years from now and I'll prove it to you. Good-day."

"One moment, McGraw. Don't go for a minute or two. I - I'd like to believe that what you say is true, but the trouble is - you see, McGraw, I have never encountered your point of view heretofore. Tell me, McGraw - don't lie to me - do you feel the slightest desire to see me suffer, or is this - er - brotherly-love talk of yours plain buncombe?"

Bob McGraw advanced toward the man he had beaten. He held out his hand. "I try to be a man" he said - "to be too big to hate and put myself on a level with a brute. Won't you shake hands with me?"

Carey regarded him with frank curiosity.

"Say" he said, "are you religious?"

"No. Only human."

"Perhaps" said Carey dubiously, "but it doesn't seem

possible that I should meet two white men in this nigger world. I think the species became extinct with the death of my friend Hennage."

"*Your* friend - "

"Why not? He liked me - I know he did. And I liked him. I'm glad he's dead - no, I'm not - I was glad an hour ago, but I'm sorry now. Had he lived I would have made of him my friend, for he was the only human being I have ever met that I could trust implicitly. He was your partner and he warned me to keep off. He meant it, and I knew he meant it - so I stayed off. Do you think, McGraw, that I would have let you beat me out of that land if it hadn't been for Hennage? I didn't dare rush those selections through for patent until he was dead - and then it was too late. Had you left your affairs in any other hands I would have crushed you, but Hennage could not be bought. I didn't even try. He was above a price."

"Is that why you failed to act immediately after you became convinced that I was an outlaw and would not dare claim the land when it should be granted to my clients?" demanded Bob.

Carey nodded. "I met Hennage in Bakersfield, and he told me to keep my hands off those applications."

"Then he bluffed you, Mr. Carey. Harley P. Hennage was my friend, but not my partner. He did not have five cents invested in my scheme. I never mentioned it to him, and neither did my wife. His threat was a bluff, and where he got his information of my land deal is a mystery, the solution of which perished with Harley P."

Carey sat in his chair, with his head bowed. He was clasping and unclasping his fingers in a manner pathetically suggestive of helplessness.

"I don't understand" he mumbled. "He told me to keep off and I kept off." He sighed. "I'd have given a million dollars for a friend like him. I - I - never - had - one."

Bob McGraw drew T. Morgan Carey's mortgage from his pocket, scratched a match on his trouser-leg and held it under the fluttering leaves. Slowly the little flame mounted, and when it threatened to scorch his fingers the promoter of Donnaville tossed the blazing fragments into a convenient cuspidor. He looked up and saw Carey regarding him curiously.

"That was your mortgage" the land-grabber said wonderingly. "You have burned half a million dollars."

"I was selling you my friendship - at cut rates, Mr. Carey. I was worthy of Hennage's trust and friendship until a few minutes ago. Harley P. Hennage never did a mean or a cowardly act, and to-day I used my power over you to extort half a million dollars from you to further a scheme of mine. I figured that the end justified the means. It did not, and I ask you to forgive me."

Carey smiled wanly. "It's up-hill work, McGraw, but I'll forgive you. What great scheme is this of yours that caused you to appear unworthy of the friend who was so worthy of you? I have a great curiosity to understand you. Who knows? Perhaps I may end up by liking you?"

And then Bob McGraw sat down by his enemy and unfolded to him his dream of Donnaville.

"Think of it, Mr. Carey" he pleaded. "Think what my scheme means to the poor devils who haven't got our brains and power! Think of the women and little children toiling in sweat-shops; of the families without money, without hope, without food and without coal, facing the winter in such cities as Chicago and New York, while a barren empire, which you and I can transform to an Eden, waits for them there in the north," and he waved his arm toward Donnaville.

"There's glory enough for us all, Mr. Carey. Won't you come in with me and play the big game? Be my backer in this enterprise and let the future wipe out the mistakes of the past. You've got a chance, Carey. What need have you for money? It's only a game you're playing, man - a game that fascinates you. You've sold your manhood for money - and you have never had a friend! Good God, what a tragedy! Come with me, Carey, into Owens valley, and be a builder of empire. Let your dead past bury itself and start fresh again. You are not a young man any longer, and in all your busy life you have accomplished nothing of benefit to the world. You have subscribed to charities, and then robbed the objects of your charity of the land that would have made them independent of you. Think of the good you can do with the proceeds of the evil you have done! Ah, Carey, Carey! There's so much fun in just living, and I'm afraid you've never been young. You've never dreamed! And you've never had a friend that loved you for what you were. Do you know why, Carey? Because you weren't worth loving. You have received from the world to date just what you put into it - envy and greed and hate and malice and selfishness, and at your passing the curses of your people will be your portion. Come with me and be a Pagan, my friend, and when you have finished the job

I'll guarantee to plant you up on the slope of Kearsarge, where your soul, as it mounts to the God of a Square Deal, can look down on the valley that you have prepared for a happy people, and say: 'That is mine. I helped create it, and I did it for love. I finished what the Almighty commenced, and the job was worth while.' Will you play the game with me, T. Morgan Carey, and get some joy out of life?"

The land-grabber - the parasite who had lived only to destroy - looked up at Bob McGraw.

"Would you trust me?" he queried huskily.

"I burned your mortgage" said Bob smiling.

"I'll think it over - friend" Carey replied. "I never do things in a hurry. It's a habit I have, and I don't quite understand you. I must think it over."

"Do, Mr. Carey. And now I must toddle along. *Adios.*"

Carey shook his hand, and they parted.

Our story is told.

San Pasqual is still a frontier town - a little drearier, a little shabbier and more down at the heel than when we saw it first. There have been few changes - the few that have occurred having arrived unheralded and hence have remained undiscovered. For instance, it is not generally known that Mrs. Pennycook has lost control of her husband. Yet, such is the fact. She is still a great stickler for principle, but she trembles if her husband looks at her. It appears that Dan Pennycook's half-hearted accusation of Miss Pickett as the author of the

anonymous note found on the body of Boras O'Rourke preyed on the spinster's mind, and when Bob McGraw started an investigation she could stand the strain no longer. She fled in terror to the Pennycook home and made certain demands upon Mrs. Pennycook; who took refuge in her well-known reputation for probity and principle and informed Miss Pickett that she was "actin' crazy like"; whereupon Miss Pickett sought Dan Pennycook and hysterically confessed to the authorship of that fatal anonymous note, alleging as extenuating circumstances that she had been aided and abetted therein by Mrs. Pennycook. To quote a commonplace saying, Mrs. Pennycook had made the ball and Miss Pickett fired it. She begged Dan Pennycook to use his influence with Donna to have the investigation quashed, else would Miss Pickett make a public confession and disgrace the name of Pennycook.

Hence, when Mr. Pennycook appeared at the Hat Ranch and asked Donna to request her husband to forget about that anonymous letter, Donna guessed the honest fellow's distress and accordingly the matter was forgotten by everybody - except Dan Pennycook. He has not forgotten. He remembers every time he looks at Mr. Hennage's watch. He has never said anything to Mrs. Pennycook - which makes it all the harder for her - but contents himself with a queer look at the lady when she becomes "obstreperous like" - and that suffices. After all, she is the mother of his children, and God has blessed him with more heart than head.

Miss Pickett is no longer the postmistress; also she is no longer Miss Pickett, although in this respect she is not unlike a politician who has all the emoluments of office without the honors, or vice versa if you will. In her forty-third year she married the only man who ever asked her - and he was a youth of twenty-five who suspected Miss Pickett of a savings account. She resigned from the post-office to marry him, and San Pasqual took a night off to give her a charivari. Two weeks after the ceremony Miss Pickett's husband, despairing of the savings, jumped a south-bound freight and was seen no more. Her triumph over the acquisition of the "Mrs." was so shortlived, and the San Pasqualians found it so difficult to rid themselves of the habit of calling her Miss Pickett, that Miss Pickett she remains to this very day.

The Hat Ranch still stands in the desert below San Pasqual. Bob McGraw has secured title to it, and safe within the old adobe walls Sam Singer and Soft Wind are rounding out their placid lives. Sam Singer is now one of the solid citizens of San Pasqual. He has succeeded to the hat business, and moreover he has money on deposit with Bob McGraw. It appears that Sam Singer, in accordance with Mr. Hennage's dying request, fell heir to the gambler's new gaiters. The first time he tried them on Sam detected a slight obstruction in the toe of the right gaiter. He removed this obstruction and discovered that it was a piece of paper money. Like all Indians, Sam was suspicious of paper money, so he took it to Bob McGraw, who gave him a thousand dollars for it. Sam Singer was well pleased thereat. He considered he had driven an excellent bargain.

In the lonely sage-covered wind-swept cemetery at San Pasqual there rises a black granite monument, severely, plain, eminently befitting one who was not of the presuming kind. There is an epitaph on that monument which is worth recording here:

Peter B. Kyne

WHO SEEKS FOR HEAVEN ALONE TO SAVE HIS SOUL,
MAY KEEP THE PATH BUT WILL NOT REACH THE GOAL;
WHILE HE WHO WALKS IN LOVE MAY WANDER FAR
YET GOD WILL BRING HIM WHERE THE BLESSED ARE.
BENEATH THIS STONE
HARLEY P. HENNAGE
RESTS FROM HIS WANDERINGS.

One day T. Morgan Carey dropped off the north-bound train at San Pasqual, and learning that he had two hours to waste while waiting for the stage to start up country, he was seized with a morbid desire to wander through San Pasqual's queer cemetery. The only monument in the cemetery attracted his attention, and presently he found himself standing at the foot of Mr. Hennage's grave, reading the epitaph. It impressed him so greatly that he copied the verse in a little morocco-covered memorandum book.

"I wonder who was the genius that evolved that verse?" he muttered aloud, and to his great surprise a voice at his side answered him. It was a woman's voice.

"I do not know the author" she said, "but if you will read Henry Van Dyke's book 'The Other Wise Man,' you will find that little verse on the fly-leaf. Perhaps Van Dyke wrote it. I do not know."

T. Morgan Carey turned and lifted his hat. "Thank you, madam" he said. "I was particularly interested. I had a slight acquaintance with Mr. Hennage, and it seemed to me that the lines were peculiarly appropriate."

"My husband and I thought so. And if you will pardon me for suggesting it, Mr. Carey, it would be - better if you would please leave the cemetery. An old enemy of yours, a Cahuilla Indian, comes here three times a week by my orders, to bring water for the blue grass on this grave. He is coming now."

"Thank you. And you are - "

"I am Donna Corblay."

Carey bowed and continued.

"Your husband told me once that he had some great plans afoot, and did me the honor to ask me to help him - " he paused, watching her wistfully - "and I want to know if you object to me as an associate of your husband in his work."

Donna looked at him gravely. "I have neither bitterness nor revengeful feeling against you, Mr. Carey" she replied.

"I have suffered" he said, "but I haven't paid all of the price. Tell your husband that I want to help him. I have thought it over and I was coming to tell him myself. Tell him, please, that I would appreciate the privilege of being a minority stockholder in his enterprise and I will honor his sight drafts while I have a dollar left."

He lifted his hat and walked away, and Donna, gazing after him, realized that the past was dead and only the future remained. Carey's crime had been a sordid one, but with her broader vision Donna saw that the lives of the few must ever be counted as paltry sacrifices in the advancement of the race. Her father, her mother, Harley P. Hennage, Borax O'Bourke and the long, sad, barren years of her own girlhood had all been sacrifices to this man's insatiable greed and lust for power, and now that the finish was reached she realized the truth of Bob McGraw's philosophy - that out of all great evils great good must come.

Truly selfishness, greed, revenge and inhumanity are but the burdens of a day; all that is small and weak and unworthy may not survive, while that which is great and good in a man must some day break its hobbles and sweep him on to the fulfillment of his destiny. She saw her husband and his one-time enemy toiling side by side in the great, hot, hungry heart of Inyo, preparing homes for the helpless and the oppressed - working out the destinies of their people; and she cried out with the happiness that was hers.

Ah, yes, they had all suffered, but now out of the dregs of their suffering the glad years would come bearing their precious burden of love and service. How puerile did the sacrifices of the past seem now - how terribly out of proportion to the great task that lay before them, with the sublime result already in sight! Surely there was only one quality in humankind that really mattered, softening suffering and despair and turning away wrath, and as Donna knelt by the grave of the man who had possessed that quality to such an extent that he had considered his life cheap as a means of expressing it, she prayed that her infant son might be endowed with the virtues and brains of his father and the wanderer who slept beneath the stone:

"Dear God, help me to raise a Man and teach him to be kind."